DOUBLE MUSCADINE

BY FRANCES GAITHER

Follow the Drinking Gourd
The Red Cock Crows
Double Muscadine

DOUBLE MUSCADINE

Frances Gaither

THE MACMILLAN COMPANY

New York   1949

To RICE GAITHER

For help without stint

The persons and the locality of this story are fictitious. The trial is modelled in considerable part on an actual case in the records of the Supreme Court of Mississippi in the 1850's.

PART I

Opening Day

CHAPTER 1

IT seemed like the dead of night when his mam started in to calling him up the ladder. She had a powerful hard time a-rousing him. "Syke," she kept a-calling up, "you, Syke. Git up now, son. Hit's most sun-up." Twice at least he answered without stirring. But at last he hauled himself up and padded over to the open patch of firelight in the floor and reached down to take the kettle she came halfway up the ladder to hand him. "I got your breakfast mighty near done," she said. "And mind you don't forget to shave now."

By that time the gray dawn was showing sure enough through the little box-square windows in the two ends of the loft. When he set the kettle down on the floor under the south one, he stood a moment looking out. Near at hand the light of his father's lantern lined off the logs of the milking-shed wall, and far away over the black belt of woods along Coon Creek color began to wash up over the pale sky. Hit's going to be a powerful hot day, he thought yawning, hot and clear, sure as preaching. As he stripped and started in to wash himself, he kept looking down out of the window. He saw his mother dart across the yard to the cowshed, like a little bitty ghost in her slack gray calico, and a moment after he heard her shrill, excited voice jawing away about sump'n other. Maybe she was after Pappy to shave, too. Syke grinned at the thought. Or maybe she was still at him about the mules. Syke had heard her in bed last night, just a-going it, wanting Syke should ride the young mule and leave old slat-ribbed Jonas to haul the rest of them in the wagon.

Whatever it was she was jawing about in the cowshed now, she

[3]

left off after a while and dashed over to the well and started in to drawing water, bucket after bucket, which she emptied into a tub on the ground, enough to scrub the whole family clean. She was bound they shouldn't shame Syke on this big day. And then she was a-hollering for two of the little chaps to come and tote the tub in for her. Something about her littleness coupled with fierce energy made a lump come in Syke's throat. Poor Mam. He'd sure like to fix things so she could take it easier—buy a nigger to take the field work off'n her, anyways. Oh, not soon, of course, but some day.

When he came down the ladder, there she was, getting the whole family washed and dressed to go. He set down at the table like she told him and began to eat without a word. When she come over from the hearth and started to fork the fried fat-meat out of the skillet on to his plate, he noticed her cheeks were shining wet. He first thought it was sweat, but when he looked closer he seen it was tears.

"Mam!" he said. "Don't be a-skeered, Mam. Win or lose, hit's something for a boy like me to be in on the biggest case ever come to trial in this county."

She wiped her eyes with the back of the hand that held the long-handled fork and sniffed hard.

"I ain't a-skeered," she said painfully. "Hit's just—oh, son, hit's just I'm so *proud.*"

He laughed and that made her laugh shakily. She went and set the skillet back on the embers and came to pour his coffee. As she poured with one hand, she let the other touch his shoulder and stray down his sleeve.

"Purty," she whispered. "It's real purty cloth. I never thought to see you in such a suit. In court when them big lawyers git to picking on you or the new judge even, outruling you and making you set down before you're good and ready, don't you bother, Syke. You just say to yourself, my mam's out there in front a-watching and she's so proud she could bust."

But for her he'd not have had that suit. He was a heap too busy, working at his case, to bother. And as to Pappy, Syke's retainer money was hardly in hand before Pappy was studying how he'd lay it out in things the family needed. But in the end Mam had got her way and Syke his new clothes—all except a hat, which somehow she'd forgotten. He stole a glance toward his torn, shapeless old

[4]

straw hanging on a peg near the door. The blame thing was fitten to follow a plow mule down a cotton row and nothing else. Oh, well, he thought cheerfully, I'll just go bareheaded, that's all.

"I bet Mr. John's proud, too," she hinted. "Any law teacher would be—to see a pupil do so well with his first case."

Syke grinned.

"Well, proud or not, he'll be in there, fightin' with me."

It was shady, almost cool, riding through the damp woods, but when he turned out on the big road the sun, up no more than an hour, was already cruel hot. With the dew still glistening on the blackberry and elderberry bushes along the roadsides, dust as dry as gunpowder whirled up from under the spinning wheels and pounding hooves to fill the air with a ruddy mist. He had hardly joined the procession of people in wagons and buggies and a-horseback, travelling toward town for court opening, before he saw his new suit powdered thickly all over. But he hardly cared. He didn't mind even the rough teasing greetings: Hi, Lawyer. Hi, Syke. Where you git them fine clothes? Where's your hat, Buddy? Syke's neck burned a deeper red and he ran one hand sheepishly across his sun-bleached towhead, but he didn't really mind. Hat or no hat, he'd won his appeal, hadn't he? And if the last man in the county —or all of them that wa'n't bedridden—had taken to the roads this morning it was, in a way, Syke's doing, wasn't it? When the old judge appointed him to defend this case, same as you'd throw a bone to a hungry dog, the judge nor anybody else ever supposed Syke could make any more out of it than the pittance the law allowed. Oh, he wasn't the big man he appeared to his mam—not yet he wasn't. But he wasn't just scrapings, either, like some seemed to think back there in November.

Passing the shady road that led off to the place called Waverley, he turned his head and peered along it. He saw nobody there really. But to his superheated vision appeared as true as life a little white-stockinged, russet mare, curvetting and prancing, flashing every stray sunbeam from her well-curried flanks and bearing on her back a figure in speckless linen and a hat of fine, creamy straw. Syke's lips twisted mischievously. Good morning, your lordship, I reckon you don't exactly relish the idea of being hauled down from up there and rolled about in the mud, now do you? At the next side road two horsemen rode out, the bachelor brothers Lee. They were gentlemen, very nearly decrepit, indifferently mounted, and by no means faultlessly attired, but they answered Syke's good morning with haughty brusqueness and an expression of distaste that left him in no doubt whatever that they considered him a bumptious upstart riding for a well-deserved fall.

The very first man to rein in beside him and ride along with him was one whose name appeared on the special venire list in Syke's saddlebags. In the instant of recognizing him, Syke clearly saw the list, his companion's name, and the note Syke had written in the margin beside it: "Challenge for cause." The cause was bias, expressed in a public saloon on an afternoon in Christmas week, and Syke believed the fellow wouldn't deny it. But now, with his excited imagination pressing ahead to the courtroom, he actually had a hard time responding to the other's easy, drawling comments on the dust and the heat and the size of the crowd.

The crowd was big, all right, even for opening day. At the junction of every byway and back road another wagon load rolled forth to swell the caravan and slow it down, until, nearing town, it seemed barely to crawl. Tempers grew short and any attempt to push ahead was bitterly resented. Driving onto the new covered bridge over the creek, where the road was narrow and fell away sharply on both sides, one wagon tried to edge past another. Their hubs locked fast and they teetered perilously while the two drivers clambered down and would have fought it out with their fists if they had not been dragged apart.

The whole procession had to pull out to let the Memphis stage by, of course. And everybody was willing to give ground, too, for Dr. Gregory on his bay horse. They knew he was returning from some country night watch and on his way to the courthouse like everybody else, knew he was, in this trial as in the first, an important witness for the State. But they would have given ground for him anyway. Dr. Gregory always had right of way on any road in this county. It was his due, inalienable, uncontested. A few called: "Howdy, Doc. Who's sick out this way?" But most of them let him pass with a nod of greeting only, because it was plain to see from his tense, lined face that he was more than ever strung on wires, thinking maybe of the sick folks he was having to neglect while he rushed back to sit in a courtroom bedevilled by lawyers and their endless tangle of red tape. Fume as he might, he couldn't get out of it. He must tell the whole painful story all over again, as he had already told it to the coroner and the Grand Jury and at the November Circuit Court term.

The doctor had barely passed when some wag shouted: "Here come the Bench and Bar! Give 'em room." Again everybody, including Syke, pulled off the road and waited, while a half dozen weary saddle horses and a buckboard, marked with the dust of the entire circuit, went by. Three of the younger lawyers, riding in front, were singing blithely: "She's a bonny, bonny lassie." One of them was smoking a pipe as he rode. Careless lads, they were content to pick up from court town to court town such crumbs of business as the older, established lawyers did not want, ready to contend by day in the courtroom and by night to drink together in the hostelry of the moment, to shuffle their worn decks of cards or to play at charades, a travelling university, throughout each spring and fall. Syke watched them go by with feelings in which envy and scorn were strangely mixed. Would he ever make one of that callow and frivolous fraternity? Did he want to?

Just behind the singing youths, serene and confident, a sprig of roadside honeysuckle in his buttonhole, rode District Attorney Tom Peters, Syke's victorious antagonist of the autumn. He rode so close to Syke as he passed that their knees almost brushed, but he did not lift his hat or greet Syke in any way. Perhaps he did not see him. He was certainly deep in conversation with the man hired to assist him this time in the prosecution: a little man with a round paunch and a big head, which a great shock of curly white hair made look even bigger. Legend said the hair had once been a ruddy gold and that was why he had been dubbed the Yam. He had a name, of course, and it was famous in the state: Dancy Boone. But the Yam was what they called him from one end of Mississippi to the other; they boasted, falsely of course, that he had never lost a case and that his brain was twice the normal size. When he was District Attorney, the Negroes used to say he carried an extra length of new rope in his saddlebags so that no shortage might be permitted to stay the execution of his fearsome convictions. Even an honest man on the witness stand was supposed to waver and break down when the Yam with his soft, silky-sweet voice got to work on him. He rarely raised that voice, but usually as he closed in on his victim in cross-examination, dropped it lower and lower instead. Old Whispers was another of his nicknames.

In the dusty buckboard with the little travelling trunk strapped on behind rode a Negro youth, who held the reins, and a stranger, a man of fifty or so with a neat small beard of iron gray, wearing a linen duster and a wide-brimmed straw hat. The avid spectators, backed off the shoulder of the road into the rank and dusty weeds, whispered: "It's the new judge! It's Judge Rusk." They all knew his name, of course, having read it in the Athens *Free Press* at the time of his appointment soon after the old judge's death: Alexander Q. Rusk, of the North Carolina bench, a comparative newcomer to this state, appointed to fill out the term of the venerable Lucius Calloway, lately dead of a coronary thrombosis. . . .

To Syke, the man now passing hardly more than an arm's length from him appeared as one vested in majesty and mystery. He strove in one concentrated moment to fathom the dark eyes, shadowy under the wide hatbrim, to spell out the meaning of the gesture of long fingers lifted briefly to pinch at the tight-pointed tuft of beard, and felt his heart contract. What was this new judge like? Who could tell? A stranger with all a stranger's unguessed potentialities for good or ill. Would he be friendly to a backwoods upstart on the unpopular side of a notorious case? Or would he, like the brothers Lee, automatically feel moved to put him in his place?

Syke knew he shouldn't let the mere sight of the judge's prim little goatee make him feel down in the mouth. But it happened all the same. In place of his early morning excitement, he felt awe and dread at the swiftness with which he and his fate were now moving at last to a meeting. Back in November, emerging, defeated, almost blinded by the District Attorney's slugging, Syke had thought of time as the crucial factor. His opponent had had two weeks to prepare his case, whereas Syke had had a scant two days. That, he had told himself, was where the overwhelming advantage lay. Time. Time. If only Syke had had time. Something like that was obsessing him when, the night after the trial, he had rushed in upon John Oliver and his mother in their sitting room up at Oxford, stately to get Mr. John's help on making out his bill of exceptions, but partly, too, to have the comfort of talking his heart out to somebody who could understand. He had poured it all out at once: the crime, the public indignation, the trial, the crushing odds against him, his defeat.

Why appeal, Syke? Mr. John had asked. From what you tell me the State's case hadn't a flaw in it. That's just it, cried Syke. Hit was too good, Mr. John. And I didn't have no case at all. How could I, with no time? But you just give me six months and I'll have one.

So he had sent up his bill of exceptions, won his new trial and gone to work.

But now those six months which had in prospect looked so infinite and even in passing had seemed so long were at an end. He had financial backing beyond his early dreams. He had Mr. John himself as ally. Together they had built a case, too. It was better in some ways than he had ever dared to hope. But it had weak spots all the same, and, but for such minor tinkering as some courtroom surprise would force them to, it was beyond their power to alter and shape. That was the thought that sobered him. The penning of his briefs on appeal; the hurrying trips about the country in search of help, moral, financial, legal; the frantic pawing at each buried bone of a clue; the searching of lawbooks were all over now. The long-prepared-for day was already long past its dawn. A little more and the spring term would have opened with the mighty Yam himself assisting the District Attorney and a strange new judge on the bench. Syke's case stood at the head of the calendar, and just as it was, with its strong points and its weak, he must defend it.

In a vacant lot at the edge of town—the circus lot, it was called —a number of farmers who lived across the river or too far off along some difficult road to make the journey to and fro daily, had arrived with their families the evening before and set up tents for the week ahead. They were now cozily eating their breakfasts around a dozen blazing campfires. On this last hill, where the road dipped downward into town, the white-faced clock in the red brick tower above the courthouse could be plainly seen, its brass hands shining in the sun. And at that very moment its majestic, booming notes came one by one to ear. Eight o'clock, just that.

In the town wheeled and mounted traffic choked the streets and the sidewalks were seething with people afoot. Every gathering place about the square was crowded: the porch entries of offices and stores, the space beneath the wooden awning before the Masonic Hall, and of course the green square itself.

Syke made his slow way through the crowds down one side of the square, across in front of the tavern, and then up again. As he turned back, he spied just in front of the north portico of the courthouse a broad space at the hitching rail miraculously vacant. He prodded his mule forward and rode into it. But he had hardly dismounted and started to loop his bridle rein over the rail when Orrin Foote, a town youth near his own age, a fellow he knew well, came running from the courthouse steps, waving his arms and yelling.

"Hi, Syke! You can't hitch there. That place is reserved."

"Who says so? What business is it of yours where I hitch, Orrin?"

"Mr. Peters says so, that's who. He just give orders that place is to be kept for the Waverley folks. And he left me here to see nobody else come along and taken it."

Already the crowd milling about under the trees in the square was taking notice, some in a friendly, teasing way calling out: "Hi, Syke. Where's your hat, Syke?" And others, more than willing to relieve the tedium while they waited for the big conflict, came crowding over to fan this small contest for whatever it was worth. "Don't let Orrin get the best of you, Syke. What right has Mr. Peters got to hold that place?"

What right, indeed? Who told Tom Peters he could pre-empt space at the public hitching rails for his favored witnesses. What if he was the District Attorney? Maybe Syke wasn't good enough for him to tip his hat to on the road, but Peters couldn't force Syke off into some little back alley just because he had taken a notion to.

A boy pulled Syke's coat sleeve.

"There's plenty of room over by the academy, Mr. Syke," he said, touching his cap, his eyes big with admiration. "I'll take your mule over there for you, Mr. Syke. Want me to, Mr. Syke?"

By that unaccustomed title and the boy's tone of earnest deference, Syke was soothed. He fumbled in his pockets and drew up a small coin.

"Why, yes," he said not without dignity. "I'd thank you if you would, sonny."

The bestowal of the coin was itself a kind of ceremonial: Although he had on this very spot in many a long-gone court term received many a tip for a like service, this was the first time he had ever been privileged to give one. The small act completely restored his ruffled spirits. He was whistling "Arkansas Traveller" under his breath as he hoisted off the saddlebags crammed with his papers. In that moment the masculine voice which of all others he loved and honored most spoke at his elbow.

"Good morning, Syke. That's a fine beginning, shows you're learning."

Syke let the saddlebags fall to the ground and whirling about caught John Oliver's hand in both his own.

"Mr. John! Gosh, Mr. John, I'm proud to see you, sir. You don't know how proud. You don't know."

IT was almost an hour yet till time for court to open. A few people bustled hurriedly about, lawyers and politicians, mainly. But for most, once the question of a place to hitch had been disposed of, there was nothing to do but relax and visit. Inside the courthouse young people took stations, sitting or standing, up and down the length of the stairways at right and left of the north entrance, ready to move upward the moment the doors above were thrown open. Courting couples strolled back and forth along the broad corridor, heads bent together. A few amused themselves reading the broadsides with which both walls were plastered from one end to the other.

The upstairs courtroom, being the only large auditorium in the county, served the community in many ways besides its official one. In between the spring and fall terms of court, it was the scene of a whole procession of events, which these posters first heralded and then commemorated. Though a new placard was put up from time to time, the old ones were rarely pulled down, so that here in graphic form was community history from the date five years ago when, after the old log courthouse had burned down, this fine new one was built. A notice of a balloon ascension of several springs ago flanked the advertisement of a travelling magician's show of last summer. There were posters of circuses in successive Octobers; handbills of theatricals, a dozen-odd at widely separated dates, some by itinerant professionals, others by local talent; spelling matches and graduation exercises; a political rally with barbecue in the yard outside; a religious revival which in an earlier day would have sheltered under a tent in the circus lot or earlier still in some brush arbor out in the country. Mixed with the record of public event ran that of personal incident, too: tax sales old and new; a music teacher's card of announcement; the promise of a hundred-dollar reward for the capture of a runaway slave. "My stallion Corporal will stand . . ." "Chalybeate Springs under new management, nature's cure for . . ."

Outside, too, people had begun to settle down for the day. Around the square farmers were loosening traces and leading off their teams to water at the town pump. Women beside their wagons rummaged in capacious lunch baskets for teacakes and sandwiches made of big soda biscuits split and folded over a good thick wedge of ham or fat-meat to hand out to their children with a firm injunction, "That's got to do you till dinnertime, remember now." Others, with young babies, sat down wherever convenient and, quickly unbuttoning, proceeded without embarrassment to nourish their infants, dreading nothing so much as that some later squalls of hunger might lead to banishment from the courtroom.

As usual on opening day, many went about greeting their friends, giving and receiving family news, debating the effect of the long drought on the young crops, chatting casually, mentioning the trial, when they did mention it, carelessly. "Did you get a good look at the new judge when he drove up? He's got a little gray pointed beard." Or: "A fellow rode up with the Yam says the Yam's got a new story about a town fellow says to the country fellow . . ." Naturally the aspects of novelty in the coming trial—the new judge, the reinforcements brought up to the battlefield since the fall by both the District Attorney and the young defense counsel, the fresh witnesses hinted at on both sides—were tidbits to pass along to a neighbor who had just arrived. Yet no one of these items, nor the sum of them all together, was enough to stir any deep feeling. Even the cheering of Mr. Dancy Boone on his arrival at the tavern just now was no more than the applause with which any public treats, as a matter of course, a renowned entertainer.

To most of these veterans court week was an old, old story. A trial was a contest like a ball game, say, or a political campaign, bigger than either, of course, and often more exciting. They seldom missed one if they could help it. Weather and personal responsibilities permitting, they attended court every day of every term and, hour by hour, day after day, sat through every case on the calendar, from that of the farmer trying to recover from a steamboat for letting his whole cotton crop perish in flames at the New Orleans wharf to that of the overseer querulously claiming: "There never was no writin's, but he was to find me. The $52.39 for that coffee and sugar and flour ain't nothin' to him hardly, but hit's a heap to me."

Not a detail was too petty to interest this audience. For the courtroom show was also drama like the stage plays these same people now and then saw unfold in the upstairs auditorium, but closer to their own daily lives, of the very same stuff indeed, its actors, their friends and acquaintances. Thus, a trial, any trial at all, was a window through which they peeped into their neighbors' affairs, gained a share in their neighbors' joys and sorrows. Such breaks in the endless routine of clearing and planting and picking were naturally prized, and a murder trial was, naturally, too, more exciting than a mere damage suit.

When one party of adventurers, four or five half-grown boys, raced off for the jail two blocks away on the rumor that a glint of gold earrings could be plainly seen through the bars of a certain window, a mother called sharply to her son: "Don't let her see you a-staring in at her. Don't give her that satisfaction, the yellow she-devil." In the pleasant holiday scene the high-pitched, woman's voice flashed out like cold steel suddenly drawn from the secret scabbard which many a woman here had with her own hands stitched inside her husband's pants for him to put his bowie knife in. That quick outcry was the more startling because, until it rang out, there had been this morning hardly a mention of the woman about to go on trial for her life again. Before and during her first trial, the whole county had seethed with angry impatience. Time and again the cooler heads in the community had feared mob action would interrupt the ordered course of the law. And if that first jury hadn't brought in a verdict of guilty, most people believed, the woman would not be alive now. But today the temper of the crowd was at first quite different. The men standing about in knots did not, as before, stare at one another in solemn silence, their hands playing nervously with their hidden knife handles, but talked and laughed together in a free and easy manner. And the women, even that one who had called her single shrill admonition, were mild and neighborly, swapping recipes and community gossip as though they had no interest at all in the prisoner and her personal fate.

Obviously they did want to see her tried again. That's what brought them together in such unprecedented numbers. Since Syke Berry, by some legal shenanigan or other, had managed to get her another hearing, not one of them wanted to miss it. But, outwardly at least, they all seemed to take her share in the proceedings for granted, as though, after all these months, she had come to seem almost negligible, the least important actor in the play about to begin.

Suddenly a voice in the crowd cried out: "Look! They're coming." Immediately people fell silent and faced toward a little cavalcade making its way along the street at the north side of the courthouse: a gentleman on horseback, a family carriage, and a farm wagon. Nobody needed to tell his neighbor: It's the Waverley folks. Everybody knew them. As the party came to rest in the broad space reserved for it at the hitching rail, there was no cheering, no uprush of shouted, neighborly greeting, but a deepening silence instead, a hush spreading back and back across the square and over the surrounding streets, all but visibly, like ripples widening over a pond.

It was as chief witnesses for the State that Mr. Kirk McLean and his party had had that space at the rail reserved for them. It was so, no doubt, that the lawyers thought of them. But the crowd knew better. The crowd beheld the principals in the real drama, the only one that counted. This arrival brought back upon them all the chill of the crime itself. And this spontaneous hush rose from emotions as intimate and profound as each one's own pulsebeat and yet as openly, as easily shared as the air they breathed. The bond which made them act as one was secret in its very nature. Perhaps, if challenged, they would have said it was something in their blood—even in their "white blood"—to which they responded. But there was none to challenge. To one another they had no need to justify or explain themselves. They simply felt and acted as they felt.

That crime at Waverley, a poisoning, was the blackest in the history of this county, maybe of the whole state of Mississippi. That it had resulted in one death only, had not wiped out an entire white household was more or less an accident—or owing, that

[15]

is to say, only to God's mercy and the speed and skill of Dr. Gregory. A slave who would do such a thing to her white folks was a creature hardly human, a monster beyond all pity. And whether any particular onlooker standing here now happened himself to own slaves as yet or merely hoped one day to own some was irrelevant. Each white man felt the mortal threat in his own bones, saw it darkly mirrored in his brother's eyes, as if the evil done out at Waverley had been done to each of them personally. Moreover, it struck at each on the side where he was most vulnerable, that is, through his own wife and children. And it struck at each woman, too, in her heart of hearts. Not one who had just a little while ago fumbled in the depths of her lunch basket and brought up for her child food prepared in her own kitchen this very morning but shared in some degree the danger her sisters there in the carriage had suffered and miraculously survived. Not one but cringed at the unspoken thought: What if we owned such a cook? What if I, sitting down to dinner on a day like any other, should pour out tea for my husband and me and our children . . . ?

Each woman saw herself as one of those in the Waverley carriage. Each man, as Kirk McLean climbed down from his saddle, felt his own bowels heave with the compunction each believed him feeling. Of course he's pitying his womenfolks for what they've been through and what they've got to go through now. And he's riled to think he can't save them from this painful public trial at least. It'd be no more than human was he to feel kinder mad, too, at that uppity Syke Berry for stirring the whole evil mess up all over again with this second unnecessary airing of their private griefs. Yes, sir, I'll bet he'd like to lick tar out of Syke Berry. I sure would, was I in his shoes.

If Kirk McLean found the rapt attention of the multitude embarrassing while he dismounted from his white-stockinged, brown mare and, his hat of fine, creamy straw in hand, went to help the ladies of his family out of the carriage, if he felt awkward in that sudden vast quiet, under that multiple, focused gaze, he gave no sign. He moved as easily, as unself-consciously as ever, with no more than a smile and a nod toward those who stood nearest. And whatever he was feeling, he apparently did not speak as he placed his hand under his wife's elbow—his second she was. A Georgia girl, a mere slip of a thing, seventeen, whom he had met and married off-at the springs last summer. Her name was Martha, although very few were intimate enough with her to call her by it. Nobody around here knew her well yet, but everybody pitied her. And why not? Imagine a bride of a few months lifting that teapot as innocent as you or me! Then he put up his hand to Miss Hat, as most people called her, his first wife's sister, familiar to them all since her childhood and yet appearing strangely long and gaunt now in her new black dress. She blamed herself, they said, kept talking about God's punishing her. For what? Was she merely wishing she hadn't lost her temper with the cook that morning and insisted on having her whipped? Or did her regrets go back to older, darker secrets? As soon as Miss Hat's shoes touched the ground, Kirk McLean turned again to the girl, bending over her in question or reassurance or maybe only to screen her from the public view. But there was no sense in that surely. He couldn't stand between her and staring eyes when she took her seat in the witness chair up yonder. He couldn't stop the lawyers then from asking her anything they taken a notion to, could he?

Then they all noticed, or the women did, at least, how it was not the parents, but Miss Hat instead, who turned back to see about the baby in its nurse's arms. That puzzled them. Was it only because the baby was named after Miss Hat that she was the one who took charge like that? Or had the little wife gone through so much she had no feeling left for her own child? Was that it? But there was no time to study her small, shy face under the wide bonnet brim. For District Attorney Tom Peters, who had come hurrying out of the courthouse, was now shepherding the two ladies inside.

Kirk McLean remained behind to look after the dozen Negroes brought along in the Waverley farm wagon to testify at the trial. It was unlikely that these Negroes felt any more concern for the accused woman than when they had so unanimously helped to convict her last fall. It was more likely that they had half forgotten her existence in the long months since the county jail had swallowed her from their sight. It was easy to imagine them confused by the white folks' necessity to prove all over again a guilt proved once already. Perhaps they had left home in the early morning gaily enough, dressed in their best, shouting frivolous good-byes to their fellows in the fields, pretending, almost believing, this a sort of holiday from cotton chopping. But now, at the courthouse door, the square a sea of intent white faces, whatever confidence they had started out with had plainly leaked away. They cowered, subdued, white-eyed, clutching their split-bottom chairs and staring helplessly down at the master.

"Get down," he said, laughing a little. "Don't be absurd. Get down at once, all of you. I haven't any time to waste on you. I want these mules watered and I want all who are to be witnesses to come with me to Mr. Peters' office quickly."

He turned his back and walked off, as if to compel obedience. For yet a long moment they held their strange frozen pose, and then suddenly it broke and they came tumbling out over the wheels, giggling and whispering and shoving, not to be first and not to be last either. The master looked back at them over his shoulder and laughed again kindly.

"Now, now," he chided. "Don't be so nervous. Nothing's going to happen to *you*—if you tell the truth, that is. . . ."

Waverley, for all it lay a good two miles or better off the stage road and one mile of that through the thick muck of Coon Creek bottom, was knit to the town by closer ties than many places more accessible. It was one of the oldest freeholds around here, dating back to the time when this part of the state was first opened up to white settlers. The older inhabitants remembered the place when it was a one-room cabin in a bit of deadening no bigger than a pocket handkerchief. And the original owner, old Hunt, Miss Hat's father, was still as vivid in their minds as when in his butternut pants and red galluses he used to come driving his mules into town with his bale or two of cotton. He raised that cotton hard, they knew, a lot of it by his own muscles, because he had at first no more than a pair of slaves that had come to him through his wife. He had been, the story was, her father's overseer back in North Carolina where they came from, but nobody here thought the less of him for that.

It was his novel-reading, lady wife—Miss Oc, he always called her—who had given the rough little clearing its fancy name. Old Hunt had been hard put to it to write his own name and ten to one he never read a book in his whole life. But a man doesn't need book-learning to be a good farmer. His land, like most land hereabouts, was only fair to middling, nothing like so rich, that is to say, as the Delta country west, but not so poor either as the hill counties northward. Yet old Hunt had steadily prospered, adding bit by bit to his acreage, building on a second room beyond a dog-trot, when his two little girls grew big enough to want it, and a cabin at a time in his back yard as the natural increase of his slaves required it. His older daughter, Harriet, known as Miss Hat, was a good manager like her father. So that now, long after he was dead and gone, to speak of Waverley cotton or Waverley hams and butter, or even a Waverley Negro, was to guarantee it as a reliable product. In a way that made the evil thing that had happened out there seem all the worse.

Kirk McLean was himself a sort of local institution. Few men in this county had such breeding and charm and not another one such easy popularity. He had come here in his early twenties, frankly penniless through his Virginia guardian's having gone on a friend's note, and, with an uncomplaining gallantry which everybody admired, had fallen to at making a living among them. Nobody before him had so much as thought of Athens' having a newspaper. But the idea was promptly recognized as sound, and he had got all the backing he needed in no time. That the *Free Press* was to this day published and distributed every Wednesday as regularly as Wednesday came was still gratefully accounted to his credit, although its current editor was the third of his successors.

Some time during his first year here he had married old Hunt's younger daughter, Honey, and gone to housekeeping with her in the little white cottage over between Judge Calloway's and Ed Ketcham's. The old judge set a heap of store by him, clipping out his editorials and carrying them around in his pocket to read to people up and down the circuit. But then Honey, about the time she was expecting her baby, got the consumption—the breast complaint, most people around here called it—and had to be taken home to Waverley for Miss Hat to look after. Old Hunt had died a short while before and Miss Hat was living all alone. At first Kirk McLean had hung on to his paper, travelling back and forth every week to get it out, but it was a mighty long road and often nearly impassable, winter and spring, and Honey got worse instead of better. So in the end he had to let the paper go, to the town people's everlasting regret. In this very court week there would almost certainly be some leading citizen or two, dissatisfied with the way Clayte Burgess was running the *Free Press,* who would draw Kirk McLean aside and try to talk him into moving back to town and taking over again.

For a long time the household out there had consisted only of himself and his little son and Miss Hat. It was common knowledge that Honey's interest in the place and the people had by old Hunt's will passed to the little boy with his father and aunt jointly named as trustees. And most people knew, too, that Miss Hat was the actual manager in all petty details. But she had the habit, familiar among women, of making use of the nearest male relative whenever she had need to bolster her authority. On the place she cited Mas Kirk to move the Negroes to any extra effort, and off the place, too, she was always saying Br' Kirk thinks or Br' Kirk wants with such eager insistence that most people got to thinking and speaking of him as the master of Waverley as she wanted them to. And Kirk McLean, besides, was a man on whom the garments of masterhood fitted easily and comfortably. No doubt it was as master of Waverley that he usually saw himself. Certainly it was so that he appeared to the people who watched him ride up to the courthouse this morning.

He was always welcomed cordially here, had his choice of half a dozen places to stay—all the best homes, that is—whenever he cared to spend the night. It was no wonder he was well-liked: The town annals were crammed with the tale of his kindnesses. The time Sam Hardy's livery stable burned to the ground in the night, it was Kirk McLean who headed and carried round the subscription paper to help Sam rebuild. If he saw a colored mammy stranded with her charges beside a muddy street, where nearly any other would ride by without noticing, he would stop his horse and insist on taking them all across, one by one behind him, even to the mammy, whom he would leave at last, bowing above her starched apron and shouting his praises to heaven. A girl at her first dance, appalled to discover herself, after all her glad anticipation, only a wallflower rooted by a wall, might well pray that Mr. Kirk McLean's eye would fall upon her. If it did, she would be led forward, gently courted (or it seemed like courting) into warmth and ease and even gaiety. Ambitious mothers sometimes misunderstood and encouraged their daughters to misunderstand his kindness, but less and less often as time went on. For most people, by

[20]

the time he got around to giving them all that big surprise last summer, had just about given up the idea that he would ever remarry. Though others changed, they didn't expect him to. They all just thought he'd go on, accepting Miss Hat's adoring ministrations, riding the best horse in the county, appearing in town in spring and fall court week and on all other festive occasions, smilingly ready to squire neglected wallflowers and rescue stranded mammies, to the end of his days.

Everybody has his faults, of course, and Kirk McLean had, or was supposed to have, one which his best friends did not so much approve as condone, saying, at least as long as he remained unmarried: Well, who does it hurt? Whose business is it but his? Certainly they didn't suppose he considered himself accountable to an old-maid sister-in-law. How could he?

When he chose last summer to treat himself like any rich river planter to a summer at the finest springs in Georgia, it occasioned no particular comment. They reckoned Miss Hat knew whether she could afford the indulgence. She wasn't old Hunt's daughter for nothing. Miss Hat was good for whatever she bought. McLean's friends were used to seeing him come and go and they had no premonition, as surely he had none himself, that this trip was any more momentous than an errand by stage to Memphis or a cotton-selling jaunt down to New Orleans. Then one drowsy afternoon at the end of last July, the *Buckeye* tied up at the town landing and he came ashore with this Georgia girl on his arm.

Now, as Kirk McLean passed close to the crowd beside the courthouse steps, Ed Ketcham stepped forward, laid his hand on McLean's arm and said warmly:

"We're looking for you all at my house to dinner. Now don't forget. My wife and the girls are putting the big pot in the little one, though I reckon they'd mighty near kill me if they could hear me tattling!"

McLean wrung his hand and thanked him, but his eyes, seen close, had an unnatural, remote expression that made Ed feel queer somehow, as if McLean hadn't heard a word he'd said. Ed said in a careful whisper to Clayte Burgess, standing beside him:

"You notice the way he looked at me, like a man not all there? Anybody'd think it was him that's going on trial."

Clayte Burgess nodded.

[21]

"In a way it is," he said. And when Ed stared, puzzled, Clayte added: "His womenfolks know it, if you don't. Didn't you see the set of Miss Hat's jaw? And as to the girl, why, man, wild horses couldn't have dragged that little thing here if his honor wasn't at stake."

CHAPTER 3

I T was hot in the District Attorney's office with the sun beating full upon the unshaded eastern window. The room was very crowded. The young lawyers sat at the long table, talking with prospective or present clients. Dr. Gregory was irritably pacing the floor, waiting for Mr. Peters. Part of the crowd seemed to be merely admirers of the Yam. They were all gathered close about him at any rate to listen, laugh, applaud— all men, of course, most with their coats off and fanning themselves with their hats or with sheets of paper caught up from desk or table. They hardly glanced round when the Waverley ladies came in. The Yam was telling a story about a trial in which he had made a monkey out of a half-baked little squirt of a doctor who didn't even know what a jugular vein was.

There was a strong smell of sweat and of chewing tobacco in the heated air, and the room looked as if it had not been cleaned for a long time. The papers stuffed in the pigeonholes of the desk and even those heaped on top were deep in dust, and the several earthenware spittoons standing about on the bare floor were circled by vast spotted areas that surely could not have been achieved in a few days only.

Miss Hat dragged a chair over near the shady one of the two windows, dusted it with her skirt, and installed the nurse and baby there. The young wife spied another chair at the other side of the room and edged her way around the gathered men to reach it. It stood in the full sun, but she made no attempt to remedy that. She only lifted off gingerly the sweaty coat she found there, dropped it on top of the littered desk, and sat down with her back to the room. She heard the shuffling tramp of the Waverley Negroes as they entered; she even sensed the odor of their profusely sweating flesh added to the already heavy atmosphere, but she did not turn around.

"All right, Mr. Peters," her husband's voice called out above the Yam's delicately whispered, sinuous narrative. "Here they are if you and Mr. Boone have anything to say to them."

There followed a minor bustle and stir in which all persons not called as witnesses for the State were asked by Tom Peters to leave the room. Those who remained shifted about and took up new positions. Kirk McLean's mild and kindly voice spoke successively the names of several Negroes as he guided one to stand here, another there, where they could hear better. Then Tom Peters, half standing, half sitting on the table edge, cleared his throat and said pleasantly:

"Now I know that to most of you, white folks' doings, and everything to do with the law in particular, are a pretty mysterious business, just about as easy to find your way around in as a black dark night with no moon and not even a lantern. So I want to explain things to you briefly before we take you upstairs, enlighten you a little if I can—"

"Yes, *suh*," cut in an old voice on a singing note, "that be a mighty comfort, Mr. Peters, ef you do. Lighten us on the law, suh, if you'll be so kind." The young wife, recognizing the voice, smiled. But then, when a ripple of laughter went around the room and the old voice, upborne on the wave of it, began to over-reach itself, she frowned. "Yassuh," it chanted on unctuously, "white folks' law like some big old miry swamp on a black night. Nigger liable trip hisself up and git hisself in up to his neck, don't some kind white gentleman lighten him where he got to put his foots—"

"That's enough, Uncle Jerry," said Kirk McLean sharply. "Mr. Peters has only a few minutes now. There will be no more interruptions."

Tom Peters smiled and went smoothly forward.

"How many of you testified at the trial in November? Let's see your hands. More than half, then. Well, you already understand, if you haven't forgotten, what I am about to say. And all of you, even those who have never seen the inside of a courtroom, remember what was said Sunday before last when I came out to Waverley and listened to your stories in Uncle Jerry's cabin. Each one of you remembers what I asked and what you answered that day—or do you? Is there anybody who wants me to let him recite again what he is going to say upstairs? Anybody who wants to change his story? If so raise your hand."

No hand went up this time. Instead there was a general lowering of eyes, a little whisper of embarrassment, rippling with giggles. Uncle Jerry spoke up firmly:

"They all remembers, Mr. Peters. They know what they going to say."

"Good."

There were, Mr. Peters gently explained, certain ways in which the law made a distinction between them and white men, but there was one way in which the law looked on them exactly the same. And that was in the field of moral responsibility. The law presumed that they knew the difference between right and wrong as well as any man whose skin happened to be white. If one of them was supposed to have done a crime, he was brought into court and tried exactly like a white man.

"And there's not one of you," said Mr. Peters, "who doesn't know the difference between the truth and lying just as well as I do. Though the law lets you off from swearing to Almighty God when you testify, the way white men have to do, it doesn't let you off from telling the truth. And, if a single one of you up yonder in that courtroom starts to putting in fancy touches instead of telling the same plain straight story already told to me, the law has power to punish him severely."

Here another voice broke in, a delicate, almost mincing voice, and Kirk McLean's wife, glancing back over her shoulder, saw the Yam reading aloud from a big book open on the table before him. As he read he was stroking the open page with one soft little pink hand in a way that gave her the creeps. The law he read, all about what was supposed to happen to Negro perjurers, she rejected as nonsense, more like a jungle incantation than a printed statute in a civilized code. Imagine nailing anybody's ears to a pillory and then chopping them off. Of course the purpose of the whole thing was just to frighten the Negroes into telling the truth. . . . She heard Mr. Peters saying smoothly: Well, of course it was just a law in a book, never enforced so far as he knew in all the years of his law practise. And, anyway, the Waverley colored people, who were known far and wide for their honesty, had no reason to be afraid of a law made just for willful liars and perjurers. He was merely preparing them for the admonition the judge would read out to each one of them in court.

"Where are they to sit, Mr. Peters?" asked Miss Hat in a fussing, worried tone. "That little witness room you've got up there's an oven on a day like this, and there are so many of them this time, too, nearly twice as many as in November. I wonder if that new judge would be willing. . . ."

"I've already spoken to him, ma'am. You know I promised you I would. He's given his permission for the witnesses to be present in the courtroom. Here, Orrin," he called to a youth loitering in the doorway, "cut around to the back door, will you, and when the sheriff comes along, remind him he's to reserve the front two rows for Mr. McLean's family and servants."

"I'll be a lot easier about them," Miss Hat said sighing. "And they are sure to be less restless and frightened if they sit close to us."

The girl Martha opened her fan and moved it slowly back and forth. When she had waked this morning, it was in the middle of a dream. She didn't remember the dream exactly—only that it was filled with an airy mountain breeze, quick little brooks tumbling down rocky slides, and the sound of her husband's (no, her lover's) voice. She found that by shutting her eyes she could put herself back inside the dream again and be for a little while far, far away from the painful present.

People flocked to Healing Springs or "the Healing," as its devotees affectionately called it, not only from the rest of Georgia but from all over the lower South. For gaiety in the height of the season, it was reckoned hardly inferior to the Virginia springs themselves. Matchmaking mothers brought their daughters here as zealously as to Charleston or Savannah in winter. Bachelors, a few with only chills and fever, but some, too, with fat holdings in land and slaves back home, dismounted almost daily in the enchanted valley. Whole families came just to escape the heat of the lowlands and stayed from the middle of May straight on through September. Many had built themselves cottages up the overhanging slopes, fragrant little Alpine chalets of the native cedar and pine, with galleries breasting a surf of laurel and rhododendron and commanding a view of the croquet matches which resounded all day long in the valley by the springhouse and of the stage unloading the newest comers before the door of the long central building which served as dining hall and ballroom. Not all who applied could be accommodated, and often, especially in midsummer, the stage departed as full as it came; many a private carriage, too, toiled up the winding valley road only to learn at the gates that every room and every bed was taken. To get in at all was to be reckoned among the blessed.

Martha's Uncle George, a United States senator, had one of the nicest cottages there, and even when, as this season, he could not go himself, always sent his wife and daughters. So when he wrote from Washington and invited Martha to spend the summer at the Healing with Aunt Charlotte and the girls and even sent in the letter the torn-off half of a hundred-dollar bill to be followed in the next mail by the second half to pay for her journey and enable her grandmother to get for her the necessary frills and furbelows, she simply could not believe in her luck.

Seventeen, released from her grandmother's apron strings for the first time, she found the place incredibly dazzling: the beribboned belles and handsome young men; the high-perched, embowered cottages; the steep little paths flowing with life and laughter; the croquet court in the valley where the crack of mallet on ball ticked off the moments of each summer-long romance; the crowding springhouse, the gallantly proffered dipper; the fiddling and dancing at night in the dining room.

Aunt Charlotte and the girls considered Martha's new clothes tacky. Oh, they didn't say so. On the contrary, they attempted consolation for this wardrobe chosen by a doting old woman. This dress was quaint, in that she looked like a girl in a story book, and so on. Nor did they tell her she was a stick. But they implied it. And she agreed with them, helpless to change. The archness and melting graces confidently practised before her mirror at home did not come to her rescue even once. Mostly she shrank into frightened homesick silence while gay flirtations gushed and sparkled all about her. When the exact hour for drinking the waters struck and the blades and belles went trooping down the paths that converged on the spring, Martha trailed along behind. When her cousins were chosen there for the croquet match to follow, Martha sat down on the children's bench to look on. After supper, when the tables were pushed back and the dancing began, she sat among the matrons except for the times when some kindhearted woman compelled a reluctant son to lead her out on the floor or one of her cousins' beaus took pity on her.

Her cousin Dessie at nineteen was a self-conscious beauty with half the young men in the place at her feet. A Mississippi planter, handsome, reputedly rich and a widower, for whom all the mamas of marriageable daughters were openly setting their caps as the brightest catch of the season, Dessie and everybody else considered her private conquest. Who would ever have guessed that, in the hottest part of the afternoons, when the senator's daughters were in their beds getting their beauty sleep, the sly puss of a cousin, with a book under her arm, was stealing away up the slopes behind the cottages to a little retreat she had found in the woods, on her way to a tryst with Dessie's lover? Why should anyone guess? She hardly believed it herself at first. It had begun by an accident or almost an accident.

Lying on the ground one day, reading her novel, believing herself alone, she had realized suddenly that she was not, and when she sat up and looked around, there he was.

"What do you want?" she asked awkwardly.

He came over and dropped down beside her, laughing.

"To be welcomed in your green parlor! I followed you. I wanted to find where you go every afternoon, that's all—or, no, it isn't. There's another thing: Why do you always run away from me?"

"From you? But I don't, not from you any more than anybody else. . . ."

"I have only to dance with you once to make you leave the hall abruptly."

"Why not? You were just being kind. It's Dessie you really want to dance with."

He shook his head, laughing again.

"Don't be too sure of that."

A vision of Dessie's fury if she could hear so overwhelmed her that she scrambled to her feet at once and said in panic that she really must go now. But he caught her arm and pulled her down beside him.

"There, you see. Running away again! Why are you afraid of me?"

"Not of you," she gasped, blushing, covered with confusion.

"Then who is it? Miss Dessie? Your aunt?" She nodded Yes. "Are they unkind to you? They seem to me such agreeable people. Surely they do not treat you badly."

"They don't mean to, I reckon. But—oh, I can't explain. I just know if they found out you were here now, talking to me, they—"

He held her arm in a firm grasp and would not let go until she promised to meet him here the next day at the same hour. She could do it only if he would give her a promise, too—his attentions to Dessie must go on just the same. He must be as nice as ever to Dessie. So then at last she promised to come back tomorrow and ran off—like a shy nymph, he always said.

Their idyl, so carefully screened at her terrified insistence, unfolded gently at first. Meeting only in the quiet afternoons, they felt themselves as alone in the mountain woods as Adam and Eve in Eden. But then came discovery: a party of children, among whom was her youngest cousin, found them one day kissing above Bridal Veil Falls. And with exposure everything Martha had feared came to pass: disgrace in the house where she was a guest, shrill reviling by Dessie for her sneak-thief behavior, an edict forbidding her lover the house, even imprisonment in her room—a sentence intended to last until the Senator, as Aunt Charlotte called Uncle George, could be written to and heard from. It would have been altogether a hopeless situation but for the circumstance that Martha was able to persuade a maid of Aunt Charlotte's to smuggle notes in and out.

That they would have to run away had been Martha's idea from the first—as the concealment had been. From the beginning she had been sure it was the only way. Her lover, who didn't know Aunt Charlotte as she did, held long to the notion that he must ask Aunt Charlotte for her niece's hand. A gentleman could do no less. It was Aunt Charlotte's own behavior at last that convinced him, showed him Martha had been right all along. So now it was he himself who proposed and planned elopement. And Martha? What could she do but agree? Miraculously granted her prince,

[29]

could Cinderella elect to remain among her filthy pots and ashes? To the end of her life it would have been, for her grandmother, as it turned out, had only a few weeks left to live, and that would have delivered Martha for good to Aunt Charlotte's keeping. Of course she didn't know that then, couldn't know in advance. But she simply and gratefully confided herself to Mr. McLean and let him steal her away one midnight from her hateful prison.

Now, in the District Attorney's office, she felt the fan slipped out of her hand and a little breeze playing over her face. Of course she had to open her eyes, and when she did she saw her husband bending over her and, alas, behind and beyond him, outside that open window, she saw, also, a dozen strangers under the courtyard trees, their faces turned in upon her and him in a curious, patient stare, that same uncanny, voiceless watching which had begun the moment they drove up. She shuddered and sighed.

"Try not to mind so much," he whispered. "Forget them if you can. They don't mean to be unkind. Really, they're all sorry for you. Whatever they think of me, they're sorry for you."

A twelve-year-old girl under the nearest tree held a double handful of popcorn up to her mouth and fed on it, slowly, thoughtfully, greedily even, yet never moving her eyes from the two people beyond the window sill.

"I don't want pity," whispered Martha fiercely. "I want to be let alone. All I want in this world is just to be let alone. Why can't they leave us in peace? Haven't we been through enough as it is?"

Her folded fan dropped into her lap abruptly. His smile faded and his lips contorted in a way that told her that once more he had taken her complaint on himself, once more she had hurt his feelings.

"You have much to reproach me for," he said stiffly, "but certainly not this. You know I have tried from the first to keep you out of this."

Tears sprang to her eyes and she could not at first answer. She could only look up at his drawn face, helpless to explain or make amends.

"I wish," she managed at last to get out, "you wouldn't always imagine I'm blaming you—as though I thought every single thing that's happened is your fault."

"Well, isn't it? I should think you might very well wish you had never set eyes on me."

The tears ached in her throat and she could only shake her head, looking sorrowfully up at him. It was given to her then to see him as others saw him, as she herself had first seen him, a handsome, broad-shouldered man, in the fairest and crispest of linen. Even now after the long dusty ride from Waverley he looked unmussed, unsullied, she would almost have said unmarked by all he had lately suffered, except for that cloud left by her fancied reproach. He wore naturally an open expression, sunny and smiling, an all-embracing, friendly look. People often remarked it. And Sis Hat said: "Br' Kirk's face matches his heart. I never know anybody with a kinder heart than Br' Kirk." Sis Hat always said. "He wouldn't hurt a fly a-purpose. . . ."

Mr. Peters came over to them.

"Well, Mrs. McLean, for your sake I'm sorry it's such a hot day, I really am. Hard enough on you without that. But don't you get stage fright now and everything's going to be all right. Like to run over that testimony with me again while we've got a few minutes?"

"No, thank you."

"Are you sure? Thorough preparation is about the best cure there is for stage fright. It would take only a few minutes."

"No, thank you."

Still he lingered, wistful, somehow touching, in a large, bustling way, a little like a benevolent undertaker wanting the necessarily painful arrangements as comfortable as possible.

Her husband turned and laid his hand on Mr. Peters' arm.

"For the last time, Tom, can't you let her off? After all, you've got Sis Hat and me and Dr. Gregory and the coroner, not to mention that chemistry professor and a couple of steamboat men and close to a dozen Negroes. How many witnesses do you need, for heaven's sake? Surely you might leave my wife out."

Tom Peters was regretful but firm.

"I want to, Kirk. Personally, I'd like nothing better than to do it. But the case needs her; the jury's got to have her there before their eyes alongside that yellow Messalina. Seeing her will do more for us than all the spoken evidence put together. But it'll take only a few minutes. I give you my word of honor. She needn't speak one word more than she feels like speaking." He turned to Martha.

"Remember that, Miss Martha: Anything I ask you is just to help you get your part of it told quickly. I won't ask you a single unpleasant question, not on purpose, and if something I ask does by accident worry you, make you uncomfortable, just you sit still and look at me and I'll help you. And under cross-examination the same thing goes. I'll jump in if there's any sign of trouble on your face. You trust me."

"I do," said Martha gratefully. "And you *will* call on me soon— let me get it over as soon as possible."

"Right after Miss Hat. I promise. We'll let Miss Hat tell the main story and leave as little as possible for you. Meantime, why don't you go over to the tavern and rest in the ladies' parlor? It's likely to be a long job, getting a jury this time, apt to take all morning, or even into the afternoon. We could call you when we seem to be nearing an end. Kirk could come over for you."

Martha shook her head. No, she said, she'd rather be in the courtroom from the first. She thought she'd get used to things better that way.

"Can you tell me where to find Mr. McLean?" a voice asked outside the open door.

"Parson!" shouted Kirk McLean, his face glowing with that special warmth he had for one person and one only.

"Mr. Banning!" exclaimed Miss Hat in the same instant and hurried forward just as he did.

Martha knew this friend of her husband's youth hardly at all yet—she had seen him actually just during the two days she and Mr. McLean had spent at New Orleans, waiting for a boat to bring them upriver. But even to her he seemed an old friend, so she smiled eagerly, too, and turned to rest her eyes on Neal Banning's trustworthy face.

"We'd given you out," Sis Hat said, wiping her eyes. "After you didn't come on the Saturday boat, we just thought you couldn't make it after all."

"Not make it, Miss Hat, with trains and stages to bring me! What sort of a friend do you take me for?"

A mighty whir and twanging set the air and the very walls a-hum as the town clock in its high tower above got ready to strike nine. At the same instant the stairs quaked and resounded to an upward surge of rushing feet. The floor overhead shook and thun-

dered as the throng poured across it. Outside under the trees someone shouted: "It's open, courtroom's open," and everybody ran
for the nearest entrance. Martha rose hurriedly from her chair.
But Mr. Dancy Boone came over and told her to sit down again.

"No need for you to hurry, ma'am," he said. "Didn't you hear
Mr. Peters say seats are reserved for you folks? Like when the
fellow was a-riding to his own hanging and the preacher was with
him said, 'Look like to me we're a little late,' and then this fellow
said, 'No mind, I reckon they can't hardly start without us. . . .' "

COURT had opened. The new judge was in his high seat, where all could see that he had, as reported, a small pointed beard, of mingled black and gray in color, and that he had also a habit of grasping and tugging at it in certain moments of tension. The several court attendants were in their several allotted places. Out beyond the railing every seat was taken and back of the benches people were standing. But the big room, though full, was very quiet. The judge had just announced that if the over-crowding to which he was consenting should result in any restlessness or disturbance tending to interrupt the business of the court, he would not hesitate to limit public attendance or even to have the room cleared. Since this was his first term here, nobody knew just how severe he really would be, but it seemed best to stay on the safe side by keeping quiet. A single stray cough among those standing drew angry backward glances.

Kirk McLean and his ladies sat in the seats reserved for them in the middle of the first row. Dr. Gregory sat on their left, and on their right were several strangers. Mr. Banning, of course, was not quite that, for, as Kirk McLean's best friend, he had been on happier occasions a frequent visitor at Waverley. Even the man next to him a few recognized as the chemistry professor from the state university. But the man beyond him had never been seen here before. In the minutes before the judge's gavel fell, he had been eagerly discussed and even now was the object of as much neck-stretching curiosity as could be quietly managed—a small-built fellow with an olive skin and dandified clothes, registered at the tavern as Mr. A-R-N-A-U-D, of New Or-*leens*. The exotic name, locally rendered Onnud, was already famous from the earlier trial as that of the family who had formerly owned the accused woman. And this was taken as proof that here in the flesh was Syke Berry's boasted rich backing—a thing only half believed in till now. An item of gossip widely shared and relished in the half hour before court opened was that the fine gentleman had been put in a room with five others at the tavern last night and had moreover found bugs in his bed. . . .

The preliminary routine moved slowly forward: the reading by the clerk of court of the calendar of cases; the lawyers' responses of "Ready" or "Not ready"; the round of sundry motions. At last the clerk called in a loud voice: "The State of Mississippi versus Aimée, a slave," and handed a sheaf of papers up to the judge. The District Attorney and the Yam took their places at their table in front of the empty jury box, busying themselves at once with disposing their books and papers and even their hats satisfactorily before them. Syke Berry and John Oliver sat down at their table. From a circular balustrade at the right and a little way back, which marked the head of a small back stairwell, the prisoner was just being brought up, a quadroon, rather slender, wearing the same gaudy flounced silk dress and gold hoop earrings she had worn throughout her first trial. As she faced the row upon row of white people who had come to see her tried again and walked the twenty steps between the stairhead and the table where she was to sit with her lawyers, she was observed to swish her flounces uppishly and to look about with the same facial expression which many on that previous occasion had found annoying—"That bold look," it was called. They all saw her, in the moment before she sat down, recognize the olive-skinned gentleman in the front row and toss her head and smile with brazen confidence.

The District Attorney asked and received permission to read the indictment.

"The Grand Jurors of the State of Mississippi taken from the body of the good and lawful men of the County of Chewalla, elected, impanelled, sworn . . ." sonorously charged that "the woman slave Aimée of the county of Chewalla aforesaid, not having the fear of God before her eyes but being moved and seduced by the instigation of the devil and of her malice aforethought . . . to kill and murder . . . at the county aforesaid, to wit in the county aforesaid, feloniously, willfully and of her malice aforethought, a large quantity of a certain deadly poison called arsenic, did put, mix, and mingle into and with a certain quantity of tea . . ."

Young Mrs. McLean found the long indictment merely boring. The whole legal procedure was to her an alien ritual, a mumbo-jumbo full of direful significance to the initiate but meaningless to her uninstructed ears. If the lawyers' doings only plunged her in apathy, however, her enforced view of Aimée at close range was experience of quite another order. Hate blazed in her. The only way she could avoid looking at Aimée was to shut her eyes. "You could wait over at the tavern, you know," her husband whispered. But she quickly shook her head and tried to take on a more appropriate expression.

Now the clerk was calling the roll of the special venire, and all over the big room men were answering "Here" or "Present." When that was over, the clerk announced that any wishing to be excused from jury duty might now present their excuses to the judge. Two men rose and went forward to confer in whispers with his Honor. One returned, smiling, took his hat and left the courtroom. The other a little sheepishly regained his seat among obviously amused neighbors.

The judge directed:

"Call the jury."

The clerk faced the courtroom and announced:

"Gentlemen, please take your seats in the jury box as your names are called."

Then he put his hand into a box on the table before him, drew out a slip from which he read a name aloud. In the righthand section of seats there was a small stir, and Sam Hardy rose and came walking down the aisle toward the railed-in part of the room. Before he reached the jury box and the seat numbered one, the clerk was calling another name and Ed Ketcham was coming down the other aisle. At the defendant's table Syke Berry was showing John Oliver his jury list with the marginal notes he had made, and John Oliver was nodding and agreeing. For, of course, being a stranger to the county, he didn't know the people around here the way Syke did and he'd have to rely on Syke entirely for getting the jury. It seemed clear that the Yam, over at the other table, took much the same attitude of detachment.

At last the jury box contained twelve men and the clerk came over and delivered to each of the rival law teams a board with twelve numbered name cards tentatively bound to it. Syke ran his eye along it rapidly. Eight owned slaves. Four had none. He looked up from the name cards and let his eyes pass along the twelve faces in the double-banked jury seats, and his lips relaxed in a slight smile. There wasn't a man among them he didn't know by sight at least. Their routine qualifications he had got by heart, and there wasn't one of the twelve who was not a freeholder, over twenty-one and under sixty, and not one who would answer affirmatively the question whether he was master of the accused or a relative of her master or of either of the prosecuting attorneys. Syke knew the set of their minds, too—or of most of them. That ought to be a big help. But all the same he dreaded his challenges for cause. Probing for bias is a mighty toucheous business. No man believes himself prejudiced. Tackle one on that score and fail to convince the court and you're liable to have saddled yourself with a juror actively and personally hostile clear to the end of the trial. . . .

"Gentlemen, you may now examine the jury," spoke the judge's voice above his head.

Syke saw the District Attorney standing up and he stood, too. His pulse pounded strongly. It's started, he thought, it's started at last!

The District Attorney questioned juror number one briefly and declared himself satisfied. Well, Syke wasn't satisfied, far from it. Sam Hardy was obligated to Kirk McLean for help in rebuilding his livery stable after the big fire and otherwise prejudiced. But before beginning on Sam, Syke had it in mind to prepare the whole twelve a little. He went over to the jury box, rested his hand on the rail and took a deep breath.

"Gentlemen," he said smiling, "you all know me. You know I'm just a plain backwoods boy, a heap more at home in the cotton field than in a courtroom." He paused and watched twelve faces relax to smiles. As he went on his voice became more earnest. "In November term when this case first come to trial and I was appointed by the court as counsel for the defense I was—I reckon you've guessed it—pretty near scared to death. I hadn't much more than passed my bar examinations. It was my first case. The crime described in the indictment was a mighty dirty one, a poisoning, aimed at a white family by, it seemed like, somebody in their own back-yard kitchen. One death had resulted. The charge was murder. If the woman cook accused was proved guilty, she'd hang. Mebbe you don't know I had barely two days to prepare her case. I couldn't find one witness to come into court and speak in her behalf. Her very owners was against her. It looked like she didn't have a friend on earth, even among her own color. The only hope she had was me, green as a gourd and scared to boot, like I say. I reckon it was no more than what you'd expect that I fought a losing fight.

"Since that time, gentlemen, the High Court of Errors and Appeals has ordered a new trial and I come here assisted this time by Mr. John Oliver, my law teacher from up at Oxford, to ask a fair trial for this woman. Evidence excluded from the first trial will, by the High Court's ruling, now be admissible. Other evidence not then available has since come to light. Now you know and I know there's no such thing as a fair trial without you've got a fair jury. As I question you gentlemen now one by one, I ask you to be patient and I beg you to look deep into your hearts and declare whether you can hear this evidence with an open mind and bring in a verdict free of all bias. . . ."

Then he spoke to Sam Hardy directly.

Q. What is your business, Mr. Hardy?

Sam's face twitched drolly as much as to say, "You know damn well, Syke Berry." But of course he had to answer politely.

A. I'm a liveryman, sir.

He contrived to stress the *sir* to get a titter out of the audience and draw a hot flush to Syke's cheeks.

Q. But you have other sources of income, too, haven't you?

A. You mean like from them two field hands hired out on a little one-mule farm south of town a ways?

Q. Yes—and don't Blacksmith Billy belong to you, too, Mr. Hardy? You get some return from his shop, don't you?

A. He belongs to my wife. Yes, Billy earns me something, more some years than others, of course. In a bad year the shop don't much more than pay his keep.

Q. You own other slaves, too, I believe. How many?

Sam counted on his fingers, his eyes twinkling slyly.

A. Well, besides Billy, my wife owns his wife Sade—she's our cook. Their three sons work around the livery stable or the two biggest ones do and the little chap, he just gets under foot mostly. And the two field hands we mentioned a while back, they've got a child but it don't bring in anything yet, being as it's under a year old. . . .

Laughter from the audience seemed to restore Sam's good humor, but the next question took him by surprise.

Q. What is the color of these several slaves that you and your wife own, Mr. Hardy? Are they full blacks or have you some with mixed blood?

Sam Hardy sat forward and stared.

A. Pure black, every one of them.

The playful, latent clowning was gone now. There was a grimness in his bearing. His face was red and puffed, his voice rumbled with anger. If Syke didn't get rid of him he'd be that dreaded enemy to the end, entrenched and formidable.

Q. Look at the prisoner, Mr. Hardy.

A. All right. I looked. What of it?

Q. She's a quadaroon. You can see that, can't you?

A. I can see she's got white blood. I can't see how much. And you can't neither.

Q. But she is obviously not a full-blooded Negro?

A. I said I see that.

Q. Now, Mr. Hardy, I am sure you recall that, a couple of years back, when you was fixing to buy the pair you mentioned just now, you discussed your plans in front of your livery stable one evening with Orrin Foote and several others. Did you tell them that you never owned any but pure black stock because one good pure black to your mind was worth a half dozen yellow niggers, that all the mixed bloods was good for, looked like, was to run away and get into scrapes? Did you say that?

A. No, not exactly.

Q. But something like it? Will you tell us what you did say?

A. No, I won't. It's too long ago. I've forgotten. Orrin has, too. I don't care what he says now. He's got no right to go around quoting a chance remark made long before this trial was ever heard of. And, anyway, if this woman's heart's as black as sin, it don't matter what color her skin is.

Q. Now, Mr. Hardy, if you feel you have been misquoted,

perhaps you will tell the court what you actually did say on that particular occasion.

A. I tell you I've forgotten.

Syke turned to the judge, but before he could speak, Sam Hardy leaned suddenly forward.

A. All right, then, I said it.

Q. Mr. Hardy, more recently, last fall, in fact, some time between the time of the crime at Waverley and the fall term of court, did you in speaking of the prisoner say to several people gathered in front of the Methodist church one Sunday right after morning services: "Anybody ain't blind can see she's a Jezebel?"

A. I reckon I did.

The Yam stood up.

"A Jezebel is merely an unchaste woman, your Honor. The question of the prisoner's chastity is surely immaterial to the issue of this trial and a juror who has formed an opinion in that regard cannot on this ground be charged with prejudice as to the issue."

The judge addressed the prospective juror.

Q. What do you understand, sir, by the term Jezebel as applied to the prisoner?

A. Like Mr. Boone said—just a woman anybody can have for the taking.

Q. Do you believe, sir, that having formed such an opinion of her chastity, or lack of it, you could, if the State fail to prove its case beyond a reasonable doubt, bring an acquittal for her?

A. Certainly, your Honor.

The judge shook his head ruefully.

"The court does not agree. You are excused, sir."

Mr. Hardy left the jury box. The clerk drew and announced another name, another man came down the aisle and the twelve seats were again filled.

Mr. Clayton Burgess smilingly told the District Attorney he had resided in the state and county five years. He was the editor of the Athens *Free Press* and a teacher in the Boys' Academy. He had formed no opinion as to the guilt or innocence of the accused and was as sure as Sam Hardy had been in response to that same question that, if accepted as juror, he would find a verdict based on the evidence alone under such instruction as to law as the court might give. Though he came of a slave-holding family back in Dallas County, Alabama, he was not himself a slave owner but was accustomed to hire such servants as he needed from his rich friends in the country. The allusion to his quasi-rich friends he accompanied with a sideways quizzical glance toward the audience that provoked the flutter of mirth it asked for. He had at present two such hired servants, a woman to cook for his family and a boy to clean up the printing office, keep the water bucket full and so forth and in his spare time to help out at home with milking, weeding the garden, washing windows, and whatever else Mrs. Burgess found for him to do. Both servants at present were mulattoes, but this was a matter of chance. In other years he had engaged blacks, browns, yellows about equally. It was his custom on hiring to pay no attention whatever to color but to rely entirely on the "character" given the candidate by owner or overseer.

The District Attorney pronounced himself satisfied and, smiling slyly, invited the counsel for the defense to examine. Syke approached the jury box, and laid a newspaper clipping on the rail in front of Mr. Burgess. Clayte took it up and looked at it, waiting for Syke's question.

Q. Did the piece you hold in your hand there, signed by the name of Athenian, come out in the Athens *Free Press* on the 25th of last November, Mr. Burgess?

Clayte turned the slip over and examined it carefully.

A. There's no date on this, and I don't remember exactly.

Q. But it did appear in the newspaper of which you have told the District Attorney you are editor?

A. Yes, sir.

Q. And to the best of your recollection was this during the very time when the prisoner now under indictment was first undergoing trial in this room?

A. Really, Mr. Berry, I should have to consult the newspaper files to answer such a question.

Q. Can you tell me the dates of the November term of court?

A. Certainly. Monday November 23 through the following Saturday.

Q. And the *Free Press* is issued on Wednesday regular?

A. Regularly on Wednesday.

Q. So the Wednesday during last November court week, which

was November 25, as this woman's first trial was nearing its end, you wrote—

A. I did not write it.

Q. No? You ain't Athenian, then?

A. I am not. The piece was left at the press office, by whom I do not know, one day when I was over at the academy, teaching.

Q. Still you was ready to publish it, seems like. Anyways you did publish, on that Wednesday, these lines assuming, the way I read 'em, the guilt of the prisoner. Will you read the piece to the court, Mr. Burgess? The title first, please.

A. "An Appeal for Justice. Even a rattler sounds a warning before he discharges his venom into his victim's veins, but the evil being in woman form who mixed her deadly brew on a bright and sunlit noon recently at Waverley struck in chilling silence. Citizens of Chewalla County, Friends, this soundless treachery aimed at the annihilation of our good friend McLean's family, was aimed at us all. Their bereavement is our bereavement. The thing that happened at Waverley can happen at any time in any kitchen on any farm or in any back yard here in town. It is the very essence of our peculiar institution that precisely those whom we trust the most we give power to deal us the greatest hurt. It is not in the humble black man chopping cotton under the eye of the overseer out in the field that our danger lies. He does his work, eats his field peas and hoecake and sleeps the sleep of lowly innocence. But the pleasant-mannered body servant wearing his master's vests, the girl in the cast-off muslins of her mistress to whose arms we trust our babes, the cook whom we praise and reward with special gifts and notice—what of them? These favorites with their secret aspirations have both the motive and the opportunity to strike us in the heart. For who can say what chance will turn any one of them against us, a small punishment for a fault, the slight preferment of one above another, some fancied tone of reproach? And once the desire to please has been transformed into malice, the deed is all too easy for the nurse who sleeps by the infant's cradle or the cook who, like the woman on trial, mixes our daily bread."

The court excused Clayte Burgess too, and again a vacancy in the jurors' ranks was refilled by drawing a new name. The next man examined disqualified himself as if purposely by declaring at once that he had attended the previous trial of the accused in this courtroom from beginning to end in November, that the evidence on any new trial, if they tried her a dozen times, was bound to be the same, and as to the law, well, he didn't reckon they had made any new laws down at Jackson that said you ought to acquit a cook that would poison her own white folks. . . .

"Excused," said the judge abruptly and stole another glance at his watch.

Getting a jury in this case, the judge saw, was going to be a long and hard-fought business, and he did not relish it. He had been up since daylight, had taken only a cup of coffee before starting out from the preceding court town, and had had, on arrival here, no time for breakfast or even rest before coming into court. So now he was hungry and tired. His pain was bothering him today, too. It was a very small pain actually, just a little nibbling and gnawing midway of his breast. But it was insistent and to some degree alarming, because he always dreaded any kind of illness out on circuit.

Since the examination of the jurors did not require his continuous attention, he took the first opportunity to open and read his daughter's letter, which had been put in his hand as he came into court.

Dear Papa:

May I introduce Alexander Quintius Rusk, Jr.? He arrived this morning a little after daylight. And, if the squalls I hear this moment are any indication, he's as lusty as any of his and my seven brothers. Mama says to tell you that, contrary to custom, she is taking the liberty of naming him without awaiting your return. And I—may I add, your Honor?—am this time on Mama's side. I advise you to yield gracefully. And why not? Having used up the names of two grandfathers, all available uncles and even a former North Carolina law partner, how can you longer decline a namesake? This letter must be brief because I am cumbered with much serving. But when you get home week after next—oh, blessed day already encircled in red on my little calendar—I mean to have a long argument with you about whether an only daughter might not be better off after all to know more about cake-making, dusting, silver polishing, the feeding and lesson-getting of the young, even at price of some Latin and Greek for herself. And, oh, yes, if a planter's first-born disappoints him as to sex, shouldn't he, especially if he intends to become a circuit judge, away from home all of every planting and picking season, also include in her education the instruction needful for the guidance of a crew of happy-go-lucky darkies, the care of livestock and such like farm matters?

Having refreshed himself at this entirely private spring, the judge put the letter away and began, with the ease of long practise, to leaf through the papers on the desk before him. As the examination of jurors ground steadily on, he familiarized himself with the case of the *State* vs. *Aimée:* the pleadings, the transcript of evidence in the former trial, the previous judge's instructions, and the bill of exceptions on which the defense had based its appeal and obtained retrial. The last-named document was very long and it made him smile a little because of the picture it brought up of a bitter battle. He could just see how young Berry there, with his frequent shouted objections, must have tried the late Judge Calloway's patience. Judge Rusk had known his predecessor only slightly, but he already felt well acquainted with Silas Berry—"that young rooster," he secretly named him. And he found considerable amusement in imagining the rough-haired tawny boy with his backwoods speech pitted against the gray and mannered old aristocrat. He himself expected to get on very well with the boy, because, somehow, he liked him—a sandhiller, they'd have called him back in the judge's native state. Here he was hillbilly, peckerwood or red-neck probably. Well, he was a fiery one, anyway, no dirt-eating there. Ten to one he had a good mother. . . .

Now he turned to the rulings of the High Court.

"One error assigned is the refusal of the court to allow the prisoner's counsel to interrogate the witness Kirk McLean on cross-examination concerning his private relations with the prisoner. . . ."

The ugly words seemed to leap off the page to strike at him, like a rattler stepped on unaware. His pain fairly clawed at him. His sweat poured. It dimmed his glasses. He had to take them off to polish them. As he did so, his startled eyes fell on the small family group who sat, as they had sat all morning, on the front center bench before him: Kirk McLean, a handsome, rather florid man in fastidious, finely worked linen, erect between the women of his household, of whom the judge's first guess had been that the younger was a daughter and the older, the wife—perhaps because it was the older who gave attention to the baby in its nurse's lap beside her. But now he saw his mistake, saw it was the other way round entirely: The role of female dependent—whether unmarried sister, aunt or poor cousin—belonged of obvious right to the older woman with her nun's face and severe black dress. The girl, though young, was after all not quite young enough to be McLean's daughter. He looked at her intently.

As always when he saw a young girl, he compared her with his own Katherine. This one, he guessed, was about the same age, not so tall and definitely of slighter build; hair and skin several shades darker, eyes bigger—or did they only look bigger because she had so recently passed through the fiery ordeal of childbirth? The color of the eyes he could not settle because she had a nervous habit of closing them often. Something about the closed, waxen lids, her almost vacant way of answering whispered remarks made to her by the other two, her lack of interest in her child, suggested want of spirit.

When he tried to force his eyes back to the words in the High Court's ruling, the young wife's shuttered face came between him and the page and a question teased him: Is this the thing that has killed her vitality? Is this what she refuses to look at? Well, it was no affair of his. He could do nothing to shield her, could not, like his predecessor, shut off the unsavory question. Whatever his personal sympathies and wishes, he must obey the High Court, which had found Judge Calloway in error for excluding testimony regarding Kirk McLean's secret relation to the accused. The High Court had ruled this testimony relevant because it "tended to show that the prisoner was not discontented with her condition and could have had no malice to lead her to commit the crime."

The clock in the tower struck twelve and the District Attorney addressed the bench.

"Shall we begin another examination, your Honor, or is it your pleasure to defer the next till after the noon recess?"

"Defer it," said his Honor, almost before the question was complete.

[46]

As the judge gathered up his papers and vanished through the door directly behind the bench, Syke whispered elatedly to John Oliver: "He gave me all I've asked for cause and I haven't used up but one peremptory." John Oliver laughed, got out his pipe and began to stuff tobacco into it. The sheriff approached the prisoner and she put out her wrist to let him clamp on the steel cuff. A young lawyer leaped the rail, sprang to the judge's platform, seized the gavel, rapped loudly and shouted:

"Attention, everybody. This courtroom will remain open for a brief debate between the candidates for the State Senate from this district. The subject is one in which every slaveholding state has a life-and-death interest; namely, that of 'popular sovereignty' and the Kansas-Nebraska question. The speaking will begin promptly at twelve-thirty in time to be finished when court opens at one. Mrs. Howell over at the tavern has asked me to announce that she's setting a first table especially for those who wish to attend the speaking and she urges them to come quickly to the tavern now."

Martha, making her slow way out along the crowded aisle beside Sis Hat, saw the Ketcham girls waiting for them at the back of the room beside the door. Evvie had on a new spring outfit that she must have been getting ready for weeks: a flower-sprigged lawn trimmed with tiny handmade folds of the same lavender color as the flowers in the pattern. And her sash and bonnet ribbons were green to match the little leaves. Evvie was fair and almost pretty, although, to Martha's eyes, she was an old maid, thirty, Sis Hat said, and more, rather than less, anxious for a man as time went on. Evvie was smiling and coquetting with everybody who passed. Clara, called "the quiet one," was actually younger than Evvie, but she looked older, being less "fixy" and more inclined to take on weight. She had on a new light dress, too, but it was a nondescript blue made plain and sacklike. It looked almost as if she had run it up the day before, and its only trimming was the same old Irish lace collar she always wore, pinned with a child's coral brooch, which seemed to be the only piece of jewelry she possessed. Sis Hat considered that Evvie's vivacious, talkative ways put poor Clara in the shade, but Martha, perversely, liked Clara better.

When the Waverley party drew near, Evvie broke off midway of laughing at the joke of some passer-by and dropped her voice to a low, serious pitch—a velvety, mournful, almost funereal tone.

"Oh, dear Harriet—and little Martha! There you are at last. I was beginning to be afraid we'd let you get by somehow. And Mr. Kirk! Mama will be so *proud*."

"Miss Evvie," Kirk McLean asked, "think your mother can have a place set for Parson, too?"

"Yes, indeed," cried Evvie and Clara in one breath and were immediately seconded by their father, who, on reprieve from the jury box, came along just then to join them.

Ed Ketcham was at all times an easy-going, hospitable fellow, and today the chance of his being soon sworn as juror and so cut off indefinitely from the comforts of home perhaps made him the more cordial as he wrung Mr. Banning's hand and reinforced "the girls'" invitation. The next moment, to Martha's secret amusement, Ed was introducing, first to his daughters and then to the rest of them, the stranger, Mr. Onnud, and blandly announcing that he had invited Mr. Onnud to stay at their house to get him away from the tavern where he had been so uncomfortable last night.

It wasn't often, as Sis Hat said afterward, that anybody got the chance to see Evvie struck dumb. But that time it happened. Evvie's mouth simply fell open and her fair face crimsoned all over. Martha almost laughed. She knew Evvie was probably worrying over how their plain little Mississippi home would strike this elegant gentleman with city ways, and maybe, too, her loyalty to Mr. McLean made her question her father's taste in proffering hospitality to the man who was footing the bills for the defense of that awful woman. Evvie's consternation lasted only a moment, of course. Power of speech returned to her and her cordiality to Mr. Onnud was, if anything, excessive. She even slipped her hand through his arm and led him off.

"Setting her cap for him a'ready," Sis Hat dryly commented in Martha's ear.

As the party passed through the lower corridor, Tom Peters came to the door of his office and asked Mr. Banning to step inside for a moment. But the interview was brief enough and Mr. Banning was able to overtake the rest of them on the sidewalk outside as they formed into ranks for the march over to the Ketchams'. Martha happened to be trailing along behind the others, and he fell into step beside her.

[48]

"I suppose Mr. Peters wanted to tell you what the defense will try to prove, what they will ask you?" she said.

"Yes. I understand fully. Please don't be uneasy. I'm not."

Still she went on, hurrying a little, becoming somehow breathless with the effort.

"They'll keep at you, you know. Or that Berry boy will. Mr. Peters says he'll stop at nothing—that Syke Berry. This is his first case. He'll do anything to win—drag Mr. McLean's name in the dirt any way he can. Judge Calloway headed him off in the other trial. But this new judge—nobody knows what he'll allow. Syke Berry may put the most embarrassing questions to you, over and over, surprise you into saying something you don't realize the meaning of—"

He laughed at her.

"Now, now, Miss Martha. Don't you know I can take care of myself? And don't you know, too, that it would be impossible for anybody on earth to make me say one word that could be twisted to Kirk's hurt—or yours?"

"Ah," she breathed. "I can't tell you how grateful—"

"Don't try," he interrupted and with swift sympathy changed the subject. In another moment her brow cleared and she was talking about New Orleans as joyfully as though she hadn't a care in the world.

Her honeymoon memories were romantic and highly colored. She often thought of herself as a bride walking with the two devoted friends along the hot, bright old streets laced with wrought iron and resounding with vendors' cries blended into one mellow chant: "Pralines, pralines, Angélique's pralines"; "L'estomac de mulatre"; "Crabs, crabs, soft-shell crabs." She remembered that special New Orleans odor, blended, like the musical cries, of many parts: scent of river water and tar and hemp and bananas, drifting in from the wharf; a mild steam of open drains and horse manure, rising from underfoot to mingle with the incense of the vendors' offerings of candy and spiced gingerbread and new-caught crabs bedded in damp gray moss; coffee from coffee stalls; wine. And every foot of the street had color: the sharp yellow sunlight, the blue-black shadows, the women of every hue from cream to chocolate brown in their brilliant *tignons;* sailors and river-boat gamblers and Creole gentlefolk in Paris finery.

[49]

"How lucky you are!" she cried ecstatically. "Just imagine *living* in such a place."

He smiled at her extravagance, but there was nothing critical in the smile. She knew there was not. His eyes were kind and indulgent.

"Oh," she appealed to him suddenly, piteously. "Why must there be such dreadful people as Syke Berry, *wanting* to destroy other people? He's just doing it out of personal spite, you know—some old grudge he's got against Mr. McLean."

"Do you know, I rather doubt that, Miss Martha. Really, I do."

"Well, maybe it's what Sis Hat says: He's just so dog poor he'll stoop to anything to get his hands on money."

"That may be. But his passion seems to me to have deeper roots than that. It's more as if he felt some real principle were involved."

They had arrived at the Ketchams' now, but Martha did not want to go upstairs to Clara's room as Clara invited. Instead she preferred to sit down in the little cluttered parlor with Mr. Banning to go on listening to his kind wise voice, pouring something human into this dreadful inhuman business.

"Isn't it possible that young Berry, being low-born himself, may be stirred to some special sympathy for this creature who has every hand but his against her? Now, mind you, I grant he's using an unfair weapon, but in a way he's forced to—if he makes a fight at all, that is—"

"Has to be unfair! Oh, Mr. Banning. You can't mean that."

"Yes, I do. Precisely because the white population is so solidly arrayed against the woman. Maybe I, an outsider, can see that better than you who live here."

"But aren't people even up North against a murderer?"

"Yes, of course. It's rather hard to express. But there's something about *this* trial in *this* place that's fundamentally different. There's a might and power released against this accused woman that's elemental in its force, like the wrath of God Himself. The whole white community is picked up and carried along by it. Listen to them talking there under the trees and on the tavern porch. Each one speaks as if he had been personally violated, outraged. And take that editorial read in court just now. Surely Moses himself, just back from the burning bush, addressed his flock with no less fervor and conviction of divine guidance."

[50]

"But it was an awful crime. Don't *you* think Aimée ought to be punished for it?"

"If she's guilty. But how can men so swept away by passion even hear a whisper of that 'reasonable doubt' young Berry insists on as her right? It's almost as though she were to that audience not a human being at all, but just a creature of straw like—like, oh, you know, the scarecrow thing they burn in England, Guy Fawkes. In the courtroom that's almost palpable. I get caught into it myself. When she turns her head, smiles at Mr. Arnaud, speaks a word to her lawyers, I am taken by surprise. I feel like springing up and crying out: see, she's not just a digit, a pawn, an effigy, set up to be knocked down like a tenpin in a bowling alley. She's a woman of flesh and blood, after all. It's that debasing, that under-valuing, of the individual that is the very root and core of the evil of slavery—Do you understand what I'm trying to say, Miss Martha?"

"Not—not very well. But I want to. Go on."

She was listening as hard as she could. To grasp this gospel he was expounding was a feat beyond her, and yet it had a flavor so new, so altogether unheard-of, that it captured and held her fast. Nobody had ever talked to her like this in all her life before. She liked him for doing it, thought he was kind and patient, too, to take so much pains for her enlightenment, like a schoolteacher or careful elder brother. She did her very best to live up to the compliment, fixing her gaze firmly in his and clasping her hands hard together on her lap. And then, alas, Evvie fluttered in to say dinner was ready and all the others came trooping along the stair and hall toward the dining room.

PART II

Double Muscadine

CHAPTER 1

To the eyes of a bride just arriving, the town of Athens veiled in the dusk of a summer afternoon and briefly glimpsed from the vantage of a hired hack seemed scarcely real. Of course she looked at the landmarks her husband pointed out in passing: especially the office of the *Free Press*, which long ago he had founded, and the little white cottage where he and his first wife had set up housekeeping. But she saw them as belonging to a past remote and dead even to him and surely having nothing at all to do with her. Waverley was his home, would be hers, too, now. Waverley was all she cared about. Besides, she was very tired. The journey from Georgia, partly overland by stage and in the cars, partly by boats down the Alabama, through the Gulf and up again along the Mississippi and the Yalohatchie, had gone on so long now that she could hardly realize this was the last lap.

Beyond the town the country road offered nothing interesting enough to point out. The tunnel bored by the rocking carriage lamps through the hot, dark night seemed to have no end. The miles of pale tree trunks and their shadows, wheeling spokelike, the twisting boughs and patterned leaves, the occasional crooked rail fences edging invisible fields, the rabbits' eyes fixed in fright between two grass-fringed ruts formed and dissolved, dissolved and formed ceaselessly. Then at last, without warning, the groping fingers of lamplight hung motionless. The racking and jolting stopped. The laboring axles, the thud of hooves, the grinding and creaking, all were silenced. In the sudden quiet, katydids and tree frogs had everything their own way.

Drugged as she was with drowsiness and fatigue, she was profoundly aware of finality. Her hand went out and strayed, groping, along the bumpy leather-cushioned seat beside her. It was warm but empty. Are we home? she said. Are we really there? But he did not seem to hear her. He had climbed out. A dog barked and he was answering: Old Hickory! It's me, old fellow. Dimly she saw a small shadow come plunging through shadows to envelop his stooping silhouette in writhings, scufflings, whinings. So you've missed me, old fellow? Well, well.

A flower fragrance lay on the air, heliotrope perhaps. Or was it oleander? Whatever it was, it was delicious. He had mentioned a garden, roses in particular. The house was quite dark, everybody in bed hours ago, of course. She bent forward and peered anxiously out at it: just a double log cabin as he had told her over and over, two hulking rooms with a dogtrot linking them, a backwoods house without a single thing to set it apart from a hundred others glimpsed from stage and steamboat—some of them even slept in—along the way. Yet there was this single, momentous difference: This one was Waverley.

"Hello! Hello!" His cheerful call battered away at the ink-black house. "Hello, I say. Anybody home?"

A light appeared in the room at the left. It flooded from an unshuttered window and leaked out around a rough door giving on the dogtrot. A woman's voice, sleepy and alarmed, called:

"Who is it? Are you lost? What you want up this road in the middle of the night?"

He laughed and leaped up the steps.

"Why, it's me, Sis Hat!"

"Br' Kirk—what in the world?"

The door opened then and the woman stepped out into the dogtrot, the lamp held up over her head, its oil-filled bowl shading her face, blotting it out, and the flame, tugged by the outdoor air, lighting only one uplifted arm thin and white in the loose sleeve of a blue lawn wrapper and the top of her head knobby with curling pins. He took the lamp from her and set it on a table near by. Then he turned to her again, caught her shoulders, and touched his lips to her forehead.

"The prodigal's returned, Sis Hat."

"Well, I never!" she cried delightedly and then, in affectionate complaint, "I reckon it wouldn't occur to you to write and say you was coming."

Her face, lit from below, wavered queerly, the shadows of her high cheekbones leaping up to mask her eyes, the smile on her lips alternately appearing and vanishing, like a mocking grimace. The girl in the carriage shivered and wiped her perspiring brow.

Sis Hat wants me to marry again. Oh, yes, she does. She's been dropping hints for years. She can't live forever, she says. And if anything should happen to her, who would take her place at Waverley? She prays for a wife for me, darling. A sort of *nunc dimittis* will burst from her lips at the sight of you. . . .

He bent and whispered at some length in the woman's ear. She gave a sharp cry and turned to stare out into the darkness. The girl drew back against the cushions of the hired hack, gripped her hands together over her damp, balled-up handkerchief, and took a deep breath. Now he was coming back for her, talking as he came. We're here, my dear. Time to wake up now. We're home. He leaned into the carriage, put both arms around her waist and half lifted, half dragged her out. As her feet touched the ground, his lips brushed her cheek and bonnet string and a whisper teased her ear. Now remember, everything's going to be all right. Aloud he said:

"Here she is, Sis Hat. Here's my wife."

"My goodness. What a surprise. What's your name, dear? Martha? Well, then, howdy, Martha. Welcome to Waverley. This is the happiest day of my life, I do declare. This the day I been praying for."

The words were exactly what he had promised. They were sturdy and true, the very shape and form of homely country welcome. But the woman's smile in the gusty lamplight still flickered unreliably, her hand felt dry and cold and so did her lips brushing the girl's cheek. After the kiss, Martha shrank back against her husband's encircling arm, trying not to be afraid of the mysterious, gaunt stranger who greeted her so cordially. Is she really glad? Oh, God, let her be. Let her welcome me in her heart.

A small creaking sound made them all look upward. A stair that was more like a ladder, rising midway of the open passage, held a boy, stopped about halfway down to frown and wonder.

He stood wholly in shadow, with the fluttering lamplight washing no farther up than the rung he stood on. Above his lean brown shanks and brief nightshirt, his wide, fixed eyes gleamed down from the upper dark like some alarmed rabbit's by the road.

"Come down and see who I've brought home with me, Son," Kirk McLean cheerfully called and then, impatiently: "Well, well, what's the matter? Not walking in your sleep, are you? I thought you outgrew that a year ago."

The boy on the ladder found his tongue and cried in a shrill voice:

"Who is it? Who is that white lady?"

"Come, Hunt," his aunt encouraged tenderly. "Isn't this a fine surprise? Your papa's gone and got married off at the springs."

"Married!" the boy wailed. "But I don't want a stepmother. I don't . . ."

His aunt's expression altered. She reached down from between the logs at her back a long switch and, swinging it grimly above her head, marched toward the ladder. The child screamed and crouched, letting the nightshirt down like a curtain over his bare feet and legs.

"I'll be good, Aunt Hat, I'll be good," he chattered, swallowing at his grief.

"You better be," she admonished tartly, returning the switch to its crevice. "Now get on back upstairs and put your breeches on. You ought to be ashamed, a great long-legged boy like you letting a lady see you half naked. And while you're about it, put on your company manners, too, you hear?"

"Yes, ma'am," he sniffled. And, turning his back, with goat-like leaps and scrambles, his nightshirt ballooning, he vanished overhead.

Harriet Hunt faced about, smiling fondly.

"Half asleep, poor lamb," she murmured, "and scared with nigger talk, too, of course. I never in all my days put such a notion in his head. I always tell him how nice it be some day to have a sweet, pretty young stepmother. He'll be all right soon as he get good awake. Here, Martha, come in my room—the old house, it is, the one Pa built first for him and Ma and me before ever Honey was born. You better set in here while I get one of the girls up to fix the other room for you. Br' Kirk, show that hackman where to set them bags, will you?"

She took up the lamp and strode off through her door, with the stranger trailing timidly behind her. They could not have entered abreast in any case, for there was barely room for them to pass single file between the big four-poster and an even bigger structure of rough timbers alongside it.

"Hardly room enough to swing a cat in here," Miss Harriet remarked offhand over her shoulder, "what with my loom and all."

"Oh," breathed Martha, stopping to stare sideways. "So that's a loom."

Miss Harriet laughed.

"Where was you raised, not to never seen a loom before?"

"Oh, I have. Of course I have. Only this one seems . . . It's a very big one, isn't it?"

The square-cut towering uprights and thick overhead beams of the loom dwarfed even the tapering bedposts which themselves almost touched the joists, and far within the mighty framework, in a very jungle of crisscross wooden bars and reeds, threads stretched like a giant spiderweb.

"Yes," said Miss Harriet proudly. She had stopped, too, holding the lamp up for the guest to examine her treasure. "It is right big. It was willed to me by a dear old friend, her that taught me to weave, Mrs. Cumby, her name was. She come here from the Kentucky mountain country. We had to take it all to pieces to get it out of her house after she died. And we like to never got it back together again. Nobody around here ever see a loom with so many treadles and shuttles. It was mighty near a year after it come to me before I got it to running right. What are you staring at?"

Martha to hide her embarrassment had bent to look at the unfinished cloth wound over the beam.

"What is it you are making?"

"Just nigger cloth," said Miss Harriet. "But, there, you ain't really interested. So don't pretend to be." She moved on at last, letting her talk flow backward. "Ma used to say what you can't do you don't ever have to. She was against white women learning any sort of drudgery: weaving, washing, milking, the like of that.

[59]

Poor Ma. She'd turn in her grave, I reckon, could she see what all I do day in and day out, woman's work and man's work, too. . . ."

They were facing each other now on a homemade hearthrug lying like an island in the mountainous seas of the overcrowded room, where splitbottom backwoods chairs strangely jostled fine old mahogany. Miss Hat set the lamp on the mantel. The flame behaved better indoors. It stood upright and steady inside its chimney, lighting the face of each for the other to stare at, two strangers thrust into intimacy willy-nilly, with everything that mattered still unsaid between them.

"You—you're kind," blurted Martha at last. "It can't be comfortable for you, being taken by surprise like this." And, she thought, maybe it's hard, too, to see me come to take Honey's place. He has told me how much you loved your little sister.

"Well, I reckon a good hearty welcome won't come exactly amiss to a girl that's come such a long ways with a stranger—"

"A stranger!"

"You never set eyes on him till a few weeks back, did you? And him a man twicet your age, nearly 'bout it, somebody you don't know nothing on God's green earth about. You must be mighty near starved for the sight of a real good woman."

Martha's fingers laced together and twisted hard.

"He's not a stranger. Not at all. I feel I've known Mr. McLean always. A few weeks is as good as years when—" when you're in love, she wanted to say, but Miss Harriet's gimlet eyes forced her to falter. "At the springs—you know how it is at the springs. Nothing to do but talk. And then all along the way, too. We talked and talked. Mr. McLean has told me all about you and Honey and your mother and father. He's told me *everything* that ever happened at Waverley."

"Humph," said Harriet dryly. Then she started and, visibly donning her company manners, cried: "My, my. What am I thinking of, leaving you standing like this, not even asking you to lay your bonnet off. Here, take this little rocker. It's the most comfortable. Ma brought it from North Carolina like everything else in this house that's anyways civilized. You must be half dead. Must a-been good dark time you left town. I wonder you could get anybody to drive you out so late over that road. And you never even stop for supper, Br' Kirk says. What make you in such a mighty hurry?"

When Martha shook her head and blinked back her tears, unable to answer, Miss Harriet looked at her, puzzled, and sitting down opposite, hands folded in her lap, made formal effort to find a more agreeable topic.

"You come by New Or-*leens*, didn't you?"

Martha brightened on the instant.

"Oh, *yes!*" she cried. "It was wonderful. I loved every minute there. And Mr. Banning—"

"Is a conquest," interrupted her husband gaily, sauntering in to join them. "She came, she saw, she conquered, Sis Hat. You wouldn't have known old Parson. Why, he's a regular lady's man after all, dancing attendance from daylight to dark, paying gallant compliments, buying nosegays—"

To Martha's horror, Harriet's lips compressed in a hard thin line and she rose abruptly.

"Well, I reckon I better be seeing about getting you something to eat. Hit's near midnight. And you must be hungry, driving all that long way out on an empty stomach."

Then she was gone. Martha sprang up and faced her husband reproachfully.

"Oh, why did you do that? Now she'll think I'm a silly, cheap—"

He pulled her to him and kissed her.

"Nonsense. Don't you suppose Sis Hat knows when I'm joking?"

"She didn't seem to. She was disgusted."

"Oh, that's just because I took the name of Parson in vain. He's not one to be mentioned lightly to Sis Hat. You should see how she behaves when he comes to visit us. Such scouring and furbishing and bed-airing and cake-baking. You'd think he was the Prince of Wales. Why, she even makes me go up to the loft to sleep with Hunt and gives him my room. Just wait till he comes the next time. You'll see. The fact is, my girl, she's jealous, she's secretly in love with him. . . ."

"Don't," said Martha trying to pull away from him. "It's only a joke, I know. But it's not a nice joke. It's—well, it's horrid. It insults both of them."

Her cheeks were aflame and tears stood in her eyes. But on him the only effect of her anger was, perversely, amused delight. He hugged her the closer, chuckling and kissing by turns, almost as if he were fondling a puppy he had teased into snapping at his finger.

Martha, tumbling into bed at last, fell at once into a dream of travelling through a dark, tangled wood. It terrified her some-how and she went hurrying to get out of it. But no matter how she strained to hurry her steps, the wood grew vaster all the while. It grew always darker, too, and was filled with strange whispering sounds, the scampering feet, even the tiny screams of little fright-ened animals. . . .

What was that? She came to with a jerk, her heart beating wildly. For one black instant she did not know where she was— they had slept in so many places along the way. Even when she remembered that she was safe at Waverley at last, her husband's arm curved close about her, she was still afraid, unreasonably afraid, straining to hear in the shouting silence of the country night whatever it was that had wakened her. Nonsense, she re-buked her cringing instincts, there's nothing to be afraid of. How could there be? Maybe some stirring bough had brushed the roof or a woods animal skittered over the shingles. Or maybe it was just something she had heard in her dream.

But, no, there it was again: bump, bump, a small quiet, and another bump, bump. Why it's only old Hickory, she thought, almost laughing. It's just the dog scratching his fleas and thump-ing his leg against the floorboards out there in the passage.

With a vague idea of chasing him off, she slid out of bed and groped her way to the door standing open on the dogtrot. The summer night was sweet with flower smells and through the open-ing at the far end of the passage she could see the moon coming up, red and lopsided, over dark tree-tops. Then she became aware of a line of lamplight, bold and yellow, under the opposite door and aware that the thumping sound she had heard went on be-yond it. At once the beat translated itself into a human rhythm. The loom! Miss Harriet's loom. That's it, of course. She's weav-ing, weaving and singing. For now the thin falsetto of a camp-meeting song, subdued to the midnight hour, muffled by door and walls, mingled eerily with the beat and thud of the batten. But faint and far as the song was, words were distinguishable, even a name, Honey's name.

> "Be faithful, oh, be faithful.
> It won't be long, you know.
> I'll meet you at the portals
> Where angels come and go.
> Oh, Honey, dear Honey,
> Be faithful, oh, be faithful. . . ."

A LONG winding blast slit the darkness: the overseer's horn, the same Pa used to blow. Morning a'ready and Harriet still sitting at the loom, studying over what all she'd say to Br' Kirk on their ride. We'll talk in the morning, she'd promised him the last thing before he went to bed. I've got to ride over to the Lees' and see is that stray bull they've taken up our Major. You go with me. Then we can talk.

After seeing to the comfort of the travellers, she had gone back to bed, herself, of course, and tried her best to sleep. But it was like she was laying on red-hot coals, the way she jumped and tossed. You'd never know it was feathers under her, good feathers picked by her own hands from fowl she'd raised, in a tick of her own weaving. Oh, she had ever hoped Br' Kirk would marry again. Of course she had. Prayed for it, like she told that girl. But she never thought it would happen like this! Never thought he'd come driving up with a stranger in the dead of night, without so much as a word of warning. Here she is, Sis Hat. Here's my wife. Cheerful as you please, like he hadn't a care in the world, a-leaving Sis Hat to do the worrying and planning, like always. . . .

The torment flung her clean out of her bed at last and before she hardly knowed what she was doing she had lit the lamp and set it up on the shelf above her loom, like so many times before. She sat down on the bench, set her feet on the treadle and reached, fumbling, one hand toward the shuttle, the other to the batten. The weaving went badly at first. Her tears came in gusts to blind her. Her muscles felt as slack as hank cotton before it's sized. Lucky hit ain't nothing but nigger cloth, she thought bitterly. But soon the familiar beat of the loom got into her pulse once more, her hands and feet steadied, her tears quit off, even her stormy thoughts began to settle down. Weaving is the best medicine of all to soothe you in sore trouble. The saying was Mrs. Cumby's, but time and again Harriet had proved it for herself at Mrs. Cumby's loom.

In one way her duty now was plain enough: Honey's long been cold in her grave. Hit's a new little wife he's come bringing home for Sis Hat to cherish, knowing she would, too, God love him. She could even see it as a mark of his trust that he had brought her home like that without a word of warning. Here she is, Sis Hat. Oh, she'd be good to the little thing. As God could see in her heart, she would. The girl, stranger that she was, should set in the wife's place now and pour out the tea and coffee. She'd be the one to mend his socks and shirts—those beautiful shirts he ordered by the dozen from a French needlewoman down in New Or-*leens*. She should even carry the key basket if that suited her fancy—Miss Oc's own key basket. She should give out whatever was to be give out. The wife's place was lawfully hers and Sis Hat would be the last to grudge it to her. Sis Hat must take a back seat now. . . . And Hunt? Well, a stepmother's only a stepmother, of course, but in time, Harriet reckoned, Hunt would leave off being afraid of his father's new wife. And his aunt must accept that, too, when it come, get used to seeing him ask another woman could he go barefooted the first warm day of spring and couldn't he sit up a little later just this once. That would come hardest of all, but when, in all her born days, had she ever been let off having it hard?

After a second blast of the horn other sounds began in the back yard: doors banging, the creak of the well rope, somebody chopping wood, a rooster crowing. Harriet stepped down from the loom bench and went to the window. Still as dark as a pocket outside. But firelight showed through the open kitchen door and there was a flight of sparks from the top of the stack chimney. Aunt Dosia was getting ready to start breakfast. The savor of wood smoke hung in air and a little cool, before-dawn freshness.

Harriet turned from the window, carried the lamp over to the table, sat down, drew toward her a gray cloth-bound ledger open at the entry she had made only the evening before right after supper. She read it through, her lips tight:

July 23. Pretty day though warm. Went with Hunt about sundown to put flowers on Honey's grave. It is now six weeks since Br' Kirk left for Healing Springs, Georgia. May Almighty God watch over him and return him soon, restored in health and spirits, to his little family.

His little family! Just him and her and Hunt. Just them three all these years. Well, that was over now. A sob swelled her throat and wrenched her shoulders, but she swallowed hard, dipped the pen in ink and wrote:

July 24. Some cooler. Br' Kirk got back a little before midnight, bringing a wife, a girl no more than half his age by the look of her and idolizing him, that's certain. God show me my duty to her and give me strength to do it.

She blotted the lines, closed the book and hid it under the clothing in the chest drawer where she always kept it. The darkness in the room was perceptibly melting now. She blew out the lamp and began, almost feverishly, to put her clothes on, with the black cotton overskirt she wore for riding. She went out through the dogtrot, down the back steps. As she passed under Br' Kirk's window she spoke his name softly but distinctly. He did not answer but she heard the creak of the bed as he stirred and turned. So she knew he had heard and, without calling him again, she went on along the plank walk to the kitchen.

Aunt Dosia was just getting her grandson Dub off to the field with the hands' breakfast in two covered pails. Lethe, also a grandchild and the old woman's prime favorite, leaned at the wall eating from a pan held laxly a little way below her chin. Harriet felt a stir of impatience at the girl's careless pose but she spoke to her kindly as always.

"Go outside, please, Lethe. I want to talk to Aunt Dosia."

Lethe put the pan down on the table and slowly followed Dub out of the door. Harriet watched until she was halfway across the yard, well out of hearing. Then she turned to Aunt Dosia.

"He brought a wife back."

"Yes'm," Aunt Dosia agreed. She was bending to stir the pot of grits cooking on the open fire and momentarily a reddish glow flooded her dark face. But it revealed there not one trace of any feeling.

"A girl, real sweet and pretty," said Harriet, "hardly more than a child. He come riding up with her like it was the most natural thing in the world. 'Here she is, Sis Hat,' he said. Martha, her name is. Now you tell the people, Aunt Dosia, so as they can call her Miss Martha right off and make her feel at home, like. I reckon hit'll soothe and comfort her to hear ever'body saying Howdy, Miss Martha, and Good morning, Miss Martha, right from the start. You tell Lethe and the others, do you hear? If any of them ain't nice to her, they'll have me to answer to."

"Yes'm."

The old woman went on stirring, inscrutable, apparently undisturbed. Harriet wished she'd express some feeling, any feeling at all, so as a person could answer.

"There'll be changes. Of course there'll be changes," Harriet went on nervously. "She's Mas Kirk's wife and you'll all have to learn her ways and study how to please her. But, land sakes, I reckon if I can take a back seat like I got to, you all can take a few changes."

The old woman made a small clucking sound, whether of deprecation or agreement, it was impossible to tell. Kirk McLean entered the kitchen yawning and fell to promptly at the breakfast Aunt Dosia was setting out for them on her table. Harriet sat down opposite and began at once talking about Major, the bull, missing since Sunday. Her brother-in-law didn't bother to answer. He must know that she wanted to get him off alone to talk to him about his marriage and those changes it must involve. But his only speech as he ate his ham and grits and drank his coffee was a greeting to Aunt Dosia.

"I brought you a present, Aunt Dosia, but Miss Hat routed me out so fast I didn't have time to pick it up."

"No mind, Mas Kirk," said the old woman loftily. "I thanks you just the same."

Her dignity did not permit her one question about the nature of the gift, and just to tease her he wouldn't tell her without being asked. But Harriet thought this was a poor time he'd picked for teasing Aunt Dosia. She watched the old woman's tight-shut face uneasily. Mother and grandmother to the entire slave family,

Aunt Dosia wielded an authority on the place second only to Miss Hat's, often superseding hers. He'd better be making up to Aunt Dosia instead of riling her if he wanted the people to like his new wife. Actually he seemed to find Aunt Dosia's grim silence amusing.

"I suppose," he hinted gaily, "you two have got up before day just to congratulate me. You both look simply delighted."

Neither of them answered. Lethe's youngest wandered naked, golden as amber, into the kitchen and diverted the master's attention. He called the little fellow to him, asked if he was glad to see Mas Kirk home again and gave him a penny. Sharp admonitions not to swallow it broke simultaneously from Harriet and Aunt Dosia. Kirk McLean laughed aloud.

"Come now. Don't set the child against me," he begged in his most persuasive, teasing tone.

The sun was just coming up as they rode off. The air was damp and cool. There was a heavy dew on the cobwebs draping the weeds by the road and the blackberry bushes in the angles of the split-rail fences. Black, wet shadows streaked the reddish dust of the road. And the hands, stopped to breakfast under a tree by the deep green cotton field, made a picnic scene, the women with their red and blue head rags, the men joking and shouting with laughter. Even Mr. Duffy, the melancholy overseer, solitary at a little distance, squatted on his heels, was smiling benignly. Harriet, feeling some compunction at having yanked Kirk out of bed while he was still exhausted from his trip, hoped he might be now a little cheered by the happy homelike scene, a little freshened by the dewy air. But she couldn't be sure.

"The cotton looks well," he remarked presently, "in spite of old Duffy's close planting."

"Well enough," she admitted. "Most any time now we'll have to begin to think of getting it pick out. I don't know how we'll manage with so many down sick."

Pehaps he did not miss the customary implication that she had borne much while he was off gallivanting. But if so, he chose to ignore it.

"More than usual at this time of year?" he asked politely.

"A heap more," she answered more shortly than she really intended. "Dr. Gregory says hit's no more than just the old summer complaint in a real violent form. But hit's crippled half our force."

He bit his lip and fell silent. They rode without speaking again past the last of the Waverley fields and turned down the narrow aisle her father had cut through the ancient woods. She could see where the wheels of the hired hack had sliced through the grass-grown ruts last night—almost the first wheels to have passed this way since he left. Waverley had little or no carriage company and cotton hauling wasn't due to begin for many weeks yet. Several times she felt him steal a sideways glance at her, but he did not again try to talk to her. If she was in no hurry to begin what she had got him out for, then, his silence hinted, he was in none either. Just bring it up in your own good time, Sis Hat. *I* don't mind.

At last she began.

"It would a-been easier on me, Br' Kirk, if you could a-see your way to letting me know ahead, so as I could make my plans. But you didn't and there's no use wasting words on that. What's done's done and what I got to do now is make the best of it. I already give her to understand she's welcome. . . ."

"You were wonderful, Sis Hat," he began, but she held up her hand to show she didn't want to be interrupted.

"She'll set in the wife's place," she announced fiercely, "carry the keys and give out what's to be give out."

"Wait, Sis Hat, wait a bit. You're going too fast. Where Martha sits at table, where you sit, is neither here nor there. If it's a gracious gesture you want to make, make it, of course. But the keys are something else entirely. You've ordered things at Waverley too long and well to make that change. Nobody asks or expects it. Martha is little more than a child, brought up, as I told you last night, in Savannah by a grandmother. She doesn't know the first thing about keeping a house, let alone giving out supplies on a big place like ours. . . . Why, the last thing wanted is for you to get the idea that you're being displaced, supplanted in your own home."

Her heart bounded with relief. But she'd have been ashamed to let him see it. With that out of the way she had only one thing left to speak of. All she had to do now was to tell him the plan for Lethe that she had painfully evolved last night in the long hours

[69]

at her loom. It, too, was at last clear and simple in her mind. She even believed he would agree—must, indeed, for what alternative was there? Yet when she tried to put the thing into words, her very tongue rebelled.

They had finished their errand at the Lees' and started home before she screwed up her courage to produce the paper she had brought a-purpose. She drew it out of her bosom, handed it to Br' Kirk and watched him read: "I leave my body to its mother earth and my soul to its father Almighty God. . . ."

"What's this?" he demanded sharply. "I was present when your father's will was opened and read. What's the idea of having me read it now?"

"Just the part about Lethe," she stammered, frightened at the change in his face but not able to draw back now. "Read what he say about Lethe, please, Br' Kirk."

Pa, in disposing of his earthly property to his natural heirs, had made one reservation: Lethe, then a child, was to go free when she reached maturity, "together with the children of her body if any there should be."

"He was ill advised," Kirk McLean reminded dryly, folding the paper and returning it. "Even when this was drawn, emancipation by will was already illegal. Judge Calloway explained that to you. Why go into it all again?"

"Still we *could* respect Pa's wishes, if we was a mind to. If you and me was to take a notion now to let his wishes guide us, if we was to want to free a woman like he set his heart on doing, long ago when she was little, we could do it, me as her half owner and you acting for Hunt. Oh, not here, of course," she put in quickly, seeing him about to speak. "I remember what Judge Calloway say about that well as you do. I know we'd have to get her up North somehow—like the Lees done about their uncle's woman. We'd have to find somebody travelling that way that was willing to take her—and the children, too. Even if Pa hadn't a-put that in, we'd not separate a mother from her children. I reckon you know I'd be the last to propose *that*. And it'd cost a heap a money, I reckon, to get them up there and settled, to say nothing of having to buy a woman in replacement—more than we can lay our hands on right away. Of course, if we hadn't a-had to borrow on our Athens gin stock for your trip we could a-used that. But like it is we'll maybe have to wait a while—till this year's crop is saved and sold anyways. Meantime I been a-wondering if we hadn't better just hire her out in town for the present. I'm sure we wouldn't have a bit o' trouble finding a good place for her. Mr. Simmons was saying only last Sunday he wished he could get one of the Waverley women to help them out. Mrs. Simmons' woman, the one she had from her folks' family—remember?—died right after you left, and Mrs. Simmons is in delicate health—" Expecting again, but of course she couldn't say that. "Lethe'd consent, and Aunt Dosia, too, I reckon, if we was to tell 'em what we was planning to do for her later. We could say we'd put the hundred a year Lethe'd earn in the bank for her and not touch it till such time as we was able to put more with it and—"

"And what about your virtuous reluctance to separate a mother from her children?"

"Oh, but this would be just temporary, Br' Kirk. And she could come home Sundays to visit them, not every Sunday of course, but, say, once a month or once every two months. The Simmonses would make any arrangement we thought fair. I know they would. And Lethe'd have a real nice home with them. We could be easy in our minds about her in every way, living with a preacher's family—"

His harsh laugh startled her. And his voice, so thick and unnatural, speaking things she couldn't have imagined from him, cut like the blows of a whip: Getting rid of her, that's what you really want, always have wanted. Oh, you put up with her while it suited your purpose, but you were only biding your time. If that's not true, why the almighty hurry? I only got home last night and here you—you— Suddenly his voice broke, his whip rose and fell on his horse's flank and he was gone. She stared after him stunned, uncomprehending. Her purpose? What purpose had she ever had but to serve Hunt and him, hand and foot? Br' Kirk. Br' Kirk. Already she doubted what she had heard. He didn't say it. Or anyway, he didn't mean it.

CHAPTER 3

SHE was ten when Honey was born and Miss Oc died and Pa first called her Miss Hat. You're the mistis now, Miss Hat, the only mother my baby's got. You'd better set in Miss Oc's seat, I reckon—the very seat she'd just offered to renounce for the little stranger bride. Fourteen she was, or near about it, when she got that shock about Pa—young enough, anyways, to have believed that old story about Lethe's father when she heard Pa tell it, but old enough to doubt it when she saw those town ladies look at each other and smile. They had drove out, collecting for the missionary society, and Honey, not much more than a baby herself, come hauling and dragging Mealy's little light-colored girl up into the dogtrot to show off to the company. Well, well, the ladies said, so hit's name is Lethe? Hit's a real sweet little thing, sure enough, pretty as a white child, near about. Who you say it's daddy is? A travelling mule drover? Well, I bet hit's mammy's proud of it. Hit beats all, the pride they take in a drop of white blood, wherever it come from.

When young Kirk McLean come to live in the neighboring town and started coming out to Waverley, coming steady like a young man a-courting, everybody, including Harriet, looked on Honey as a child, a heap too young to marry. But Harriet always thought she might have known the truth sooner, hadn't a-been for Pa. Pa never suspicioned how it really was. He just taken it for granted it was Hat the young man was after. He teased her day in and day out. Honey, he would say, how you reckon we make out when Miss Hat marry her beau and go to live in town? You better get Hat learn you 'bout sausage making, pickling, and what not before she leave you here high and dry, run this big place all by yourself. Miss Hat, what you want for a wedding present from your pa? I'll bet you got your eye on Miss Oc's silver coffee pot right now, planning on them parties you going to give the town ladies.

And Harriet, God love her for a fool, what must she do but turn to and dye up a lot of good wool hanks and draw in her web for a fine coverlid for her bridal bed, the very finest she had ever attempted. Double Muscadine the pattrun was called. It made her cheeks burn this minute to recall it. Well, leastways, even Honey never suspicioned what she aimed to do with it. Nor nobody else. A heap of people seen the coverlid in the loom, of course, for she was a mighty long time a-working at it—weeks and weeks it must a-been. And ever'body come to the house had to examine and admire. She was setting there on the loom bench with her bride's cover more'n half done, a-weaving away and just a-singing, when Honey come in and stood beside her, her hands twisted together and her eyes bright.

"Sis Hat," she said, "Sis Hat, stop a minute and listen to me. I've something wonderful to tell you, the most wonderful thing in all the world."

Honey never knowed what went with the half-finished coverlid, although of course she asked.

"Why, Sis Hat!" she cried, staring at the empty loom next day. "What have you done? Where is your beautiful coverlid?"

"I botched it, Honey. I found a bad mistake in the weave clear back at the beginning. So I got to ravel hit out and start hit over some day."

Even Pa come close to guessing.

"What's that I smell?" Pa said, his nostrils flaring. "Seem like hit's wool a-burning. Miss Hat, who's been burning up good wool around here?"

"Why nobody, Pa, nobody as I knows of anyway. I reckon your nose is fooling you. Or maybe Aunt Dosia's a-swingeing the pinfeathers off that gobbler she kill this morning."

Honey sat on Pa's knee in the dogtrot one day, badgering him to give her one of the Waverley people for a wedding present. Lethe, peeking in from the back steps, hopped up and down on one foot, making signs to show Honey she was listening.

"You'll have them all when I'm gone, miss, you and your sister between you. What's your hurry?"

Honey twisted at his rusty mustache ends and kissed his leathery forehead and said:

"But, Pa! I want one now. Why won't you?"

"Because I can't spare air one, that's why. Since Jerry and Dosie quit a-goin' to the field and I got this misery in my leg, hit look like I can't hardly manage to git a crop in the ground, let alone save it and gin it."

"Well, one of the little ones then. The little ones are no good to you. They're just eating their heads off. You're always saying it."

He joggled her up and down.

"Which one you got your eye on? And if hit's no good to me, miss, what good'll it be to you? What would you do with it if I was to give it to you?"

"Oh," cried Honey, just a-laughing, "it could pick up chips and be company for me in town when I get homesick."

"Well, run and take your pick then, anyone that's playing out there now," he said, giving her a push to set her on her feet. "Quick now, before I change my mind."

She went running out, laughing, caught hold of Lethe and ran back up the steps, leading her by the hand, both of them giggling at the trick they'd played on him. He was furious. He half rose from his chair.

"Dog my cats. I meant one of the dark ones and you know it. You know I never meant Aunt Dosia's favorite—mine, too, for that matter. You take my little Lethe and who's to light my pipe for me and fan the flies when I set eating? No, I won't have it. No, sirree. Even if I was willing, what'd Aunt Dosia say? That girl's the apple of her granny's eye."

Honey began to chatter to Lethe about going to live in town with her and Mas Kirk: "You'll have all the pretty dresses you want, Lethe, and store candy. And we'll take you down to the river every time a boat lands. How'd you like that, Lethe?"

Lethe twisted her apron and bored at the floor with one bare toe.

"I like it, Miss Honey." Her voice was faint but firm. "I like it if Mas Will let me go and if my mammy and my granny get on without me. Can I, Mas Will? Can I go live with Miss Honey and Mas Kirk?"

"Come here," he roared.

She drew her hand out of Honey's and went to him. She did not sit on his lap like Honey, but of course she was no more afraid of him than Honey was. The story about the travelling mule drover had maybe fooled her whilst she was little. But she was half growed now. She more than likely knew who was her real father. She rested her two hands on his arm and looked up at him, smiling.

"Can I, Mas Will?"

"Listen to me, Lethe. In town you won't have any other children to play with."

"I have Miss Honey," she said and smiled around at the sound of laughter.

"I hear tell a editor sets a mighty lean table—no buttermilk, no hams and souse," Mas Will warned. "You get mighty hongry for your granny's fried chicken and good old Waverley watermelons."

"I have store candy like Miss Honey say and ever' time a steamboat come up the river, I be there to see it," Lethe argued.

"All right, all right," he grumbled at last. "But she's not a gift. She's a loan. I call on you all to witness that."

Harriet worked her fingers to the bone, mighty near, a-gitting ready for the wedding, a-making sheets—there was no time for a coverlid—and Honey's dresses. To this day she hardly knew how she got through the weeks before the wedding. But at last the cakes were baked and even eat, down to the last crumb, and the bride and groom were on their way home—that little cottage in between Ed Ketcham's house and Judge Calloway's, it was, with crape myrtles a-growing in the yard all around it, small but real pretty. And the Waverley wagon followed after, carrying the two linen sheets wove on Sis Hat's loom, Honey's dresses, Miss Oc's silver coffee pot, six hams, and ever'thing else Sis Hat and Pa had been able to imagine a young pair could need to set up housekeeping, including Lethe.

Lethe's residence in town didn't last long. Harriet had feared from the first she'd be spoiled by town ways. And sure enough she was. One day Br' Kirk caught her and some white boys—Syke

Berry, Orrin Foote, and two others—up in Judge Calloway's loft, thrashed the boys with a riding whip he found there and bundled Lethe off home in disgrace.

In less than a year Pa was dead and Honey ailing and Br' Kirk brought her home to Waverley to have her baby. In some ways it was easier for Harriet, having them where she could look after them all instead of way off in town out of reach. But in some ways it was harder. Br' Kirk, like lots of menfolks, was a regular fish out of water when it come to a sickroom, and Harriet was apt to be short of patience and temper at his faults, especially any that related to Honey.

One warm day right after dinner she lowered Honey's pillows, drew the shutters half closed to keep out the light but not the breeze and, taking Honey's tray with her, went out through the dogtrot to the table where she was shredding cabbage and cucumbers and peppers for chow-chow pickle. She'd remember that pickledy smell to her dying day. Lethe, having come in for the tray, stopped a moment beside the table and stacked the dishes more securely. She made a little clatter and Harriet looked up quickly and shook her head in rebuke.

"Sh-sh. Not so loud, Lethe, please. Miss Honey's just about dropping off."

"Yes'm."

Lethe set the tray on her head and turned to go, but her apron pocket caught on the corner of the table. She couldn't let go the tray on her head, couldn't even look down. She fumbled blindly with her free left hand, made a twisting movement of her hips, got loose at last and then saw Miss Hat staring at her waistline.

"Lethe!"

"Yes'm."

"When did you get in this fix? Who got you that way?"

A tremor ran through Lethe's form and the dishes on her head tinkled lightly.

"I don't know'm."

"Nonsense. You're bound to."

"No'm. I don't."

Harriet's suspicions swept her off her feet with the force of a gale. Sternly she ordered Lethe not to set foot in Miss Honey's room again without she give her permission. And she told Mr.

Duffy to put Lethe in the field—not at heavy work, of course, not at any job that would hurt her, just light tasks such as all the older children did alongside their mothers: gathering field peas or the last sprinkle of late cotton and later, as cool weather came on, knocking down the dried cotton stalks and clearing the trash to get ready for the plows. Oh, it wasn't done to *hurt* her, putting her in the field wasn't. It was done to shame her. And Harriet reckoned it did shame her the worst of anything that ever happen to her. Her, that had been a pet child from the first, learned to read and write, dressed in Honey's own clothes, turned now into a dirty, barefooted field hand. . . .

Harriet tried to be as nice to Br' Kirk as ever, but it was like she couldn't. One day when he came home from town without the medicine for Honey she had asked him to bring, she stood right in the middle of the back yard and spoke her mind to him. She was tired, of course, and worried because Honey was failing so fast, but that didn't excuse her. Even while she was railing at him, she got ashamed of herself and broke off short. As she came back into the dogtrot, shaken with rage and wanting a good cry, she was shocked to see Mr. Banning sitting there in the patch of sunshine, his blanket around his knees: Br' Kirk had brought him back from New Orleans the week before to get his strength after a bad spell of malaria, and he was so quiet a body sometimes forgot he was around.

He looked up from his book and smiled at her. Then he reached out and pulled a chair up close beside him and patted the seat invitingly. She sat down, her cheeks burning with shame.

"I don't know what you must think of me," she managed to say. "Poor Br' Kirk. He didn't go to do it. And me taking on like an old squawking hen. I reckon it's something nobody could understand."

He said maybe he understood better than she realized. He said he liked her all the better for not being *too* good. Saints with haloes are all right in a picture on the wall, he said. But in real life he preferred human beings, always did relish a bit of vinegar and salt in his diet. After he'd made her laugh at that, he said seriously:

"A little scolding here and there means nothing anyway. I know you love Kirk."

Saying it out loud in the broad daylight while he looked out at an old hen at the foot of the steps giving herself a dust bath in the sunshine, saying it, not like it was a shameful thing, a temptation from the devil, to be wrestled with on one's knees in the dark at midnight, a treacherous sin against her little sister lying sick beyond the log wall, but nearly like it done her honor, in his eyes at least. . . .

"Don't I see what you do every day of your life, Miss Hat, for Kirk and Honey and their baby and even for a lorn stray like me? Don't you know the last thing you have to do is to explain yourself to me or to apologize for what you are?"

One bitter cold day in December, when they was killing hogs and the back yard was seething with business, they heard the tinkle of Honey's little bell. Harriet couldn't spare the time to run in and throw a log on the fire and see what else Honey wanted and, without half thinking, she sent Lethe. But the next time the bell rang Harriet went herself. Honey seemed to be asleep, although her frail fingers still hung at the handle of the bell on her bedside table. Harriet moved as softly as she could, building up the fire. But when she straightened and turned, Honey's eyes were wide and her white hand lifted from the bell in a beckoning gesture. Harriet went nearer, crooning:

"You cold, Honey? Want me hunt out some more quilts for you? Uncle Jerry say we haven't had such a hard freeze since the winter you was born. You want Sis Hat make you a nice hot toddy?"

Honey shook her head.

"Lethe's going to have a baby. She's going to have it soon. Why didn't you tell me?"

"Why, I don't know, lamb. I forgot it, I reckon."

"Why have you kept her out of my room all fall?"

"Kept her out! Mr. Duffy needs her. We've got the biggest crop ever been raised on Waverley. Look like it take ever' hand on the place get it saved."

"Who is the father, Sis Hat?"

Harriet laughed.

"Mr. Who'd-a-thought-it," she said airily, but she was beginning to tremble and a cold trickle of sweat crawled down her spine. She wet her lips and stared, helpless to go on.

Honey put out her little clawlike fingers and hooked them around her sister's wrist.

"Who? Tell me. Who?"

"Lord, child, how do you expect me to know—with so many a-hanging round her?"

The birdclaw grasp turned loose at last, the waxy lids fluttered wearily down, and Honey lay back, sighing.

Well, then Honey died when her time come, along in February it was, and Lethe's first, the one she named Lucas, was born soon after, with a clef' in hits chin like the Lees' overseer had. And he toed out like him, too, soon as ever he come to walk. Harriet felt terribly ashamed then about her first suspicions. She taken Lethe out of the field for good and all and put her back at housework like before.

After Honey's death, for a while, anyways, it had seemed to run in ever'body's mind Br' Kirk would marry again. He could have had his pick of the county at any time, of course. There was even those as thought he might do a heap worse for himself than to marry Honey's sister, and they was always letting out sly little hints about it that Harriet just made out like she didn't hear. Oh, her life wasn't no bed of roses. But she got used to things the way they was and they got on, him and her, better than many a married pair. Mr. Banning's visits were a treat to her as to him. And there was a lot, besides, that they shared. She set in the wife's place at table, of course. And surely an own wife could hardly have looked after him and Hunt any more devotedly.

What she done for them was pure pleasure, God knows. Br' Kirk had no call to be always so grateful. But he was grateful and, in the easy, generous way that come as natural to him as breathing, he was always finding ways to let her know it. She couldn't darn a sock or sew a button, look like, without him noticing and taking on about it. Hit was real funny to see Hunt, who was his spittin' image, picking up his ways: "Thank you for a nice dinner, Aunt Hat," the dear lamb would say, or, looking at some patch or other she'd been putting on his little old breeches: "What kind fairy's been a-mending my pants?" Sometimes it was all she could do not to burst out laughing at mealtimes to see the child standing stiff as a board behind his own chair, waiting till his papa had seated her and casting looks of dark scorn at poor old Duffy when he'd

[79]

haul himself in to the table first of anybody and even reach out for the victuals that was nearest to hand.

Well, hit went on like that for mighty near two years, with her grief for Honey getting easier to bear and her peace and contentment deepening all the time, until one morning, along in the spring it was, when Mr. Duffy was fixing to go into town for some things they needed. She had made up the list for him the night before but, careful as she was, she had forgotten she was slap out of black sewing cotton. Right after breakfast, hurrying about the house, she caught the hem of her dress on a chair rocker and ripped it a ways, and the minute she done it she remembered how she'd used the last inch of her black thread on the vest she'd finished for Br' Kirk yesterday and she went running right out to see could she catch Mr. Duffy before he got off. Br' Kirk, reading in the passage, looked up to offer to go for her. Hunt and Dub were playing school on the back steps in the sun, Dub holding the book and Hunt singing "B–A, ba, B–E, be, B–I, bi." But Hunt broke off to echo his papa's offer: "Let me go, Aunt Hat. Mr. Duffy's at the stable, hitching up. Want me to run and tell him?"

"No," she said. "No, thank you, lamb. I'd better write it on his list. Here, lend me your pencil."

It was a real pleasant morning to be outdoors, with the fields, far as you could see, all greening over and the sky so blue and warm. The shade tree down by the well was out in full leaf and the Negro children playing under it looked as fat and happy as the chickens and guinea hens that scattered out of her way. Uncle Jerry sat on his doorstep weaving a cornshuck rug and singing some sweet hymn about the river Jordan. The wistaria over the well house was all misty blue, humming with bees and smelling the sweetest she ever remember.

She called out to Mr. Duffy over in front of the stable to tell her where the list was and then she stepped into the shade of the well house where he'd hung his hat and coat on a nail in one of the posts and ran her hand into his left-hand pocket like he told her and took out a scrap of paper. But it wasn't her list. It was something she wouldn't have read a-purpose for anything on earth. But she did read it, God love her, in one swift glance without intention: "One skillet with a lid, five yards of red calico dress goods, and four yards of white baby flannel." The handwriting was

Lethe's. There wasn't many on the place that could write worth mentioning and not one but Lethe could write as neat and plain as this. And down underneath in a different, but equally familiar, hand there was a note to Ed Ketcham, reading: "Dear Ed, please charge these items to my private account, K. McL."

"Find it, Miss Hat?" Mr. Duffy called.

Hastily she put the piece of paper back, fumbled in another pocket, drew out the list she had made the night before and called: "Yes, I found it." But for several minutes to save her life she couldn't remember what she had meant to write on it. Her thoughts made her dizzy, look like. At last she was able to remember that it was black sewing thread she was a-needing. She held the paper up against the post, wrote, returned the list carefully to its proper pocket and made her slow way back to the house, past Dub and Hunt keeping school on the back steps and Br' Kirk in the passage, looking up to smile and ask: "Catch him all right, Sis Hat?"

She never let on what she'd found out. Outwardly nothing was changed. The rhythm of her days never missed a beat. She went steadily forward, sewing on buttons, mending pants, planning nice meals for Aunt Dosia to cook, directing Lethe in the housework, but her heart wasn't in it like before. And Br' Kirk's agreeable manners, even his frequently expressed thanks, which had ever been so satisfying, often seemed hollow, empty of real feeling, a barren ritual performed on purpose to keep up a front.

If now, on the morning after his homecoming with his little bride, tears stood in Harriet's eyes as she watched him ride furiously from her, they were, she knew, as much for old and buried griefs as for any present one. She hardly blamed him for unjust reproaches flung off at her in a moment of sudden temper—so well she understood him. She knew that she had shocked him. To him and practically every other red-blooded man of his acquaintance, the question she had raised was one scarcely so much of morals as of taste. Such things should be kept out of sight. His own obedience to that law had been scrupulous and exact largely out of respect for her. So her boldness in dragging the forbidden topic out in the open at last had caught him at a complete disadvantage. He felt as outraged as if she had cast to earth ancient tablets of stone. She saw it as no more than natural that he would go plunging off from her, r'aring and charging like he had a cockleburr under his saddle. All the same she stared after him ruefully.

The Waverley gate checked his headlong flight. In a way it was funny. There he was galloping off from her in a fury of repudiation and suddenly there was this gate. He couldn't jump it, couldn't just go through it and close it in her face or even leave it open for her to close. No, whatever else, he couldn't do that. His manners got the best of him, or his real self, as she put it, the self that was a kindly gentleman no matter what. He climbed down, opened the gate and remained there on the ground beside it, waiting for her to come up with him and ride through. She heard it close behind her and then she listened with a small secret smile as he came on at a more seemly pace. Presently he rode alongside, put out a hand to her knee and spoke.

"I'm sorry, Sis Hat. Forgive me."

"I was just thinking of Martha's peace of mind."

"I know it, Sis Hat. You sort of took me by surprise."

Surprise! He, to talk of surprises!

"Well, Br' Kirk, you must a-known something had to be done, you must a-seen when you come bringing a bride home, a wedded wife, you must a-thought—"

He interrupted with a rueful laugh.

"No, Sis Hat. Believe it or not, I didn't. As Parson always says: Kirk is one of these fellows who acts first and thinks not at all."

Then, haltingly but honestly, he tried to explain why he had acted so impulsively. Item one, there was he in love and more of a fool maybe than a younger man would have been in his shoes. Item two, there was Martha loving him and being made to suffer for it by her cruel relatives, locked up, reviled and persecuted day and night. She had to be rescued. . . .

"You do see that, don't you, Sis Hat? I couldn't just leave her there and let those harpies pick the skin from her poor little bones, could I?"

His actions were, as always, simple and obvious to him.

"We-ell," she said slowly, "I reckon you couldn't. With your kind heart, I reckon you had to do it the way you did. Anyways, hit's done now and we'd maybe just be wasting breath to go talking back over it and figuring if you could a-done it some other way. If you was a little short on foresight, maybe you'll have to use a little extra hindsight. Hit's now we got to think of. She's your wife and she's here and we don't want her to get to wishing she was back there with her mean kinfolks if we can anyways help it. That's all I was aiming at."

"Give me a little time, Sis Hat, I'll think over what you suggest and let you have my answer. All right?"

"Of course, Br' Kirk."

Mr. Duffy rode toward them across the fields and hailed them. When he came up to them, he said he wanted to speak to Mr. Kirk on a private matter if Miss Hat would excuse them. Of course she would. Sighing deeply, more shaken than she could quite take in, she rode on toward the house alone.

MARTHA, waking late and finding herself alone, was startled at how quiet the house was. Then she remembered the plan her husband and Miss Harriet had made for an early ride and she lay still, feeling lazy. The only sounds came from outside: a babble of children at play and the "pot-rack, pot-rack" of guinea hens, a continuous murmuring flow as of water running. She got up at last, drew on her wrapper and went to the window overlooking the sunny, grassless back yard. When she called Good morning, the little darkies, some in shirttails, some naked as they were born, tumbling like puppies in the dust, stopped still and stared at her in silence. One, lighter in color than the others and the youngest of all, seemed less shy than his playmates. He came a few steps toward her, not speaking, but holding up his hand to show her something.

"What is it? A penny? Why, how nice. Where did you get it?"

"Mas Kirk," he confided, lifting the coin on his open palm as high as he could reach and smiling.

"Where is Mas Kirk?" she asked. "Hasn't he come home yet?"

But he grew shy and ducked his head and would not answer. A little old woman came to the door of the nearest cabin, splashed water toward the roots of a near-by fig tree and then, with the empty dishpan dangling, stood and, like the children, stared at Martha. She was of indefinite age, her face showing dark brown, like a tiny wrinkled walnut under a mammoth white head rag coiled and built up half a foot high. She didn't somehow look friendly, but Martha smiled at her.

"You must be Aunt Dosia," she guessed.

"How come you know my name?"

"Why from Mas Kirk, of course. He's told me all about you. I'm Mas Kirk's wife, you know—Miss Martha."

The old woman curtsied stiffly.

"Miss Hat say to let you sleep long as you can and not bother you about eating till you get your rest out. I'll bring you a li'l sump'n now if you're ready."

"Why, thank you, Aunt Dosia."

The promised breakfast was a long time in coming, so long that Martha, after getting dressed, returned several times to the window to see if she could discover any cause for the delay. Once, to her horror, she heard sounds of strife, male and female, inside the kitchen cabin. There was shouted violent language and the sound of things being slammed furiously about. It frightened her into full retreat not only from the window but even from the room. She ran out into the dogtrot, her heart thudding, and looked off up the road in the hope that the riders might be at hand.

Then at last her breakfast came and it was extremely good: coffee, fresh and hot, with thick cream, broiled ham and red gravy, grits and hot biscuits with plenty of butter. While Martha ate at the corner of the big table in the open dogtrot at the end over-looking Miss Hat's garden, Aunt Dosia both ministered there to her table wants and between whiles, in the room behind her, briskly made the bed and tidied up. But her manner continued aloof. Either she was really too busy to respond to the newcomer's several overtures or she was downright unfriendly. Part of the time she pretended not to hear what was said to her. Or maybe she actually didn't hear. Maybe she was deaf. At last as she stood by the table, stacking the dishes on a big tray preparatory to carrying it back to the kitchen, Martha made one last effort.

"I enjoyed my breakfast," she said warmly.

The old woman made no answer but turned her back and moved off along the passage, her spine stiff. Martha knew it was absurd to care. These old servants were all the same—toucheous on a point of family honor, prideful, arrogant even. It was Martha's own fault if she let offense take root and grow between them. She called after the old woman already at the end of the dogtrot.

"Wait, Aunt Dosia. Please wait. I have something to say to you."

[85]

Aunt Dosia stopped and turned.

Martha hardly knew what she said: Aunt Dosia must not think she had come here to take Miss Honey's place. The people who had loved Miss Honey—and of course that meant every soul who lived at Waverley—simply mustn't feel like that. But she was Mas Kirk's wife now and she did hope they would all like her, a little bit at first and more as time went on, first for Mas Kirk's sake and later for her own. Surely she could make a place for herself in their hearts, if they wouldn't just shut her out. But Aunt Dosia's dark gaze remained unaltered and no word of response came from her. Making another movement to go, she merely said with chill politeness:

"Mebbe you want somebody do up some things for you? On the road mebbe you never have any chance to get washing done? Want me send a girl in for your close?"

"Why, yes," said Martha. "Thank you very much."

The woman who came presently for the clothes to be washed was the same comely young mulatto who had served the travellers' midnight meal and whose name, Martha recalled, was Lethe. She appeared to be more friendly than Aunt Dosia. Over the business of gathering the washing, she showed considerable interest in Martha: where she came from, how old she was, how long she had been at the springs before meeting Mas Kirk, and so on. And of her own accord she offered to flute Martha's ruffles, a gratuitous attention for which Martha felt grateful.

Alone again, Martha wandered out to the front steps and stood once more peering off along the road through the woods. Below her Miss Hat's garden looked very pretty, jewel-bright in the sun with the dense, almost inky shade folded close about it. The crape myrtle, rosy with bloom, grew higher than her head against the log walls of the house in two great clumps by the side of the steps. Beyond, roses and a tangle of all sorts of annuals spread in two sprawling beds around the inner edge of the drive. The idea of gathering some flowers came to her and she easily found shears, basket, and even a sunbonnet in the dogtrot.

Her basket was nearly full when a man's voice called:

"Hi, Miss Hat!"

Martha straightened and pushed the sunbonnet off as a man whom she took to be a neighboring farmer rode out of the woods toward her. He swept off his hat and scrambled down from the saddle, embarrassed.

"You ain't the lady come last night, Mr. McLean's new wife!"

"Yes," she said, laughing a little. "Why not?"

"You're powerful young," he said helplessly and stared, turning his hat in his hand. It was a dilapidated hat, straw, burned by the sun of many summers, greasy about the band and frayed to a fringe along one side. His blue-checked shirt was faded, dirty, torn in the sleeve and lacking several buttons. His unshaved cheeks wobbled uncertainly with a quid of tobacco which clearly he regretted, but did not know how to dispose of. And he had, she thought, the strangest eyes she had ever seen in her whole life, blue, deep-set, darkly clouded, sad to the point of melancholy. "Pleased to make your acquaintance, ma'am." The quid shifted from cheek to cheek and muffled his words distressingly. "I manage for Miss Hat." The Waverley overseer, then, not a neighbor. "Duffy's the name, Aloysius Duffy."

"That's an Irish name, isn't it?" she said politely.

"Yes'm. My folks come over from the old country before I was born."

He worked a filthy red handkerchief up from his breeches' pocket, held it before his mouth, took it carefully away and smiled broadly, his stained, broken fangs lightening the somberness of his face not at all. Well, so much for that, thought Martha. He'll feel more comfortable now. But even with the quid safely out of his mouth he still seemed uneasy, shaking the red handkerchief out in careful secretiveness behind him and then slowly cramming it back into his pocket again without once relieving her of his curious, concentrated gaze. To lessen his embarrassment or to rid herself of his hypnotic, melancholy stare, she turned to snip another rose and laid it in her basket.

"You goin' live here? You come to Waverley to stay?"

She laughed.

"Why, naturally. Of course I'm going to stay."

He shook his head mournfully.

"I wish you happiness, ma'am. I do that."

"Thank you, Mr. Duffy. Thank you very much. I *am* happy."

She didn't know what to say after that. So she bent to cut another rose. Still he lingered.

[87]

"Hot weather," he observed over her head. "Good for cotton but mighty hot for travel. I reckon you all found that out."

She shifted from one foot to the other.

"Yes, we did."

There was a long silence and then abruptly he bent toward her, made a funnel of his hand and whispered through it.

"Seen anything yet of that old woman does the cooking?"

"Yes, I have. She gave me breakfast just now, a very fine one. She's a good cook."

"Humph. Cooking's one thing, conjuration's another."

Martha straightened up to look at him and laughed. But Mr. Duffy's face looked gloomier, more inscrutable than ever in the shade of the hat he was putting on again, preparatory to leaving her.

"Well, good morning, ma'am. I better be getting on back to the field. I got good, study hands, but like all niggers they're eye-servants and slack off a little when your back's turned. An' more'n half of 'em's puny now from summer sickness. If I can ever serve you anyways, let me know." He swung into the saddle and turned his horse back toward the road. "Anyways at any time," he said, touched his hand to his hatbrim and rode off.

As she was sitting at the table in the dogtrot, arranging her flowers in the random array of pitchers and toothbrush mugs and even bottles which she had assembled, she heard hoofbeats. She sprang up and ran to the head of the steps, gladly waving a spray of larkspur.

Harriet's sharp eyes noted how the flower flag drooped and fell when the girl saw that she was alone, but she pretended not to notice.

"Hello, Martha. I reckon you thought we never was a-coming. Br' Kirk'll be along in a minute. He had to turn out in the field to speak to Mr. Duffy. So you've been picking flowers, have you? That's good. I want you to feel ever'thing on this place is the same as if you planted it with your own hands. What's flowers for if it ain't to give pleasure? We'll have to get you some real nice vases next time anybody goes in to town. I hope you got a good break-fast and was well served and didn't get noways lonesome. I hope Aunt Dosia and them remember to say 'Miss Martha' like I told 'em. I want them all to make you feel right at home from the start. If you ain't happy here, it won't be anyways my fault. I aim to make you happy if I can. . . ."

"Yes, ma'am," faltered Martha falling back before her, step by step, in a way that made Harriet long to seize her shoulders and give her a real good shake.

For the land's sake, what kind of treatment was the girl used to that she couldn't take an honest welcome like it was meant? Harriet wiped the sweat off her face and put on her most beaming smile.

"I been studying about what I could give you for a wedding gift. How'd you like a coverlid, a real pretty one? The one I got in mind to weave for you is called Double Muscadine. I don't know as you ever saw one in that pattrun?"

Martha caught her breath.

"For me? You would do that for me? Really and truly? Oh, Miss Harriet."

"Don't call me 'Miss,' child. Say 'Sis Hat' like Br' Kirk does and Honey ever did."

"Yes, ma'am," said Martha again, and again retreated.

Harriet sighed, stripped off her long black cotton overskirt, smoothed the crumpled folds of her clean gray calico dress, smiled again and said:

"Maybe you'd feel more at home like if I was to tell you what's expected of you right from the start: Well, you're to set in the wife's place and pour out at mealtimes. But I'll keep the keys and do the giving out and order what we're to eat. Looking after the peoples' rations I'll go on with, too. Hunt, I reckon, will keep on asking me what he can and can't do, for the present anyway. If he change, it won't be fast. And we won't crowd him. You'll maybe want to do your own mending and Br' Kirk's. And I reckon I won't miss it much, not after I get at that coverlid. A coverlid can fill up a right smart of time. . . ."

Kirk McLean found his bride weeping on the bed when he came in. He pulled her up and kissed her.

"What is it, darling?"

"You were gone so long. I thought you'd never come."

He laughed, dried her tears with his own handkerchief, and kissed her again, her cheeks, her eyes, her lips.

"Why, Martha, child, you're trembling. What is it? Tell me.

[89]

Did anything happen to distress you? What are you afraid of? Surely you can tell me."

She wanted to tell him. She tried hard. Her eyes closed with the effort of it. Aunt Dosia? No, it would be silly to name Aunt Dosia. She wasn't afraid of Aunt Dosia, no matter how she behaved or what Mr. Duffy said. Mr. Duffy, then? No. That would be just as silly. Mr. Duffy was crazy. Some time she would ask Mr. McLean if he wasn't. But not now—no overseer, even a crazy one, had anything to do with her really. . . .

"What is it, dear? You must tell me."

"Sis Hat," she blubbered.

"But Sis Hat's so full of kind intentions toward you she can hardly wait to get them started. From beginning to end of our ride she was making plans for you."

She shook her head.

"She—oh, she feels *terrible* about your marrying. Yes, she does, inside. I can tell. It's because she feels like that that she. . . ."

He held her off and looked straight into her eyes.

"You poor silly. You are all wrong. Yes, you are. Her one prayer has been that I should marry. For years, I tell you. And now that I have married *you*—why, you little goose, can't you see she's crazy about you?"

Martha tried to laugh, too.

"Is she—honestly? I don't want to be silly. But it's partly because she's so kind—oh, I don't know. It's almost as if she were too kind. I don't want to take her place at table. I'd much rather not put anybody out."

He laughed, hugged her close, and started in all over again to warm her face with kisses.

"But, Mr. McLean, really, I mean it. Does she like me a little? Isn't she just trying to force herself to put up with me?"

"She's good and kind, honestly good, the best woman I ever knew. She hasn't a thought but for our happiness. And if you want her to like you more and more, let her sacrifice herself for you body and soul, wait on you hand and foot, give up her place at the table to you, and anything else, too. Never cross her. Understand? Never cross her."

Somebody was knocking.

"Well," called Kirk McLean impatiently, "Who is it? What do you want?"

"It's me, Papa," said a small voice. "Aunt Dosia wants to know if you're ready for her to dish up."

"Ask your Aunt Hat."

As they were about to sit down at table in the dogtrot, Mr. Duffy stumped up the back steps, halted to wash his hands in a tin washpan on the shelf with the water bucket, and with no further ceremony but a brief "Howdy, all," seated himself at the family board. In his sweat-darkened, ragged shirt, with the dirt of the cotton field still in the deeper creases of his neck and along his hairy forearms, he took a large helping of everything that was offered him, as a hungry working man should. But he had, after all, no appetite. Instead he was peckish and finicking. Breaking open a piece of Aunt Dosia's crusty cornbread, he held it not to his mouth but to his nose, sniffing it in an animal-like way. Suddenly he turned to her.

"Where you get the water to make this bread, old woman?" he demanded suspiciously.

"Outen the well, Mr. Duffy."

"You scald that bucket like I told you?"

"Yass'r, Mr. Duffy."

He laid the bread untasted at the side of his plate and with his knife poked doubtfully at the tiny pickled beets and mounded yellow squash thereon. Kirk McLean laid down his own knife and fork and watched him in disgust. Seemingly unaware of offending, Mr. Duffy addressed himself to Martha.

"I like to show you my cotton, ma'am, sometime. I got a fair to middlin' crop, if I do say it as shouldn't."

He hefted a hearty bit of squash on his knife point, but as it neared his lips, his nostrils flared and he dropped the knife noisily back on his plate. Kirk McLean exclaimed with exasperation and Miss Hat spoke sharply.

"If you don't find what's set before you to your taste, Mr. Duffy, maybe you can keep from spoiling other people's appetites."

Mr. Duffy flushed darkly and they all sat in strained silence, broken only by the creak and swish of the fringed paper fly fan which a dark boy in a white coat, addressed as Dub, faithfully kept in motion over their heads by means of some cord and pulley

[91]

arrangement while Hunt, between mouthfuls, stole fearful glances at his father's darkened face and Martha strove to eat as if she did not suspect anything had gone wrong.

An old Negro man with a cane stumped up the back steps and stopping there, bent over his cane with one hand pressed at the small of his back, spoke suavely.

"Excuse me, Miss Hat. I begs your pardon for coming whilst youse eating. But Mr. Duffy say I got to help out in the field. He say he so shorthanded I got to."

Kirk McLean turned, frowning, to Miss Hat.

"Well, why not? After all, Sis Hat—"

The old fellow giggled.

"Lord, Mas Kirk. You been away so long you plumb forgot about the misery in my back? All that bowing and bending liable lay me flat in my bed. This old nigger's past such as that. . . ."

"Go along, Uncle Jerry," Miss Hat said, getting up. "We'll talk about this outside."

Uncle Jerry withdrew reluctantly, groaning and muttering, with Miss Hat at his heels and Hunt, too, trotting along to hear her judge the case. Whereupon Mr. Duffy revived—conversationally at least. He nodded and winked at Martha pleasantly and, without waiting for Uncle Jerry to pass out of hearing, not even troubling to lower his voice, sketched the old fellow's character for her in broad, sure strokes.

"As spoilt a old darky as ever I run up against in the thirty year and over I been a-managing. He ain't earn a honest meal of victuals since I come on Waverley. Not to my knowledge he ain't. I try to git him lay off corn rows or lay the worm for a new fence or whatsoever light, piddlin' work I got to give out, but you think he will? No, ma'am. The least little hint anybody want him to do something useful more than apt to put him right down in bed for Dub here and Miss Hat to fuss over. It beats me how the old chap's got the wool pull over Miss Hat's eyes. She ain't what I'd call soft in ginnerl but when it come to old Jerry she's downright chickenhearted. . . ."

"If you aren't going to eat any more, Mr. Duffy," Kirk McLean hinted, "I'm sure my wife will excuse you. I know you want to get back to the field."

Mr. Duffy rose and departed. Martha, left alone with her husband, looked nervously at his clouded face and put a timid question.

"Is he—is he *crazy?*"

"In a way," he answered absently. And then, when Martha continued to sit staring at her dessert of peach cobbler smothered in cream, he said almost crossly: "Now, for heaven's sake, don't start getting notions about old Duffy. He's quite harmless, I assure you."

Martha ate a morsel and laid her spoon down.

"He said such a strange thing to me about Aunt Dosia this morning. I'm sure it wasn't true, of course. But she *is* peculiar, isn't she? Or maybe I just thought so because of being frightened already. . . ."

Kirk McLean roused himself with visible effort to smile at her.

"Frightened, child? What on earth are you talking about?"

"Well—before I had my breakfast there was a regular fight out in the kitchen, angry voices, a struggle—"

"Look," he interrupted. "Do you want to please me very much?"

"Of course I do."

"Then don't begin life at Waverley by bothering about backyard doings that don't concern you."

All the same she felt concern, even regret, in the late afternoon when the agreeable Lethe brought her washing back with all the ruffles beautifully crimped and announced that she was leaving Waverley for employment in town.

"Oh, Lethe," she said with real wistfulness, "I wish it were one of the others—why, you have been nicest of all to me."

CHAPTER 5

THE hiring of Lethe to the
Methodist preacher's family was a gesture sincerely applauded in
town. Spontaneously, and so generally that it was impossible to tell
who had the idea first, there sprang up among the town ladies a
plan for giving a sociable to compliment the Waverley bride. The
Ketcham girls, delegated to carry the invitation, returned to town,
bringing armfuls of Miss Hat's roses and larkspur and a glowing
report of the Georgia girl. Though shy, they said, she was real
pleasant—and pretty, too, dressed in a little flowery lawn dress,
all over ruffles crimped with a fluting iron. She had soft, bright
hair and appealing, childish ways. Mr. Kirk could hardly take his
eyes off her, and if she went out of the room one minute he was
after her, calling "Martha! Martha!" Hunt, too. It beat all, the
way that child took to having a stepmother, though, of course,
being so young, she was a lot more like a sister, really. He called
her Martha, too, just like his papa. Miss Hat? Well, she acted like
Mr. Kirk's getting married was something she thought of for herself and planned out for him from the beginning. It was Martha
this and Martha that the whole enduring day.

Kirk McLean rode in with the carriage when the Waverley
ladies came in for the sociable, and if ever he thought he was
popular before he must have realized now that he had had no
notion what true popularity was. He couldn't move a foot along
the plank walk in front of the stores without somebody stopping
him to wring his hand and congratulate him.

The Ketcham girls had got the party up, or Evvie had, really,
but the whole town had a hand in giving it, one lady bringing

a coconut cake, another a chocolate, another the blancmange. Each had brought the bride a gift, too. One present was a little red, padded autograph album. They all wrote in it. Sitting each in turn at the table by the window, turning to a new leaf, dipping in the pen, each wrote one of the standard rhymes and her name. Then they made the bride sit on a little sofa, holding open in front of her a flowered bag, as big as a pillowcase, into which the guests, notified in advance, each dropped an offering of quilt scraps, walking before the bride and singing like children, "We're marching round the levee."

Harriet was downright proud of the way the ladies made over Martha and proud, too, of Martha's response. She was warmly grateful for each single thing that was given to her. To see her pleased and happy face when they was all marching past her, throwing quilt scraps into her bag, you'd have thought it was diamonds and rubies they was giving and she was collecting. She kept that scrap bag in her lap the whole way home.

In those early days the girl seemed to Harriet like somebody living inside a private fairy tale—and not just in town with ever'-body making over her, but out home, too, when there was nobody by but the family. She was as happy as the day was long, hunting muscadines for Sis Hat to make into wine, picking her little flowers and fixing them in mugs and bottles, humming to herself, breaking off to run out to call after Hunt when him and Dub started off with Mr. Duffy's old gun, to remind them of their promise to bring her back a rabbit foot; or leaning up against Br' Kirk's shoulder, looking up at him and laughing and teasing him about those poor, lovelorn girls in Athens, who said he couldn't find anybody good enough for him in Chewalla County all these years and at last had had to go travelling away off to the Georgia springs to find a wife that suited him. With Harriet she was as open and easy as blood kin. While Sis Hat was at her loom, working away at the Double Muscadine coverlid, Martha would sit beside her, sewing on a grubby little square for the quilt she had already started by a pattrun Sis Hat made for her or throwing it down impatiently to jump up and gaze at the beautiful design slowly winding out on the crossbeam of Harriet's loom.

"I could never make anything so beautiful if I tried my whole life long," she cried ardently.

Of course Harriet was pleased and flattered, but she tried not to let on.

"Hush your foolishness, child. You talk so much you're liable to make me botch my work. This pattrun is strange to me. I started a coverlid by hit once but something happened and I never finished. . . ."

Mrs. Cumby's directions lay at Sis Hat's hand. Martha bent down to study reverently the notations in faded handwriting on the long snakelike paper—the back of an old letter it was, cut into strips and sewed together with coarse black cotton thread, the numbers written close and fine all along it.

"Why, it's like a musician's notes," Martha declared. "You're a musician, Sis Hat. When it's all in your head you can play from memory, but when it's a new tune you need your notes."

"You're sure talking a heap of nonsense, child. What's got into you? That sociable addle your brains?"

One day when Martha alone in her room was tumbling her quilt scraps about on her bed, searching for a blue of a certain shade, humming happily to herself, her hand felt the prick of paper and her fingers closed on a tiny peaked triangle. It was a small, innocent cocked hat such as children make to carry their messages about a schoolroom or neighbor women send by a servant's hand. Printed in crude childish letters across one triangular face was her name: Mrs. Kirk McLean. Some game of Hunt's, she guessed, smiling as she unfolded and read. The single line inside was unsigned and lettered with the same awkwardness as the address. But she knew now that it was not the work of a child. The hand that had penned it was almost certainly one of those twenty-three that had set down in flowing or cramped feminine script a trite rhyme or good wish in a bride's album.

When you are old and cannot see, put on your specs and think of me. Evelinda Mabel Ketcham. Roses are red, violets blue, sugar's sweet and so are you. Kate Ashe Burgess. May you live to a good old age and be *very* happy is the wish of Sue Ella Foote.

There was no earthly use in comparing, as she did so painfully over and over, the anonymous note with those assorted, carefully signed messages. The lettering was a perfect mask. Yet surely one of those hands had written this, too:

Who is the father of Lethe's children?

Harriet was puzzled by a change in Martha. At first, as regularly as Mr. Duffy would set off for town, she would come running out with a long fat letter to her grandmother for him to post. And in the evening when he got back she'd be watching for him and calling out: "Anything for me, Mr. Duffy? Are you sure the Georgia mail had come?" Harriet thought her kinfolks were real mean not to write to her even once. But Martha seemed not to care now. She give over writing and taking any interest in the mail when it came. Once when Mr. Duffy did bring a letter for her, not from Georgia, alas, but from Athens, she wasn't even to be found to receive it. Harriet put it in her pocket and forbade Hunt to mention it to Martha until she had paved the way in order not to rouse false hopes.

"I shouldn't wonder," Harriet announced carefully at the supper table, "if you was going to have some more fun in town, Martha, another sociable or candy pull or something, because Evvie Ketcham's been writing to you. Leastways it was Evvie that backed this letter if my eyes don't deceive me."

Martha accepted the letter indifferently, although it was the first, to Harriet's certain knowledge, that she had got, backed with her new married woman's name. She laid it on the table by her plate. Hunt watched her all through supper, his eyes popping. At last, when the little fellow couldn't stand it any longer, he drew a deep breath and said:

"Ain't you going to *read* Miss Evvie's letter, Martha? Ain't you going to find out what she's inviting you to?"

That got a smile out of her, anyway. She opened the letter, barely glanced through it and folded it up again.

"It's just a quilting, Hunt," she said in a flat kind of tone that told Sis Hat right off she wasn't a bit interested.

Harriet spoke up.

"Why, a quilting in Athens can be real lively, Martha, especially for somebody that's just come here and all, with the whole town in a fret to make over her and give her a nice time. When does Evvie say they're going to have it?"

She had to open the letter again to see.

"Next Friday," she said in that same dead tone.

Then Br' Kirk tried to get her interested.

"Well, that's kind of Miss Evvie. And it's lucky, too," he said.

"I was meaning to see Judge Calloway. I could take you in with me. Friday would suit me fine."

"Thank you," she said in a touch-me-not tone. "But I think I'll just ask you to take a note to express my regrets."

Harriet said right out she felt like giving her a good shaking, seventeen years old and talking like that. You'd think she was forty with a dozen young 'uns to keep her housebound. But Sis Hat's cheerful urgency only drove Martha off, seem like. She never sat by the loom now. She even shrank from Hunt begging her to come out and pick muscadines, stole away by herself instead on long solitary rambles, from which she returned wide-eyed and disheveled to sit through Mr. Duffy's mealtime monologues of conjure talk. Worst of all, of course, was her shrinking from her husband. "I cannot," was as much as her stiff lips could manage once when he asked her to go for a ride. Sis Hat heard her. " 'Cannot' is starvation victuals to a man hungry with love," she chided curtly. His eyes showed such a deepening hurt that Sis Hat could hardly bear to see them. And once him and her quarrelled right out before everybody.

Martha in the long privacy of a rainy afternoon had done her hair a new way, copied from a picture in a *Godey's Lady's Book* that Clara Ketcham had given her at that now legendary sociable. Hunt at supper drew attention to her high, ribbon-decked coiffure by saying: "Oh, Martha, you look funny!" Even her husband laughed. Martha sat up very straight, biting her lip and saying,

"Do I look funny to you, Mr. McLean, just funny?"

"Yes, my dear," he said in his careless way, "as funny as anything I ever laid my eyes on outside a tent show."

She pushed back her chair and left the table, sobbing.

"Go after her, Br' Kirk," Sis Hat urged. "Do go and tell her you didn't go to hurt her feelings."

He only shook his head and gave a hard answer.

"A wife has other ways to please her husband than by trussing herself up in bows and streamers."

Harriet knew that he slept in the loft with Hunt that night—as how could she help knowing in that small, intimate house? And her heart was wrung between pity and blame for Martha. Mostly the girl did not weep. Mostly her eyes were dry and staring as she moved, unseeing, about the house. Even when her uncle's letter came at last with the news that her grandmother was dead, she did not shed one tear.

It was about that time that Kirk McLean made his plan to get away. Harriet was sitting, writing up her diary one night when he come and stood just inside the door.

"May I speak to you, Sis Hat?" he said and then, coming in, "I'm thinking some of going away. . . ."

"Well—" she tried to make her voice cheerful and natural— "why not? A real good hunting trip might do you good. Get Horace Lee or Ed Ketcham and have you a nice hunt. Stay overnight and don't hurry. . . ."

But it wasn't just a hunt he had in mind. It was New Orleans. She noticed the pupils of his eyes. They were small, no bigger than pin points. Downright miserable he looked.

"Well," she said again, "that might be nice, too. Ever'body needs a change at times. And hit always does you good to see Mr. Banning. When was you aiming to get off?"

"On the next downriver boat that goes," he said grimly.

CHAPTER 6

A HOUSE can seem mighty lonesome with nobody in it but a child and two women, and one of them so turned in on herself she can't rightly hear when a person says Good morning. Harriet, having ridden off right after breakfast one day on an errand of mercy, stating she would not be home before sundown, returned instead at midmorning. The house was quiet. She opened the door to her own room and, somewhat to her surprise, found Martha there sitting by the fire in Miss Oc's rocker. Martha looked round, startled, and said hurriedly and somewhat incoherently something about the wind's being from the other side of the house.

"It made the smoke come down my chimney in great puffs. I had to come in here, Sis Hat."

"Well, you're welcome, child. You know that," Harriet said placidly, moving toward her along the narrow lane between the loom and her bed, untying her bonnet as she came.

"You came back so soon, Sis Hat. I thought you'd be gone all day."

"Half Chewalla County was there before me, look like, house full and yard full, too, ever'body getting in ever'body else's way and poor Mrs. Berry already worrying and fretting about what all she can find for them to eat come dinnertime. She was bound I should come inside and look at the sick child. And that I done, of course. It would a-been downright hardhearted not to. Why, Martha, what you got there?"

From the first she had noticed that Martha was sitting in a peculiar way, hunched over something in her lap, something she

kept her arms over as if to hide. It was, apparently, a book, open
on her knees, a very large book. It . . . no, no, it couldn't be.
Harriet's eyes leaped from Martha to the chest beyond her, where a
drawer stood open, its contents tumbled. Harriet marched forward,
her hand out.

"Give it here," she demanded. "Give me my diary. How dare
you meddle in what don't concern you?"

Martha closed the book and handed it up to her. She stood
up, too, and her head turned from side to side as though she
would have liked to run away, but Harriet stood squarely in front
of the opening between bed and loom, blocking her one escape
as securely as a cork driven hard into a bottle.

"So," said Harriet, very angry, "that's how I get paid back for
being as kind to you as if you was my own flesh and blood. The
first time I turn my back you go to snooping and prying in amongst
my private things. I wonder what you're trying to find out, anyways. And I'd also like to know what Br' Kirk say when he come
back and I tell him what a sneak he marry. . . ."

"No!" cried Martha. "No! You can't tell Mr. McLean. If you
do I'll kill myself."

She buried her face in her hands and rocked back and forth.

"We was brought up different, I reckon," Harriet said on a
milder note. "Maybe being an orphan with only an old woman
to look after you, you never was taught that picking over a person's diary is the same as stealing—or was you? Maybe you do
know I'd as soon you'd stolen my mother's breastpin?"

Martha shook her head, helpless to answer. Harriet passed her
to put the diary away again in its accustomed place. As she did so
she went on speaking over her shoulder.

"I intend to forgive you. I was never one to harbor grudges.
You just tell Sis Hat you're sorry and won't do it again and . . ."

She broke off as she turned around again and faced the empty
room. Beyond the dogtrot a door slammed and a bolt fell.

It was right then that Mr. Duffy come in the house and said
he'd found Aunt Dosia a-laying on the floor in her kitchen. She
was unconscious and he had no idea what had happened. Nor had
Miss Hat when she went running out. Aunt Dosia been shelling
cornfield peas, seem like, because there was the pan turned upside
down on the floor beside her and the peas all run out ever' which-

a-way. Mebbe she just reach over to chunk the fire and taken dizzy, what make her fall. The little old thing weighed scarcely a hundred pounds, but now, a dead weight, she seemed twice that, and Harriet thought of her own heart several times while she was helping Mr. Duffy get Aunt Dosia up off the floor and into bed. Guard against strain, Miss Hat, Dr. Gregory had said. That's what you'll have to learn.

Harriet had no more than got Aunt Dosia bedded and Duffy started off to town when Hunt came flying to call her to come to Martha. Martha was laying on her bed, half undressed, white as the sheets and complaining of griping pains, but when Harriet said Mr. Duffy was already on his way to get the doctor, Martha had a hard crying spell and said she wasn't sick and wouldn't see the doctor.

So then Mr. Duffy come back, bringing Dr. Gregory with him— round about four o'clock it must have been by then. The doctor attended to Aunt Dosia first. It was a stroke, he said, as soon as he seen her. She's just about outlived her usefulness, Miss Hat, and I wouldn't be fair to you if I was to tell you any different. Well on in her seventies by now, isn't she? Oh, we can maybe get her up off her bed again, fix her so's she can sit on a splitbottom chair by the kitchen fire and order some strapping young wench around. You got some daughter or granddaughter of hers ready for promotion from field work? No? Well, then, you'd better get Kirk to look around down there at New Orleans and buy you a woman for the old lady to train. . . .

Harriet knocked on Martha's door and opened it for him, but as soon as Martha spied him satchel in hand at Sis Hat's elbow she began to cry: "No, I don't want the doctor. I won't see him. . . ." Harriet dropped back and, leaving him to enter alone, went into her own room, built up her fire, sat down by it and took up her mending basket. But she was too fidgety to sew a patch on straight, look like. Old sorrows kept rising up to plague her. Martha's sickness had put her in mind of the day Honey had the first bad hemorrhage from her lungs and Dr. Gregory and Kirk was shut up with her crost yonder in that same room. That time Dr. Gregory come in here and set down by the fire and said: "Well, Miss Hat, I've got hard news for you. I'd rather take a whipping than to be the one to tell you. But the fact is Honey's got consumption."

By the time Dr. Gregory knocked at her door today, Harriet was in a cold sweat all over. Her voice shook when she told him to come in and take a chair and asked him about Martha.

"Nothing dangerous, I hope."

He frowned and it was like he was angry about something, his voice rasped so.

"Yes, it's dangerous." And he had hardly set down before he was up again and over by the medicine shelves. "Is this castor-oil bottle the one I sent you by Duffy last Saturday?"

"Why, yes, Doctor. Of course it is. Why?"

"Why? Why? My God, Miss Hat, haven't you got eyes? You'd have had to dose every pickaninny on the place twice around to make it waste away like that!"

It was a quart bottle and sure enough it was half empty.

"But I never even opened it," she said aghast. "I never so much as pull the cork, let alone give out one dose of it."

"No?" said Dr. Gregory furiously. "And you haven't the least idea where it's gone, have you? Wake up, Miss Hat. You're a woman. A Christian. You don't want to stand by and see murder done. If an unborn child's life is not sacred to you, maybe you'd be willing to lift your hand to save that poor, silly girl in yonder from death. . . ."

Harriet felt her cheeks on fire.

"Death! Why, Doctor, you sure can't mean that. Castor oil don't kill."

"Don't it?" he roared. "Well, ma'am, I assure you it does, taken under proper conditions and in sufficiently large doses. No, don't try to put me in a good humor by smiling, Miss Hat. When a young woman tells me she'd rather die than have her baby, I take it seriously. It's my business to. And if you can't put that girl in a different frame of mind mighty quick, I tell you, I won't answer for the consequences."

Standing on the outside steps in the cold wind, watching him ride off, Harriet got a fit of shaking like a hard chill. And her teeth were still chattering when she came back to her fire and leaned over it to warm her hands. Then a glimmer of understanding flashed far within her. Suspicion! That's the name of the secret disease been eating away at Martha's heart like a cancer. That's what made her run her husband off and sent her poking and scrabbling through my diary, made her even try to get rid of her baby. She suspects. Ain't nothing else could make a sweet girl like her act like that. No use to ask how come. Hit could a-been anything set her off—a glance out of her window at Hunt playing alongside Lethe's young'uns and seeing, or thinking she saw, a resemblance. Well, thought Harriet, sighing deeply, if that's what ails her—and I'm mighty near sure it is—ain't but one antidote on God's green earth as I ever heard of and that's a dose of plain and undiluted truth. . . .

But first I reckon I better give her some supper or she'll never be able to hold a medicine strong as that on her stomach, weak like she is. Le's see now, what'll I fix? A real good chicken broth and a little toast and a light, nourishing dessert, say apple and tapioca. That's it. And a pot of weak tea, fresh and hot. By the time she got the tray ready she had it all clear in her mind what she aimed to say to Martha, and the very moment the girl swallowed her supper Sis Hat sat down beside her bed and, folding her hands in her lap, began:

"Well, now, Martha, I got to tell you something I never before told a human. I don't aim to beat about the bush or do any mealy-mouthed shilly-shallying. I just aim to let you have it straight. Hit's got to do with Br' Kirk—"

"No. No. I don't want to hear it. Not from you. If I have to know—anything—it should be from him. He should tell me. He should have told me long ago."

"Now, lamb, maybe he can't and never could. Young as you are, you ought to know there never was a man his age topside of earth but have sump'n other on his conscience he'd find too hard to tell a innocent young wife. . . ."

"No matter what you say, I'll never forgive him."

"No, lamb? Seem like that's a strange thing to say, seeing you got so much on your own conscience needs forgiveness. When a sweet girl like you can change overnight, in a manner of speaking, into a sneak thief and mighty near a murderer, seem like you'd know in yourself the power of sin and have some charity maybe for other folks. Br' Kirk ain't perfect, Martha. I know that maybe better than you do, living beside him like I have all these years. He's got his faults like anybody else—one mighty bad one in particular. We own a woman by the name of Lethe—I don't know

as you even remember her because she was sent off this place by Br' Kirk himself soon as he brought you here a bride. . . ."

"No, no. You shall not tell me. I won't believe you. Don't say another word. It's not for you to say such things to me. I won't let you. I won't listen."

Harriet's determined bluntness was not due to any want of mercy for the girl wincing and cringing there on the bed, even putting her hands over her ears to shut out the unbearable truth. Poor lamb. Sis Hat was plenty sorry for her, but she just couldn't afford to show pity, that's all, lest it weaken them both. She was like a brisk-mannered, competent nurse who must do her painful duty of dressing a wound or whatever it is, exactly as if she could not hear the patient's groans and cries.

After it was all over—even that filthy anonymous note dug out from where the poor child had hid it under the newspaper lining of a bureau drawer, given to Sis Hat and burned—Sis Hat swep the hearth, took up the tray of dishes, and started toward the doc Martha, till then wrapped in sodden misery, able only to writ and weep, stirred, raised herself on one elbow, sopping at streaming eyes with her already soaked ball of a handkercl and gulped:

"Thank—thank you, Sis Hat."

Sis Hat set the tray down and came back.

"There," she said, "that's a heap better. Oh, it's har Hat knows that. But being a woman is hard when you com down to it. You ain't the first to find that out. And mayb pray, the good Lord will ease your burden or give you to bear it." Her tried and true recipes she proffered as t into her mind: The greatest of these is charity. Judge n be not judged. If thy brother offend thee. Forgive and f

"You see, Martha, you was meant for Br' Kirk's salv wouldn't a-sent you to him if He hadn't meant him through you. Was he to lose your love, there'd be noth but backsliding. That's a big responsibility for a wife full-grown woman to shoulder it. I seen women so so selves they just push their menfolks down to shame the way they take on: complaining and blaming f end to the other or either moping and acting the r till a poor man's got no choice but to take his co

find it—in drink, if that happen to be his weakness, or with some handy yellow girl, if that's the way his taste run. . . ."

She patted Martha's hair in an awkward caress and that started the poor child off to crying again. She flung both arms around Sis Hat's spare waist, nuzzled her head into her apron and sobbed and shook.

"You're so good to me," she gasped. "So good. Why? Why are you?"

Sis Hat laughed, ruffled her hair foolishly, even bent down and kissed it.

"Now, lamb, what a question. After all the years I prayed for you, why wouldn't I be thankful when God sent you? You see, Martha, there ain't a mite of use of dodging pain. Like Mrs. Cumby used to say to me: 'Daughter,' she'd say, 'God's going to find you wherever you're hiding and hand you the cup, and then you got to dreen it if it's yours to dreen.' Mrs. Cumby *knew*. How come her to leave the Kentucky hills was by her losing her husband and three oldest sons in one night. . . ."

"You've told me," said Martha wearily, turning her head away.

"They was shot in a feud," Harriet went on. "And then she run off here with her youngest that was all she had left to save him from his mountain enemies. But one night in town Caje, that was her son—"

"Was killed," said Martha and shut her eyes.

Well, there's times a body's own trouble is so bad it's like they can't bear hearing about other people's. Harriet knew that. So she kissed the girl on her forehead and left her without another word.

That night was one of those when Harriet couldn't lay in her bed. She hadn't much more than got herself down, it seemed like, when she was up again, lighting her lamp and building up her fire. She even put her clothes on, because it was a chilly night and her old wrapper was none too warm. It ran in her mind that Dr. Gregory's advice about getting Br' Kirk to look around down there in New Or-*leens* for somebody to do Aunt Dosia's work was good counsel. With Lethe gone and Martha expecting, she'd need an extra woman. So she took pen and paper and got the letter written or Mr. Duffy to take in first thing tomorrow. Then she carried the mp over to the high shelf Pa had fixed just right for her to weave and eased herself down on the loom bench.

She had ever been a poor sleeper. The lightest squirrel patter on the roof was enough to make her start wide awake, rigid and listening. The soft footfalls she used to hear, or imagine that she heard, even in her girlhood, along the dogtrot and through the back yard had power to destroy a night's sleep and leave her next day irritable and drained of energy. And if she'd worried about Pa's sins, when it come to Br' Kirk's, it was like she couldn't stand it. Nights when she couldn't sleep, weaving was ever a mighty comfort. Like all natural-born weavers, she had only to draw in her web to begin to find peace. Busying her hands was a soothing thing, and the beat of the loom kept her from hearing what she didn't want to hear. . . .

Mr. Duffy's horn sounded outside her window, and she became aware that the lamplight had grown pale, weakened down by the whitish dawn washing in through the panes. She stared at the work under her hands. It was pale, too, dimmed by that watered-down light, very nearly faded to a dun monotone, but it was—and the fact was as surprising as some holy miracle—finished. The last thread in the faint, almost dreamlike pattern of Martha's coverlid was in place.

PART III

King's Yellow

CHAPTER 1

AT four o'clock on Tuesday, the second day of court week, the twelfth juror was chosen, the twelve stood and took the familiar jurors' oath, and a bailiff returned the battered old Bible to its stand. A long sigh went up from the audience. The cast was complete at last and the play could now begin. The day had clouded over rather suddenly and there was a rumble of thunder, but, though a good many people stirred in their seats and exchanged uneasy glances and some of those sitting in the windows got up to stand at the back of the hall, nobody left the courtroom. This was the moment they had waited for all yesterday and today, or rather for six months. They had no real concern for the threat of the elements.

The new judge said:

"Gentlemen, you may proceed."

The defense, by John Oliver, made a routine motion to dismiss on the ground of insufficiency of indictment. The court denied the motion but granted an exception. Then the judge looked at District Attorney Tom Peters and he rose.

"May it please the court and the gentlemen of the jury," he began smoothly.

The morning rosebud had wilted in the course of the day and hung now dejected against his lapel. But he had quite forgotten it. And his forgetting had a human, ingratiating quality somehow. He was a big, genial man with simple, easy manners and a voice that carried, without his making any special effort, it seemed, not only to the back of the big room, but even at times to the courtyard and streets outside. He put his discourse easily, too, in short, clear sentences, like a father telling his children stories. There wasn't a word Tom Peters spoke that couldn't be readily heard by any but a deaf man and readily understood by any present over the age of ten. He never hesitated. He made his statements so distinctly that they rang as good coin rings. If any one of them was not pure truth, but contained instead a small alloy of counterfeit, it was impossible to detect it, at least while his frank voice echoed at your ear.

"The crime described in the indictment is one of poisoning, the punishment for which by the laws of this state is hanging. The State will present evidence to show that the prisoner, a woman slave Aimée, is the person who committed the crime, the only person with motive and opportunity to do so. And the jury will be asked on this evidence to bring in a verdict of guilty against her. These are the facts."

He told about the domestic crisis out at Waverley the autumn before that had made necessary the purchase of a woman servant. Aunt Dosia had had a stroke—"good old Dosia," he called her—and Miss Harriet, whom the community valued as they had always valued every member of the Hunt family, had written to Mr. McLean, in New Orleans at the time, and asked him to buy a servant in replacement.

When Mr. Peters came in his story to the point where the prisoner was offered to Mr. McLean in sale, he bade the jurors look at her and try to see her as a prospective purchaser would: young, erect, neat-appearing, the very sort described by the traders as a likely wench, certified as to health and character by the family in whose uninterrupted possession she had been from birth and who were selling her only to settle the estate of her late master.

"Why wouldn't she seem a bargain at $650? Who wouldn't have closed the deal on the spot just as our good friend McLean did?"

Having himself the kindest heart on earth, as this town and county knew from long experience, Mr. McLean was far from suspecting what depths of black evil could be hidden beneath that prepossessing exterior.

Syke Berry stood up.

"Your Honor, counsel is arguing his case. Will you advise him to reserve persuasion for his summing up?"

The judge, smiling a little, murmured a perfunctory caution

[112]

and the District Attorney proceeded as blandly as though there had been no interruption.

The likely-appearing new servant, so trustingly bought by the master of Waverley and sent off home on the first northbound boat, had scarcely set foot on his place before she had begun to reveal herself to the ladies of his household in her true colors, as would be told presently by the ladies themselves on the stand, Mr. McLean's wife, that is to say, and Miss Harriet Hunt, his sister-in-law by his first marriage.

As Mr. Peters then read off the list of witnesses for the State, he made a running commentary, supplying a descriptive word or phrase for each to help the jury keep them all straight and to show in advance how each one's testimony would fit into the case as a whole. He did it very deftly, tactfully, almost like a gracious host in his own parlor, presenting to his family the guests whom he has invited to meet them. He smiled at the Waverley Negroes sitting in the second bench and paid them the compliment of saying they were the finest stock anywhere around here; but he did not call them singly by name except old Jerry, whom he dubbed the patriarch of the tribe and represented as outraged at the dishonor that had come on that fine old homestead through this evil stranger.

The prisoner's conduct in her brief sojourn at Waverley he merely outlined, assuring the jury there would be abundant testimony to prove the details he mentioned and many others equally damning. He only touched on the high points of the State's case, such as her having got the poison into her possession the night before the crime, her attempt at flight in the hours following it, and so forth. The crime itself he referred to with awestruck solemnity in a lowered voice that moved his audience deeply. Not a woman in the courtroom but had to reach for her handkerchief.

Then, barely twenty minutes after rising to begin, he bowed gravely to judge and jury and sat down.

The judge said: "Call the first witness."

The clerk called: "Dr. Gregory."

Dr. Gregory rose from his seat beside the Waverley family and went forward. The bailiff waiting with Bible in hand near the witness stand was a youth the doctor had been treating for more than a year for a painful rheumatic condition, and they exchanged smiles of mutual trust as the pale young man held the Bible forward and the doctor put his left hand on it, raised his right and attended carefully as he was asked if he solemnly swore to tell the truth, the whole truth, and nothing but the truth, so help him God.

The doctor smiled again as he sat down and everyone in the courtroom smiled, too, even the Yam as he rose to question. As if Dr. Gregory could tell anything but the truth, the smiles seemed to say. The District Attorney handed the clerk three articles, asking that they be labelled Exhibits A, B, and C; and the Yam waited until Mr. Peters was back in his seat before he put the first question to the witness. The questioning, once under way, went very fast, but not fast enough to suit Syke. He fumed and twisted. Everybody in the courtroom except maybe the judge knew that the witness' full name was Malcolm A. Gregory, that he was a graduate of a medical college in Philadelphia, a practising physician for twenty-five years, for twenty of which he had resided in this county. . . .

"We concede the doctor's qualifications!" shouted Syke.

The Yam smiled and went on smoothly.

Q. You have been, I believe, the family physician out at Waverley all that time, were the one they always called in case of sickness?

A. Yes.

Q. Then you know the folks out there very well, don't you, Doctor—white folks and black folks, too?

A. Yes.

Q. You were called to Waverley in the emergency of November 10, last?

A. Yes.

Q. Will you tell the jury about that?

A. Well, I got the call the middle of the afternoon, half past three—about. I know it was about that time, because I had just got in from another country call down the river near Bates Bend and was sitting down to a late dinner. They told me there was a little darky outside badly excited. They said—

Q. Tell whom you mean by "they," please, Doctor.

A. The servants, my children, I don't remember exactly, members of my household, whoever reported the boy's arrival. They reported his excitement, said his horse was so lathered it looked as if it had been soaped all over. I went out at once, of course. And it was true—the horse had been ridden hard. The boy, a child by the name of Dub—although I didn't right off recognize him—was crying so that I had some trouble getting out of him who wanted me and why. Then I made out he was from Waverley and what the trouble was.

Q. What did he say, if you please, Doctor? Not the exact words necessarily, but the sense of the message.

A. That the white folks out there had taken mighty sick all of a sudden. I think he said they were all dying.

Syke leaped up to object.

"The statement is prejudicial, your Honor."

The judge nodded agreement, ordered the remark excluded, and directed the witness to proceed.

A. The messenger said that Miss Hat, or Miss Martha, I believe it was, wanted me to come as quick as I could.

Q. And you did go quickly?

A. Of course, without dinner. It was lucky he found me at home. It was a miracle I wasn't off at the other end of the county. And mercifully Sam Hardy was able to let me have a fast saddle horse from his livery stable, or two, rather, for my own poor nag was dead on his feet from our day's work and the boy's horse was even worse off. It wasn't much past four when we left town, and we made the best speed possible not to overstrain Sam's horses.

Q. And how long did it take actually? What time did you arrive?

A. Around six. I didn't look at my watch. Just about sundown, though—still good daylight. I heard them calling their hogs as I passed through the Lee place and I saw the Negroes travelling in from the field—

Q. The Waverley fields?

A. Oh, no. The Lees'. There hadn't been much work done at Waverley *that* afternoon. The darkies were too excited by the lamentation at the big-house.

Q. The lamentation, Doctor?

A. Well, that's what the Negroes called it. The sickness in the big-house had set in right after dinner and by the time I got there the whole place was a bedlam. Old Jerry had tears streaming down his face when he met me in the back yard to take my horse. "The shepherds is all stricken, Doctor," he said, "and the sheep is astray," which they were, milling around the back yard, wailing and praying and hanging on to me, begging me to save Miss Hat, save little Mas Hunt—

Syke stood up. The judge motioned him to sit down and in a low tone admonished the witness that he was again on forbidden ground. The doctor was embarrassed and could not go on until the Yam gave him a fresh start.

Q. When you did get into the house, Dr. Gregory, how many did you find ill?

A. Mr. McLean himself, just back from New Orleans the day before, and the whole family: his wife, Miss Hat, little Hunt, and —oh, yes, old Duffy, too.

Q. The overseer?

A. Yes. He was the overseer at that time. I looked in on him in his own house before I went in to the others. But he had only an ordinary upset stomach—apparently nothing more. I thought him more mentally excited than anything else. I tried to make him get up and help me wait on those who were really ill. But he wouldn't do it. He believed he was dying. Had some fool idea as usual about being conjured, blamed old Dosia, the poor soul. I told him he ought to be ashamed of himself, talking so about a helpless paralyzed creature.

Q. Aunt Dosia was the old cook? The one who had had a stroke a while before and who, I understand, died along about Christmas?

A. That's right. I reckon she had never got on too well with Duffy. He claimed she had evil powers of some sort.

Syke had been standing for some minutes. At last he got the court to recognize him.

"Surely, your Honor, all this testimony relating to Duffy and old Dosia is irrelevant and moreover prejudicial."

The court agreed. The objectionable testimony was excluded and the Yam sternly instructed to keep his witness to the crime and its consequences. The Yam smiled at his witness.

Q. Well, then, Doctor, I suppose you went on to the big-house. Tell how you found matters there.

A. I found Miss Hat up, trying to look after the others. But she wasn't able to, of course. So the first thing I did was to order her to bed and send one of the Negroes off across the creek to call Mrs. Berry—

Q. Mother of Mr. Berry, counsel for defense?

A. That's right. She was the nearest white woman in the neighborhood, there being nobody but men over at the Lees'.

Q. And after you sent for Mrs. Berry what did you do?

A. Well, I took stock of the sick first of all, found Hunt, Mr. McLean's son by his first marriage, by far the worst off, and the three grown members of the family in no apparent danger. Then I cleared the house of wailing Negroes, kept two or three to build up fires, heat water, wait on me, and ordered the rest to stay out. And I got to work administering relief.

Q. What symptoms did you observe in the boy, Doctor?

A. Purging, vomiting, excessive cramps, dryness about the mouth, thirst—all of the sick had about the same symptoms except as to degree. And the child, Hunt, was also affected by spasmodic action of the extremities.

Q. Convulsions?

A. Well, not complete convulsions, only the limbs. His skin was very cold, too. And his condition altered rapidly for the worse after dark. He suffered collapse some time after the lamps were lighted, went into coma and never came out, poor little fellow. I could do no more. Along toward midnight—eleven-ten to be exact—he—he died. . . .

The doctor's voice broke. He got out his handkerchief, blew his nose, and cleared his throat. The Yam, with his sure sense of drama, turned his face away and respectfully waited for the witness to master his natural emotion. The momentary silence, so much more eloquent than any spoken words, brought home to every listener anew the enormity of the crime which had cost an innocent child his life. Visibly and audibly, too, the whole courtroom pulsed to revived grief. In the solemn pause there rose a low hum compounded of the suppressed groans of men and the stifled weeping of women. After a long moment the Yam lifted his chin in a resolute manner, again faced the witness and spoke in a low, measured tone, weighing every syllable.

Q. From the symptoms you observed, Doctor, you give it as your opinion that the boy died as a result of poison?

A. I do.

The Yam took a sip of water, relaxed his posture, and went on in a more natural voice.

Q. The grown people suffered, then, no serious damage?

A. I wouldn't say that; Miss Hat's heart has not recovered yet. And Mrs. McLean was left with a digestive impairment for which I treated her for several months.

Q. You spoke just now of immediate relief measures, Doctor. What exactly did you do for the sick?

A. Emetics, sedative, castor oil.

Q. You carry all these things in your saddlebags?

A. No. I don't. I carry a lot, but I rely on the old plantation stand-bys wherever I safely can. There'd be no sense in my carting castor oil around. I found that on Miss Hat's medicine shelf.

Q. You found it or she got it for you?

A. I looked for it myself. I had just got her to bed and didn't want to trouble her. But she watched me and, as I was standing there in front of her shelves, I saw her dye chemicals up there with the medicines and I started in scolding her for keeping them together. How did she know, I said, she wouldn't get up to take salts some night and take blue vitriol or verdigris by mistake.

Q. She had those chemicals?

A. Oh, yes, and any number of others: alum, copperas, indigo, cochineal. She got up, came and stood beside me and asked me to point out which ones were really dangerous to have about, and suddenly she missed one particular bottle and cried out: "Oh, merciful God, my yellow is missing. That man who sold it to Br' Kirk *told* him it was poisonous . . . arsenic, I think he said, it had in it." I had already questioned her a little while before about ratsbane and fly powder, and she had said she was sure there was none on the place.

Q. Now, Doctor, at what point did you assign the cause of this sudden family illness to poisoning?

A. As soon as I saw the patients, observed their symptoms, heard how they had all been stricken immediately after eating their dinner. I thought it was poisoning, and by arsenic.

Q. That is your opinion as a medical practitioner?

A. It is. I treated them for arsenic. Of course, as I went along I kept asking questions, and then Miss Hat missed her arsenical dye and I suspected the tea—

Q. Excuse me, Doctor. I am not sure that I quite follow you and perhaps the jury does not either.

A. Well, I learned that tea was drunk that day by the white

[118]

household and by nobody else. Mr. Duffy was at the dinner table with the rest of them, shared everything they ate, but took no tea. He alone of those at table escaped poisoning.

Q. Now, Doctor, in your capacity of family friend, during that night at Waverley you performed certain acts in regard to the prisoner and I want you to tell the jury what they were. But you must understand that by the rules of evidence you cannot in this part of your testimony express any opinions or conclusions but must relate happenings only, tell what you and others said and did and only that.

The doctor nodded, coughed into his handkerchief, pocketed the handkerchief, shifted his position slightly and told how he had crossed the yard to the kitchen to question the cook who had prepared dinner that day—the new cook he called her, explaining that she was a recent purchase of Mr. McLean, bought by him in New Orleans and sent up a week earlier to do Aunt Dosia's work. He told how he had found the kitchen empty and the shedroom in the rear, too. Disturbed by this, the witness said, he had then reported to Miss Hat and, at her order, sent all the grown males on the place out in every direction with lanterns and lightwood torches.

Q. This was after dark then?

A. A little after. But it was some time before she was brought in. They had caught her a long way down Coon Creek—

Q. You are speaking of the prisoner?

A. Yes. But she didn't look as she looks now. Her hair was loose and wild, her clothes torn. She had on field hands' clothes and she had torn them to tatters in the bushes, her stockings, too. Her eyes, when they first brought her into the lamplight, looked like cat's eyes. We couldn't question her at first. She was in such a state— hysterical, hitting out at whoever came around her or screaming and crying and throwing herself about. I gave her a mild sedative and left her tied up to that big loom of Miss Hat's with Uncle Jerry to watch her. Later, when I went back and found her quiet, I had one of the women search her. She had no poison on her, but we did find inside her dress a very interesting document.

The Yam asked permission to present in evidence Exhibit A. Counsel for the defense objected. All in the audience who had attended the earlier trial knew that the famous stolen "free papers" were now in debate once more. Judge Calloway had excluded this paper, but there was absolutely no telling what the new judge would do.

The wrangle between the lawyers grew so heated that the judge had the jury led from the room until the question could be resolved. The "free papers" taken from the prisoner when she had been captured in full flight on the night following the crime were, of right, not her own at all. They bore not her name but that of a woman who, according to the prosecution, had been a fellow passenger on a steamboat coming up the Mississippi when the prisoner was on her way to her new home. The State contended that the theft of this document which would facilitate escape tended to prove premeditation and so bore on the issue. But the defense insisted it was collateral evidence only and should not be admitted. The court ruled at last, as the earlier one had done, for the defense. The paper was again excluded. The jury was brought back and the doctor went on.

After the prisoner had been searched on the night of the crime, he took pen and paper and sat down beside her to question her. He questioned her from three in the morning till daylight. He wrote down her answers carefully. Relating this now, he described these written answers as a "confession," but the defense got the word stricken. Then the Yam attempted to introduce Exhibit B and another tussle between him and Syke got under way. The judge did not this time send the jury out, but himself took over the questioning of the witness.

· Q. Dr. Gregory, were the statements made to you by the prisoner on the night in question and by you then and there written down made of her own free will?

A. Yes, your Honor.

Q. She was not whipped or threatened with whipping or other punishment to get her to make them?

A. No, your Honor.

Q. Did you on the other hand cajole them from her by promise of reward—as to say, if you say such and such things, I will see that you are acquitted on your trial?

The doctor twisted uncomfortably.

A. I am a medical man, sir. These fine points of the law escape me entirely. Perhaps I didn't handle it the way a lawyer would. I don't know. It seemed all right at the time, seemed the kindest way of getting at the truth or maybe the only way. . . .

Q. Then you did offer her some sort of reward?

A. Well, yes, I suppose it might be called that. I let her think she could be got out of the country on a boat.

Again the court ruled for the defense. Exhibit B, informally known as the confession, was also for the second time excluded. And Syke Berry, with cross-examination on his mind, felt a surge of confidence. He tried to master it, because he knew that if he was the least bit too cocksure with Dr. Gregory he'd have every juror against him from the start and, what was maybe even worse, his own mam.

The doctor had now got to the bottle, which he himself had found in the hour of dawn in the ashes of the kitchen fireplace: a glass bottle or the part of one, empty, of course, with the label burned off and the glass partly fused by heat, the Yam's Exhibit C. Syke objected to admitting the bottle fragment. He said the State could not prove that any given blob of glass, misshapen by fire, without name or other identifying mark on it, had ever contained poison or had ever been in the prisoner's possession. The judge asked the Yam if he expected to prove this, the Yam said he did, and Exhibit C was ruled admissible. "You may take an exception," was all the defense got this time. Watching the expression on the faces of the jurors as they fingered the small twisted and discolored thing, passing it along from hand to hand, Syke popped his knuckles and ground his teeth. It was all so like the first trial that it had for him a nightmare quality. The judge returned the witness to the Yam and the Yam went on.

Q. It was by the prisoner's direction that you searched the ashes, Doctor?

A. It was.

Q. She told you to look for the bottle there and you went and found it where she said you would?

A. Yes, sir.

Syke sprang up.

"Your Honor," he cried passionately, "the court has excluded the prisoner's so-called confession. Surely you cannot permit counsel to get into evidence by the back door what he is forbidden to bring in by the front."

The judge's gaze rested a moment on Syke, shifted away to the Yam, and then to the clerk.

"Strike the last two questions and answers from the record," he ordered.

The Yam said bitterly, "Cross-examine," and sank into his chair.

Syke looked at the big wall clock above the bench. The hands showed twenty to five. He addressed the judge in a pleading tone.

"Your Honor, the questioning of this witness is very important to us. It will be a distinct disadvantage to the accused if we are forced to hurry it. May we put it off till tomorrow morning?"

Dr. Gregory twisted in his seat and claimed the judge's attention testily.

"Your Honor, I have already sacrificed two days' time and perhaps the welfare of several patients to attendance on this trial. Surely you will not require me to come back tomorrow. I'd rather get on with the thing now if it takes till dark."

The judge frowned. The threatened thunder shower had gone round after all. The air in the crowded room seemed closer if anything, the heat more intense. That pain was gnawing again in his breast. His daughter's letter was unanswered. If he went over to the tavern now he had the chance of a little rest and quiet before supper. He might even write his letter.

"Court is adjourned," he said, "till nine tomorrow."

CHAPTER 2

As the courtroom slowly emptied, the olive-skinned Creole stranger, boarder in the Ketcham home locally known as Mr. Onnud, made his way forward to have a word with the prisoner before the sheriff led her out. Many people turned and watched him attentively. His thin patrician features, his fine linen suits, for the laundering of which the Ketcham servants were said to receive fabulous tips, his general appearance of substance and high standing had already shed some measure of light into the dense blackness that hitherto had surrounded the accused woman. To see a gentleman of such degree going up to the rail to speak to her, however briefly, as now, was to realize that she was not quite the unregarded, utterly damned and degraded being she had formerly appeared. Nobody knew that any better than Syke. He drew a profound satisfaction from it. His exotic patron seemed to him a miracle and no less.

Back in the slow December weeks when Syke was waiting to hear the High Court's ruling, he had had to help his pappy clean up their deadening for planting. It was hard work, logrolling and burning all day long, and mighty mean weather, too. But, hard as his body worked, his mind was busy with what he then thought of as his lost case. All the time he was working, it kept turning in his head that a nigger that's got white folks' backing in court is the only one's got a bare chance. One day he saddled old Jonas and rode clear into Athens to the jail and made one more try at the prisoner.

At first all he could get out of her was the same thing she'd said to him a hundred times before. Her New Orleans master had been her one friend and he was dead, in him she had lost her only hope. His widow hated the wench. She sold her because she hated her. No help there. But Syke kept on: Wasn't there somebody else in the dead man's family then, a brother maybe? So then for the first time he heard of Mr. Onnud, or Monsieur Achille, as Aimée called him. By his lamp in the loft at home that night, Syke wrote a letter: Sir, you do not know me, but . . . It was a short letter boldly asking if Monsieur Achille would consent to appear as a character witness at Aimée's second trial if ever there should be a second trial. Syke hardly dared to hope for an affirmative answer. But it came in a courteous letter of thanks for Syke's efforts past and to come in behalf of a creature so nearly friendless and with an enclosure of what Achille Arnaud called a small token of appreciation. The token was $25—as much as Syke's original fee, only just paid somewhat grudgingly by Miss Hat.

The letter with enclosure reached Syke on the same day as the news that the High Court had ordered a new trial. With $50 cash money in his hands, Syke was able to make a momentous decision: He would go to New Orleans. His pappy opposed him bitterly and with reason. It was a wild-goose chase, and he couldn't spare Syke. Singlehanded, he'd never get that deadening ready in time to plant. Syke's law learning the year before had been got at untold family sacrifice. And this money had ought to be laid out in things they needed. Even Syke's mam said his clothes wasn't anyways fitten for such a journey. It was a bad season for travel: no boats on the Yalohatchie since November and none likely before the spring rise. Still he went, by stage to Memphis on the day after Christmas, and as a deck passenger on a downbound steamboat from there, went in the same butternut homespun pants and outgrown jacket he had worn for the past three years.

Achille Arnaud was clearly a rich man. He lived in a fine old house with a parlor like no parlor Syke had ever seen before. There were bright brocade hangings and tinkling chandeliers and a parrot, in a little swing, that called, "Bon jour, Monsieur, bon jour," to Syke as he sat waiting. His host in a silk dressing gown (which made Syke blunder into asking if he was sick) received a stranger graciously, without noticing, or seeming to notice, his backwoods clothes, asked him to be seated and listened patiently, if at first non-committally. But at last he spoke.

"As I understand it, you believe the wench didn't get a fair trial?"

"That's it. A fair trial's what I aim to get her next time."

"Well, she should have that, certainly. However damning the circumstances against her appear—and even to me they do appear quite hopeless—she should have a fair trial. Yes, it would be too bad if she should perish, the victim of local prejudice. Now, Mr. Berry, what do you think you need to get her simple justice? Money?"

Syke popped his knuckles and his voice was strained.

"Well, if you was to come up yourself, sir, like you've promised, to show she had good white folks' backing, that'd help more than anything. But money'd help, too. Oh, not just for me. I'd fight the case for the fee the court allows me from her present owners, like before. But I need help, sir, somebody that knows more law than what I do."

"You know such a man?"

It was then that Syke hurriedly introduced John Oliver's name, painted his portrait in swift, passionate strokes. . . .

John Oliver laid a hand on Syke's shoulder now and nodded toward the door of the empty courtroom where Orrin Foote and Mr. Duffy stood waiting for them.

"Didn't you promise them a drink as soon as court let out, Syke?"

"Sure did, Mr. John," said Syke cheerfully, stacking his papers into a neat bundle. As they went out together along the aisle, he said soberly: "You know, Mr. John, I been so lucky in this case up to now it sorter scares me: having Mr. Onnud's backing and you to help and ever'thing. Why, you take now that matter of the old judge's office. I know it's a little thing. I know it was your writing Mrs. Calloway done the trick. All the same, it's luck."

Judge Calloway's white-pillared, high-verandahed brick house was set back at the end of a long mossy walk made also of bricks and bordered in violets and shoulder-high sweet olive and calycanthus shrubs and shadowed by magnolias that almost hid the house from view. But the judge's office, theirs for the duration of court term through the kindness of the judge's widow, stood at the street line and only one step above the plank sidewalk. Syke had the key in his pocket, and when he had proudly opened the door he

[125]

stepped down to the walk again and let the others pass in before him: Mr. John and Orrin Foote and old Duffy. Mr. John and Duffy, of course, had slept here with Syke the night before, but Orrin was seeing the place for the first time. He whistled and let out an "I'll be goddamned," as he looked round him at the book-lined walls, the horsehair sofa, the cot bed Mrs. Calloway had had set up for Mr. John, the chairs, the desk with the pitcher of fresh water and glasses on it and, beside them, a lunch basket spread over with a clean towel.

"Nice, ain't it?" Syke said as he busily brought out the brown bottle he had hidden behind the Mississippi Code last night.

"Nice," agreed Orrin accepting a glass and sinking to the sofa.

Duffy pretended not to want his drink. He went to the open back door and stood staring out along the bricked path that led toward the kitchen door of the main house. Mr. John left his drink untouched, too, while he took down a volume from the shelves and began to look up something. Syke closed the street door and, glass in hand, sat down, waiting. Whatever was on Mr. John's mind he'd know pretty soon. As to Duffy—well, a second day was ending with him sober and that was enough for Syke. When Orrin finished his drink, Syke would slip him the dollar agreed on for watching over Duffy through the day, and get his promise to take over again when court opened tomorrow. Duffy, with Syke and Mr. John on guard was safe enough at night. A drink a day wouldn't do him no harm. His rambling, conjure talk was mighty weari-some, but Syke and Mr. John would manage what all they had to say to each other in spite of it—especially if Duffy went to sleep early like last night.

Orrin was in no hurry. He made his drink last as long as he could, gossiping between his slow sips, about the trial: the jury, the whole panel, one man at a time, the new judge—"a rich man, I hear. Got a big plantation down in Copiah and fifty slaves, they say." Syke took his drink slowly, too, holding a swallow in his mouth and letting it slip lingeringly down his throat as he an-swered lazily, "Umph-humph," or "Yeah," or "You don't say." All the time he kept one eye on Mr. John, bent over that book on the desk, and one on Duffy. Once Syke got up and unobstrusively lit the lamp at Mr. John's elbow. But Mr. John was too absorbed to notice.

Duffy turned round, his face glowering in the lamplight.

"I ain't a prisoner," he suddenly announced. "I ain't under arrest. I been subpoenaed as a witness, that's all. I'm a free white citizen. You got no call to set a guard on me and say what I can and can't do. I don't want my drink measured out to me. If you can't trust me, what's the use putting me up on that stand a-tall?"

Syke set his glass down and went over to him.

"Look, Mr. Duffy. I'm your friend. You know I am. If you're here, subpoenaed like you say, ain't it your own doing? Didn't you, 'way back last winter, write to me . . . ?"

Actually the letter was right there in amongst his papers and Syke could have got it out and showed it to him. Only that wasn't anyways necessary. Duffy remembered it as well as he did:

I seen in the Athens paper where you aim to git a new trile for that pore retch they come so near hangin at the faul term. I attend that trile they give her befor and hit dont seem anyways likly to me you can git her off. But I dont think she the one done the business. I will tell you more when I see you. . . .

Syke's voice went on wheedlingly: "I trusted you then, didn't I, Duffy? A man don't take a twenty-mile ride a-muleback in January for fun, does he? If there's those didn't think enough of you to call you to testify in the first trial after you a-offering to, I'm not to blame, am I? And if it's measuring out your drink you don't like, why, look, hit's no more than we do to ourselves. We got a fight on our hands, man. We can't none of us afford a drunk right now. You know Tom Peters and the Yam could keep you from testifying if you wa'n't sober. They're already gunning for you. You heard Dr. Gregory just now, what he said about you. And you told me yourself Miss Hat been going around, telling you're crazy. They're trying to fix that jury not to believe you even before you take the stand. Keeping you sober is our one chance. . . ." Mr. John had left his book and turned to listen. Orrin was listening, too, and grinning. Syke went back and picked up the two glasses, his own and Duffy's. "Come on now. Drink up, like friends, which we are."

Duffy drank and, if he did not smile, he ceased to glower. At the second gulp he was launched on his favorite theme: his sufferings at the hands of Aunt Dosia, who was certainly a witch.

"From the time I come on Waverley, I never know a minute's

peace from her bedevilmint ontwel I went to a root doctor down beyond Bates' Bend and got me a bag to wear with stronger stuff in it than Dosie's stuff. But she work on me right up to the day she die, I know. How come her to plague me at first was by me a-having a young nigger feller by the name of Dave when I come to Waverley to manage, going on ten year back. This Dave taken a notion after Lethe, the old woman's fav'*rite*. Dosie have nine head of chillern all told and I never stop to count up how many gran'-chillern besides this here Lethe. But Lethe the one she set the most store by a-count of her white blood. Now my Dave was as black as your boot, and her granny didn't want Lethe to have no truck with him. So the first thing the old witch done to me was to put a conjure on Dave and he run off and I never see him again. He cost me $700 back in Alabama. And she conjured my gun—as good a gun as you'd want to see—so hit never shoot straight again. And she conjured my mule. A real study plow mule he was, year in and year out, up to the day Dosie conjure him, and from then on twel he die not worth the feed he et or the iron it take to shoe him. . . ."

When they had finished their drinks and Orrin had left, Syke opened the basket of food his mother had fixed and left there for them: fried chicken and biscuits, wild-plum preserves and fresh cake. She had got up at daylight, Syke knew, to get it ready. While they were eating, an old Negro woman in a red head rag and a clean white apron came through the twilight down the bricked path at the back, bringing, with Mrs. Calloway's compliments, a pot of coffee on a tray with cups and saucers and sugar and cream. Mr. Duffy scowled at the woman. He wasn't sure her coffee was to be trusted, but when Syke and Mr. John had each drained off a cup without apparent harm, he accepted one, grumbling. However, he was in a relatively good humor now and continued talkative.

"Syke," said Mr. John, "I'd like to see your notes for the doctor's cross-examination."

Syke fished up his notes, his mouth too full to answer, but his eyes eager and intent. Then he swallowed with a gulp.

"I knowed you had an idea," he crowed gratefully.

Mr. John pushed the lunch basket aside and drew into the cleared space under the lamp that book he had been consulting. It was still open and he indicated—carefully, with his knuckles only, since his fingertips held a half-eaten piece of fried chicken—a section headed: *Collateral facts affecting credibility.* Syke bent over the page and his eyes sped along it.

Mr. Duffy sighed, took up from the sofa the folded quilts allotted to him, spread them down on the floor in a corner and began to make ready for bed. First he took off his shirt, revealing his dark hairy chest and the cord from which was slung just under his left armpit a small leather bag containing probably another of red flannel encasing God knows what mixture of hair, dried and powdered toad, graveyard dirt, salt and pepper to ward off evil spells. Then he took off his shoes and carefully inspected the silver coin he wore in one of them. If any friend turned hostile on any day, Duffy would know by the blackening of his luck piece. Fortunately for the cause of the defense, the silver now showed bright and undimmed and Mr. Duffy replaced it in his shoe. Then he stretched himself out on his bedding and relaxed at once to peaceful snores.

CHAPTER 3

ARRIVED at Waverley, Martha sat on the front steps, her bonnet hanging from its ribbons looped over her knee, and Mr. Banning stood in the path before her. Behind him Sis Hat's garden was brimful of sunset brilliance and summer bloom: tiger lilies, poppies, marigolds, ragged robins, roses. Their smell was hot and pungent. The encircling woods were steeped in silence and evening shadows. Martha found it pleasant after the day in the stuffy courtroom with its mysterious wrangling, its greedy, staring eyes, its barely concealed personal threat, to sit here, relaxed and free, alone with a trusted friend.

"I always liked the creek," he said, "used to roam off there with a book or, in summer weather, go for a swim with Hunt. On hot nights in the city I often think of it, so cool and green and deep."

Martha stood up and smiled. Supper would be delayed because her husband had stopped in at the Lees' on the way home.

"Let's walk over there. Sis Hat can blow the horn for us when Mr. McLean comes."

She went through the dogtrot to the kitchen to leave word with Sis Hat, came back, and led the way down the drive that circled the garden and along the path through the woods. When they stepped out of the deep shade beside the shining scimitar of the creek, she winced and drew back.

"It's the wrong hour entirely," she complained. "We'll go blind, looking at that glare."

She turned rightabout and even moved a step back upon the shadowed path, but he caught her arm.

"No, no. Don't go back yet. Stay a little. Sit down—here's a patch of shade. Absorb this peace."

So they sat, she on a fallen log, her back toward the sun-struck water, and he on the ground at her feet, digging out of his pockets his pipe and tobacco. He did most of the talking. Like many lonely men, in intimacy with a good listener, he could become almost loquacious—the man of words, Kirk McLean called him at such times. He was in reminiscent mood today and Martha encouraged that. She never tired of stories of his and her husband's student days in Connecticut, although she already knew so many of them now in superficial, anecdotal fashion: how Parson had got his nickname from his father's calling, what larks they used to have at Mrs. White's boarding house, and so on. Even the memory he dwelt on now she had heard before, but she kept him talking about it just the same.

The two men very nearly lost each other after their college parting. The erratic and dwindling correspondence of the next year or so lapsed entirely through a mishap. Kirk McLean's one and only letter sent back to New England from the Southwest, beginning in careless exuberance: "Well, Parson, here I am in the Mississippi backwoods, editing a newspaper, of all things, and engaged, or nearly so, to the prettiest girl in the region," had contained, after all, no address. Martha could picture the young New Englander some time later, making his own way South for the first time, pacing the deck of a Cincinnati packet, passing a gay group of young people, hearing the thrum of a banjo and a familiar song: Possum up de gum tree, Coony in de hollow. . . . Among the voices was one as familiar as the well-remembered song, but he hadn't realized that. He had thought he was only reminded of his lost friend by the nostalgic strains. But then at supper in the dining saloon, he had felt somebody looking across the table at him, heard: Parson! I'll be a son of a gun. Where did you drop from?

Martha agreed it was a minor miracle but no more amazing, when you stopped to think, than their being friends in the first place.

"You're so *different*," she insisted. "How did it ever happen to start with? Did you like each other from the first time you met?"

He laughed.

"Heavens, no. We had no use whatever for each other." He leaned back on one elbow, watched a gray squirrel flicker up through the lower shadows, green as ocean depths, to the topmost branches bathed still in a golden light, and tried to explain. "The Virginian, they called him, and he hadn't been in the place a week before he was the most popular man there. He was like nobody we had ever known: so warm and genial, so kindly, so full of small gracious courtesies that we hadn't even the imagination to think of, and a leader, of course, born to command, born to be first in everything, dancing, even ice skating and sleighing—although I'm sure I don't know how he managed that—"

"But *you* were first in classes. Mr. McLean always says so."

He waved that aside with his pipe.

"Only because classes didn't interest him particularly. He'd have been first there, too, if he'd cared to be. The human scene was his. How he shone there! That banjo of his and his plantation songs alone would have made him the center of every gathering. Then there was his playful charm with women and girls, his considerateness for them, his forthrightness with men, his knowing by some sixth sense how to put any and everybody, high or low, at ease. Most of us came from little New England villages, more or less alike, with their town meetings and their white church spires and elm-bordered streets, where everybody knows everybody else, sees them every day, face to face, you know, even over and over in a day. There's not much chance for illusion about one's neighbors. And here was a man from an unknown and, to us, unknowable society. It seemed a fabulous, feudal order and he, a knight of sorts. I never saw anyone so generally and easily liked. Only I held out against him, from jealousy, I have always supposed. There was no other reason. So it must have been that I felt envy of a man who was everything that I was not, easy where I was stiff, charming where I was shy, gay where I was dull. And he thought I was a terrible stick. Ask him some time. He'll admit it. Oh, we were the last two people you'd ever have thought could become lifelong friends. I used to avoid him religiously. He had only to come into a room for me to leave it. If the fellows were planning a sleigh-ride or a skating party I made sure to find out if the Virginian's name was on the list before I'd let my own be put down. To myself I justified my prejudice by my anti-slavery sentiments, which in those hot-headed days were intense. But I can see now that hardly made sense—you'd as well say you couldn't abide the smell of a rose because of the manure it took to grow it."

"And then you changed—why?"

"Out of perversity, maybe. Anyway, I began to like him only after others ceased to."

"Why, what happened?"

"Nothing at all. Mostly, I think, it was just the fickleness of the crowd. In our second year a fellow from Boston was the cock of the walk. The tide of Kirk's popularity ebbed pretty fast, once it had turned. You see he had been an interesting novelty that first year. He could never be that again. Having lost his novelty, he simply did not appeal to the—er—New England taste. He couldn't understand that any better than you can. Deprived of his stellar role, he could play no other. He grew frightened, unsure of himself, imagined slights where none was intended, began failing in his classes, got into one absurd scrape after another: used his fists on a farmer who jostled him in the street; quarrelled at a card game and challenged an inoffensive little Vermonter to a duel—"

"The duel you prevented?"

"As it happened, yes."

"You saved his life—or that other young man's."

"Maybe I just saved them both from getting expelled. But, no matter—the point is, he went floundering into one idiotic mess after another until the whole place was down on him, all but me. The more the rest turned against him, the more I was for him. Don't ask me why. I don't know—or, no, perhaps I do. It was his veneer that had always put me off, you see, the manners, the graces, and now at last I glimpsed behind the gentleman a real, live man—" He broke off sharply as she buried her face in her hands and wept. "What have I said? How have I hurt you? Oh, Miss Martha, do forgive me. I'm a clumsy idiot. What is it, please?" She could only sob and shake her head. He sprang to his feet and bent over her. "Perhaps you are thinking people may turn against him here, too? Thinking this trial may cost him dear? If that is it, I have tormented you needlessly. Loss of prestige in that callow schoolboy world was something very different. His popularity there was superficially grounded, but here he has true friends— like the doctor, like Sam Hardy. Such men will be no more affected by a bit of gratuitous mud-slinging than you or Miss Hat."

"Or you?"

"Or me," he agreed. "Here he is the embodiment of the local

ideal. Men admire in him the qualities they would like to have themselves. Why, the other day, that first morning while I was waiting at the tavern, I heard two men talking. I have no idea who they were, but not personal friends of Kirk's, I'm sure. They said they knew him only by sight. I wish you could have heard them. I can't possibly reproduce the words, let alone the heartiness of their homespun manner. But the gist of their comment was this: It's a burning shame that lawyers should be allowed to resort to such trickery as the defense is using. Either the accused woman put the poison in that tea or she didn't, and the law ought to make the lawyers stick to that instead of permitting them to attempt to get sympathy for her by blackening the name of the finest gentleman in the whole county. I got the impression that they thought the trick was far more likely to turn the jury against the prisoner than win their sympathy for her. They said, I know, that Kirk McLean is as solid in this county as the courthouse itself. . . . And in this affair, besides, the truth makes him invulnerable."

"But what is the truth?"

She barely whispered it. Yet he heard and, hearing, seemed profoundly shocked. He began to walk up and down before her, frowning. For a startled moment she thought she had forfeited his liking forever. Devoted as he was to his friend, perhaps he could only resent that murky hint from her. Oh, now he would surely hate her. He came and stood above her, sternly, she thought, but she didn't dare to look up.

Her moist bit of handkerchief hung in her paralyzed fingers. And she would have recalled the words she had spoken if she could. They must have sounded to him like treason. She heard herself go stammering lamely on, qualifying, amending. Even if the defense charge about Aimée is without foundation, she faltered, the jury may believe it. You see there is something else that the defense means to bring out in this trial, something you don't know yourself, I reckon, something about another colored woman, a woman named Lethe. . . .

"I do know," he said gently.

"Well, then, that *is* true and all the jury probably knows about it and that may influence what they believe about Aimée—"

He interrupted her.

"Leave the jury out of this and what they believe and why. Ex-

[134]

plain yourself to me. Surely you do not believe this trumped-up charge against Kirk?"

"Do you?" she whispered.

"Certainly not. Do you think I'd be here if I did?"

Her eyes fell before his steady, honest gaze. Now she felt confounded indeed—unwilling to deceive him and unable to explain herself.

"Now you will think badly of *me*," she said forlornly. "And I don't want you to. You—well, you see, in New Orleans, I thought, I mean you seemed so happy about our marriage, nearly as happy as we were ourselves, and I got an idea you really liked me—"

He laughed gently.

"That's true, Miss Martha. I did. I do."

"Oh, then, don't you see? I hate to—to have you think I can't trust him the way you do—and Sis Hat, too. But I can't. I don't even know why I can't. It's all so mixed up."

Again he walked away from her, up and down, up and down. Again he stopped. You love him very much. You are very brave. It takes a great love to accept the worst, or the possibility of the worst, in the beloved and yet stand with him against the world. But that troubled her somehow. It seemed far more than she deserved. She stood up, too, to meet his eyes more nearly on a level. She put out her hand.

"No, no. You still don't understand. I—oh, it's impossible to explain. I can't talk about it."

His eyes were compassionate. No, they said. You can't. Not to me, a man. You would have to break too many taboos of ancient tribal hallowing.

"Perhaps," he hinted, "I understand anyway."

"Not if you think what you said. Not if you believe I *want* to—to back him up in that courtroom. I never have wanted to. Before the baby came I prayed to die to get out of it."

"Then why are you doing it?"

"I have to," she cried feverishly. "I have no choice. Sis Hat and Mr. Peters both say if I stand by him publicly everybody will think I don't believe what the defense will charge. That's what I want them to think. After all, if anybody is very unhappy, it's their own business, isn't it? It only makes everything harder to have others know. Even at first—I mean when I learned about that other woman, the one I thought you didn't know about—it would have been much easier if I hadn't felt that everybody around here knew. I reckon the worse things get to be in private the more important it is to keep up a front."

He took in his grasp the cold hand she had all this while been holding out to him in pleading.

"And is that all you're doing it for, Miss Martha—just to keep up a front?"

He still held her hand but she turned her eyes away. She laughed, a small, hard laugh without mirth.

"Oh, well. I've told you so much. I may as well make you dislike me utterly. What does it matter? No, that's not all I am doing it for." Her words rang defiantly. "I'm going through with that trial partly because I want to find out. I have to."

"Find out what?"

Still she could not look at him.

"Oh," she said wearily, "not just what happened or didn't happen. I reckon I could forgive him anything he *did,* if only I could understand what he *meant* by it. Buying that woman, for instance. I nearly go out of my mind trying to figure it out: why, why, why?"

"Have you asked Kirk?" he asked gently, giving her hand a little squeeze and dropping it. "Does he know how this question troubles you?"

"Oh, *no!* No, indeed. Why, the only thing he has to cling to is my faith in him. He often says so."

"A faith you have already lost? Ah, Miss Martha, surely with him, the—the sham should be laid aside."

She sat down again and bowed her head over her knees. Oh, that was the real grief. And he in his kindness had uncovered it now to the very quick. It was the sham that was breaking her heart, the being a stranger to her husband and no more, never, never anything more. The first secret had overgrown their life as weeds overgrow a pond and at last shut out the daylight. Maybe it's not all his fault, Miss Martha. No, I suppose it isn't. Maybe it's partly mine. Anyway, she mourned, we cannot talk now about *anything.* Her life was emptied of meaning. Her days were built on lies to Sis Hat, Dr. Gregory, Uncle George, everybody but Mr. Banning. And maybe she ought just to have lied to him, too.

Maybe she shouldn't have let him see how wretched she was. Maybe she was selfish to spoil his pleasure in Waverley, when, as his hostess, she should be thinking only of entertaining him and making him have a nice time. He said soberly that she had showed him her true feeling and surely she should not reproach herself for that. . . .

"For the love of God, are you two stone deaf?"

He was standing on the path, staring at them, half laughing, the horn in his hand. Old Hunt's horn, it was, shorn from the head of some Waverley cow in the dim, lost past, and still kept, when not in use, hanging by a leather thong from a peg in the dogtrot. It was the time-honored household summons. Every soul at Waverley obeyed its imperative. Mr. Duffy's successor, even as Mr. Duffy, used the horn every morning to waken the hands at crack of dawn. Miss Hat took it down in the old days to call Hunt and Dub in from their far-ranging sports in woods and stream, and now to apprise Martha on some aimless ramble that there were unexpected callers at the house, to trumpet abroad to any or all of the absent family: come to dinner, come to supper.

"Is supper ready?" said Martha with false alacrity and added: "Did you blow?" quite unnecessarily, because it was perfectly obvious that he had done so and more than once, too.

"Like Gabriel himself, after poor Sis Hat had given up, exhausted," he said, looking from one to the other curiously, waiting in smiling politeness for some sort of explanation of their amazing oblivion and Martha's tear-blotched face.

"We fell into a conversation," Neal Banning said promptly. And Martha was glad that he could explain, since she felt she couldn't have managed to. She had, under her husband's gaze, such a feeling of guilt she could not meet his eyes. "Miss Martha has been upset about the trial. I have been trying to reassure her."

"Good old Parson. Why are you upset, my dear? That's entirely unjustified. Tom Peters says the case is shaping up very well. He's even more sanguine than he was the other time. However, it's a shame you have to be dragged into it. If I'd had my way, you never should have been. This time tomorrow, anyway, you should be well out of it and then you can stay at home the rest of the week."

"No," she interrupted quickly. "No, Mr. McLean. I'm not going to stay at home at all. My place is there with you to the end."

He put his arm about her shoulders and appealed to his friend. "Hear that, Parson? You old hardshell bachelor, you, can you understand how it strengthens a man in the face of his enemies to have his wife wholeheartedly at his back?"

CHAPTER 4

MARTHA sat with Sis Hat in the District Attorney's office, waiting for court to open. It was Wednesday, the third day of the trial. Her husband, who had run across to the post office with Mr. Banning, dropped a letter in her lap. She recognized her cousin Dessie's handwriting and her face burned before she even opened the letter or read one line of it. When in December her uncle George had written apologizing for his delay in settling her grandmother's estate and saying he hoped he had occasioned her no inconvenience in her "new life, which he was unable to picture because so uninformed," she had seized upon his obvious ignorance of even her most public sorrows and fiercely determined that he (and Aunt Charlotte and the girls) should never know. Replying, she had not only omitted mention of any shadow whatsoever upon her new life but had yielded to the temptation to paint her circumstances in colors romantic and false. She was ashamed of that letter as she opened Dessie's now.

Dessie was engaged and very, very happy. She and all the family were relieved and delighted to hear that Martha's match had turned out so ideally—"especially Mama, who, under Papa's reproaches, had begun to feel that, if you were unhappily married, she was somehow to blame. Now about my Charles." A long page. The wedding—another long page. The bride's dress—another page. "And so you see, Martha, that although I was fated to be, not the wife of a rich Mississippi planter, but of a poor Charleston lawyer instead, I am happy, too, and I want you to write and tell me you are as honestly glad of my good fortune as I am of yours. . . ."

There were tears in Martha's eyes when she lifted them to Mr.

Banning standing in front of her, his kind face marked with concern.

"No bad news, I hope, Miss Martha?"

"Well," she evaded, "unless you'd call it bad news to hear your kinfolks are getting on fine without you, don't really care any more what happens to you."

As she stood up to take the arm he offered, something fluttered off her lap to the floor. He retrieved it. It was half of a hundred-dollar bill. Their eyes met above it as he handed it to her. His were smiling.

"It looks as if the kinfolk did care a little after all," he hinted gently.

"Oh," she said, hurrying to hide the half bill in her bag and glancing over her shoulder toward her husband and Sis Hat, who were talking to Mr. Peters at the other side of the room, and then back at Mr. Banning. "You won't tell?" she begged him. "You won't mention it to anyone? Promise. It's my own—from my uncle. I need it very much for—for a private reason. I don't want anyone to know."

"No one shall know from me, Miss Martha."

Court opened with Dr. Gregory again on the witness stand. At a word from the judge, Syke rose, passed behind the prosecutors' table, took his stand at the end of the jury box nearest the audience and farthest from the witness, and began.

Q. Dr. Gregory, you have said that on the evening of November 10, when you were called to attend the sick at Waverley, you made a diagnosis based on their symptoms?

A. Yes.

Q. But isn't it true, Doctor, that symptoms resembling those you described and which you attributed to arsenical poisoning may result from disease: gastritis, gastroenteritis and Asiatic cholera [Syke read the names carefully from the card in his hand] for example, or from eating foods which have developed poison from decay or from being cooked in copper vessels that ain't been cleaned properly?

A. Yes, of course.

Q. Haven't you treated a lot of people around here toward the end of summer and in the early fall mighty sick from "summer sickness," as we call it?

A. Well, yes, but in diseases, in cholera or in attack from food-poisoning causing dysentery and nausea, we rarely find traces of blood in the ejections as we do with arsenic poisoning.

Q. You found such traces of blood then?

A. I did.

Q. So you are willing to swear that the boy who died, died from taking arsenic?

A. I give it as my medical opinion that he did.

Q. I reckon you know, Doctor, that in some of the most famous poison cases the doctors themselves have been in disagreement as to whether death occurred from poison or natural causes?

A. Of course I know it. The only absolute certainty would be a post-mortem chemical examination of internal organs, for which, of course, Chewalla County has no facilities.

Q. Then, without that kind of test, could you swear the boy's death come from arsenic?

A. Nobody could. I can only give you my honest conclusion based on twenty-five years of medical experience.

Q. Have you in those twenty-five years attended many persons who had been poisoned?

A. By arsenic? Fortunately, no.

Q. But some? One or two? Or more?

The doctor reddened, rubbed his palms together, and glared at Syke.

A. I don't recall. How would a man riding from one end of the county to the other every day in the week and Sunday, too, remember all his cases?

Q. But you would certainly remember it if you had appeared in court like this to testify about somebody's commiting murder by poisoning. . . .

A. Oh, that! That has never happened before. Certainly not. I have never before been involved in a case where poison had been maliciously administered.

Q. Then how did the others whom you have treated get hold of it?

A. By accident—like a child swallowing Jimson weed seeds or an ignorant darky dosing himself with ratsbane or fly powder. And I have attended a couple of suicides.

Q. In these cases of accident and self-administered poison the symptoms were the same as those you observed among the sick at Waverley?

A. Where the poison was arsenic, yes.

Q. Did Mr. Duffy the overseer tell you when you went out to his house in the yard that he believed they was all poisoned with Jimson weed put in their food?

A. He did. But that was just his ignorant, superstitious—

Q. Excuse me, Doctor. But I believe the court will not allow you expressions of opinion except medical ones.

A. Well, it's my medical opinion that Jimson weed was not in this case even a remote possibility. Jimson weed, stramonium, acts more like belladonna, extremely dilated pupils, and so forth. It is what is called a narcotic. Arsenic is an irritant. No doctor would confuse the effects of the two.

Q. Did you report Mr. Duffy's suspicions to the Grand Jury or the District Attorney?

A. Not that I recall. They were quite baseless.

Q. In the case of the child you just mentioned, the one that got hold of Jimson weed by accident, was the result fatal?

A. Yes.

Q. Did you in that case, as in the present one, diagnose by symptoms only?

A. Yes. Also we found Jimson weed in the ejections. And the mother then recalled the child's playing in a patch of the weed the afternoon before it was stricken. . . .

Tom Peters stood and appealed to the court. The tenor of counsel's questions seemed to be to impeach the witness' competence as a medical expert. In view of the witness' position of high trust and long-standing professional fitness, surely the cross-examination as conducted was only wasting time. The judge asked Syke if he hadn't about covered the ground, but Syke said, No, he had not finished his questions in the medical field. And since the witness had also testified in his capacity as family friend, acting in the matter of the prisoner's capture, the finding of the bottle, and so forth, the defendant must have a right to cross-examine on those matters as well. The judge said go ahead and Syke went ahead.

Q. In your testimony in this courtroom in November when the same person was on trial accused of the same crime, you stated, I believe, that arsenic is found in many different preparations on the pharmacist's shelves, among them ratsbane, fly powder, and certain dyes, as Schweinfurt green [Syke was reading again from the card in his hand and having a hard time with that German name, and he heard somebody, Orrin Foote, he believed, chortle in the back of the courtroom. He flushed but drove on.] Scheele's green and king's yellow. You did testify that there's arsenic in all these products that would kill if swallowed?

A. In sufficient quantity, yes. There's arsenic in some medicines, too, as Fowler's solution. A lot of medicines contain poisonous elements. Strychnine, foxglove, and so on, are all healing in proper quantity, deadly in ignorant or malicious hands. The question of poison is rather a matter of dosage than of chemical content, you know.

Q. Well, then, Doctor, would this here king's yellow kill if taken in sufficient quantity?

A. Positively, yes.

Syke crossed to the clerk's table, picked up the bottle described as Exhibit C, brought it back and handed it to him.

Q. Is this the bottle or the fragment of a bottle that you found in the kitchen fireplace on the night of the crime at Waverley?

A. Yes.

Q. You are sure?

A. Of course I'm sure.

Q. What size bottle should you say it was before it was half burned up?

A. A two-ounce bottle.

Q. I hand you now a one-ounce bottle undamaged. Will you say if you think the fragment is certainly part of a bottle of larger size?

Dr. Gregory turned the piece of glass around and around in his hands, held it up to the light, ran a forefinger measuringly around an angle, considered it beside the one-ounce vial Syke had given him and looked embarrassed. Syke hinted that the doctor's telling this jury as well as the jury at the November trial that he believed the fragment belonged to a two-ounce bottle had been a trifle hasty. Perhaps he had not, until now, compared it with a whole bottle as he now did? He nodded, but he looked wary. Syke put his next question very gently.

[143]

Q. Is there a possibility that you have made a mistake in your estimate of the size of the bottle?

A. Yes, of course. My guess on that is no better than a juror's, say, or anybody else's.

A juror in the front row put out a hand for the bottle and the fragment and Syke, out of the corner of his eye, watched him weigh, consider and pass on to another hand already outstretched.

Q. Did the fact that Miss Hat told you a two-ounce bottle of king's yellow was missing from her shelf of dye chemicals have anything to do with your first assigning that there burned scrap of glass to a two-ounce size?

A. It may have.

Q. Now, Doctor, seeing as you have testified that quantity is very important when we come up on a question of poison, I take it you won't deny there'd be a lot of difference in the potency of one ounce and two ounces of king's yellow introduced into a six-cup pot of tea to be drunk in teacup quantity? You know the exact quantity of arsenious acid in king's yellow? The degree of solubility? You have made these calculations of course.

A. Well, no, I haven't. But an accredited chemist is here to testify. He is much better qualified to answer all such questions than I am. However, I don't think there's a doubt that even one ounce of arsenic dye put into that quantity of tea would be highly dangerous, could prove lethal—to the child, anyway, who seems to have taken two cups of the mixture.

Q. Then you give it as your medical opinion that the size of the bottle, whether one or two ounces, is not important? You believe the smaller quantity would be sufficient to bring about the acute illness of the grown people and the death of the child?

A. Yes, I do.

Q. Now, Doctor, I want to question you on that part of your testimony which is not a matter of medical opinion.

Syke paused and took a deep breath.

Even at the November trial he had been deeply embarrassed at having to cross-examine the doctor. It wasn't easy for a young fellow like him to face up to a man who stood as high as Dr. Gregory. Like most people in this county, Syke was personally indebted to the doctor. Times without number he had come to Syke's home day and night in every sort of weather and never, in all these years, sent them a bill for his services. Oh, they gave him what they could—Syke's mam seen to that: a melon in melon season or a bushel of yams when yams were dug, even a dollar now and then if they could get hold of one. Syke could see his mam right now, fingering a dollar she had got by selling a half dozen fryers maybe, turning it in her fingers, saying: Spend it? Of course I could spend it. But this time I aim it's Dr. Gregory should have it. But whatever she gave him wasn't enough.

"Mr. John," Syke had said last night, "Listen, Mr. John. If it's impeaching Dr. Gregory's credit you're fixing to plan out, mebbe you'll have to take over that cross-ex your own self. My mam looks on the doctor as a close second to God Himself. She ain't whup me in a good long time, but if I was to try any monkeyshines with the doctor I declare I believe she'd wear me out, grown man that I am."

John Oliver had laughed at him. "You'll do it all right, Syke." Before Syke's eyes now ran the lines in the book Mr. John had opened under the lamp:

Where the question goes clearly to the credit of the witness . . . where the inquiry relates to transactions comparatively recent, bearing directly upon the present character and moral principles of the witness . . . a witness may be bound in some cases to answer an interrogatory to his own moral degradation, where, though it is collateral to the main issue, it is relevant to his character for veracity. . . .

Q. You have said, Doctor, that when you conducted your interrogation of the prisoner, following her capture on the night of November 10, you "let her think you could get her off on a boat." But actually you promised her to do that, didn't you?

A. Well, yes. I suppose I did. I had to, to get her to talk.

Q. You knew, of course, that to connive at the escape of a person suspected of murder would render you yourself liable as accessory after the fact?

A. Of course I did. Obviously I could not and would not negotiate such an escape. Nobody in his right mind would really take the law in his hands like that.

Q. Then you planted false hopes in her mind, made her a promise you had no intention of fulfilling?

A. Well—don't we all say that circumstances alter cases?

[145]

The doctor attempted an ingratiating smile.

Q. You mean, don't you, Doctor, that the law of the truth, the whole truth, and nothing but the truth, as applicable to other men, is in certain circumstances not binding upon doctors?

Dr. Gregory was actually too angry to answer. A low buzzing sound came from the audience. Syke out of the corner of his eye saw his mam lift her folded sunbonnet from her lap and bury her face in it. The reaction of the jurors he simply could not appraise, although he was aware that several bent forward and that all were intent.

Q. Shall I repeat the question, Doctor?

A. NO!

Q. Then will you be good enough to answer it?

The muscles in the doctor's cheeks showed as hard as iron. His fists were clenched upon his knees. Still he managed to get his answer out very slowly.

A. There are circumstances in which I believe the exact truth as dangerous as a deadly drug to a patient. In such cases I withhold or soften it, as any other doctor would do. But the matter of planting false hopes, as you call it, in the prisoner's mind is in a different category. It had nothing to do with professional ethics. I grant you it may have been a mistake. I regret it. More I can not say.

Syke thanked the witness and excused him.

CHAPTER 5

WILL STOKES, after being
sworn, stated that he was a resident of Athens and coroner of
Chewalla County, that Dr. Gregory called by his home soon after
breakfast on the morning of Tuesday, November 11 last, reported
to him what had happened the day before, and that he, the witness, in turn reported to the sheriff and set off for Waverley, reaching there a little before noon. His first duty was, of course, to view
the body of the dead child and his second was to question the prisoner who was then still tied in Miss Hat's room and who was, as
soon as her questioning was over, arrested and taken away to jail
by the sheriff, who arrived only about an hour behind the witness.

When the witness wished to proceed with his duty of questioning all others present on the place at the time of the crime,
he met with annoying delay. It seemed that a strange rumor had
sprung up among the suggestible Negroes, spontaneously, as it
were, upon his appearance. Whereupon every grown hand on the
place had simply absconded. So, although the witness had seen the
whole force as he rode in, picking late cotton or gathering peas and
digging potatoes, when he was ready to lay hand upon them, they
were nowhere to be found. The overseer was gone—fired, Miss Hat
said—and the small fry playing in the house yard gave the coroner
the only help he had in rounding up the hands. And even when he
got hold of them at last, about all he could get out of them was
hysterical protestations of innocence punctuated by fervent appeals
to heaven. Miss Hat had to get up out of her bed and come out in
the yard to quiet them down enough to hear and answer the
coroner's questions. However, by sundown, he had a rough sum-

mary in writing of testimony by both white and black, sufficient to submit to the District Attorney.

The defense by Mr. Oliver cross-examined this witness in regard to that rumor he had spoken of and its peculiar effect on the Waverley Negroes. As near as he could make out, the witness said, it was some nonsense they had got up about his official powers. It seemed that on seeing him ride in they had passed the word about that an inquest was to be held, by which they understood they would be required to pass before the corpse and lay their hands on it and that blood would follow the hands of the murderer. But, Mr. Oliver suggested, if they believed it, believed the true murderer could be detected by the coroner in such magical fashion, why had it frightened them all so? Wouldn't innocent people, trusting such primitive justice, trustingly, too, lay their hands on the corpse, confident they would come away bloodless?

The State objected to this question. Obviously the witness should only report the rumor as he heard it, could not be made responsible for interpreting it or gauging its effect on others. Surely the jury should be left to make its own inferences of innocence or guilt from behavior as reported. The objection was sustained.

The defense had no further questions and the witness was excused.

The District Attorney removed the paper wrappings from a squat brown earthenware teapot and asked leave of the court to put it in evidence. Syke Berry rose to object on the ground of incompetence and, before the court could put a question, stepped close to the judge's high desk and urged that discussion of this proffered evidence be kept from the jurors' ears. A stir of excitement and curiosity spread through the courtroom. The teapot had not been brought into the earlier trial. Here was something new and unpredictable. Every soul in the courtroom craned to get a glimpse of the vessel that had held the deadly brew. The judge listened carefully to Syke's lowspoken plea, nodded agreement and gave the order for the jury to be led out.

As soon as they were gone, the judge asked Mr. Peters if he could prove competence. He said he could. Syke argued that if it was admissible now, that pot had surely been admissible in the earlier trial, too. Why had the State not brought it into its case in November? Things had moved too fast before, Tom Peters said. There had been no time then to get a proper chemical analysis. Now an analysis had been made and the State had at hand a qualified chemist to testify as to what he had found on examination of the teapot. Then Syke protested the lapse of months, six since the earlier trial, six and a half since the crime. Anything on God's earth could have been put into that teapot in that interval. But Tom Peters assured the court he would prove the teapot had been in safe custody, under lock and key, from the date of the crime to that of its delivery to the chemist for analysis. "How will you prove that?" the judge asked. "I have witnesses, your Honor." Throughout the wrangle the teapot sat in its nest of wrappings on the prosecution table, like a silent witness waiting to be sworn.

The judge at last ordered the jury to return, ruled the teapot admissible, the District Attorney lifted it proudly from its paper folds, carried it across to the clerk and had it labeled Exhibit D. Syke took his exception and sat down, mopping his hot face and sighing. In the audience fans fluttered and the knowing checked on their invisible score cards: "One point for the State."

Professor Elliot Starnes from the state university at Oxford took the stand, was sworn and stated that he was a chemist and that the teapot now shown to him as Exhibit D had been examined by him. He said when it was delivered to him on April 5 last it had contained no fluid or tea leaves, but he had found in it, on the bottom and sides, a yellowish brown crust, which he had submitted to chemical analysis. By evaporating this material at high temperature and collecting the sublimed product, he had procured octohedral arsenical crystals and sulphur, both ingredients of the commercial coloring product known as orpiment, or king's yellow. He gave it as his opinion as a chemist that this compound, comparatively tasteless and soluble in hot water to considerable degree, could be intermingled with the tea leaves in a pot of tea with small possibility of detection by those drinking the infusion and with consequences highly dangerous, perhaps fatal, to them. The drink would be somewhat, but perhaps not noticeably, clouded. The less harmful, insoluble sulphide would be hidden by the tea leaves and the arsenious acid element of the compound, a very severe poison indeed, is soluble even in cold water to the amount of three parts per 100 parts of water. Conceivably the boiling water used for tea could release as much as 4.2 grams of arsenious acid to every cupful, enough to kill seventy people. Even 0.1 ounce, or approximately 2.8 grams of king's yellow, containing a minimum of 10 per cent arsenious acid, could make of each cup of the poisoned tea a lethal dose for four people. He therefore concluded that a pot of this size, namely six cups, containing tea holding in solution even a fractional part of one ounce of king's yellow could readily account for the disaster at Waverley last fall.

Under cross-examination by Mr. John Oliver, his friend and neighbor at Oxford, the witness was asked in the friendliest, off-hand way to tell how the teapot had been delivered to him.

A. Why, Mr. McLean brought it up to Oxford when he was making a trip to Memphis on April 5, as I said, and picked it up again on his way home a few days later.

Q. Six and a half months after the crime, then. Tell me, Professor—I am no chemist, of course—would a crust of arsenic trioxide and sulphur such as you describe retain its original character all that time? Wouldn't it suffer deterioration or alteration?

A. No. Both ingredients, the sulphide or pigment and the orpiment, are very stable substances. They would not undergo change.

Q. Then you, a chemist, consider a test made so many months after the event entirely reliable, accurate enough to allow you to swear in court that king's yellow was the poison in that pot of tea November 10 last at Waverley?

A. What I swear to is what I found in the pot, not when it was put there, sir.

Q. Ah, then, if the teapot had meantime been tampered with, if some other poison had been used on November 10 and the dangerous substance that yielded you this yellow pigment and arsenical crystals had somehow got into the pot some time after the crime, or even some considerable time before it, you would have no way of determining it?

A. No.

Q. There are no more questions. Thank you, Professor.

CHAPTER 6

Neal BANNING was called
next. He appeared tense and uneasy—so much so that Tom Peters,
who was questioning, believed he must have made a tactical error
in preparing this witness. Forewarned is forearmed, he had genially
said when he had called him into his office on Monday to tell what
the defense would try to get out of him on cross-examination. And
now Mr. Banning was, it seemed, so unhappy about his coming
interrogation by the lawyers for the defense that he conducted
himself under Mr. Peters' mild and friendly prompting almost like
an adverse witness. Yet the events he was asked about were superficially unimportant, normal in a slave-holding society, and, so to
say, innocent. Moreover, they had not taken place so long ago that
they could be in any way difficult to recall. What was the matter
with the witness? Why did he hem and haw like that?

Q. Will you look at the prisoner, Mr. Banning? Will you tell
the jury when you first saw her and under what circumstances?

The simple question struck him dumb.

Q. Weren't you present when she was bought by Mr. McLean
on October 26 last?

A. Yes. Yes, of course. It was late October, perhaps, as you say
the 26th. I'm afraid the date has slipped away from me. Of course
if it's important, I might try . . .

Q. Never mind the date. The date will be proved by the bill
of sale, which will be introduced in evidence later. Now will you
be good enough to relate the circumstances of the purchase as you
recall them?

The truth, if Mr. Peters could have known it, was that Mr.

Banning was thinking of him and what he had said on Monday hardly at all. Much less was he considering the judge or jury or even Kirk McLean, for whose sake he was here. He was thinking almost entirely of the girl sitting with downcast eyes on the front center bench and he tested each answer as he slowly gave it, for its effect on her and her only. For, whatever he said or however carefully he said it, he knew there was a danger that she might read into it some unintended significance. That, and that alone, was why he met every question as though it were a snake that might strike him. Least of all was his hesitation due to uncertainty of recall. He remembered only too well, with, indeed, a peculiar and personal vividness a great deal more than he had the slightest intention of revealing here in open court.

On the October day when he and Kirk sat in the French market having coffee and Kirk looked up and saw coming toward them the man he was expecting to meet him there, he said:

"Oh, Parson, I forgot to tell you. I've got an errand to do for Sis Hat. Mind coming along?"

He didn't mind because he didn't guess what the fellow had to sell. When he did presently realize, he tried to excuse himself. Really, Kirk. Let me off. You'll be no end of a long time. I've got things to do at the bank. See you at lunch. But Kirk said it would take only a few minutes. All he meant to do was to stop in and have a look at the wench. That was absolutely all. He had no idea of concluding such an important deal in a hurry. So Neal Banning let himself be persuaded. But he didn't like the errand, was, in fact, squeamish, he supposed, about being present at even the preliminaries concerning the purchase of a human being and he resented Kirk's obtuseness in forcing him to come along.

Piloted by the representative from Slade & Torrey, the slave-traders, they passed through a shadowy tunnel from the street to a green and sunlit enclosure, a court like an outdoor sitting room, furnished with tables and chairs and Spanish water jars, regular Ali Baba jars, each one big enough to hide one of the forty thieves; a court partly paved, partly planted to oleanders, yucca and a dozen sorts of vines climbing to the surrounding upper galleries. The stable doors were open and a groom was currying a pair of sleek-flanked horses on the pavement toward the back; and up and down stairs, in and out of doors, servants went busily all the while the guests, seated at a small iron table, were drinking coffee with the mistress of the mansion. Madame Arnaud was dressed in black, her husband having died only the week before; and every word that she spoke in her French-accented English in gracious answer to the Mississippi planter's questions echoed clearly now in Neal Banning's mind—although he, the innocent bystander, was at the time so affected by distaste for the whole proceeding that he tried not to hear, not to see what went on. The wench, on being summoned for inspection, appeared promptly. She was dressed, as now in court, in silk, with a snow-white organdie neckerchief and gold breastpin and earrings. And he automatically thought: She cannot have been doing anything useful, wherever she was when they called her. What is her real position in this house? But no question of that or any other seemed to trouble Kirk McLean. Suddenly, unexpectedly, he said he'd take her and did take her. . . .

It wasn't the kind of thing you forgot. And the sequel, also, was perfectly clear in Neal Banning's mind. On the morning after the purchase Kirk presented himself at Banning's door, appeared at the elbow of the servant who brought Banning's coffee, before Banning was out of bed, sat down while Banning drank and gave every evidence of a man beset by regret. The price was too low, Parson. I should have known something was wrong. And now I've found the nigger in the woodpile: She was old Arnaud's mistress. How do I know? Oh, she told me herself just this morning. Isn't that a pretty kettle of fish? Picture her at Waverley among our lowly blacks. And Sis Hat! Parson, can you imagine Sis Hat when she sees her? He didn't mention his young wife, nor did Banning mention her. But they both thought of her. Oh, Kirk, what a rash fellow you are. Surely you ought to have considered all this yesterday. Well, I didn't. I can't help it if I was born impulsive, Parson. No, Kirk. Certainly you can't. But, look here, now that you're doubting your judgment, why not sell the woman? Slade & Torrey could handle this thing for you so you wouldn't be out of pocket. Kirk seized on the idea and they parted. Two days later when Banning saw him next, Aimée was already on her way upriver. But I thought you meant to sell her, Kirk. Well, I did, Parson. When I left you I was completely resolved. I even stopped by Slade & Torrey's and discussed it with them. But then, you see, when I announced my decision to the wench she took it so hard—well, the plain truth is, I weakened. She'd already begun to attach herself to me, you see, and the idea of being sold again so soon to an utter stranger simply frightened the life out of her. . . .

Neal Banning now surveyed this richly colored fabric of detailed memory, surveyed also his sworn obligation to tell the truth, the whole truth, and nothing but the truth and carefully, in answer to Mr. Peters' request, enunciated one stark sentence:

A. I was with Mr. McLean when Slade & Torrey's man came to take him to Madame Arnaud's residence, accompanied them, and was there present, as I have already said, when Mr. McLean bought the prisoner.

Q. What was the prisoner's attitude as shown by her actions?

A. She was crying.

Q. Hysterical, eh? Rebellious and taking on considerably?

A. Why, no, sir. Rather quiet on the whole. Just weeping and dabbing the tears away with her handkerchief.

Tom Peters made an impatient movement of his shoulders and said, almost bitterly: "Cross-examine."

Syke Berry smiled confidently at the witness as he approached him.

Q. Mr. Banning, you have testified that you was surprised to see Mr. McLean. How come that—considering he was in the habit, as you also testified, of paying a visit to the city mighty near every fall?

A. Well, he usually came at a later date, and besides, this year, he had gone through such a short while before on his way home from the springs, you see, with—with his wife.

Q. You met his wife then? You saw them while they laid over at New Orleans, a-waitin' to get upriver?

A. Yes, I did.

The witness clenched his hands and this mention of Mrs. McLean he resisted by pitching his voice so low that one juror ostentatiously cupped his hand to his ear and another called out: "Louder, please," a plea which Syke repeated with careful politeness to the witness.

Q. And if you would please turn your face toward the jury, so that man setting farthest off can hear better. Thank you, sir. Now, Mr. Banning, on this later visit, the one in October, when Mr. McLean got you to go with him to buy the prisoner here, did he mention to you any special requirements or qualifications he was looking for?

A. Perhaps he did. I really don't remember.

Q. Well, what did he tell you, the sense of it—that he was wanting a likely young wench?

A. No. A cook. He said Miss Hat needed kitchen help right away.

Q. You are sure he said a cook?

A. Of course I'm sure.

Now that this dreaded question had been asked and answered, the witness actually gained confidence. His voice saying "Of course I am sure" rang clearly through the big courtroom.

Q. Was that what he told Slade & Torry's man, too, when you all went around to Madame Arnaud's, did he tell him he was in the market for a good cook?

A. Yes, sir.

Q. And Madame Arnaud—did he tell *her* a cook was what he needed, ask her what experience this wench had had in her kitchen?

A. I don't remember.

Q. Did Madame Arnaud mention the girl's relation to her late husband?

A. No. I am positive she did not. Mr. McLean had no suspicion of that until afterward—after the deal was concluded. He was, we both were, completely unaware of anything of the sort.

Q. Well, what did they talk about, him and Madame Arnaud, setting there, drinking coffee, discussing the deal, with you there, setting alongside?

A. I don't remember.

Q. Come, now, Mr. Banning, a man don't buy a pig in a poke, not when the price is $650. He must have asked some questions about this girl. What were they?

A. He asked her age, how long she had been in the family, whether her health was sound, if she had a good disposition, and the price, of course. It seemed to be the price that decided him. He made his decision quite suddenly.

Q. But wasn't he told that this girl Aimée owned by the Arnaud family from her birth had been around their kitchen about as much and no more than Madame Arnaud herself?

[155]

A. No. Positively not. I tell you he had no idea of her station when he bought her.

Q. Now when you all left there, taking the prisoner along, with her a-weeping and a-grieving to leave the only home she ever know, did Mr. McLean take her right down to the wharf and put her on a upriver boat?

A. No, sir. There was, I believe, no boat leaving that day or the next, which was a Sunday.

Q. None before the *Buckeye* sailing Monday? That right?

A. I think so.

Q. During that two days, Mr. Banning, what was the prisoner's conduct as you observed it?

A. Why, I did not see her again.

Q. Did not see her after the morning of her purchase until you saw her here in this court two days ago?

A. No, sir.

That was all of the cross-examination. The witness looked around at young Mrs. McLean as he returned to his own place, and the judge, at least, saw her smile at him gratefully.

CHAPTER 7

$\mathbb{S}$PANISH FRANK, a mulatto,
cook on the steamboat *Buckeye* plying between New Orleans and
the Yalohatchie River country was, like the chemist and Mr. Banning, a new witness. He testified under the Yam's leading that he
had first seen the prisoner when she was put aboard at New Orleans
on or about October 28 last by her new owner, Mr. Kirk McLean,
and had heard from her in the ensuing days and nights a good bit
of talk, which he called wild. Encouraged by the Yam to be more
specific, he said for one thing she claimed to be a free woman sold
into slavery by trickery. She even waved in his face what she claimed
was her free papers. But she laid mighty low on that subject after
another colored woman passenger raised a hue and cry about losing
some free papers. To all the prisoner's big talk about what all
she'd do if they didn't treat her right up where she was going, the
witness listened with only half an ear, putting it all down as a
pack of lies. Whenever during the journey she would appear in
her big earbobs to lean in the door of his galley or would ease
alongside him when he stood at the stern rail for one last pipe
before turning in for the night, he just listened to her carryings-on,
rather entertained by her tall tales of the rich New Orleans gentleman who had valued her so highly he had, according to her,
promised her her freedom at his death and would rise right up
out of his grave now if he knew his widow had sold her as a slave
instead of giving her the promised freedom. Mostly she boasted of
his riches: a big sugar plantation on Bayou Vache, and two hundred slaves, a fine city home with crystal chandeliers, horses, car-
riages and what not. Once, on the night before they got to Athens

on the Yalohatchie, she got to talking wilder than usual and made like she was going to throw herself in the river, but the witness just laughed at her. And he was right, because next day he saw her alive and undamped by river water when the captain delivered her to her owner's representative at the Athens landing.

Spanish Frank's story was so irrelevant, so downright prejudicial, that Syke, left to himself, could, he believed, have got very nearly all of it declared inadmissible, leaving only a few shreds and tatters in the record. And, at the start, he had kept popping up like a jack-in-the-box with valid objections. Sustained by the court, he was preening himself on his success. But it was Mr. John's idea that in too much and over-excited protest lay the danger of making this testimony, unimportant in itself, appear important to the jury. So he gave Syke a sharp, whispered caution. After that Syke kept still. So the latter part of the testimony, except for two or three elisions of grosser faults ordered by the court, would go to the jury as spoken.

This witness, turned over to Mr. John Oliver for cross-examination, was brought to admit that the prisoner's talk of what she would do if treated badly at Waverley had not included any threat of harm to any living soul but herself. Even the talk of drowning herself she indulged in only that once on the last night of her journey. Mostly it was running away that she threatened if she should be ill treated. Counsel then led the witness back to the subject of the free papers alleged to have been lost by another colored passenger on the *Buckeye* and bore hard on the witness for implying that the lost or stolen paper was the same as that he had seen in the prisoner's possession.

Q. Can you read, Frank?

A. No, sir. At least not much.

Q. When the prisoner let you see a paper which she told you was her free papers given her by her late master, did you hold the document in your hand, have any opportunity to spell out the name on it? Can you state positively what that name was?

A. Well, no, sir. She never let me catch a-holt of it.

Q. When you later heard that another woman had lost such a paper, did you go to your captain and suggest to him that he have the prisoner searched?

A. No, sir.

[158]

Q. Why not? If you believed her a liar and perhaps a thief, surely you were failing in your duty not to report her to those in authority. Isn't it true, Frank, that your suspicions of the prisoner didn't really bother you enough to make you mention them to anybody, or at least to your captain, until some weeks later when the news got back to New Orleans of a crime up the Yalohatchie River and the trial there of a certain quadroon woman who had lately come there from New Orleans? Take care now, Frank. You will be severely punished if you testify falsely. Wasn't it after the prisoner's first trial that you went and told your captain the story you have just told here?

Spanish Frank stared at him. And when he spoke at last it was slowly, weighing every word.

A. Yes, sir. I reckon it was. It was after I got to thinking it all over, putting two and two together, you might say.

Captain Hastings, also of the *Buckeye* and also testifying for the first time, told how he received the prisoner from Mr. McLean at the New Orleans wharf, how, during the run up the Mississippi and the Yalohatchie to Athens, he perceived nothing out of the way in her conduct, indeed paid very slight attention to her, and took no precautions in her regard other than to instruct his crew to keep a sharp eye out to see she didn't give them the slip at any of the various landings on the way up. While he was making fast at Athens, the witness hailed old Duffy, whom he recognized among the crowd there to meet the boat, with the purpose of turning over to him promptly responsibility for the woman. In reply to Duffy's question whether Mr. McLean was aboard, Captain Hastings had called back: "No. But I got a letter to his wife, a hogshead of kitchenware, a barrel of molasses, some rope and baling and this here lady with earrings." His calling her a lady meant nothing special. It was broad daylight, four o'clock or such a matter, and the sun shining bright. Anybody could see the wench was colored by looking close and the whole town of Athens most likely knew from Mr. Duffy about the woman he was expecting from Mr. McLean. But everybody on the landing started in to laughing as though the captain had said a mighty funny thing and there were catcalls and whistles and a stray comment or so: "A fancy piece of goods." "I'll bet she set Kirk McLean back a pretty penny." Whereupon the woman behaved resentfully, flouncing her-

[159]

self around and glaring at the captain, muttering to herself in French, and so on. "Well now, she's a real handful," he said to his engineer, who had just come on deck, "liable to make somebody a heap of trouble."

This comment proved too much even for John Oliver. He rose and got it stricken. The witness was admonished to refrain from expression of opinions and went on.

So then Duffy came aboard and signed a receipt for the woman and he and the captain concluded the bill of lading business for the freight, and the last the captain saw of her was when she and Duffy had some sort of argument on the landing alongside of Duffy's wagon. The witness was too far off to hear what was said but he got a kind of idea from her gestures that she didn't like the look of that wagon a bit—an upcountry farm wagon it was, with mules hitched to it and full of all sorts of farm plunder. Maybe she thought her silk flounces were too fine to risk in contact with the mud-clotted plows Duffy'd brought in for mending and that molasses keg.

John Oliver got all these conjectural remarks declared inadmissible and then, again cross-examining, brought Captain Hastings to expand his statement that the prisoner's conduct aboard the *Buckeye* prior to that moment of leaving the boat had been in no sense unseemly; that for the several days she had been in his care she had borne herself so discreetly as practically to escape his attention. This point having been well established by several mild questions, Mr. Oliver thanked the witness and smilingly excused him.

CHAPTER 8

MISS HAT took the stand next.
Her upright bearing, her big-boned, honest face, her homely backwoods speech, her simple downrightness made her a fine witness.
The State did well to call her first of the Waverley family group,
well to let her tell her story more or less as she wanted to tell it.
Her full name was Harriet Ralston Hunt, the Ralston for Miss Oc,
her mother. Her home was Waverley, of course, the only home she
remembered clearly, for she had been a small child when her parents brought her with them out to the Mississippi country.

Q. You are sister-in-law to Mr. Kirk McLean, mistress of his
household for some years?

A. Yes—since the death of his first wife, my sister Honey.

Q. His second marriage some time last summer did not make
any change in that arrangement? You have still continued to manage household matters just about as before?

A. About as before.

Q. You did not turn over your responsibilities to his wife then?

A. Certainly not. Town-raised, only seventeen, what would she
know about running a big old farm like Waverley?

Even a stranger like the judge could see plainly she was a strong
character on whom others leaned. And most of those who heard
now knew her so well that they were able to fill in the simple outline of her life story from their own memories with a hundred
details of church work done and sick neighbors attended.

Q. Now, Miss Hunt, will you tell the jury as briefly as possible
the domestic situation early last fall which precipitated your decision to purchase a cook?

A. There was sickness both in the house and out in the cabins. It caught me shorthanded. I hadn't had no house help worth mentioning since I'd hired out one of our girls here in town a while before that. Mr. Duffy was behind in his picking and needed every able hand he had anyways. Br' Kirk was off at New Or-*leens*. Seem like if we was ever to buy, now was the time. So I wrote off to him, he bought a woman the very day he got my letter, and sent her right on back.

Q. This was the prisoner?

Miss Hat turned her face toward the defense table, took a deep breath and said explosively:

A. Yes—God help us all.

Q. Just the story, Miss Hat, please, without comments. It's easy to realize your emotions are deeply involved. But you will not be allowed to express them to the jury. Just give us the bare facts. Tell us how you heard that Mr. McLean had made his purchase immediately on arrival and—

A. Oh, we didn't *hear*. I had Duffy meet every boat just on the chance. If there wasn't anybody for us on the first boat, I figured, mebbe there'd be on the next. . . .

Q. And she was actually on that one of Saturday, November 1, as has been testified already. Now, Miss Hat, tell us what happened after the prisoner reached Waverley. Tell only her behavior within the field of your own observation, what you did and said, what she and others said and did. . . .

Miss Hat began with the arrival of the Waverley wagon—along about dust-dark it was—with the prisoner aboard. The Negroes in the back yard sighted it afar and one of them came flying to Miss Hat with the news that Mr. Duffy was home from town bringing "company," and Miss Hat went hurrying out as the wagon drew up in the back yard. As near dark as it was, she seen right away that her informant, in spite of the woman's fine clothes, her dress, her bonnet and veil and shawl, was mistaken. She knew at once who it was, because Mr. Duffy sat perfectly still on the wagon seat and watched the woman scramble out over the wheel without making a move to help her.

Q. You mean the circumstance of his not offering to help her suggested to you that this was the woman you had asked Mr. McLean to buy and send or bring back?

[162]

A. Yes, sir.

Q. And it was the prisoner?

A. Yes, sir.

Q. Well, go on, if you please. You asked her her name, I suppose, gave her some sort of welcome, told her where to put her things.

A. She say her name was—well, hit's a Frenchified name that sounded more like May than anything else. So that's what I call her, and we all did. Just May. I said: "Well, May, I'm right glad to see you. I been having a time with our good old cook down sick and Mas Kirk's wife, Miss Martha, ailing, though she's up and about now, thank God. . . ." I talked to her like I would to one of our own people, trying to make her feel at home like. Then I show her the shedroom behind the kitchen where she would sleep and told her to git off her bonnet and things and put on an apron so as she could help with supper. It was right then she put on her first show—

Q. Just a minute, ma'am. What do you mean by show? The jury here want to understand this woman. They are fair men and they want to give her a fair trial. You have told them what you yourself said. Now tell them what the prisoner said.

A. She said nothing, not a word. She looked at me in a uppity way while she was winding off that veil of hers and taking off her bonnet. The only way I keep myself from slapping her was to turn my back and walk back into the kitchen—

Syke leaped to his feet.

"I move that last remark of the witness be stricken as incompetent. Surely the court will not permit a witness to give the jury her own interpretation of the prisoner's facial expression. . . ."

The District Attorney smiled and addressed the judge.

"The High Court has explicitly ruled, your Honor, that the conduct of the prisoner toward the witness and the members of her household in the days preceding the crime is admissable in evidence."

The judge grasped his beard, thought deeply, cleared his throat and gave his ruling. Beginning with some general remarks on the fact that English law failed to supply precedent in cases of this kind because it took no account of the special conditions of slavery, he said:

[163]

"Even our own legislative acts on the subject of slaves leave much to interpretation. Police regulations for the most part, having to do with overt law infringement, they make no provision for such shadings as are involved in the point in controversy between counsel now. What act in a slave will amount to insolence it is manifestly impossible to define. It may consist of a look, the pointing of a finger, a refusal or neglect to step out of the way when a white person is seen to approach. But each of such acts violates the rules of propriety and if tolerated would destroy that subordination upon which our social system rests. The witness' description of the prisoner's manner is, therefore, competent, and must remain in the record. Counsel for defense may take an exception."

Syke scowled darkly as he subsided into his seat. He couldn't meet John Oliver's eye. His high hopes of the new judge had received a shattering blow. That subordination upon which our social system rests! A human life is neither here nor there then? The social system is what we must save, we bulwarks of the God-given order, we judges, we planters and slave-holders. "Pay attention, Syke," John Oliver whispered anxiously. Syke nodded and roused himself. Tom Peters was saying smoothly:

Q. Where were you when she looked at you as you say in that uppity or insolent manner?

A. In the shed where she's to sleep. We was in there when I was talking to her like I said.

Q. Then you turned your back and went into the kitchen, leaving her in the shed?

A. Oh, she followed all right. She knew she had to help about supper but she was bound she'd give all the trouble about it she could. . . .

Q. Not what you thought of her actions, please, Miss Hat. Just what she did or said. Let the jury form their own conclusions.

A. Well, I don't know what conclusions anybody could form but insolence from her not answering one word when I say I hope she will be happy here amongst us, I hope she have a pleasant trip, I hope she won't be too homesick . . . and not a word out of her. And when I say she's to put on an apron of Aunt Dosia's hanging on a peg in there and she refuse to do it. . . .

Q. Refuse, Miss Hat? She said she would not?

A. Said nothing, I tell you. But she didn't put it on all the same. And coming back into the kitchen she kicked over a chair. Then when I showed her the pot of grits I had boiling on the fire for supper and told her about stirring in some milk just before she take it up, what does she do but upset it. I seen right away she was a troublemaker. . . .

Q. Wait a bit, Miss Hat. Let the jury decide whether her conduct was troublesome or not. Confine yourself to the prisoner's specific words and acts, such as upsetting the chair and the pot of grits.

She frowned and said slowly:

A. I'll try to tell it like it happened. I don't know as I can remember what all she done because it was just so many little things like them first two. If it was to keep her fire up you told her, she'd let it go down. If it was to watch something cooking and not let it scorch like oatmeal, she scorched it. If you said you liked the biscuit made small, she'd make them big. If there was anyways to spoil anything, she'd spoil it. Give her an order—like Hand me this or Reach me that—she'd walk off into the shedroom like she hadn't heard. Sometimes she'd answer in French and from the way she'd smile, saying it, you'd know it was some impudence she didn't dare put in plain English. And then she'd have these spells. . . .

Q. Spells?

A. Crying fits, or crying and laughing both together, and praying to the Virgin Mary.

Q. Did you attempt to reason with her, reassure and quiet her?

A. Of course I did. Time and again. I tried ever'thing: kindness, patience, reasoning with her, telling her she wa'n't so bad off if she just let herself see it that-a-way. I tried not noticing her in them hysterical fits, just walking out and letting her cry hit off. Oh, I try ever' way I could think of to make her behave.

Q. But you did not, during that week before Mr. McLean's return, resort to punishment?

A. I did not.

CHAPTER 9

MARTHA, sitting in the front row with downcast eyes, was immersed in her own thoughts. Now and then she would dart an upward glance at the clock over the judge's head. Her own turn would come next. Mr. Peters had said so. Each time she pictured herself up yonder in Sis Hat's place, she went cold with dread.

Her knowledge that the defense meant to explore the secret places of her husband's life laid her open to imaginings of the most preposterous sort. In her inexperience, her ignorance of the nature and limits of the laws of evidence, she fancied the most shameful and cruel inquiries being flung at her defenseless head. However she had been schooled to expect the coming attack, she was incapable of understanding its strategy. But if the defense lawyers really wanted to get at Mr. McLean, she reasoned, how could they do it so advantageously as through her? Suppose they asked her the most dreaded question of all—Why did he buy this woman?—what would she answer? What could she? Better never take the stand at all than to betray him publicly as she had betrayed him privately yesterday in confessing her doubts to his friend.

Good Dr. Gregory, who, to shield her, had forbidden her appearing as a witness in the other trial, had offered this time, too, to supply an affidavit excusing her. But she had declined to accept that way out. And if her motives for being here were, as she had admitted to Mr. Banning yesterday, sadly mixed, now that she was here she wanted, at least, to play her part as well as she could. However meager the office of wife had privately become, this public duty which she assumed of her own free will she hoped she could perform without mishap or humiliating tongue slip. But she was afraid, awfully afraid, when she thought of facing all those intently listening people and being catechized on such a subject.

Part of the time she didn't listen to Sis Hat's testimony at all. At best she listened vaguely. She had heard Sis Hat tell all this before many times over. Not even the circumstance of hearing it now in new and somehow unreal surroundings, and punctuated too, by questions in important legal language, could vary it enough to compel her attention except intermittently. So she did not so much listen as, hearing, relive in her own memory those still incredible events which had led her step by step along devious, hidden ways to this seat in this public arena.

She was not on the place the afternoon of the new cook's arrival. She had gone for a long walk with Hunt and Dub and the dog Old Hickory. Coming back through the woods Hunt was chattering away about the gun his father had promised to bring him. Often he and Dub would dart off into the high brush alongside the twisting path and play at shooting rabbits with sticks they had caught up. Bang. Bang. Bang. I got him. No, you didn't, Hunt, you ain't aim anyways straight. H'ist it to yo' shoulder fo' you say bang. Well, then, I'm h'isting it now, ain't I? Bang. Bang. Martha smiled and filled her lungs with the cool fresh air smelling of dried leaves and moist earth.

She was well again and strangely at peace. The storm of grief and resentment had played itself out days before that. The will to save her husband, as Sis Hat put it, had taken the place of all selfish anger. Now her whole being was knit into one intense purpose—all she wanted now was that Mr. McLean should come home soon and let her prove her dedication. A boat was due that very day. What if he should be on it?

It was late when they got back, dusk already. They could see Mr. Duffy, returned from town, in the shadowy cave of the stable, moving about his wagon.

"Did Papa come, Mr. Duffy?" Hunt called.

"No, Hunt, he didn't. But a letter come from him for you, Miss Martha. And he sent Miss Hat that there woman she asked him to get—a real likely looking gal."

Crossing the hard and grassless back yard between the double row of cabins, Martha looked in at the kitchen, where she expected

[167]

to find Sis Hat busy about supper, with Martha's letter perhaps in her pocket. But Sis Hat was gone. A creamy-skinned young woman with rouged cheeks and big earrings and rustling taffeta flounces turned from the fire and stared in a strange bold way and Fender, the little kitchen errand-girl, danced cricketlike about her, squeaking:

"Hit's the new cook, Miss Martha. See? Mas Kirk bought her and sent her on the boat. Name, May . . ."

Martha murmured a greeting, a welcome of sorts, and withdrew in some haste, bewildered by the sudden commotion in her heart.

Firelight streamed from all the windows of the dwelling house, but the house was quiet except for the placid thud and thump of Sis Hat's loom. Martha, crossing the yard, stopped a moment, far enough off to look in on Sis Hat weaving beneath her lamp. Sis Hat sat with her shoulders bent forward over the beam, her hands and arms moving purposefully, evenly as a clock, over the taut, harplike strings. Her face, a little tilted, shining in the lamplight, was rapt, uplifted, like a musician's under spell of his own harmonies. She was not singing as often she sang. Sometimes if one stood close at her elbow, one could hear a whispering sibilance, light as insects' wings, when the shuttle flashed from hand to hand, but at this distance, of course, there was no swish of shuttle and, through the closed window, even the beat of the batten came muffled to Martha's ears. Yet, listening, Martha felt her heartbeats quiet and her breathing steady. Without going to her own room first to lay off her bonnet and cloak, she went straight in to Sis Hat.

"The new cook . . . I . . . I just saw her."

Sis Hat turned around on the loom bench and smiled.

"A real sight, ain't she? Uppity as they come. I reckon I got a job cut out for me, learning her her place."

Was there a false note in Sis Hat's cheeriness? Or did Martha only imagine it?

"Sis Hat," she implored, "Sis Hat, please tell me. *Why* did he buy her?"

"Why, you know that, lamb. I wrote and asked him to."

"But a woman like that, Sis Hat—so light-colored, so—so—"

Sis Hat got up and faced her.

"Now, Martha, surely it ain't fitten to turn against a human

[168]

creature just for her color. As to Br' Kirk, well, I reckon he's like most men, paying more mind to the way a package is wrapped up than to what's inside it. It ain't sensible, of course, but it ain't a sin."

Then she nodded pleasantly toward the mantel, where, propped against the vase crammed full of twisted paper spills, the letter stood. And Martha, running to seize and open it, forgot all about the new cook and her own vague misgivings. It was a wonderful letter and it brought her husband very near to her. He already knew about the baby. Dr. Gregory had written him. He was very proud and happy. He would be home on the next boat. Even so she must wait a whole week—a week and a day, really. For the river was falling so fast that the next boat went aground twice on its way up the Yalohatchie.

Late Sunday afternoon Dub came into Martha's room to set the table for supper. (They had to eat all their meals indoors now that it was so much cooler, and of course the loom left no space for the family table in Sis Hat's room.) Sis Hat moved about the table, giving Dub minor directions. Martha thought she heard wheels and looked up from her book questioningly. Sis Hat smiled and nodded.

"Now, lamb . . . you'll just wear yourself out with impatience."

That very moment they heard Hunt in the dogtrot, screaming: "Did you get it? Did you get my gun, Papa? Oh, you *did!* Dub! Dub! Dub!"

The happy shouting died off into contented murmurs as Martha ran out of the door with Sis Hat at her heels.

He was looking particularly well and handsome. His eyes seeking Martha's were so loverlike, his kisses so warm and tender, his embrace so close that she could almost feel they had never been parted, either by physical distance or by that more compelling shadow which had separated them during the weeks before he left. She had rarely seen him in such high spirits. He didn't seem even annoyed at Sis Hat's flying up at him with her reproaches: "A cook! My goodness, me, Br' Kirk, I just bet you bought her without asking anybody could she cook."

He was so used to Sis Hat's ways, he just laughed at her. "I wouldn't know I was welcome if Sis Hat didn't greet me with a scolding," he said, winking at Martha. And then he set his parcels down and started rummaging for the presents he had brought: a

[169]

length of fine dress goods for Sis Hat, and a dear little pair of scissors in a velvet-lined morocco case for Martha. "Are you all right?" he whispered under cover of Sis Hat's strictures.

She nodded and felt happy tears washing down her face. Almost at once he drew her apart to talk to her privately. He squeezed her shoulders in his hard grasp and shook her in pretended anger. My poor silly darling. Of course you were frightened, even rebellious, at first, but that's no excuse, you little idiot, for treating your husband like that, letting him go off imagining ten thousand horrors that weren't true. Oh, what if you'd done yourself or the young 'un real harm? Shall I punish you or will you promise me that as long as you live you'll never again keep anything from me?

"Never," she promised. "Oh, never."

But in the act of promising she did keep something from him—that question about why he had bought May. Over and over she had planned how she would ask it: Were you just rash and thoughtless? Was it only that? Tell me and I will believe you. But the moment was too sweet, too much their own, to risk spoiling.

The breakfast next morning was poorly prepared—the coffee as strong as lye and muddy besides, the saucer-sized biscuits soggy, the fried ham charred and flinty. Sis Hat was quite put out. She had wanted things especially nice in honor of Br' Kirk's homecoming. She had wanted his first breakfast with his family to be a fine one, and look what happened. Well, she aimed to give the new cook a good talking-to, sure as her name was Harriet Hunt. Hunt giggled and choked: "Ain't that what you been giving her ever' morning and evening, too, since she come, Aunt Hat?"

As bad as the breakfast was, nobody minded really except Sis Hat. Kirk McLean said, "Oh, forget it, Sis Hat. The wench will learn. She looked very intelligent to me." Then he changed the subject by asking Hunt how he'd like to try out his new gun this morning. Hunt, of course, was delighted and asked Martha if she wanted them to bring her back another rabbit's foot.

Breakfast over and the menfolk gone, Sis Hat came into Martha's room to get her advice about making up the dress goods Br' Kirk had brought her. She held the shining black satin against her, standing before the mirror, and then stretched it out on the bed with the sections of a tattered old newspaper pattern placed on it first one way and then the other. She was so pleased with her present that for an hour at least she forgot to harp on that no-count yellow wench Br' Kirk had saddled them with. Then the door pushed open. Sis Hat glanced first at the clock and then at Aimée, silent in reproach upon the threshold.

"My goodness me!" cried Sis Hat. "How I do gabble. Here it is ten o'clock and our dinner not give out yet. Go 'long, May. I'll be there in a minute."

She snatched up a shawl for her head and shoulders, picked up her keys and flew. In a trice she was back again, looking very strange, her face drawn, her lips white. She looked positively ill. Martha's first thought was Hunt: that new gun, he was only nine. . . . But, no, it wasn't that.

"I've quarrelled with Duffy," Sis Hat said, looking rather as if she didn't believe her own ears. "I've told him to get off the place."

"Oh, Sis Hat!"

It seemed incredible—after ten years. Crotchety as he was, crazy in some ways, still he was a part of Waverley.

"Don't 'oh, Sis Hat' me, like I was guilty of some crime. I done it and there's no help for it."

"But why? What had he done?"

"Defied me, that's what. Refused pointblank to do what I told him to. Taken the part of that yellow wench against me in my own kitchen or just the same as . . ."

"I don't understand, Sis Hat."

"Well, she gave me some more of her sass, only worse this time. She said such a thing to me as no white woman's got a call to take."

"What, Sis Hat? What did she say?"

"I wouldn't soil my lips to repeat it. Well, then after she say it, trying me out to see how far she *can* go, I reckon, Mr. Duffy happen to look in to see if his boots was dry he had setting by the fire. When he see me in there and hoppin' mad, too, he was all for slipping right out again, but I stopped him. 'Wait a minute, Mr. Duffy,' I says, 'I have a need of you. This woman has been uppity to me once too often and I won't stand it. Take and tie her and give her a thorough dressing. . . .'"

"A whipping?" cried Martha, startled. "Did you mean it?"

"Certainly I meant it. But he refused. Pointblank to my face he said he wouldn't. Oh, of course he give his usual reason: said she was conjured, what make her act so ornery, said whipping was no good against Aunt Dosia's conjuration. Well, I just come to the end of my patience, look like. I told him when the time come he couldn't do what he is hired to do, he'd better go and let somebody else have the job."

Fender knocked and came in, wiping her nose on her sleeve and coughing from the cold.

"Well," said Miss Hat impatiently, "what is it now?"

"Hit's about the tea. May say, do you want tea for dinner, you have to give it out. May say you forgot when you was giving out before."

Harriet took up her key basket and shawl again and went out. Martha, standing at the window, saw her pass the kitchen and go to the storeroom. Fender ran behind with an empty teacup in her hand and stood, jigging about to warm herself, while Sis Hat for the second time that morning unlocked the storeroom door. Just as Fender on her spidery legs flitted back to the kitchen with the cup holding the tea leaves, Hunt and his father climbed the back fence and came across the yard, meeting Sis Hat as she turned from locking the door.

Martha watched Sis Hat send Hunt off and stand talking to Mr. McLean, or arguing, it seemed, rather vigorously. At last he left her in front of the storeroom door, shivering in her cotton dress and small shawl, and came toward the house. His face had a dark look. It frightened Martha. She ran out into the dogtrot to meet him.

"What is it, Mr. McLean? What are you going to do?"

"Whip the wench," he said brusquely and, putting the gun down, reached from its crevice between the logs the switch Miss Hat kept there in pickle, as she said, for Hunt and Dub.

"*You* are going to whip her, you, yourself? Oh, no, Mr. McLean!"

He put her aside without looking at her and went out again to the back yard. Returned to her window she saw him go into the kitchen and shut the door behind him. She saw Sis Hat standing as before, rooted to the ground, clutching at her shawl, staring toward that shut door, waiting for the ends of justice to be fulfilled. She saw Uncle Jerry sitting on his doorstep watching, too. She saw no more for, suddenly, she left the window and ran to her chair beside the hearth and buried her face in her hands.

Sick, exaggerated fancies flooded her mind. He would make

[172]

May unbutton her dress and bare her shoulders. He would lash her naked yellow flesh. Oh, it wouldn't really harm her, wouldn't even hurt much, a little lithe switch like that. But it would shame her. And him. Oh, it was a vile, vile thing Sis Hat had made him do. And why, why, why? What were the intolerable words the woman had spoken? Had Sis Hat repeated them to Mr. LcLean? Was that how she got him to do the shameful thing?

Hunt ran in, excited, babbling.

"He's whipping her! Papa's whipping her now. Listen. Can't you hear her holler?"

Martha drew him close to her and held him tight.

"Don't listen. Please don't listen. Think of something else. Your gun. Tell me about your gun. Does it shoot well?"

Then Dub set the table and began to bring in dishes. Sis Hat stood and inspected the job. Mr. McLean entered, red of face, a little disheveled and unwilling to meet Martha's eye. Hunt was sent to call Mr. Duffy. When Mr. Duffy arrived, elaborately silent as if, though he still must eat, he was no longer one of them, they sat down to dinner.

Now in the courtroom Mr. Peters was showing Sis Hat the brown earthenware teapot and having her identify it as the one in which tea was that day brought to table. She told minutely how it was stood on a trivet on the hearth to keep it hot while she was carving and then brought by Dub to the table and set down before Mrs. McLean. Martha heard Mr. Peters interrupt the testimony to ask: Not before you, Miss Hat? And she heard Sis Hat's answer: Oh, no. She set in the wife's place from her first day at Waverley. She ever poured the tea or coffee, whichever we was having. . . .

The handle of the teapot had been turned near the fire and was very hot, but with a napkin folded around it, Martha poured tea, even for Hunt as a special treat, and began to eat her dinner. Very likely, as Sis Hat was testifying now, the tea was cloudy and did have a funny taste. Martha didn't know. She hoped Mr. Peters didn't mean to ask her too many questions. All she could really remember was her husband's vacant expression, his eating hardly at all, his not looking at her and her own throat aching with grief for him. Maybe Martha poured Hunt a second cup absent-mindedly as Sis Hat was saying now. Maybe he drained it off, too. It was possible. She almost remembered pouring a second for herself, but she was sure that if she did she never took a sip of it. For suddenly Hunt stood up startled and appealed to his aunt. I think I am going to be sick, Aunt Hat. Then Sis Hat pushed her chair back and ran to him and held her napkin to his mouth.

Martha hurried ahead to make the bed ready for Hunt and when she turned round there was her husband standing up, looking from side to side, with his napkin crushed to his mouth. Martha was too busy at first, helping Sis Hat wait on them, to notice that she felt ill, too. Then she found herself alone in Sis Hat's room, bending over a slop pail.

"Sis Hat! Sis Hat!"

Nobody came for a long time. Then it was only Dub with eyes rolling and white.

"Miss Hat, she sick, too. Miss Hat laying in yonder by where Hunt at. I think she dying, if she ain't dead a'ready."

Martha caught hold of him.

"Get Mr. Duffy."

"He sick, too, Miss Martha. He gone lay down long ago."

"Then saddle a horse, Dub, and ride in for Dr. Gregory yourself. Do you understand?"

"Yass'm. I understand. . . ."

MISS HAT'S testimony was incomplete when twelve o'clock came and the noon recess was declared. As soon as the afternoon session began, she sat down in the witness chair again and went on with her story. It was past two when Syke Berry rose to cross-examine.

Q. Where was the table dishes kept, ma'am, in the dwelling house or out in the kitchen?

A. Both places. The best china and the silver—my mother's things mostly, brought from North Carolina long ago—we've always kept in a kind of press with doors to it in Mrs. McLean's room. The press is kept locked and the things we put in there we use for company, not every day. The plain dishes stay on shelves out in the kitchen.

Q. And the teapot which, you have testified, was in use at dinner November 10—where did it stay?

A. In the kitchen.

Q. On the open shelves?

A. Yes, sir.

Q. Then it was washed, right after you use it, I reckon, and again when you take it down to use the next time?

A. Why, I don't know—when I make tea myself I rench out the pot with a little hot water just before I brew the next. . . .

Q. And when, to the best of your belief, had this teapot last been in use prior to dinnertime November 10?

A. I don't remember. How could I remember now the last time we had tea before, such a little thing as that, all these months . . . ?

Q. At breakfast that morning maybe?

A. Well, no. We never taken tea for breakfast, none of us. Coffee was what we drank then, except Hunt, of course, and he had milk. And Mr. Duffy, too—he never taken tea or coffee either one lately.

Q. Had you had tea at supper the night before perhaps?

A. No, we all drank milk at supper, buttermilk or sweet milk, one or the other.

Q. But you always had tea for dinner?

A. Not always, but usually we did, in cold weather, anyways.

Q. Was the day before, November 9, that is, cold?

A. Why, yes, it was. Real sharp, near as I recall. We had fires going all day.

Q. Now, Miss Hat, this new cook, the prisoner, give you, as you have testified, a mighty unsatisfactory service all round, scorching the oatmeal and spoiling good food one way or another ever' meal. Whether that was because she didn't know kitchen ways or whether she done it just to plague you, as you seem to think, we'll leave to one side for a minute. What I want to get at is this: When she taken the teapot down from the shelf that day of November 10, mad like she was and resenting that switching Mr. McLean had give her, however little or much it really hurt her, do you think she taken the same pains as you would a-done yourself or do you think she maybe just dumped in the tea leaves and sloshed in some scalding water without renching or even looking to see if the pot was good empty like it was when she washed it and set it on the shelf after the last using?

A. I wasn't there. How can I tell you what she done? Fender, the little girl helped out in the kitchen, she the one better tell you that.

He kept on and on at her about the teapot, trying to shake her story. When had she put the teapot under lock and key in the press? Who cleared up after dinner? Wasn't the darkies streaming in and out and the white folks, including herself, too sick to know what was going on for the best part of the afternoon? She reckoned so and she reckoned they never thought to clear the table. But she knew for certain she herself took and locked up the teapot. *Before* the doctor come, Miss Hat? But wasn't it him suspected the tea first of anybody? Surely you wouldn't a-thought to lock the pot up *before* that? Well, yes, seem like she had. . . .

When he had got her really confused about the teapot, he began to question her about the missing dye bottle, showed her, as he had showed the doctor, the bottle fragment and the whole one-ounce bottle, and badgered her to describe her lost king's-yellow vial more exactly than she was able to do. Then he drew off from that and started in to wheedling her with questions on her favorite subjects, weaving and dyeing. You do a lot of weaving, don't you, ma'am? You got the finest loom anywheres around here, haven't you, ma'am? And so on. When he had got her to talking freely on her most beloved topic, he circled back to the bottle of dye stuff.

Q. This here king's yellow, ma'am—how come you to have such a dangerous poison as that around the house?

A. Well, you see, a good pure yellow is right hard to get in dyeing. I make out all right when black-eyed Susans is in bloom. They make as pretty a yellow as you'd want to see—a real sunshine yellow. I make out with peach leaves if I have to—or smartweed. But they're all things you got to get in season. Out of season you mighty near got to use boughten dye. Some favor fustic but I never have no luck with fustic, seem like—never got a fast color with it. And I hear king's yellow was real good and I always did hanker to try it. So I got Br' Kirk to bring me some back from New Or-*leens*. . . .

Q. You mean you had only just got it the day before?

A. Oh, no. That was several years back when I ask him and he brought it to me—three years, mebbe four. I think it was the last time Mr. Banning come back with him to rest up at Waverley from the fever. Four years.

Q. And you had kept it all that time? Or maybe you had used a lot of it? Maybe the bottle was nearly empty?

A. I had used a little mite, just to try it out once. But it was near full. Hit was near like it come out of the store.

Q. So, all this time, four mortal years, the nearly full bottle of this deadly arsenic dye stood there in easy reach on your open shelves?

A. Yes.

Q. Miss Hunt, when the accused was first brought to trial, did you take any precautions to see that she had a fair trial?

A. Why, she had a jury, like any other criminal, didn't she?

And dear, kind old Judge Calloway. I'm sure a fairer man never lived.

Q. Did you provide the accused with counsel?

A. Well, it come to that. She was asked in court if she had a lawyer and when she said No, Judge Calloway appointed you. But you know yourself it was me had to pay you the $25 charges. I had to under the law.

Q. Who provided that the District Attorney should this time have the assistance of Mr. Dancy Boone in the prosecution, Miss Hunt?

A. Well, I did. But I don't see what that's got to do with May getting a fair trial. I heard you was getting in a second lawyer to help you this time. I don't see no reason against the prosecution having two.

Q. Well, it's a fact, ain't it, Miss Hunt, that, for some private reason of your own, you are so eager to see the prisoner hanged that you have been willing and anxious to pay the fees, no matter how high they may be, of an outside lawyer to help the District Attorney with this case?

The prosecution lawyers leaped up to object. The judge sustained the objection and directed counsel to pursue that line no further. Syke took a swallow of water and eyed the jury speculatively as he framed his next question.

Q. Now, ma'am, if the District Attorney and the brilliant and able counsel you have so generously employed to assist him are successful in getting this woman hanged for you, you stand to lose half her value. For I reckon you expect to put in a claim on the state treasury for the half allowed you under the law, don't you?

A. We certainly do.

Q. We, Miss Hat? We? You are the sole owner of this woman, aren't you?

A. Mr. McLean and I bought her together, share and share alike, like we ever done all our Waverley business.

Q. I understand that. Mr. McLean was acting at that time as representative of his minor son. But didn't Hunt's half interest in the land and the people, under the terms of your father's will, revert to you at the child's death, Miss Hat?

A. Yes.

The admission came hard. She seemed visibly to shrink and

[178]

age as she made it. Many a person out in front smiled in rueful sympathy. Kirk McLean's position as master all these years had been, they all knew, her proudest illusion. Her always having tried to make it appear that nothing was ever done out there but by his orders had become a by-word and a joke hereabouts. Part of the joke was the way he had never crossed her, even in the control of his little son. What she relinquished now was an empty shadow—and yet there were those present who pitied her.

Q. You taken a dislike to the prisoner the minute you laid eyes on her, didn't you, ma'am?

A. Well, I seen she had a devil in her, if that's what you mean.

Q. Because this high-strung creature, weary from her long journey, panic-stricken with loneliness and fear, awkwardly turned over a chair and even a pot of grits you had put to cooking on the fire?

A. That and other things.

Q. Her speaking French, for instance, the language she is most at home in, speaking it with a smile, too, you decided was surely her devil speaking?

A. Well, what else could it be? She know I can't understand her. Why should she use French, if she wa'n't saying something she's shamed to say in plain English?

Q. Isn't it true that you had some reason for disliking this woman besides the way she act, ma'am?

A. I don't understand you.

Q. Well, was you afraid she'd make trouble in this new marriage you set such store by?

A. I don't know what you mean.

Q. Look at her, please. You'll grant she's what they call a likely wench: young, straight, vigorous, good-looking, like many of these here quadaroons. Did her good looks have nothing at all to do with your dislike, Miss Hunt?

A. Certainly not.

Q. When you taken away her clothes and locked them up and gave her a gray osnaburg wrapper to wear like a field hand, did you do that to humiliate her and make her look as ugly as possible—

The District Attorney objected. The question as framed contained implications of motive on the witness' part in no way relevant to the issue. The objection was sustained. Syke reframed his question.

Q. You did take her clothes away, the dress and bonnet that were her own, bought for her by her indulgent former master?

A. Yes. I did. That dress she's got on now is what you're talking about. I taken and put hit up like any other woman would for her to wear Sundays. It wasn't anyways fitten to *cook* in. . . .

Q. Isn't it true that you demanded her earrings, too, and the only way she managed to retain possession of them was by hiding them, saying she had lost them?

A. Saying somebody stoled 'em! Accusing Lethe, a perfectly innocent—

Q. Now, let's get back to May, if you please ma'am. You don't deny that you and her got on just about as bad as mistress and servant ever did that whole enduring week?

A. It was *her*. I'd a got on all right with her if I see the least sign of her being biddable or willing.

Q. Well, anyway, this girl May, whom you disliked from the first, whose every act was displeasing to you, was completely in your power, wasn't she?

A. I don't know what you mean. She was in nobody's power, that girl. *I* couldn't manage her.

Q. But you believed you could manage her if you could have her whipped by Mr. Duffy or, after he refused, by Mr. McLean himself, didn't you?

A. Yes. I've already said I did. Why should you keep on at me about it, Syke Berry? The next thing you'll be saying I drove her to her desperate crime! Well, of all things. Of all the unjust, outrageous. . . .

The judge tapped his gavel. Syke hid a smile with his hand.

Q. Just a minute, please, ma'am. You had no use for the girl from the first. You have said so yourself. But you haven't really told us why. Was it because she couldn't or wouldn't cook properly?

A. Well, I just couldn't make out why Mr. McLean ever come to buy her.

Q. Oh, then you did suspect he wanted her for some other reason?

A. No. I did not. That isn't true. But I didn't like her. Her looks, her fine clothes, her way of laughing when I corrected her for anything just about drove me crazy. Ever' time you mention any fault to her, instead of looking sorry or scared, she looked like the cat that swallowed the canary. I had a hard time putting up with her insolence as long as I did.

Miss Hat fumbled in her reticule for her handkerchief and, after finding and unfurling it, blew her large nose daintily. A flutter of amusement passed over the tense courtroom.

Q. Now, ma'am, having put up with what you call her insolent behavior for more'n a week, your patience the morning after Mr. McLean got home failed you all of a sudden. Will you tell the jury, please, ma'am, what specific thing she done that made you decide at last to have her whipped?

A. It was something she say—a thing I'd cut off my right hand before I'd repeat, a thing no white woman's got a call to take.

Q. Was this unquotable remark insulting to you personally, ma'am, or was hit a insult to others—like Mr. McLean maybe?

The District Attorney objected and his objection was sustained. Syke excepted and went on.

Q. Did she say to you that she had pleased one white man from the time she was sixteen years old to the day he died, and that she reckoned, from what she learn of her new master during one night in New Or-*leens,* that white men was mighty near all alike in one particular, wherever they happen to live?

Miss Hat looked at the judge.

"Do I have to answer such as that, Judge Rusk?"

The judge said No and admonished counsel to refrain from questions offensive to a white lady's finer feelings.

Q. Well, ma'am, after you had her whipped and that terrible thing happen a half hour later at the family dinner table, you hadn't a doubt but it was May done it. That right?

A. Yes.

Q. Did you, quick as the doctor's medicine give you some relief, raise your head up off the pillow and say: "Take and tie May, somebody. She the one can explain this mysterious sickness if anybody can?"

A. I reckon so. But the doctor thought himself the cook done it. He said so.

Q. And later, some time after dark when the news was brought in about them catching May down Coon Creek a ways, did you say to Mrs. Berry: "She shall hang for this day's work?"

A. Yes, I did. And why not? Poisoning's murder, ain't it? And they do hang people for murder. She killed the being I loved most on this earth. . . .

Q. But when you made that remark about hanging, nobody had died. That was an hour or so before the death of your nephew. Wasn't it?

A. Yes. But Dr. Gregory had already told me he was mighty near sure we was all poisoned. Don't the law hang for trying to kill?

Q. Well, yes, Miss Hunt, when it's a slave who done it, the penalty is hanging. But what I'm trying to get at is this: There was twenty-odd other grown Negroes on the place. How come you was so sure that this particular girl—even if you had disliked her on sight, even if you feared her in ways you wouldn't care to mention—how come you so sure hit's May and nobody else done the mischief?

A. Because there was no one else could a-done it or would a-done it, that's why. Our people are old family servants. I trust them the same as I trust my own self.

Q. All of them, Miss Hat?

A. Every last one of them.

Q. So you found the new girl guilty, without no trial, without no judge or jury, all by yourself you tried her and sentenced her to hang—just like you had sentenced her to a whipping before she'd blundered into that first chair?

A. I see what you're driving at and I reckon the jury sees it, too, by now. You are making out I'm just blind with prejudice, but why do you pick on me? I'm not the only one believes she done it. There's hundreds, maybe a thousand by now, think it was her. Even the twenty-odd people her own color out at Waverley you been talking about can tell you it was her.

Q. What about the overseer, Miss Hat? Mr. Duffy? Does he agree with you?

A. Well, I don't see as it's of any importance what Mr. Duffy believe, crazy like he is.

There were no more questions and the witness was excused.

YOUNG Mrs. McLean was the
next witness. Many people in the courtroom had never seen her
before this week. Since the big welcome sociable at the Ketchams'
right after her coming, she had scarcely ventured into town. Even
the Ketcham girls, who knew her best, still regarded her as a
stranger, a timid little thing at best, secretive almost, mighty hard
to get to know. But they all felt sorry for her. And however greedy
they were for every crumb of evidence in this case, they all suffered
compunction at seeing her put to the torture of appearing here
publicly to give up her sad little story. She gave her age as eighteen
but she looked less, and she had a way of glancing toward Miss
Hat as each question was put to her like a child watching its
mother's face for approval. That suggested innocence and help-
lessness to a degree hard to reconcile with the fact that she was
herself a mother.

Tom Peters began with an expression of thanks to her for consenting to come "and help ferret out the truth" and an assurance
that he would make his examination as comfortable for her as
possible. His tone was gentle and he did not speak to her without
an encouraging smile. He took a great deal of pains to begin slowly,
letting her tell her first impressions of Waverley and the Waverley
people at considerable length just to put her at her ease. As long
as he kept on that tack she got along pretty well, speaking out
distinctly and even smiling a little.

When he got to the facts in issue, however, asked her to tell
the jurors her side of the story of events from November 9, when
her husband returned, through November 10, the day of the crime,

[183]

her voice dropped to a whisper and after a few faint attempts stopped altogether. She could not or would not go on. Beyond a nod for Yes or No, she could only twist in her chair and touch her wadded-up handkerchief to her lips. A painful ripple pulsed at her throat. Her breathing grew rapid and shallow. His most soothing, fatherly guidance could not give her confidence. When he asked her specifically about the whipping, she found her voice again but it was only to refuse to answer: She didn't know anything about the whipping, anything at all. She was in the house, in her room the whole time. And questions about the dinner and its consequences brought a bare "Yes, sir" or "No, sir," or "I don't remember." At last Tom Peters was getting nothing out of her at all.

Syke Berry, looking up from making notes for use in cross-examination, saw her staring at him with eyes dilated in stark terror. Abruptly he scribbled: "Will she bear cross-ex.?" and slid the note under John Oliver's hand. John Oliver wrote: "It's the jurors I'm worried about—can they bear it?" Then Syke studied his jury. Middle-aged and over, most of them, they were all gazing at the girl with a rapt and stricken expression. Even the judge wore a harrowed look. You'd think she was the beloved daughter of each one of them, that in her suffering each experienced a father's helpless heartache. . . .

When Tom Peters finished and proffered the witness to the defense, Syke had already torn up his notes. He stood and said the defense had no questions to put. The breath of relief that ran through the courtroom was like a mighty single sigh. Several jurors smiled and nodded approval. John Oliver squeezed Syke's elbow. "Great," he whispered, "magnificent. You couldn't have done a more popular thing."

As the witness, obviously confused by her sudden unexpected release, did not rise, Tom Peters spoke to her in an undertone and smilingly put out his hand to help her down. She got up then and stepped gingerly to the floor. Her husband was already on his feet hurrying to meet her. With her hand on his arm he led her, not back to her former seat between his own and Miss Hat's, but out along the nearest aisle toward the main door. The clerk, reading from the list of witnesses, was already calling his name in a clear voice: "Mr. Kirk McLean." He left his wife at the door and, frowning, hurried back to the prosecution table, where he spoke insistently to the lawyers. Tom Peters, on the very point of sitting down, straightened up, walked back to speak first to the judge and then to the clerk. The clerk called: "Uncle Jerry." Kirk McLean went up the aisle again, rejoined his wife and they left the courtroom as Uncle Jerry, leaning on his cane moved toward the witness stand.

Martha and her husband had barely reached the foot of the stairs when they heard footsteps coming down behind them and, turning, saw Mr. Banning smiling and signalling them to wait and behind him, following more slowly, the nurse with the baby. Mr. Banning brought a message from Miss Hat: She suggested that Mrs. McLean and the baby should go on out home without waiting for her. There was a matter of private business on which she was seeing Mr. Peters after court adjourned and, since it might take some time, she preferred to spend the night in town at the Ketchams'.

"Good," agreed Kirk McLean. "Then we can get started right away. Tom Peters says they won't call me now till after the last of the Negroes and that'll be some time tomorrow morning. You'll go out with us, won't you, Parson?"

Outside, a boy was selected from a half-dozen eager aspirants to summon the driver, reported to be over on the porch of the Emporium, and the little party moved toward the carriage waiting in the same spot where it had stood daily from the first. Dr. Gregory rode by and turned down the street toward his office. Kirk McLean remembered he had wanted to talk to him. This seemed a lucky chance to catch him.

"Mind waiting a few minutes for me?"

The question was addressed to Martha, on the point of getting into the carriage and already painfully aware as usual of the intent faces turned her way in square and street. Only stragglers were about, of course, since court was still in session, but the few concentrated upon her and her husband. An old colored woman shepherding a trio of white charges along the sidewalk stopped with them an arm's length away to look and listen.

"Here?" asked Martha in a haunted whisper. "Do you mean wait here, Mr. McLean?"

He frowned and then smiled, but the smile was bitter, as if he thought: Is the smallest thing I ask too much? Does every simple request lay an insupportable burden on you? At that moment the driver came hurrying up and Martha said a little more naturally:

"Couldn't I drive on ahead and wait for you just outside of town, at the top of the hill? It would be cooler there."

"Certainly, my dear."

He made his consent somehow elaborate, ceremonious, exaggerating her wish into a command and his submitting into a gallantry false and excessive. He even bowed, keeping his hat in his hand and looking at her in that mocking way that said: Lady, your caprice is my law. It was a manner that thrust her upon a bleak, unwanted eminence and it never failed to wound her. Instant tears stung her eyelids and she had valiantly to exert herself not to let them pour down her cheeks. That Mr. Banning stood so near, looking bewilderedly back and forth between them, contributed to her humiliation and confusion. He knows we are quarrelling, she thought in dismay. I hope he doesn't blame *me!* She could clearly see he was embarrassed and uncomfortable, hadn't the least idea what to do with himself, didn't know whether he ought to ride on with her or wait here. As her husband handed her up into the carriage, she swallowed hard, strove to smile, said: "You wait, Mr. Banning, wait for Mr. McLean," and sank back into her place beside the nurse.

Her husband's face suddenly cleared and warmed as it always did when it turned toward his friend.

"Look, Parson. Martha's really tired. She ought to get on home. How about your riding out with her and leaving me to follow when I can?"

"Why, of course," Mr. Banning agreed.

As the carriage turned and wheeled her away, Martha let the tears flow unchecked down her cheeks. She really should be feeling more cheerful. She had given her testimony. There had been, after all, no cross-examination. Her public responsibility was over. Her private unhappiness was her own concern and it was nothing new. Her husband's ironic politeness she should be used to by now. Well, why wasn't she? Why did it hurt her so—still as much as ever? In a sense she understood those brittle graces, knew they were a sort of armor put on in defense against pain itself and the mob's onset, but that didn't save her from heartache when he used them against her personally. Back in the days when disaster like a tornado from God's hand had been loosed on them, she had even pitied him because, allowed no time or place for private grief, he had had to withdraw from human touch behind his own protective shell. But then she had hoped he wouldn't go on and on shutting *her* out. . . .

Surely in his own home, with her and Sis Hat, he should be able to lower his guard.

"My goodness, Br' Kirk, you needn't be as polite as all that," Sis Hat said once, as coming in weary from hog-killing labors, she sank into the chair he sprang to set for her. "Hit's like it wears a body out to be always saying thank-you to homefolks."

That was partly how Martha felt, too. His never-ending punctiliousness wearied her, but, because she was his wife, it wounded her as well. After the trial in November she had tried repeatedly to reach him. With burning face and stammering tongue she humbled herself to ask him why he always slept in the loft now. In a tone of wounded dignity he said it was out of consideration for her condition. She had fled to Dr. Gregory for enlightenment and, encouraged by him, had returned with, not a question this time but an invitation. He accepted—perhaps a gentleman cannot decline to accommodate a lady? He came back at once to share her room, even her bed, but with such ceremonial deference to her wishes as to dishearten and humiliate her. The wall of glass seemed, in intimacy, more, rather than less, impervious.

Dr. Gregory could give no further help. A doctor isn't God, you know. The stuff was never bottled that would cure an unhappy marriage. If it's a love philter you want, you'd better visit Aunt Dosia. I'm told she's quite a hand at— Why, there, my dear. Forgive me. I'm a blundering old fool. For God's sake, don't cry like that. What I should have said is: "Can't you exercise a little patience? You're very young. You've got a lifetime of happiness ahead of you. Give nature a chance. Kirk—well, you see the poor fellow blames himself for all that's gone wrong. He's staggering under an inhuman load. Bear with him, can't you? You've got your own job cut out for you. Stop worrying about your husband and stick to your knitting."

The baby he meant. But how could expecting a baby make up to a woman for the loss of her husband's love? Or even the baby

[187]

itself after it came? For still nothing was changed, nothing at all. Her husband was an aloof and stilted stranger, elaborately alert to all her minor needs in regard to chairs and doors and the ordering of the carriage, but blind and deaf to her real feelings. If she were starving before his eyes, she thought, he would not, perhaps could not, put out his hand to save her.

It was all very well for Mr. Banning to say she should not seek private light from this so-public trial. But where else could she find it? Not, as Mr. Banning urged, from her own husband. Least of all from him. If ever she could have done it, the time for that was long past. Now he dwelt forever beyond an impenetrable mask. Sis Hat was little better. Before May's coming Sis Hat's honesty had seemed to clear the way for womanly confidences. But that, too, was over long ago. Now, girded for conflict, single-minded, Sis Hat would have made short work of Martha's vapors. There was no use turning to the doctor again. Yesterday for a little while Mr. Banning had seemed on the verge of helping her to understand her husband. She had almost felt he held the key in his outstretched hand. But Mr. Banning, for all his kindness and his wish to help, couldn't understand *her* difficulty. How could he? She couldn't possibly confide in him fully as she had done in Dr. Gregory. Oh, if there were somebody, anybody at all to advise her. If only she weren't so alone.

She opened her locket and stared at the two faces inside it. She did not remember either of her parents. But she believed that if they were living now they would share her grief and tell her what to do. It must be wonderful to have a father to stand by you. The young man in the locket had sure, steady eyes and a small pointed black beard. In spite of his youth he reminded her of someone much older. At first she couldn't think who and then suddenly it dawned on her: if he were living now, he would look very much like Judge Rusk.

The locket clicked shut and fell out of her hand. She opened her reticule, drew out Dessie's letter, and reread the postcript:

Enclosed is from Papa, the other half to follow. He says you are to spend it however you like, but, oh, Martha, I wish you'd let it bring you to my wedding. . . .

The half bill itself, wrapped in a handkerchief, was pinned safely inside Martha's dress now. She had attended to that at dinnertime alone in Clara Ketcham's bedroom, where she had gone to wash her hands and brush up her hair. The other half would be here soon, in a few days perhaps. By the time the trial ended, maybe, by the time she was able to make up her mind what to do, the money would be in her hands, a whole hundred dollars, actually the very sum she had longed for, had more than once thought of asking Uncle George to lend her. Dear Uncle George, could you spare me a hundred dollars, as a loan against my share of Grandma's estate? Of course, if I asked my husband he would give it to me. . . . Well, she had never written those words, after all. What was the use, when every time she started to write them she came up against Uncle George's inevitable question: Well, then, my child, why not ask your husband? But now Uncle George had sent it anyway. . . .

IN the courtroom Uncle Jerry stood, leaning on his cane and looking gravely up at the judge, who read:

"You are brought here as a witness, and by the direction of the law, I am to tell you before you give your evidence, that you must tell the truth, the whole truth and nothing but the truth; and if it be found hereafter that you tell a lie, and give false testimony in this matter, you must for so doing, have both your ears nailed to the pillory, and cut off, and receive thirty-nine lashes on your bare back, well laid on, at the common whipping post."

The old fellow's wrinkled dark face was a study in solemn reverence, but once, as the judge read, Jerry's gnarled left hand lifted from the knob of his cane and crept up to finger an ear just under his creamy, lamb's-wool thatch, and he darted a roguish glance at the assembled white folks. A ripple of mirth at his gentle clowning ran over the audience but the judge cut it short with a single stern look above the steel rim of his spectacles. There was absolute silence then till he had finished reading.

Q. Do you understand the meaning of what I have read, Uncle Jerry?

A. I understands, Mas Judge.

Jerry collapsed in his chair so fast that he let fall his cane and was then so undone by the alarming rattle it made that he seemed to take no comfort in it when it was restored to him by the Yam, himself, smiling graciously.

Q. Now, Uncle Jerry, don't you go to feeling anyways embarrassed. We are all inclined to drop things as we get older. It happens to white folks, too, you know, getting old does. By the way how old are you, Uncle Jerry?

A. Well, sir, Miss Hat she say seventy, but Miss Hat's pa, he say Miss Oc's pa—

Q. Never mind your exact age. You came out to Mississippi with Miss Hat's father and mother, in your prime, didn't you?

A. Yassuh. Me and Dosie come with 'em, us and our chillun, our biggest boy and girl and—

Q. Never mind, Uncle Jerry. I know you have a fine large family now, children and grandchildren, more than we've got time to hear about. Mr. Peters called you the patriarch of Waverley the other day. We all know what a good and faithful servant you have been all your life to your white folks and we trust you to tell us whatever you can to help us get at the truth in this trial that's going on here now. Look at the prisoner, Jerry, and tell me if you know her.

A. Law, Mas Yam, know her? Of course I know May. That the girl Mas Kirk got down in New Or-*leens* for Miss Hat to try to make a cook outer. She the one put the poison—

Q. Wait a bit, Uncle Jerry. Did you see May the night before the crime?

A. Yassuh. She come to my cabin bring me my supper like Miss Hat told her she got to do. My joints been troubling me some that day and I was laying down.

Q. Was anyone else in the cabin with you?

A. Fender was there, seem like, roasting her a yam—excuse me, please, sir—I means, a sweet potato in my ashes. . . .

The inevitable flutter of laughter with its inevitable judicial rebuke barely interrupted the flow of the examination.

Q. Fender is your granddaughter, a child who will presently testify here?

A. Yassuh. But I reckon Fender my great-grandchild. That what Miss Hat say. She my daughter Mealy's grandchild. Her mama, Fender's mama—

Q. Never mind, Uncle Jerry. We'll have to hurry this a bit. Was anybody else in the cabin besides yourself and the child Fender when the prisoner, May as you call her, came in to bring your supper?

A. Lethe come in right behime her.

[191]

Q. Lethe, one of the witnesses in this case? What was she doing there? Isn't she the one that works here in town for the Reverend Mr. Simmons' family?

A. Yass'r. Lethe work for the Reverend's folks. But they lets her come home see her chillun Sundays, not ever' Sunday, but sometimes.

Q. And this was one of those times? She had come out home for a visit?

A. Yass'r. Mr. Simmons brung her that evening a little fo' sundown and leave her. Well, so then Lethe come in whilst I was setting up eating. May was waiting round to carry her dishes back, and I says, "Lethe, honey, fix me my medicine Dr. Gregory gi' me." So then Lethe started to look where I told her to look up on my shelf and she rattled things around up there and didn't find it and she laugh and say: "I give you a dose of my medicine you don't look out. I got a medicine here put a end to your troubles for good and all." And then she taken a little bottle outer her pocket and May put out her hand and say: "What is it, sho nuff, Lethe?" And Lethe say, "Anybody take that medicine they never have no more pain." She say hit's some kind of coloring stuff Miss Hat use to dye her wool with. Lethe pick it up off the ground one time by where Miss Hat been boiling her dye-pot over a yard fire and when Miss Hat don't never miss it or ast her for it, Lethe jes' kep it. And she give it to May for her to look at. And May reach over where the fire shine bright and look at it and she say, "For Jesus' sake this here is pure poison. Hit's even got a death's head and bones on the label." Lethe laugh at her and say, "Didn't I tell you?" And then May study over the bottle some more and put it in her pocket—

Q. *May* put it in her pocket? You're sure she didn't give it back to Lethe?

A. She didn't give it back, May didn't. She put it in her own pocket and then she pick up my dishes and flounce out. I say, "Lethe," I say, "that's a bad thing you done, girl. She liable do herself some harm with that stuff." And Lethe laugh again and say, "What if she do? Good riddance of bad rubbish." Then she find me my medicine and dose it out and give it to me and go on off.

Q. The child Fender was there all the time?

A. Yassuh, peeling her yam and eating it and staring and listening. But she run off home when Lethe lef' out of there.

Q. You live alone in your cabin, Uncle Jerry?

A. Nawsuh. Dub live in there, my daughter Mealy's youngest boy. Miss Hat put him there after I got so feeble I need a heap o' waiting on.

Q. Dub, the boy who is a witness in this case?

A. Yassuh. Dub, a witness, too.

Q. Dub was not in the cabin during the time you have just been telling us about, while you were eating your supper and May got the bottle from Lethe?

A. Nawsuh. Li'l Mas Hunt come git him right after supper to play round with the new gun his papa just brought him, and Dub, he—

The Yam interrupted to show the witness Exhibit C.

Q. Did you ever see this bottle, Uncle Jerry?

A. Yassuh. Hit the one May taken from Lethe or a piece of it.

Q. What was the size of that bottle, Uncle Jerry, as nearly as you recall from seeing it that night?

A. About as long as this here fust finger and twicet as thick.

Q. Could you see the contents, see what was in the bottle?

A. No more'n just to see hit was some kind of little shiny yellow lumps like.

Q. Now, Uncle Jerry, tell us what you recall about the next day, the day of the crime, tell only what you yourself saw and heard of the happenings.

Uncle Jerry settled his hands firmly on the head of his stick, nodded to show he understood and launched into a rambling account of how Mr. Duffy had come soon in the morning and routed him out of bed and put him to fixing the palings in the back-yard fence, how he still was working at the fence when Mas Kirk and Hunt come back along toward dinnertime and Miss Hat met Mas Kirk and tell him he got to whip May. . . .

Q. You heard this, Uncle Jerry, heard what they said? You were working near enough to hear?

A. Yassuh. I hear what all they say. But I wa'n't working then. I quit when I see Mas Kirk and li'l Mas Hunt coming home for dinner. I jes' lay my hammer down 'longside the fence and come along right past where they was talking. I see Mas Kirk go on off up to the big-house and go inside and come back out with a switch in his hand.

Q. You are sure it was not a leather strap or whip?

A. Nawsuh. Hit jes' a little green switch, peach bough or hickory mebbe, what Miss Hat burn the boys' legs with if they slip off swimming when she tell 'em not to: hickory tea, she call it when she switches Dub and Hunt. "Come here to me, boys, and git your hickory tea," she say.

Q. Where were you when the whipping of the prisoner took place?

A. Setting on my steps, near as to where the white folks is setting out yonder. And Mas Kirk pass as clost as from me to—to— Mas Syke Berry there, when he come by with that there switch in his hand.

Q. You could see into the kitchen?

A. I could see if the door open, but Mas Kirk shut it behime him when he went in. I couldn't see nothing but I hear plenty.

Q. What did you hear?

A. Tussling and screeching. That May take on like he half killing her . . . but I know she jes' putting on because I seen the size that little switch.

Q. Did you go into the kitchen yourself that morning, Uncle Jerry?

A. Nawsuh, no more than jes' to put one foot over the thrash-olt to see can I git me a cup of coffee before I went to work. But that May claim hit was all gone. I try to get her boil me up some fresh. But she won't.

Q. You hadn't had breakfast?

A. Oh, I had me my breakfast. Dub, he bring me breakfast when the hands wus starting out to the field soon after sun-up. I had me my hoe cake and fat-meat. But I hadn't had me no coffee.

Q. Did the hands come back for dinner? Were any of them about the yard?

A. Nawsuh. Dub taken 'em their dinner where they's working over in the field that jines the creek, Creek Field, we calls it. Hit's the furtherest-off field we got. Dub, he jes' come back from taking their dinner.

Q. How many of the force were working over there on the creek that day?

A. All of 'em, all as could work. Nobody lef' on the yard but the chillun and me, piddling at them palings, like I say, and May to cook and Fender to wait on her and Dub, of course, a-coming and a-going twixt the field and the yard.

Q. And Aunt Dosia, who was in her bed then, I believe? And perhaps someone to wait on her?

A. Dosie in her bed in Mealy's cabin. Mealy wait on her when she at home but Miss Hat and the chillun tend to her when Mealy in the field with the balance of the hands, like that day.

Q. And Lethe—where was she?

A. Oh, Lethe lef' out of there a little past sun-up. Overseer from over to the Lees' come after her like he promised the Reverend and taken her with him back to town.

Q. Now, Uncle Jerry, what happened after the whipping?

A. Mas Kirk and Miss Hat they went in. Dub carry the white folks' dinner up. Hunt come down to Mr. Duffy's house and knock on the door and say dinner's ready. May come out and set on the kitchen steps a while but when I holler over to her and tell her Ise hongry, too, and how about bringing me a little sump'n t'eat, she sulky-like and won't answer. And right after that Dub come running out and say Mas Hunt was taken mighty sick and Mas Kirk, too, and Miss Hat want some hot water quick. He taken the kettle back in the house, just a-running. And pretty soon he ridden off after the doctor. He ridden out by Creek Field I reckon, because it wa'n't long before all the hands come streaking back home, hollering and taking on. Us do what us can for the sick, but it ain't much. Hit was a bad time, Mas Yam, like the doctor and Miss Hat done told you, a time of suffering and lamentation. Look like all our white folks bound to die.

Q. Where was May all this time? Did she help the rest of you in waiting on the sick?

A. May? May? I don't know where May at. Seem like nobody got time think about where May at till the doctor come and started 'em out hunting for her.

Q. Have you discussed these happenings with anyone since they occurred—with the members of the white family at Waverley or with the other Negroes on the place?

A. Nawsuh.

All the time old Jerry was testifying Syke had been scribbling busily. Now he felt a sharp tug at his sleeve and the prisoner's hand came between him and the close-scrawled page before him. He looked up and saw the Yam taking his seat. Syke rose hastily, without picking up his notes.

"No cross-examination," he announced bluntly and sat down again, his ears reddening.

This time there was no pleasant stir of relief and approval through the courtroom. The Yam turned and stared. The jurors looked mystified. The prisoner's whispered protest at Syke's elbow was sharp and insistent. Out in the audience people looked at one another, trying to understand. Mr. Arnaud, employer of the lawyers for defense, frowned critically. Some rows back of him Syke's mother and father began a puzzled argument. Wait, Syke longed to signal them, just you wait and see. I know what I'm doing all right. Yet some childish longing for understanding now, this moment, compelled him to push the sheet he had written over to Mr. John. John Oliver read it, smiled, and pushed it back. The next witness was already on the stand.

She was the woman Lethe, a mulatto, twenty-odd, rather comely, with a soft, agreeable voice. She was, she said, the child of Mealy, Aunt Dosia's eldest daughter. Mr. Peters, who questioned her, discreetly refrained from any mention of her father. But there were few in the courtroom who did not hold old Hunt responsible in spite of the legend so often and insistently recited by Miss Hat to account respectably for the girl's light color: "A man come through here selling Kentucky mules one spring soon after we come to Mississippi and he was stuck at Waverley a good long time. Such a fresh there was as nobody round here ever see the like of before or since, bridges out, Coon Creek a mile wide in places. Well, then this man and his drove put up on us mighty near three weeks and he run up such a feed bill he had to leave a pony for Honey in settlement with Pa and about nine months later we found he'd left, too, this here other rememberance. . . ."

Under Mr. Peters' circumspect guidance Lethe merely said she had been born at Waverley and had always lived there except for a while when Miss Honey was a bride and keeping house here in town, and more recently, during the months since last summer when the witness was hired out to work for Mr. Simmons' family, as testified by Uncle Jerry.

With these biographical facts out of the way, Lethe was then permitted to relate without interruption the events in Uncle Jerry's cabin on the night before the crime. She told the story almost exactly as he had: how she had entered and found him eating his supper brought by May; how he had said, "Lethe, honey, fix me my medicine Dr. Gregory gave me"; how she had looked for it on the shelf where he told her to look without at first finding it; how she had then taken from her pocket or out of her stocking, it may have been, a bottle of Miss Hat's yellow dye stuff she happened to have and teased him by saying, "I'll give you a dose of my medicine if you don't look out and it will put an end to your troubles for good and all"; how May took the bottle and studied the label in the firelight and commented on the skull and crossbones, saying, "Jesus, it's pure poison, sure enough"; how May put the bottle in her pocket and went off with it; how Uncle Jerry scolded her, Lethe, for letting May have such a dangerous thing and how she, Lethe, laughed and said, "Good riddance of bad rubbish"; how she then found Uncle Jerry's medicine, gave him a dose of it and left; how Fender was there all the time, cooking and eating a sweet potato. The witness had slept that night in her mother's cabin. Of what happened next morning she could not testify, because she had, as Uncle Jerry had said, left the place not much after sun-up. Like Uncle Jerry she had not discussed the matters to which she testified with any one since the crime occurred.

This was all of Lethe's testimony. Again there was no cross-examination. Again Syke and John Oliver were the targets of puzzled, and, in some cases, critical glances and comment. But Syke saw one juror register a faint gleam of what he fondly hoped was understanding.

Lethe was followed on the stand by a child. Her tiny head, scored off into a dozen-odd segments and the separated locks tortured by the process known as "wropping" into intricate, knobby cocoons, reached, even while she stood, no higher than the level of the judge's desk. Her eyes stretched wide and white in her dark, minute face as she heard the judge's reading of a perjurer's fate. She was barely able to gulp assent when asked if she understood. She gave her name as Fender, her age as eleven, but she looked no more than eight or nine and her bare little shanks dangled forlornly over the edge of the chair when she was told to sit down. She twisted frantically at a fold of her Sunday dress of clear blue homespun all the time she was testifying and her story was told in a high, shrill monotone that suggested she had rehearsed it over and over, perhaps in her cabin bed every night since the awful crime.

Yes, sir, she was Mealy's grandchild. Yes, sir, she was there in Uncle Jerry's cabin that night, yes, sir, roasting her a potato in the ashes and eating it, too. She saw it all, heard everything, heard Uncle Jerry say, "Lethe, honey, fix me my medicine Dr. Gregory gi' me," saw Lethe look for it and, not finding it, git that li'l bottle of yaller stuff out'n her stocking and say, "I gi' you some this here an' you never have another pain on this yer yearth." Yes, sir. An' May stoop down over the fire, studying the bottle and see the li'l black skull and the li'l black bones crossed up on it and screech out, "Sweet Jesus, this here pure poison! Where you git this here?" And Lethe say, "Hit some Miss Hat's stuff what she use for dyeing." An' tell 'bout where she find it. An' May take it an' go. An' Uncle Jerry say, "Youse one bad girl, Lethe. Don't you know she liable swallow hit down and hit liable kill her dead and Mas Kirk pay a heap o' good money for that girl I bet." An' Lethe go on laughing an' say, "What I care what he pay. I hope he do lose her. She rubbish right on. Rubbish what you sweep out," Lethe say. An' off she go.

The next morning Fender was in the kitchen when Mas Kirk come in and say, "May, take down your dress, girl, I'm a-going to switch you." "What I done, Mas Kirk?" May say. An' Mas Kirk say, "You been talking sassy to Miss Hat again," he say, "an' you been giving her trouble, too, ever' living day sence you fust come on this place. Take down your. dress." So she open her dress and let it down off her back a ways an' he cut her crost her bare shoulders with that there li'l switch and she scream an' run round behime the table and him after her an' he cut her again an' she try to run again an' bang into the table where the dishes was set out for dinner, but then he grab her and push her 'gainst the table so she can't get loose and lam, lam. . . .

Q. After the whipping what happened, Fender?

A. Mas Kirk went off to the big-house. An' May set down, sniffling an' say, "You dish up, Fender. Seem like my heart broke," she say. So I dish up. The dishes was all ready like I say and the teapot, too, on the table, with the tea in it—

Q. The tea was already made, Fender?

A. Nawsuh. The dry tea what I mean. May, she shaken it in the pot when I give it to her from Miss Hat 'fore Mas Kirk come in with the switch. Hit was the dry tea was ready in the pot. An' then Dub he started to carrying in the dinner.

Q. And when was the water poured on the tea? Who poured it?

A. After Dub carry in the rest of the dinner, May got up an' say she make the tea now an' I see her take the bottle out'n her pocket an' shake it over the pot real quick an' turn around an' throw it in the fire an' pick up the kettle an' pour the hot water in the teapot. An' Dub come back an' say Miss Hat say is the tea ready an' May give him the teapot an' he take it in. An' I go right behime him with the hot biscuits. . . .

Like the two witnesses who had preceded her, Fender declared nobody at Waverley, white or black, had talked to her about the poisoning. Again the defense forbore to cross-examine.

It was now ten minutes to five. The judge discussed with the District Attorney the question of whether to introduce the next witness with the prospect of delayed adjournment or to wait until morning. Tom Peters preferred early adjournment, the defense agreed and court adjourned. John Oliver did what he could to quiet the prisoner's distress before she was led out. Syke, partly to avoid talk with Mr. Arnaud, his own family or anybody else, went on writing and did not look up as the courtroom emptied with the usual outbreak of buzzing voices. A shadow fell on the page. He looked up and saw the Yam standing above him. Syke hurriedly stood up, but not before he had reached for a book to cover what he had written.

The Yam was smiling in what seemed to be a patronizing way. "Very smart," he said. "Very smart indeed. And I reckon you got it out of some book you read in your law course. This being your first case, you can't have learned from experience."

"I don't know what you're talking about," said Syke feeling his ears burn.

"No? Well, I'll bet Mr. Oliver does." As John Oliver now turned toward them, he addressed him next. "I was just telling our

[199]

young friend here that his game of not cross-examining our Negroes is a very smart move."

Mr. John didn't seem particularly disturbed. He just laughed.
"You think so?"

"Well," said the Yam, "it's a shrewd play in certain circumstances. I've never used it myself with country jurors. . . ."

Then with a shrug of his shoulders he rolled smoothly away
from them. Syke stared after him and sullenly took up the page
he had written as if to crumple it. Mr. John caught the paper out
of his hands.

"Good Lord, Syke!" he chided. "Surely you can't expect an experienced lawyer like the Yam not to see through your little game
before the jury gets it."

"Well," said Syke sheepishly, "how do we know the jury ever
will see the point? They're backwoods, like he says. And now he
knows what we're up to, hit's no good, anyways. I'll bet him and
Tom Peters are outside now telling the ones that's to testify tomorrow how to change up their stories and make 'em not sound so
much alike."

"No. It's too late for that now. They wouldn't dare. They'd be
afraid of making them nervous. After all, they'd a lot rather let
us claim they've over-coached their witnesses than to risk having
something unpredictable slip into evidence." Then he lifted Syke's
written sheet and read from it: " 'Gentlemen of the jury, you have
heard these docile darkies, who have not discussed their testimony
with anybody white or black, reciting one after another their
parrotlike stories and I ask you. . . .' Good, Syke. Very, very good."
Then he took up his hat. "Now, how about our daily drink? I see
the faithful pair is waiting for us."

THE Ketcham girls waited at the foot of the stairs for their house guests. They spied Mr. Arnaud first and Evvie hailed him happily, careless of the smiles her warmth called forth in the passing crowd. Evvie's open angling for the dapper bachelor was now a town joke. Miss Hat was only a few steps above and behind him. Evvie greeted her cordially, too.

"We'll wait outside for you, Harriet. . . ."

"I'd a heap rather you didn't, Evvie. Mr. Peters may have others he has to see first. And I don't want to feel hurried. My business with him is right important—I told you." She glanced quickly about and lowered her voice. "I'm seeing him about my will, Evvie."

"Well, then," Evvie gushingly agreed, "I'll walk on home with Mr. Arnaud, and Clara can wait. You won't feel hurried with just Clara waiting. And Clara wants to wait for you, don't you, Clara?"

Harriet frowned and her lips thinned.

"No," she said quickly before the good-hearted Clara could answer. "I don't want anybody should wait, not even Clara. I reckon I know my way round to your house by now."

So then Mr. Arnaud bowed to Harriet in his outlandish way, clapped on his hat, offered an arm politely to each of the sisters; and the three went off, leaving Harriet at the open doorway of Mr. Peters' office.

She went in and sat down at the table to wait. She was real glad Syke Berry had showed the Christian forbearance, or whatever it was that moved him, to let Martha off from cross-examination. But he had certainly had no mercy on Harriet and she felt real done in now, like somebody that's had a beating and is sore all over. The worst was his hints about her wanting to get May hanged just to get rid of her as a temptation to Br' Kirk. Of all the low-down, mean slurs to put on a person—as kind as she'd ever been to his mam, going to her day or night if there was sickness or any sort of trouble! And right before that new judge, too, a stranger here and not knowing, like ever'body that live around here, the long years of Harriet's carrying a cross a heap heavier than that there hateful May with her false claim. It was like Syke Berry held her, Harriet Ralston Hunt, responsible for the murder they was trying the woman for, making out it was Miss Hat's mistreating the girl made her do it. Lord love us. Pa used to say a smart lawyer can twist things round to make black look white. And seem like it was so. . . .

Tom Peters came hurrying in.

"Well, now, Miss Hat, here I am—at your service." He went directly to his desk, unlocked a drawer and took out two sheets of paper and laid them before her. "This," he said, "is the old will with the corrections you made on it yourself. And this is the fair copy. Read it carefully—though of course there's but slight difference in the two: just the bequest to Mrs. McLean and the substitution of the little girl's name for your nephew Hunt's. But you look through it anyway. If it's all right, I can call in some witnesses and you can sign right now."

Harriet nodded and took the papers from him. But she couldn't get her mind off the trial, seem like.

"Is it going off all right?" she asked timidly. "Did we do all right, testifying?"

"Do all right, Miss Hat? Yes, yes, of course. You, in particular. You were fine. You stood to your guns. Several times I wanted to rise and cheer."

"Wasn't you pleased they didn't cross-examine Martha? Seem like I been more worried about her than myself. And I feel mightily relieved, too, they didn't ask Lethe a single question."

He frowned.

"Well, don't bank on that too much, Miss Hat. You can be pretty sure they aren't through with Lethe. Maybe they figure they can do more with her on direct. They are almost certain to call her as witness for the defense."

[202]

"I didn't know they could," said Miss Hat, badly taken aback.

"Oh, yes. And to prove their allegation about May's relation to Mr. McLean, they will not scruple to rake old embers."

She sighed deeply, got out her glasses, wiped them, put them on and studied the papers under her hand. ". . . to my beloved brother-in-law Kirk McLean my father's gold watch and chain; to my dearest friend, his wife Martha, my mother's silver coffee pot and sugar bowl and creamer; and to their infant daughter, Harriet Hunt McLean, all the property in land and slaves of which I die possessed, to wit: the farm called Waverley, consisting of one hundred acres bounded on the south by Coon Creek, on the east by the section line . . . yet other one hundred and twenty acres, beginning at a stake . . . the slaves, Jerry, Mealy. . . ."

"Is it all right?"

"Yes," said Miss Hat.

Mr. Peters went to the door and looked out into the hall. The lawyers for the defense were just passing on their way home with Duffy and Orrin at heel.

"Oh—Mr. Berry, Mr. Oliver, I wonder if you'd be good enough to witness for me. Take only a moment. Your friends won't mind waiting, I'm sure. Matter of a will. Thank you, gentlemen."

It took hardly any time, as he had said. Harriet on the street outside, where home-going wagons and buggies were only just backing out and getting started, could hardly believe a thing so important could be concluded so quickly. She glanced up at the clock in the tower: only five-fifteen. More than an hour till supper-time at the Ketchams'—an hour which Evvie and Clara would likely fill with hanging over Mr. Arnaud at the piano while he sang Creole songs in a rich New Orleans dialect. Or maybe Mr. Arnaud would try again to negotiate about buying May back in case of her acquittal. She needn't go there just yet if she wasn't a mind to. From where she stood she could see the porch of the Emporium over on the west side of the square. It was crowded with late afternoon customers and yet she believed she could get waited on promptly. She usually could, and today it would be groceries for supper that most wanted at this hour. She thought it might cheer her up to buy a present for Martha.

At the Emporium, just as she'd expected, it was before the counter with the cheese under its fly net at one end and the candy jars at the other, that the crowd was gathered, jammed in between the pickle and herring kegs. The shoppers parted readily to let her pass and in no time at all she was in the shadowy rear of the store with no competition, facing Sue Ella Foote across the dry-goods counter.

"What can I show you, Miss Hat?" Sue Ella asked respectfully. "Something cool, I reckon. We've got in some lovely book muslin and if it's black you're wanting, we got that, too, in lawn, a real good quality. . . ."

"Oh, not for myself, Sue Ella. I'm looking for something for Martha this time."

Sue Ella turned to the shelves behind her, pulled out a bolt of flower-sprigged lawn and as she lowered it to the counter, deftly unwound a length to lie in folds over her arm and along her shoulder, pink as a cloud in the late sunlight streaming through the window at the back of the store.

"There," she said, beaming down at it through her glasses. "The very thing. Prettiest piece of wash goods in stock. I been wanting a dress off it ever since Mr. Ed first unpacked it."

"Hit's real pretty," Miss Hat admitted, staring at the thin, rosy folds draped over Sue Ella's sturdy blue gingham. "And Br' Kirk was ever mighty partial to that shade of pink. . . ." When Honey wore it, she thought a little wistfully. It used to bring out the color in her fair cheeks. "But seem like something else would suit Martha's skin better."

Sue Ella took down another bolt. Miss Hat recognized it instantly.

"Oh, no, Sue Ella. That's the one Evvie's dress was cut off of. I wouldn't want her to have a dress like *Evvie's!* I don't know as lavender'd be any more becoming than pink, anyways."

"Yellow?" suggested Sue Ella, obligingly tugging at the lowest bolt of all and speaking back across her shoulder. "Dotted Swiss launders prettiest of anything and wears, too. I've got a dotted Swiss I'm fixing to wear the third summer if mama'll just get time to let out the hem a little. And yellow goes nice with a brunette complexion."

Somewhere behind Miss Hat a voice murmured: "King's yellow." And several people laughed. It was like she'd been stabbed in the back. All the pleasure went out of her errand.

"Don't get it down, Sue Ella," she said in a voice she tried to keep from trembling. "On second thought, I believe Martha might like it better to pick out the color she wants herself. We'll come in together some other day. There's no hurry."

Outside, as luck would have it, she ran spang into Miss Minnie Calloway, the old judge's sister and, by vocation, long followed and universally acclaimed, the town gossip. At sight of her, Harriet set her lips. Never one to bear a grudge, she hated to admit how hard and unforgiving she still felt toward little old Miss Minnie for what she done to Martha. Even Martha said: Sis Hat, I don't see how you can be so sure—printing's not a bit like handwriting. No mind, lamb. This here—she had waved the ugly anonymous note in air before dropping it into the flames—belong to Miss Minnie as plain as them little purple satin scraps she slip in your scrap bag at the same time. I'd know it anywheres, like I'd know her cane or her ear trumpet. To this good day Harriet had a mighty hard struggle to speak civilly to Miss Minnie.

"Well," said Miss Minnie, bobbing and beaming, "I hear you're staying in at the Ketchams' tonight, Miss Hat. Mr. Kirk told me. I met him in front of the doctor's just now. He said he sent his wife home in Mr. Banning's care. I said, 'Sir, you trust that gentleman like a brother, don't you, Mr. Kirk?' And he said, 'Miss Minnie,' he said, 'Parson's a heap more to me than any brother could be,' he said. . . ."

As the farmers' families got out of their wagons and buggies in the square on Thursday morning, the fourth day of the trial, they spoke first by habit of the weather: the hottest day yet, ninety-two by the courthouse thermometer and not yet nine o'clock. Then the men plunged straight into their daily debate on trial strategy. As the State's case drew near its end and the defense was getting ready to begin, speculation, reasonable and unreasonable, ran rife—especially about Mr. Duffy, popularly called the dark horse, because he had not appeared in the earlier trial and because Syke had kept him under such close guard this week as to suggest there would be some gratifying and dramatic surprise when he took the stand. The women, who certainly would have been more comfortable shelling peas or churning in their own breezy dogtrots, released from stays and Sunday clothes, showed no more signs of flagging interest than the men. After begging the children not to run about and get overheated, they eagerly foregathered with their town sisters to circulate those richer personal items in which the occasion abounded: what Evvie Ketcham had by now told concerning Miss Hat's will, speculations as to whether young Mrs. McLean had had any idea of anything like that when she named the baby Harriet, and what Sue Ella Foote had said about events over at the Emporium yesterday evening just before closing time.

As hot as it was, Kirk McLean in the District Attorney's office for his final grooming exhibited that coolness which such men can usually summon in the face of actual danger. He claimed to have slept well and appeared, in his fresh, well-ironed linen, as one armed cap-a-pie. Tom Peters at his desk, making aimless arcs and whorls on a writing-pad with his pencil, did most of the talking.

"Now, Kirk, for the last time: You understand that the defense in your cross-examination will attempt to establish an intimate relation between you and the prisoner. Oh, I know we've been over it all before. But let me sum up: Syke, after getting you as angry as he possibly can, will put to you the same question he asked you at the other trial and he'll no doubt have a whole hell of a lot of circumstantial detail to surround it with since he made that midwinter trip to New Orleans. He'll make it as hot for you as he can anyway. Your Yes or No is strictly a private affair, between you and your conscience, naturally. All I want to get over to you is the legal aspect. Whichever you answer, we're prepared, the Yam and I, to fight it out to the end just the same and we confidently expect to get a conviction. If you answer in the affirmative, we'll take the seduction line, a quadroon Circe, so to speak, and I expect to win the jury's sympathy—their natural feelings are with you and against her. Now, on the other hand, if you answer No, we can assume that the jurors, seeing it is clearly your sworn word against hers, must take yours. Well, that's all. Any questions?"

"Just one—Will they put Aimée on the stand this time?"

"I think not. It's possible, of course, but unlikely. Her previous appearance only damaged her case. Why should they risk that again?"

Upstairs every window of the courtroom stood open but not a quiver of breeze came in. The leaves outside showed stiff and still, as though they had been carved on the hard blue sky. Most of the men in the audience were in their shirtsleeves. The Yam wore a coat of gray cotton crash and even the judge had changed to a black alpaca one. Mr. Arnaud, like Mr. McLean, had on a whole suit of finely laundered linen. It was noted that young Mrs. McLean wore a new dress, a rose-sprigged dimity and a hat with matching ribbon. When she came in with Mr. Banning, everybody saw Miss Hat turn and watch them pass down the aisle, saw her question the girl in whispers, probably about the baby, left at home today, but even the Ketcham girls wouldn't know for sure about that till noon recess, if they could know then.

The tower clock finished striking nine. The judge took up his gavel. It was rumored that he had suffered an attack of something like colic the night before, sharp enough to have the doctor to him. He was a little pale this morning and his lips had a set look.

The State had several more Negroes on its roster, but Tom Peters got the judge to let him march them up in a group to be admonished all at once concerning the punishment for perjury; and then he and the Yam, questioning by turns, hustled them along through their testimony at a great rate. Dub, the Waverley house-boy, questioned about the dinner of November 10 and the tea, corroborated facts already proved by others and added no new ones. His older brothers, Jim Crack and Lemon, successively related in almost identical words how they had captured the prisoner on the night of the crime in the woods down Coon Creek, brought her back and tied her up to the loom in Miss Hat's room. None of the three witnesses had talked about their testimony with anyone. None was cross-examined.

Jason, father of the three, testified concerning the morning after the crime while he was guarding the prisoner in Miss Hat's room. It was warmer that day, the witness said. There were no fires, the house doors stood open and there was a good deal of passing back and forth between the cabins and the big-house. At one time Mealy, wife of the witness and present now to testify on her own account, come in and got after May about the poisoning. Several others were in the room at the time, among them his and Mealy's girl Precious and their son Jim Crack's wife Josie, both witnesses in this trial, and maybe others, too, but he didn't remember. They was all asking May why she done it and they kept on at her about it. May was crying and taking on. And she said: "For God's sake, people, shut your mouth. You raise more fuss than the white folks. I'm not the first that's ever did a crime by ten thousand."

This was all of Jason's testimony. He gave it as he himself recalled it, not having talked it over with anyone. He was not cross-examined. He was followed by the three women he had named, Mealy, his wife; their daughter-in-law, Josie; and their daughter Precious, who in that order, related after him the scene in Miss Hat's room on the morning after the crime, quoting the prisoner's words, "For God's sake, people, and so forth" exactly as Jason had quoted them, except that Precious, a flighty creature of sixteen and the last to take the stand, introduced a slight variation. According to Precious, what May said was: "*If* I had did it, I would not be the first, and so forth"—a slip which caused considerable stir at the prosecution table until the Yam, who was interrogator of this witness, got her to repeat the quoted remark. And Precious, who was really very intelligent though careless, repeated it then word for word as the others had done, with the startling *if* clause entirely omitted. None of these witnesses had discussed the events to which they testified with anyone. As each concluded her story, Syke Berry, who was busily writing, looked up only to shake his head and say: "No questions."

Actually the seven witnesses, thanks to the dispatch of the State's attorneys and the non-intervention strategy of the defense, had been disposed of in a few minutes less than an hour. Yet the repetitious character of the testimony, unrelieved by the customary legal sparring or by any variety except the quickly corrected tongue slip of the witness Precious, was beginning to wear on the spectators' patience visibly. Even the jurors showed signs of boredom. But when Mr. Kirk McLean's name was called, there was a reviving breeze of interest through the steamy air. The audience leaned forward with whispers and fan fluttering. Syke Berry hastily shuffled his papers and conferred with Mr. Oliver. The jurors straightened their spines and prepared to give their full attention. The two who wore glasses took them off and polished them. One man blew his nose. Another cleared his throat.

Tom Peters adjusted the flower in his buttonhole—a clove pink it was this morning—made a smiling comment to the Yam and rose to his feet. This was their last and most important witness. But Mr. Peters was not a bit worried. Women—and Negroes, too, of course—are skittish and unstable, prey to their own emotions of fear or anger. With one of them on the stand, a lawyer has forever to be on guard for the unpredictable. But Kirk McLean would not let his lawyers down.

The ripple and stir of excitement subsided to abrupt silence as soon as the witness faced about and raised his right hand to swear that he would tell the truth, the whole truth and nothing but the truth.

Tom Peters moved toward him as he sat down and, smiling, led him adroitly through the preliminaries of name, place of residence, and the like, straight into the facts pertinent to this case.

The witness did not look toward the audience or often toward the jury, but mostly kept his eyes on Tom Peters, answering whatever he was asked in an easy informal manner that made their colloquy sound almost like a friendly chat in a cozy sitting room. The bill of sale introduced as Exhibit E, without objection from the defense, was verified by the witness as the instrument by which he had come into possession of the prisoner on the date named upon it and was then handed over to the jury to examine. While they were looking at it, Tom Peters got the witness to relate the circumstances of her purchase already outlined by Mr. Banning the day before and, though they did not linger over this part of the testimony, they contrived to put color and life into it, to make it seem fresh and interesting. And all who heard felt as though they themselves had actually visited the rich Creole widow in her paved and palm-decked courtyard and bought from her that fine-looking quadroon wench for $650 between one sip of coffee and the next. They accompanied the witness step by step as he started his new purchase off for home in keeping of Captain Hastings of the steamboat *Buckeye* and, having himself delayed in New Orleans to conclude certain routine farm and personal business, followed, arriving at Waverley one week and one day behind her.

By now Tom Peters was hardly interrupting at all and when he did speak it was only to drop in an omitted date as when he would say "This was Sunday, November 9?" or to make sure a personal pronoun was properly pointed, as, "you are referring now to the prisoner?" The witness, entirely untroubled by this legal exactness, merely nodded each time and went smoothly on. When he mentioned Miss Hat's complaints of the prisoner's refractory conduct and his own reluctant consent to administer what he called light punishment, Tom Peters stopped him and asked him to be more precise. For the first time he hesitated and then defined the phrase as about a half-dozen licks across the shoulders with a hickory switch. He accompanied this particular detail with a smile genuinely and disarmingly rueful. That he regretted giving in to Miss Hat in that matter was as plain as day. His face clouded and his voice became grave when he told of the family dinner and its immediate direful consequences. He stated that his own seizure had been, throughout the afternoon in question and half the night, so acute that he honestly could not now remember clearly the order or nature of events as related by others here. He believed the doctor had given him a sedative very early. Anyway, he had slept through the time when the teapot was suspected and put away and the prisoner first missed, then sought for and brought in. He had roused only with the greatest difficulty when the doctor stood by his side and told him his son was dead. Now he identified the teapot as the one used at dinner on the day of the crime and then locked up by Miss Hat until he, the witness, had received it from her hand and delivered it in early April to Professor Starnes, as previously testified by the professor.

Martha, from the moment that her husband had taken his seat in the witness' chair and begun to speak in his smooth, even tone, had sat like a person in a trance. Not that she had not attended, for she had. Not a single word he spoke had been lost on her, not an inflection of his voice or one trusting glance toward Mr. Peters, not a gesture of his long-fingered hands or turn of his well-brushed head. She had noted how easily he bore himself, how he relied on his careless grace to carry him through what, apparently, he considered no more than an awkward social moment. If the significance to her of his testimony touched him at all, she at least discovered no sign of its doing so. If he had been discussing the price of cotton or plans for a deer hunt with Mr. Peters, he could not have been more nonchalant.

Now, when Tom Peters faced toward the defense table and proffered the witness for cross-examination, she was aware that her husband's manner altered. An expression of condescension, almost of scorn, crept over his face as Syke Berry rose and came toward him. His lax pose stiffened and his eyes grew wary. She thought: Is he afraid? If he is innocent, invulnerable, as Mr. Banning, says, surely he can't be afraid. An unexpected thrill shot through her heart—pity, sympathy, fear on her own account? A plea, almost a cry of longing, fluttered from her heart. Tell the truth. Oh, please tell the truth. Whatever it costs you, whatever it costs us both, tell the truth. . . .

THE judge, who could not see the clock above his head, drew out his watch and looked at Syke.

"We have fifty minutes, Mr. Berry. Is that enough time for you?"

Syke nodded.

"I'll do my best, your Honor. But I want to go through without interruption if it's anyways possible. . . ."

His heart was pounding and he believed that he must look pale. The handling of Kirk McLean was the one point on which he felt Mr. John did not wholly trust him. Their debates on the subject reached as far back as that first visit to Oxford right after the other trial. Look here, Syke, why are you so insistent on the McLean angle? It's almost as though you had a grudge against him. No, Mr. John, I got nothing against him—only that he rides a fine horse and wears French shirts and has a condescending way of speaking Good morning when we meet on the road like I was dirt. Well, watch it, Syke. Animosity is a tricky weapon in a lawyer's hands. It's got a back-kick like an old-fashioned musket. The prisoner's accusation against this man is a serious charge. You would do well not to believe it too trustingly yourself. But, Mr. John, I do believe it. Why? Well, because I know this here fine gentleman and his ways. It's not just a notion I got up. His habits is common knowledge. Why, there's a yellow woman on his place out there that he. . . . Wait, Syke, wait. What you call common knowledge in such cases is all too often base slander. Many an innocent man has been the victim of such a local prejudice. Why, Mr. John, he had her and he had her for years, I tell you. At least

two of her children are his. The whole county knows it. She had
the best cabin at Waverley. She was the only soul on the place besides Aunt Dosia who never went into the field. Oh, she was his,
same as her mammy was old Hunt's. Well, then, Syke, admit that,
even that the whole county knows his long relation to this other
woman. It proves nothing whatever about him and Aimée. Besides,
did that old half open, half clandestine business with the other
woman ever cost him one friend? Not as I knows on, Mr. John. All
right. Your first jury was sympathetic to him, wasn't it? Solid for
him, seem like. Well, Syke, there'll surely be several on your next
of the same mind. Moreover, our society being what it is, there may
be some who'll have a strong personal distaste for seeing a man's
private morals dragged up in a courtroom, several who'd hate
like the devil to have their own secret habits exposed to public
view. Even those who don't know McLean personally will be irked
at seeing any man's dirty linen washed in public. This isn't just
legal procedure, Syke, like a game of chess or a problem in an
arithmetic book. It's a human question and the most ticklish ever
brought up in court since the Lord God walked in the garden of
Eden and discovered what the first man and woman had been up
to. Jurors are kittle cattle, Syke. Win one point at price of offending them and you'd as well make up your mind your case is lost.

Only this morning he had reminded Syke once more of that
ancient axiom that, regardless of particular persons and issues,
jurors by instinct side with the underdog. By nature's law, which
is so much older than even common law itself, their sympathy
goes to the badgered witness as against the attorney who handles
him too roughly.

Syke glanced along the double row of men facing him from the
jury box and felt his sweat start and a dryness take hold of his
throat as he politely framed his first question.

Q. You bought the prisoner on Saturday morning, October 26,
as you have testified, Mr. McLean, and then on Monday, roughly
about forty-eight hours later, you turned her over to Captain
Hastings of the steamboat *Buckeye* then about to sail upriver as
testified?

A. Yes.

Q. Now, Mr. McLean, I want you to account to the court exactly for that forty-eight hour period of your guardianship. The

more explicit you are the less I aim to question you. Just begin at the moment when you and Mr. Banning stepped out into the street with your new property in your possession.

Kirk McLean stared at him and answered slowly.

A. I didn't know when there would be a boat with a captain I knew and trusted. It might be several days, even a week, before I could get her off. Slade & Torrey's man offered to take her down to the slave pen and keep her there. But she was pretty badly upset—

Q. How you mean, upset?

A. Crying, taking on. I thought the slave pen might have a bad effect on her nerves. Or she might even catch some disease. So I said No, thanks, to Slade & Torrey's man and he left us.

Q. Left you and Mr. Banning alone with the prisoner?

A. Yes.

Q. Go on with the story, please: what you said and did.

A. Well, Banning asked me what I was going to do with her. And I asked him if he would be kind enough to fetch a cab. So then he went around the corner to try to find a cab. He was gone for some time. . . .

Q. While you was alone there with the prisoner in the street, was she secured in any way, her wrists bound together with rope perhaps?

A. Oh, no. Certainly not.

Q. Did she continue to, as you say, cry and take on?

A. She did, increasingly at first. People passing stared at her. And I kept wishing Banning would get back with the cab.

Q. Did you make any attempt to soothe and reassure her in her distress?

The District Attorney sprang to his feet.

"I object. The witness is being led to discuss his feelings, the prisoner's feelings."

The objection was sustained, and Syke directed to reframe his question.

Q. Did you, while you were waiting there on the street for Mr. Banning to get back with a cab, talk with the prisoner? If so, what did you say to her and she to you?

A. Oh, I said the usual sort of thing: that Mississippi wasn't the jumping-off place after all, that she had nothing to fear if she behaved herself and did her duty, that naturally she could expect to feel a little homesick and strange at first, living in the country, but that good white folks were good white folks, city or country, and if she'd just be a little patient, she'd soon find she wasn't so badly off. . . .

Q. And what did she answer when you said these things to her?

A. Nothing that I recall. But at least she left off that wild weeping and looked at me in a watchful sort of way that told me she was paying attention.

Q. She quieted down then?

A. Quite noticeably. So much so that I made a joke about it to Banning when he drove up in the cab. "Aimée has decided to behave like a lady," I think I said, some such thing. And he nodded and smiled at her and said, "That's good. . . ."

Q. And then?

But Kirk McLean seemed unable to go on. He looked toward his own lawyers and back at Syke, unwilling apparently to get on with his story. He cleared his throat twice. The left hand inside his pocket moved coins or keys or both and set up a thin tinkle. The right hand, with its beautiful seal ring, its tapering fingers and clean, shapely nails rose from his knee to anchor itself at the lapel of his coat. He uncrossed his legs and crossed them again in the opposite way. Syke said to him gently:

Q. I suppose you told the prisoner to get into the cab?

A. Yes.

Q. Well, go on, please. You said good-by to Mr. Banning, got in after her, gave the cab-driver an address?

The witness looked at him without answering. Syke was insistent.

Q. What address?

A. Madame Claire's, three doors beyond the Ursuline Convent.

Q. Is this Madame Claire, as you call her, white?

A. No—about three quarters, I should say, and free, of course.

Q. The jury has a right to know what sort of establishment you was taking the prisoner to, Mr. McLean. Was this free woman, Madame Claire, a virtuous woman, keeping a respectable house?

Kirk McLean's half lolling attitude changed convulsively. In one instant his feet were planted squarely on the floor, both his hands were doubled fists braced against his knees, his shoulders

[215]

bent forward above them, almost as though he were squaring himself to leap upon his persecutor. Automatically Syke recoiled a step or two and shot a questioning glance at the jury. But his voice went relentlessly on.

Q. If the house is respectable, surely you can't have no objection to telling the jury so, Mr. McLean.

A. It is, then. One of the cleanest and best-run rooming houses in the city. Ask anybody. Down there it's the mulattoes and quadroons who keep these rooming houses. Claire's clientele, bachelors, of course, represents the best class possible. All gentlemen, and nearly all permanent residents. As a rule she takes no transients. She makes an exception in my case. I have stayed there for years. Prefer it to hotels.

Q. So it was to your own personal lodgings you taken the prisoner?

A. Yes. It seemed best—in the circumstances.

Kirk McLean forced himself to lean back in his chair and cross his legs again, but his pose had now nothing relaxed about it. His eyes, darting off now and then to his lawyers, swiftly returned to Syke and clung watchfully. It didn't take any particular cunning to follow the trend of the questioning, even to shape the implication. All who had been at the trial in November knew the very words in which Syke's climax question would be framed and they didn't blame the witness for twisting about, his young wife for veiling her eyes, or Miss Hat for flapping her fan faster and faster as the question drew nearer. In November, of course, Syke had displayed no such finesse as he was now doing. He had not, in fact, feinted and sparred at all but had dealt his body blow at once. And, in a way, that had been easier on his victim. This, by contrast, was slow and exquisite torture. Sweat sprang out on Kirk McLean's forehead and along his upper lip. He swept out a big snowy handkerchief to dab at it. His friends in the audience wondered what was the matter with the Yam and Tom Peters anyway. What are lawyers for if not to prevent this sort of merciless grilling?

Q. And what disposition was you able to make of the wench there? Did this remarkable Madame Claire install her in her best bedroom?

Kirk McLean's voice was low and reluctant.

A. She put her in the attic, a small room, but clean and comfortable.

Q. You saw it?

A. Yes, I went up. The room was all right.

Q. Well furnished? A bowl and pitcher, chairs, a table?

A. I'm afraid I hardly noticed.

Q. There was a bed?

A. Really, Mr. Berry . . .

Q. All right. You may skip that. The attic room you put her in seemed to you better than the slave pen, is that so?

A. A long sight better.

Q. Were the windows barred?

A. I didn't notice. However, it was a long way to the ground, if that's what you mean—too far to jump.

Q. Was there a lock on the door, a good stout one, with a key?

A. Certainly there was.

Q. So then you locked her in, put the key in your pocket?

A. Oh, no. I gave it to Claire.

Q. Well, go on from there.

The witness relaxed slightly as he related rapidly how he had had lunch, how he had gone to his factor's and from there to several shops, how he had had dinner at the home of certain friends and afterward gone to the opera with them. It was, he said, past midnight when he got back to his lodgings. He stopped abruptly.

Q. You found the house dark, I reckon? Ever'body gone to bed?

Kirk McLean stared at him without answering.

Q. You are under oath, Mr. McLean. Was ever'body gone to bed when you got back to this here quadaroon lodgings? Did you go straight up to your own room and to bed without meeting nobody a-tall?

A. No. Claire was waiting up for me. She said that wench of mine had been giving her trouble.

Q. What sort of trouble?

A. Disorderly conduct, screaming out of the window to people about being a free person trapped into slavery, begging to be rescued, a lot of lies such as only a hysterical woman could think of and very humiliating to Claire, whose house, as I have said, was everything that was discreet,. correct. It had gone on as nearly as I could make out most of the afternoon and evening, too, with Claire expecting to have the police arriving at any minute. But only an hour before I got in, it seemed, Claire had got her quiet.

Q. How? How did she get her quiet?

Kirk McLean, both hands in his pockets, leaned far forward to inspect the toes of his shoes or perhaps to conceal a smile. Then he straightened up, looked his persecutor full in the eye and answered.

A. Why, by threatening to whip her. Unfortunate to have to use such a threat of course. And I'm sure it wouldn't have come to that in any event since Claire expected me home so soon. . . .

Q. So this here near-white woman threatened to whip this poor woman of her own color? Well, well. And when you come in and hear what all been going on, what did you do?

Syke walked close to the witness stand, put his foot up on the edge of the platform and stared straight into his victim's face. Kirk McLean patted his forehead with his snowball handkerchief and forced a smile.

A. I took the key and went up to talk to the girl.

He spoke so slowly that the words seemed wrung from him one by one.

Syke took his foot down and turned away, his shoulders twitching. In his pocket lay the affidavit of one Claire Berliot, free woman of color, licensed keeper of a rooming house in New Orleans, attesting that the undersigned had held in trust for her lodger Mr. Kirk McLean of Mississippi on October 26 and 27 last a certain slave girl by name Aimée, that she had on request given Mr. McLean the key to the girl's room about midnight October 26 and gone back to bed. Now that the witness had admitted these facts himself the affidavit was useless. But it might have made things awkward for him if he had perjured himself on any detail.

Q. So you took the key and went up to May's room?

A. Yes.

Q. Alone?

A. Yes.

Q. Well, go on. . . . Tell what happened, tell what you found. Was she asleep, awake, in the dark or what? Tell what she did, what you said: if you threatened to whip her or what.

A. The room was dark. I couldn't see her, but she was awake. I knew that at once.

[218]

Q. How?

A. She was weeping. I could hear her. I did not mention punishment. I merely begged her to stop crying, said she would only make herself ill. I told her again she had nothing to fear, that she would be treated kindly at Waverley.

Q. Kindly! Do you call kindness the treatment this poor homesick creature got on that lonely farm you sent her to?

The District Attorney interrupted to protest that Syke was arguing his case. The judge admonished counsel to reserve argument for his summation. And Syke continued.

Q. Well, go on, Mr. McLean. What was the girl doing when you unlocked the door and went in on her? Was she setting in a chair over by the window maybe or was she laying in her bed while you was talking to her?

A. I don't know. The room was dark, I told you. I couldn't see my hand before me.

Q. And you didn't go no nearer? You just went on standing there by the door?

A. Yes.

Syke wheeled about and leaped toward the witness.

Q. Did you or did you not have sexual intercourse with the prisoner that night of Saturday, October 26, in that attic room in the house of the other yellow woman, Claire?

The Yam stood up. He was smiling broadly, as though Syke had just said something extremely funny. He ran his fat, rosy little fingers through his white, unruly locks, bowed slightly toward the judge and said in a voice so low and sweet that it sounded almost womanly:

"We object."

Judge Rusk sighed, rustled his papers, tugged at his beard and bent forward.

"When this same question was put to this witness in a former trial, the State objected just as you do now, Mr. Boone. But in the meantime this case has been up to the High Court of Errors and Appeals and come back again with that court's opinion attached as must be well known to counsel for both parties. Surely you realize, Mr. Boone, that if the High Court found this court in error for excluding the answer to this particular question in November, I can do nothing but allow it now."

"But, if your Honor will excuse me," Mr. Boone went smoothly on, "was not the objection in the previous trial taken on the ground of irrelevance?"

It was, the judge agreed, and read from a paper which he had ready at hand the ruling of the High Court:

"It is to be observed that the State objected to the testimony sought by this question . . . but we think that the question was competent and should have been allowed by the court, leaving it for the jury to determine whether, if answered in the affirmative, it was a sufficient answer to the imputation of malice on the woman Aimée's part against Mrs. McLean. . . ."

While the judge was reading, Mr. Boone teetered lightly on his toes, his little round stomach touching the table and leaving it like a rubber ball or a tethered balloon kept delicately in play. When the judge's voice stopped, Mr. Boone's rhythmic swaying stopped, too.

"No one could claim irrelevance after that, your Honor. Certainly not. But my objection now is taken on the ground of the nature of the question itself. Is there not good legal precedent for excluding evidence that is indecent, offensive to public morals or injurious to the feelings or interests of innocent persons not themselves parties to the issue? A question deliberately calculated to disgrace this witness, to wound his family's sensibilities, and prejudice him in the eyes of the jury can surely be allowed only if it impeaches his credibility as a witness. And this question, even if answered in the affirmative, has no bearing whatever on the witness' veracity. Your Honor must see that."

Kirk McLean sat with downcast eyes. Syke Berry moved his shoulders and hands. Judge Rusk tugged and plucked at his wisp of a beard. As the Yam finished and sat down, Syke moved a step nearer the high desk and waited, his face uplifted. The judge said:

"All that has been argued so ably by the counsel for the State does not persuade me that his objection should be sustained. After this opinion of the High Court it would seem to me impossible not to allow the question. I am, however, aware of the dangers that have been pointed out and I am quite willing, if Mr. Boone desires, to have the courtroom cleared while the witness answers the question."

The honorable Dancy Boone stood up again and directed a

questioning glance toward the witness. The witness shook his head slightly and they both smiled.

"Thank you, your Honor," said the Yam in his silkiest tone. "It will not be necessary to clear the room."

The judge addressed the witness.

Q. We will hear your answer to the question, Mr. McLean. Do you want the clerk to read it to you?

A. No, your Honor. That is unnecessary. I remember it quite well. My answer is NO.

Martha drew a deep, shuddering breath. So he had lied after all. There was no hope for him then. None for her. Behind her a long-drawn "A-a-ah" rose from the courtroom, and a wave of movement rippled through the audience. The rigid pose of the jury altered convulsively. A single note of shrill laughter flashed, bright and sharp as a drawn blade, at the defense table. It was the prisoner who had laughed. It was plain that the sound, very nearly obscene in the circumstances, shocked the audience deeply. Syke turned and frowned at the woman in sharp reproof. Then he took a few steps nearer the witness and bent over him.

Q. No? No? You are under oath, Mr. McLean. Can you swear to this court that you went into that room that night of October 26 where the prisoner was a-laying in her bed in the dark and left without touching her?

A. I do swear it.

Q. And you expect us to believe that you bought this woman for a cook and nothing else. . . .

Before Syke could speak another word, Judge Rusk leaned forward and checked him.

"That will do, Mr. Berry. The witness has answered you."

That, by a standard of literal truth, the witness' denial might be a lie, the judge at his age was privately willing to concede. But if it was, then privately the judge was none the less glad of it. It was bold and final. It set a limit to the public humiliation this man would submit to. And, humanly speaking, why not? If in his frailty the handsome and likable fellow had once been tempted beyond his power to resist—for it is well understood that in these situations the seduction may very well be mutual if it is not indeed wholly the woman's—then surely that single lapse had now been expiated in full. The question of his purpose in buying the woman should not be forced on him. The defense, of course, was fighting for a human life, and an old lawyer could but respect and uphold its right to find the Achilles' heel in the prosecution and aim directly at it. Even without the direction of the superior court, the judge believed he must have allowed the single obnoxious question. But more he would not permit. The very strength of the witness' *No* evidenced a firm, considered intention. True or not, that was a statement he would stand by. He would hold fast to it in the face of all questioning. He could take care of himself. But the judge's duty, as he saw it, was to shut off here and now the needless humiliation of a proud man.

"I shall not permit you to belabor this point further, Mr. Berry. Please confine the remainder of your interrogation to other aspects of the witness' testimony, as, for instance, the crime and the events immediately before and after it."

"We have no further questions, your Honor," said Syke meekly, returning to his seat.

As Kirk McLean stepped down from the witness stand, Syke's eyes were no longer on him but on the jury. How many of them had swallowed that bold *No?* How many believed, as Syke did, that it was a barefaced lie? How many, believing, yet condoned? Had Syke, as Mr. John had feared, only prejudiced his case by crowding McLean into that unsavory corner from which a lie was the only escape? How much harm had the prisoner's unseemly mirth done her cause?

Judge Rusk followed the witness with his glance and noted how, as he regained his seat beyond the railing, he smiled round at Miss Hat and how her nervously flapping fan sank still upon her lap as she smiled back. Since court had opened this morning the judge had watched the young wife with anxiety. But now, with that question he had been dreading since the beginning of the trial answered for good and all, he looked at her hopefully, wanting to see her young face light up in pride at sound of her husband's ringing, manly answer. He saw it instead close-shuttered and still, as lifeless as a carved mask.

The District Attorney was standing up.

"The State rests, your Honor."

Defense Counsel Silas Berry rose and, by the immemorial ritual of the law, made the customary motion allowed at this point: that the case be dismissed on the ground that the evidence brought against the accused did not prove beyond a reasonable doubt that she and no other person had committed the crime charged in the indictment. The routine motion overruled and the defense granted an exception, the judge looked at his watch. It lacked ten minutes of twelve. The crowd, wearied by the ever-increasing heat and the intensity of the conflict, barely waited for the judge's gavel to release its pent-up feelings. The outrush of talk was nearly deafening. Some young toughs in the back of the room whistled shrilly and let themselves go in catcalls and cheers for "Syke! Syke Berry!"— whether in compliment or derision for his share in the just-concluded hostilities, it was impossible to tell. Syke mopped his face and was surprised to find that he was trembling all over as if with a chill.

At the foot of the stairs one of Syke's sisters was waiting for him with a message. John Oliver left them and walked on ahead down the corridor and out of the door. When Syke crossed the outer portico alone, he was aware of a knot of townspeople, Mrs. Sam Hardy and Mrs. Simmons, the preacher's wife and one or two other ladies, who at his passing broke off talk. His hackles rose at what he took to be a veiled expression of distaste for what had just happened upstairs. It was almost as though they avoided looking directly at him. Maybe he only imagined that emanation of feminine disapproval. A country neighbor at the edge of the steps was smiling broadly, waiting on purpose, it seemed, to clap an arm about Syke's shoulder and whisper in his ear: "Good boy! You sure lammed the gizzard outen him." And Syke stammered in deprecation: "Well, I don't know as that'll please Mr. McLean's town cronies any too well. . . ."

Out beside the hitching rail the Waverley wagon, with its load of Negroes, their dubious holiday at an end, was getting off for home under the care of Andy Scales, the overseer. Beside a near-by carriage which also seemed on the point of departure, Miss Hat and Evvie Ketcham were talking to the people inside and Mr. Kirk McLean was waiting for them. As Syke passed, having no hat to tip, he touched his forelock politely to the two ladies. They both looked straight at him without acknowledging the salute and Evvie laughed and said something to Kirk McLean, who stood facing her. He turned abruptly. Syke saw him in turning take the buggy whip

[223]

from its socket on the dashboard of the carriage, but he did not impute any meaning to the action. Even when McLean started directly toward him Syke was slow to take in what it meant. Not until the lookers-on began to gather in ringside formation, did Syke realize. Automatically his hand strayed to his belt for the familiar comfort of his knife handle. But there was no hidden scabbard in his fine new clothes, no knife handle, no knife.

"Mr. Berry," said Kirk McLean in a loud, thick voice entirely unlike his natural pleasant one. "Under protection of the court up yonder, you made a slur on my good name. I demand retraction and apology."

"And if I was to say I don't owe you neither one?"

"Then take the thrashing that I do owe you, sir."

The whip lashed Syke's temple and the flesh along his cheekbone in one searing blow, but it never struck a second time, for Syke, cursing and snarling, his head low, got a grip above and below McLean's hold, wrested the whip from him, broke the butt in two and flung the whole thing out over the heads of the spectators. Then he went at that handsome face with his bare fists. But in an instant they were dragged apart by John Oliver, who had come running back, and several other men whom Syke, with a trickle of blood in one eye, failed to see clearly.

PART IV

Jimson Weed

THE apartment dignified as the judge's chambers was a small, square room, ten by ten, little more than a box, dusty and hot, its one window propped open with a stick of firewood and provided with no shade against the hot noon sun now shining fiercely on it. For furniture the judge had a chair and table, both unpainted and rickety, a cuspidor, long unemptied and rank in smell, and a ragged but highly colored wall calendar considerably out of date, advertising Hardy's livery stable.

The judge's own body servant Joe brought his tray over and set it down in front of him with an apology from Mrs. Howells. She say she sure hate to send you such a sorry little sump'n t'eat, Mas Sandy. But if that doctor say that's all you got to have then that's all she can make out to send you. She just hope it tasties good. The judge twitched the napkin off, eyed the poached egg cooling on its sliver of toast, the saucer of stewed fruit, the small pot of tea, cooling, too, and almost certainly too strong, smiled and said that was all he wanted and more, and told Joe to run along and get his own dinner. But he did not eat the food. He only stared at it.

It was not merely that he lacked appetite. He was in pain. The hurt was like a live coal in his breast. His very throat closed against swallowing. This case was more distasteful to him than any that he could recall. He would be glad when it was over and he was travelling homeward. Meantime he sat there staring at his untasted dinner and thinking of that girl. Like an apparition, a ghost, a vision, she haunted him. He had barely entered his room and shut the door, had not so much as sat down, when he heard the timid knock, called: Come in; and there she was.

She apologized for breaking in on his hour of rest and promised to take only a few minutes. She had slipped away from her party to manage this small chance to speak to him alone. Not about the trial—she knew she must not embarrass him that way. It was about something else, something entirely private. And she hoped he'd understand when she said that he didn't seem after all this week quite like a stranger, but more like an old friend whom one could trust and turn to. Maybe she had guessed he had a daughter about her age? Had he really? Oh, then, that did make it easier to say what she had to say, might even make it easier for him to understand how ignorant she was. She had some money, a gift, to do with exactly as she pleased, but she simply had no idea whether it was really enough for what she wanted. Maybe a hundred dollars looked a lot bigger to her than it would look to any lawyer. But the judge could tell her. And actually—as silly as it must sound to him—she had never in her whole life known a single divorced woman.

Well, he had, God help him. He had known as many as three. But one would have been enough, the one he had helped through the courts back in North Carolina twenty-five years ago as a young lawyer too hard pushed to refuse any sort of case. He could see her right this minute all too clearly: her raddled, thin cheeks, her desperate eyes, her dyed hair; could see the wretched little shop where year after year she had vainly tried to make a living for herself and her child. Oh, yes, they let her keep the child. It was a case of gross infidelity on the husband's part, not her fault, as they say. But that didn't make it any better for her, poor creature. Millinery was what she turned to to try to keep body and soul together, and of course no decent woman would set foot in her shop and there weren't enough of the other sort in a town the size of Raleigh to keep her afloat. She failed. Last he heard of her, she'd gone North, where, he supposed, she'd hardly done any better, her story being bound to come out sooner or later wherever she went to escape it. Fair? Of course not.

"I'm not saying what is fair, my dear. I'm only saying what *is*. There's not a place in our society where the divorced woman can rest the sole of her foot. And if ever she should find a man brave enough to marry her, she would only go through the hell of seeing him come to regret it. If they should have children, she could only expect their lifelong reproach. Maybe some day in some other society it won't be like that. But here and now it *is*. Believe me."

It was not that he lacked sympathy. Indeed it wasn't. If it were his own daughter Katherine sitting before him now, he'd say the same to her. Yes, he was sure he would—he'd rather see his daughter in her coffin than see her divorced. Every marriage is in one way or another a compromise. Some are happier than others, of course. But even the unhappiest is better, a thousand times better, than divorce. And you, my dear, have your child. Surely you cannot realize you'd in all likelihood be giving up your child. Her being provided for by the aunt is of no importance. What is wealth compared to a mother's love? He talked about the sacredness of the words till death do us part. He even got up and brought the Bible and leafed through it until he found and read: If thy brother trespass against thee, rebuke him; and if he repent, forgive him. And if he trespass against thee seven times in a day and seven times in a day turn again, saying, I repent, thou shalt forgive him.

"It isn't just a question of forgiveness, Judge Rusk. Really, it's not. I reckon a woman can forgive a man nearly anything he does, if—"

"If she loves him enough?" he challenged.

But she shook her head woefully. If she understands what he feels, she amended. It's hard to love enough for two. Maybe any woman, to go on and on till death do us part, would have to have something more than her own feelings. How could she stand it if he couldn't *talk* to her?

She left that absurdity echoing at his ears as she sprang up hastily, far too hastily, when Joe came in with his tray, said she mustn't keep him from eating his dinner and ran out—but not before she had thanked him. Oh, yes, she thanked him prettily enough, said he was kind to have talked to her as he would to his own daughter and she knew he had done that. Yes, she said she was sure he had advised her for her own good, just as he would have advised Katherine, speaking the name easily, naturally as though she and Katherine were old friends.

She forgot to close the door, and when he moved to do it himself he saw beyond her the reaches of the courtroom, which looked so much bigger with the emptied benches stretching away to the farther wall. And he saw, too, the man who had been sitting alone there rise and step forward to meet her inside the railing, recognized him: the husband's friend. The old pattern, he thought dismally: the unhappy wife, the comforter at hand. The Yankee fellow, What's-his-name, who on the stand yesterday couldn't speak much more than a bare Yes and No. But I reckon he's glib enough alone with her. Yes, that's what she meant by that last strange confidence. This one *talks* to her.

Are you quite sure you did the best you could by this girl, Judge Rusk? Weren't you rather chill and elderly, a shade on the self-righteous side, a little too much the judge, not enough the human being? Didn't you let her hand slip out of yours a little too quickly after all? If the unhappiest marriage is so much better than divorce, what about elopement? Out of your vast store of experience and wisdom, what advice can you give about that? Take it easy, Judge. After all, you can speak quite freely and simply, as you would to your own daughter. Now that you have slammed the door of divorce, locked it fast, take for discussion another avenue by which a trapped creature may seek escape. How many runaway wives have you known? Did they all live happily ever after? There's a whole chapter in Proverbs about a good and dutiful wife. You might have read that one to her. How *did* you happen to overlook it? And, oh, yes, Judge: is a good woman born different or are there sometimes circumstances in which a woman born to be good loses her way and finds herself following the happily titled primrose path? You didn't even mention infidelity, Judge, clandestine, of course, ending with the inevitable surprise by the betrayed husband and a bloody vengeance. Strange oversight on your part, for surely you must have followed many honor killings through the courts? Perhaps the fact that the outraged husband is generally exonerated kept these cases from making any deep impression on your memory?

Martha had gone in with something very nearly like confidence, her mind almost made up at last, clutching the knowledge of Uncle George's gift like the key to—well, not happiness, certainly, but freedom at least, escape from Waverley and Athens and the everlasting curious faces spying on her pain. Maybe it was a childish plan, but the judge had destroyed it too fast, too utterly, too—too sternly, somehow, with his Bible reading and that part about the baby, when the baby was no problem at all. So careful she had been from the first not to get fond of it, never protesting when Sis Hat to conserve Martha's strength had got the doctor to say the child should be put to nurse at a dark breast. She had *given* the baby to Sis Hat. Its cradle stood in Sis Hat's room. And if she, the child's own mother, was willing to have another woman lavish love and care and even a very good property in time on that child, wasn't it precisely *because* she loved it too much to drag it off on the hard road she chose to follow herself? Surely even a stranger should know Sis Hat could do more for the child than she could. . . .

When she came out of the judge's door, she found Mr. Banning waiting for her.

"Oh—" she gasped—"who set *you* to spy on me?"

He led her into a little room alongside the judge's and made her sit down on a chair until her storm could quiet. And when she couldn't find her handkerchief, he gave her his own to staunch her tears. He didn't say one word about her slipping off secretly to confide in a stranger. He said very little in fact—only that he had been surprised not to find her when he had overtaken Sis Hat on her way to dinner, that he had turned back to look for her and had been directed upstairs by the watchmen in the courthouse porch. At last, when her tears had stopped, he took her along to dinner at the Ketchams' as calmly as though nothing had happened. There he contrived a fiction about her having had to go back to look for something left behind on the courtroom bench.

CHAPTER 2

D R. GREGORY saw the fight
or rather the clotted crowd surrounding it as he rode by. But he
contented himself with a passing inquiry. Since the combatants
had been separated without serious injury to either, the doctor
preferred to duck the unpleasantness. He was tired and out of sorts.
He had just lost a patient, a little girl down by Bates' Bend. It was
the parents' fault, of course, fooling around with that ignorant
steam-doctor a whole precious week before they sent for him. All
the same the loss had got under his skin—a sweet little thing she
was and her unnecessary death angered him.

His office, like old Judge Calloway's, stood in the dooryard of
his home. He looked in as he passed. For once he found nobody
waiting and the note on his desk to remind him that he was expected that afternoon out at the Lee place was hardly news. He
put his saddlebags down, set the door slightly ajar, pinned up a
note: "At dinner—come in and wait," and went on home, where
he was treated as he ate to the story of the fight in full detail by his
two young sons, who had been privileged to witness it from the
ringside. His wife would have hushed them: Your father's tired.
Can't he have his dinner in peace and quiet? But he shook his head
at her. Boys have to have these excitements. For a small blessed
while yet they are privileged to be onlookers, not participants. Let
them enjoy their brief immunity. The housegirl came in to say
there was a white gentleman waiting over at the office. She didn't
know who it was. He didn't give no name. But he had said he was
in no hurry and the doctor should finish eating.

When the doctor crossed his yard again and by the back door

entered the shuttered twilight of his office, the man sitting on the lumpy horsehair sofa sprang up and began nervously:

"I hate like thunder to bother you, Doctor, but I got into a little trouble when I come out of court just now—"

"Never mind, Syke. I know all about it. Here, sit down, in the light where I can have a look at you. . . ."

His hands were as gentle and sure as ever but his eyes avoided Syke's and the few remarks he barked, rather than spoke, were intended to leave Syke in no doubt whatever that the doctor considered he had got off lighter than he deserved. A quarter inch nearer the eye the gash might well have been serious, might have injured the ball, even endangered his sight. As it was, of course, it was nothing, a mere flesh wound, needing a couple of stitches, a bit of plaster, that was all.

"I don't suppose it would do any good to warn you to be careful how you insult people in the courtroom," the doctor said at last, putting his instruments away. "If you have no awareness of the amenities, my advice ain't going to supply the lack."

Syke's cheek reddened under the white plaster and he swallowed hard.

"I'm fighting for a life," he said painfully.

The doctor turned his back and washed his hands. His voice, directed back over his shoulder, sounded, even to himself, cold and censorious.

"Whether that particular life is worth as much as the peace and quiet of an innocent young wife and mother already considerably bludgeoned by fate, I strongly question. But, as I said before, you don't care what I think. You don't even believe I'm honest—or it suits your purpose to pretend not to. Legal ethics would cover such minor insincerity, I suppose?"

"Oh, pshaw, Doctor," blurted Syke childishly. "Please don't get hard down on me. Wait till the trial's over anyways. Maybe, time you see more what we're driving at, you'll even make out to forgive me for what I done to you. . . ."

"I'm not thinking of myself—or not entirely anyway," said the doctor grimly. "But I couldn't expect you to grant that."

"Aw, Doctor, look—I taken one beating today. And I've sure got one coming to me from my mam. If she don't take a stick to me about me and you yesterday, she'll sure blister me with a tongue lashing. You know that. I dread to go home. I really do. Can't you make out to let me off a little easier?"

Syke had barely gone when a tap sounded at the half open door and Kirk McLean came in. His nose had stopped bleeding and begun to swell. He was inclined to laugh at it. All the same it embarrassed him to think of the stares in the courtroom this afternoon. The doctor made sure there was no fracture and then made his patient lie down on the couch with a cold compress on his nose to reduce the swelling while he himself moved about the room, preparing his saddlebags for the trip he had to make this afternoon. He talked as he got ready. Surgery: He had to take a leg off. Negro fellow belonging to the Lees. Mean case. Accident. Foot lacerated in gin machinery. Two days ago he had thought he could save the leg. But this morning he'd got word of the danger signals he'd told them to watch for. Infection had set in and amputation was necessary. He hated such a job as he had to do it: a scrubbed kitchen table, a kettle of water on the kitchen fire, some Negro cook or chance neighbor white woman to hand him what he needed. It was better, of course, when he'd had his sleep out the night before, but this morning he had been routed out at three to attend Judge Rusk. . . .

He had thought his audience wasn't hearing a word he was saying but suddenly the man on the couch stirred and spoke.

"Judge Rusk, you say? What do you think of him, Doctor?"

"As a judge, or a man?"

"Well—both. How does he strike you?"

"I don't know. He hasn't got the stature of Judge Calloway— not by a long sight. But then he hasn't been on the bench as long. I reckon most of us make the mistake of expecting too much of judges, see them as a special order of humans with some God-given wisdom and pure justice. We're apt to forget a judge is just a lawyer lucky enough to have been promoted. And any lawyer's thinking always does seem to me kinder tricky. And I'd be a little easier in my mind, I own, if his gall bladder weren't kicking up. But allowing for all that, this man Rusk seems to me—well, a good deal better than average, a gentleman, of course, decent, wanting to see fair play according to his lights. Yes, I think you can count on that much, Kirk. He's got an upright look about him and he's wide awake, I'd say; wouldn't be misled more than another

[234]

by his prejudices. And his class would incline him to sympathy with you—"

"He showed me none this morning, God knows."

"No? I had to leave town at sun-up and just got back. How'd it go?"

"All right, I reckon. I didn't see Peters or the Yam on my way out. But from what Peters said this morning when he was giving me my last instructions before we went upstairs, I take it everything is going so far about as they were expecting. Peters seemed pretty confident."

"How far along are they?"

"The State rested just before adjournment. I was the last on its list, the climax as it were."

His laugh was short and bitter.

"It was a tough grilling I take it—from the public demonstration of your resentment in the street afterward."

"It was."

"Syke asked you the expected question, I hear, and you answered it with a good round *No.*"

"Yes—God help me."

Dr. Gregory rested his two hands on the edges of his open bag and stared at the still figure with the snowy compress mounded over its face. For a long moment he was too angry to speak. At first he was mistaken in the cause of his own fury. He thought he lost his temper because if he was still liable to recall into court as Syke had hinted, then Kirk had embarrassed him with a confidence he could do a lot better without. But no, that wasn't it. Was it because he was so sick and tired of other people's troubles that this unburdening was the last straw? What did the fellow think he was anyway? A priest for every sinner to run to, expecting absolution? Well, he wasn't, goddamn it all. He was an overdriven country doctor covering a territory three times bigger than he could do justice to and not even able to afford a spare horse to give him a little extra speed and comfort. But when the fumes of his rage had cleared a little, he was able to see that he had been angered less at the confession than at the act it revealed. That Kirk McLean had really done what he was accused of doing stunned and revolted him.

On that sofa where Kirk now lay, clutching that compress to his

[235]

handsome nose, the doctor saw instead little Mrs. McLean, sitting upright, white-lipped, her hands gripped in a hard double fist on her knees. It was a very distinct memory because it was less than a week old. No, doctor, she was saying. You're just as kind as you can be. And I do thank you. But I don't want any excuse to stay away from this trial. You see this—this slander about Aimée and my husband—well, just as Mr. Peters says, if I go into that courtroom and stand up for him everybody will see that I am on his side and they'll all know, every last one of them, that I couldn't be if this horrid thing were true.

To the doctor the yellow woman on trial for murder was, by brutal contrast, an object of extreme repulsion. He'd as soon have thought of fondling a rattlesnake. Her glistening white smile, her gold ear-hoops rolling in some stray sunbeam through the courtroom windows had become during these last days so obnoxious to him that he could very nearly have shared old Duffy's belief in black magic. She seemed to him not human but demoniac. Kirk's careless copulation with her appeared to him shameful, incredible, even monstrous. . . .

He closed his bag with a snap, walked around his desk, came close to the couch and said:

"I feel like going out and finding Syke Berry and apologizing. Oh, don't worry. I won't betray you. But I'll tell you this: I wish that whip Syke snatched out of your hands had not broken in the tussle. I wish he might have had the opportunity to give you such a God-almighty thrashing as—"

Kirk McLean swung his feet to the floor and his hand holding the white compress plunged away from his eyes with a jerk. He scowled at the doctor, looking for all the world like a boy gripping a snowball on the point of hurling it.

"Doctor!" he warned.

"Oh, don't 'doctor' me. I'm everlastingly sick of everybody's running to me to confess their sins. If you were going to commit this perjury why, in the name of all that's holy, couldn't you do it and shut up?"

"They can't prove perjury. Not in a thousand years. Peters says so."

"All right, all right. You expect to evade legal punishment for that. I hope you will. It's a crime all the same, a damned serious one. And how any man with the most rudimentary sense of honor—"

"Look here, Doc, didn't you say yourself on the stand under oath that there are circumstances when the truth constitutes a danger to someone, you—"

"Poppycock. When I go out yonder this afternoon and that poor old darky shows the whites of his eyes in mortal terror of my knife and asks me if he is going to die and I, as scared as he is, say No, I do it to rally his tired forces to make some sort of stand for life while I'm doing what I can to save him. It's not the same thing as blowing smoke in people's eyes to keep them from seeing my secret indulgences. And you know it."

"Doctor, do you despise me?"

"Despise you! Man, I love you like my own son. That's why it pretty near sets me crazy to see you behave the way you do. You scare the life out of me.

Kirk's brow was lined, his eyes, staring at the doctor, showed pupils narrowed to mere dots. The poor fellow had of course no real philosophy to sustain him. The doctor recalled a saying he'd heard Kirk make use of a hundred times: Well, I reckon we all get in the long run about what we deserve. That did all right as long as the sun shone on him—and that with certain exceptions was pretty well all his life till now. No doubt it had been a comfortable idea: If pleasant things happen to me, if most people like me, if I have more good luck than bad, there must be some reason for it. I must deserve it. And he could have thought this without any special vanity. Why should he take credit for being what he was? But now, to turn the old rule of thumb hind part before was proving obviously a painful business. In a way, the doctor understood that. Kirk was a man of instinct and action, rather than of thought. A side of his life which he himself had never really faced was now exposed to public view and he knew of no way to defend himself but by lying and physical blows.

Kirk saw the doctor's expression soften and he longed with all his heart to confide in him and have this one friend at least understand.

"Look here, Doctor," he said, "the thing that happened that night in New Orleans was outside my will, very nearly outside my consciousness. Even now it doesn't seem somehow to belong to me."

He had found the woman weeping on her bed in the dark, had gone in and leaned over to speak to her the ordinary words of comfort the situation called for. It was all he intended, absolutely all. Her desire—well, they were all alike, these poor creatures. Back in his own room afterward he had been filled with revulsion, self reproach, regret. And the next day he wished to God he had never seen her. That was why he had suddenly decided to send her on alone. He couldn't have borne to travel up in the same boat with her. . . .

"Kirk, why did you buy her at all? Answer me honestly."

Kirk's brow cleared and a sunny, engaging smile touched his lips.

"Damned if I know myself," he said cheerfully.

"Look, Kirk. This trial has a peculiar angle to it. Judge Calloway shielded you before. But this time you're out in the open, under fire. I know it's hard to take. But can't you at least refrain from striking out with your fists? Your recklessness gives me goose-flesh. You're exactly like some fool nigger leaning up against a gunpowder keg, enjoying his innocent pipe. After the explosion has blown you to bits I don't want it on my conscience that I didn't at least warn you. How can you be so cocksure as to come red-handed from perjury and accost the leading attorney for the defense at the courthouse door with pompous nonsense about a slur on your good name and a retraction?"

"I didn't know you were near enough to hear."

"I wasn't. My boys were admiring witnesses. You're a great hero to my boys. I gather they're just living to grow up and have some low-down white-trash cur insult them and make him eat his words. Only they don't aim to let him get a-holt of the stick. Not them. They aim to thrash the sorry poltroon within an inch of his life—"

"Like father, like sons."

"Eh? What's that? Well, I guess I did sorter lose my temper with you, Kirk. I'm sorry. But when I see you blind to consequences, I—well, after all, what if one of my pair ten years hence should act as rashly as you do, wouldn't I scold him?"

"Whom the Lord loveth, he chasteneth."

"Stop it, Kirk. This is no laughing matter. Promise me you'll try to exercise some self control for the rest of this trial at least.

Look where you're going, man. When the need for direct action comes on you, count ten, count twenty, ask your wife's advice, ask mine, Miss Hat's, What's-his-name's, the Yankee fellow's, Uncle Jerry's. . . ."

"Meaning anybody at all would know better what I ought to do than I know myself?"

"It looks like it—mightily like it."

The doctor pulled out his watch and started.

"Well, I've got to go if that old darky's to have daylight on his side. I'll kill him sure if I do it by a kerosene lamp."

He went over and clapped his friend on the shoulder, tried to speak, gulped instead and turned abruptly toward the door. Before he opened it he said:

"I suppose you know you've got only ten minutes."

Kirk yawned.

"It would be no great deprivation to miss the Honorable Syke Berry's brilliant opening. Mind if I rest here a while?"

"Make yourself at home. Why don't you duck out for the afternoon? Leave the others to hold the fort. Go home. Spend the rest of the day quietly. Do you good to have a little time to yourself in peace and quiet. But keep that compress on as long as you *are* here."

"Thanks. I will. So long. Good luck to your next victim. If you see Tom Peters on your way out, you might tell him I may play hooky."

The doctor's horse was waiting, saddled and ready, in the street outside. He undid the hitchrein, flung the saddlebags over the broad, chestnut-colored rump, patted the firm-muscled flesh, murmured a brief: "Here we go again, old fellow," and was about to swing himself up to the saddle when a thought struck him. He turned back. Kirk was sitting with his head sunk in his hands and the compress already cast off, forgotten on the floor. The doctor felt a twinge of compunction. Had he been too hard on him? We are as God made us.

"Kirk, my boy, I forgot something: Lethe was in yesterday afternoon." Kirk did not take his hands from his face but of course he heard. "She's pregnant—"

Kirk lowered his hands and showed tortured eyes.

"Doctor, if I believed for one minute that you—"

"Hold on, my boy, hold on. I know who the father is. I know as much as Lethe does anyway. The calendar just about narrows it down to two contenders. You mustn't misunderstand me. She came in to see me about her condition, worried, not unnaturally, about what her white folks will have to say when the matter gets beyond the stage of further concealment. It seemed to me a good time to take up with her Miss Hat's and your plan for sending her up North."

He got no answer to this and, still suffering compunction for Kirk's sagged and beaten look, he laid his hat down on his desk, stooped to unlock a drawer, took out a bottle and two glasses, poured a couple of drinks, handed one to Kirk and, as he sipped his own, went on:

"I intimated that now that Aunt Dosia is gone, the idea might appeal to her more favorably. I explained that you hadn't pressed the question lately because Mr. Peters felt she should be kept here until after this trial. But, I said, if she should want the gift of freedom for herself and her children, and I should think she would, now was her chance. I was rather surprised at the way she took it. I had understood from Miss Hat that she had greeted the suggestion from the first with bitterness and resentment."

"She does not now?"

"Not at all. She seemed—well, not grateful, exactly, but definitely interested. She wanted to get off at once. I explained it could not be till all this blows over. I thought it might comfort you to know she'll go and not unwillingly. It should, I think."

"Meantime, outcast and defenseless, she is preyed on by every Tom, Dick and Harry in this foul dump?"

"Lord, Kirk. Be realistic. You can't help that. And there's as many Tom, Dick and Harry's to the square yard in Yankee land as in this foul dump. You'd better not fool yourself on that score. Lethe will be what nature intended her long after she's passed from our view, the same as she was before you ever laid a hand on her. There's some responsibilities God himself doesn't put on us."

"Thank you, Doctor. You're a good friend. I wish I deserved you."

"Poppycock. Well—good-by."

He glanced about for his hat, remembered the whiskey bottle, put it away and again departed—this time for good. Passing the courthouse he saw Miss Hat just going in with Mrs. McLean and Mr. Banning. Miss Hat hailed him, he drew rein beside her, gave her Kirk's message for Tom Peters, and then rode on.

He was a good piece out of town when a small disturbing memory struck him: something intent in the way Kirk's eyes had followed his movements when he was putting the whiskey away. But surely he had locked the drawer. He put his hand in one pocket after another and found no keys. He halted and looked back. There, beyond the down-sloping fields, a patchwork quilt of brown figured with the various greens of new cotton and corn and sweet potatoes, lay the town in the steel-bright, curving sickle of the river, the gray shingled roofs and red brick chimneys just showing among the thick-mounded darker green of tree-tops with the courthouse clock thrust high over all. One-thirty. He'd come a mile or better. He couldn't go back. He simply could not.

CHAPTER 3

BY the time court took in after dinner the story of the fight had already been told so often and with so much exaggeration that the absence of Kirk McLean was taken by some to mean that he had abandoned the field to his foe. These, seeing that Syke Berry was able to walk down the aisle to his accustomed place at the defense table and that the plastered area on his tawny, freckled face was not eight inches long as reported but a scant three, seized the occasion for a salute. The salvo of scattered applause was really very small, like a quick flutter of rain before a storm, and what little there was was abruptly shut off by the judge's gavel. But all the same it was heartening to Syke and he grinned delightedly as he slid into his chair.

"They ain't all down on us, Mr. John," he whispered eagerly. "Must be a dozen at least that's for us."

"Whether the tribute is to our principles or your brawn remains to be seen," murmured John Oliver dryly, pushing across a paper he had found on their table when he had come in.

It was a handbill such as travelling actors' troupes used to announce their offerings. It was addressed to the gentlemen of the bench and bar, Circuit Court, Chewalla County, spring term, and it announced for this evening of Thursday, May 26, promptly at eight o'clock, at the Phoenix Tavern in the room of Judge Rusk and the two lawyers for the prosecution, an Entertainment, in three parts. "Part I. Shakespearean readings. 1. The Balcony Scene from *Romeo and Juliet,* with the Honorable Dancy Boone as Juliet [this in capital letters] and certain named younger lawyers [listed in more modest type] as Romeo and the Nurse. 2. Court

Scene from *The Merchant of Venice,* with Judge Alexander Q. Rusk as the Duke, District Attorney Tom Peters as Shylock, Mr. Boone as Portia [all in large type], Bassanio and sundry minor characters by sundry minor attorneys [named in small type]. Part II. Charades, in which all attending will participate. Part III. Plantation Melodies, sung by all to banjo music supplied by the talented District Attorney Tom Peters [not this time capitalized]. There will be cigars and whiskey to the amount justified by a collection taken at the door. This handbill has been struck off gratis by our good friend the printer at the office of the Athens *Free Press.*"

Syke was too cumbered with care to see any fun in the thing. He shoved the handbill aside with an expression of deep disgust.

"Do we have to go, Mr. John? I was aiming to have a heap of help from you on my summation tonight. God knows I need it more than all this here high jinks and cutting up."

"Look here, Syke. What I do makes very little difference. But this is your home circuit. This is your first case and your side of it none too popular, I'm afraid. You'll be working with these men every court term in every possible combination of association and rivalry. You're going to have to make friends with them somehow in court and out. Hadn't you better begin?"

He broke off to nod significantly toward the judge, who was addressing Syke. The hour for opening their case was here. Syke drew a deep sober breath, rose, cleared his throat, carefully addressed his Honor and the gentlemen of the jury and began.

His opening was almost as compact and neat as Tom Peters' own. But it had not the easy spontaneity, the casual, almost impromptu effect of the older lawyer's. It had so obviously been written out and carefully memorized that many of Syke's hearers guessed it to be the work of the man they had dubbed his "sleeping partner." But they were mistaken. The address was Syke's own composition. Mr. John had merely gone over it to correct it in matters of law and syntax. But he had done his work thoroughly. In particular he had been watchful lest Syke in his ardor should run ahead of himself and commit the legal sin of arguing his case prematurely. All passages with the heat of pleading had been cut out and, not thrown away, of course, but reserved for that other fast-growing packet of notes headed "Summation." The result,

[243]

legally irreproachable and with all Syke's uncouth, everyday language carefully pruned away, was regrettably somewhat colorless. And the unfamiliarity of the precise diction had the effect of rendering Syke's delivery halting and unsure. Yet for all that the case for the defense as outlined was simple and clear.

The speech began by conceding the State's contention that, at the time and place named, a poisoning had indeed occurred, by which one white person had died and the lives of three others been threatened; that it appeared likely the poison used was a certain bottle dye called king's yellow containing arsenic; and even that the deadly substance had been administered in a pot of tea from the back-yard kitchen, as alleged. But there the concessions of the defense stopped. It held and respectfully begged the gentlemen of the jury to note that the State, with all its elaborate multiplication of circumstantial evidence had not answered beyond a reasonable doubt either of two highly important questions concerning the introduction of the lethal chemical into that teapot, namely: When had it been done and was it by hand of the prisoner and no other? Actually the only testimony thus far on these two essential points was the unsupported statement of a child claiming to be eleven years old but looking considerably younger.

As to the prisoner's supposedly incriminating behavior, the defense held her reported conduct prior to that noon of November 10 to be not other than was normal to a sensitive, perhaps even hysterical, person abruptly snatched from the only home she had ever known and plunged into a strange and hostile environment; and her subsequent flight to be at least no better proof of her guilt than that mass evacuation by which the twenty-odd other Waverley slaves had reacted to the coroner's inquest was proof of theirs. In conclusion the young advocate declared that the High Court's having set aside the prisoner's earlier trial and summary conviction constituted a mandate to this court for greater fairness. The State's hypothesis of guilt surely rested on partial evidence. Indeed the High Court's decision was based, as already shown, on the previous exclusion of testimony perhaps vital to the prisoner's case. Moreover, new facts which had lately come to light through persons not appearing as witnesses at the first trial also deserved to be heard and weighed. It was upon this additional evidence that the defense would chiefly base its plea. And if the jury, after hearing this evidence now about to be presented, should feel a reasonable doubt that the prisoner was guilty as charged, it would be their duty to acquit her.

The first witness for the defense, under John Oliver's questioning, accounted for himself smoothly: His name was Achille Arnaud, his residence the city of New Orleans and the plantation called La Côte Fleurée in Conception Parish, Louisiana. Any relation of the late Victor Arnaud? Brother. Look at the prisoner and say if you know her. Yes, sir. She was formerly the property of my late brother. Will you look at this bill of sale and say if the signature is, to the best of your belief, that of your brother's widow, Madame Victor Arnaud? It is. And the slave herein sold by her to Mr. Kirk McLean of this county is the woman Aimée, the prisoner? Yes, sir. The date of this sale, Mr. Arnaud, is October 26 last—will you tell the court the date of your brother's death? October 19, one week earlier, that is. Mr. Arnaud, did you during that week attempt yourself to buy the woman Aimée from your sister-in-law? I did, several times. But she would not sell to you? As you see, she sold her to Mr. McLean. Now, Mr. Arnaud, it is obvious you would not have tried to buy this woman yourself if you had believed her an evil being capable of criminal—

"We object," the District Attorney interrupted. "Counsel for the defense is leading his witness."

The objection was sustained and the question reframed.

Q. Well, it is granted that you made an attempt to buy her, or, I believe you said, several attempts. Do you recall how many? Two or three, maybe?

A. Half a dozen, more or less. I brought up the subject every time I saw my sister-in-law that week.

Q. How long have you known the prisoner?

A. All her life, about twenty-five years.

Q. Was she considered insubordinate, rebellious?

A. On the contrary—rather docile, affectionate, a little spoiled perhaps, particularly of late years because of her special status.

Q. What was her status?

A. She was my brother's concubine.

The State asked that this remark be stricken: This is a relation essentially private, about which even a brother can have no more than an opinion. He cannot testify to this of his own knowledge, therefore he cannot testify. The court sustained the State's contention, the remark was stricken and the examination proceeded.

Q. Has the woman Aimée any children?

A. She had—one, a boy, who died of yellow fever several years ago, a fine little fellow named Victor.

"Stricken," cut in Judge Rusk. "Really, Mr. Oliver, you surprise me, sir. Surely you understand the court's ruling that allusions to a private relation between the prisoner and the witness' brother are inadmissible."

"Yes, your Honor," said John Oliver and with a gesture toward the prosecution tendered his witness for cross-examination.

The Yam rose.

Q. Mr. Arnaud, did you in offering to buy the prisoner name to your sister-in-law any sum that you would be willing to pay for her?

A. Why, yes, naturally. I went as high as $2,000.

Q. Yet she preferred to sell her for $650 to a stranger. Obviously she was moved by considerations other than money. Did it occur to you that she was concerned for her own personal safety, that so long as this woman remained in the family she, your sister-in-law, believed her own life in jeopardy?

Syke Berry objected hotly. The question was improper. It dealt with feelings and motives and not even those of the witness but of a person too remote to be called into court and questioned as to the truth or falsity of the implication. The court sustained the objection and the interrogation went on.

Q. Is it true that you are footing the bills for the prisoner's defense?

A. You have heard me say that my brother valued her highly. His wishes are still important to me. He was a wealthy man. He was very generous to me both during his life-time and in his will. Naturally I . . .

Q. Never mind all that about your brother, Mr. Arnaud. It's you I want to hear about. Just after the retrial of this case was ordered, some time along in January past, you received a visit at your home in New Orleans from the counsel appointed by the court to defend the prisoner at her November trial, Mr. Berry there. Is that correct?

A. Yes.

[246]

Q. Did you at that time pay him a retainer to continue his connection with the case? And did you agree to pay him and the counsel now associated with him, Mr. John Oliver, a certain sum whatever the outcome, win or lose, that is to say, and certain other specified sums in the event they secured a mistrial or full acquittal?

The witness bit his lip, twisted his ring and cast a glance of deep reproach at his two lawyers. Syke, who had committed the sin of boasting of his client's illustrious backer, writhed guiltily and bent to his papers. But John Oliver stood up.

"Your Honor, the witness' employing counsel to defend the prisoner, like his coming so great a distance to testify personally for her, is the normal action of a high-minded gentleman who feels himself the natural protector of a human being in peril of her life, perhaps unjustly, and, but for him, defenseless. The exact terms agreed on between the witness and ourselves may surely be omitted from evidence as fairly as the amount of the fee Mr. Boone himself expects to receive from Miss Hunt for assisting this time in the prosecution."

The judge directed the Yam to restrict his question to the fact that the witness had employed counsel to defend the accused. The question reframed was answered in the affirmative and the witness was then excused.

CHAPTER 4

THE clerk called, "Mr. Aloysius Duffy." Everybody turned to search the courtroom.

Mr. Duffy rose from a seat far in the rear and made his way down the left-hand aisle with his slow straddling gait. Halfway down he remembered his tobacco cud and, to the audible amusement of the spectators, made obvious disposal of it by means of a not-too-clean red handkerchief drawn from and returned to his breeches pocket. He even acknowledged the merriment bubbling along his path by a wide and friendly grin and a half bow first to one side and then to the other, almost like an opera singer responding to his public's applause. His sweat-darkened, blue-checkered shirt, his slack and sliding galluses, his shambling walk made of the bowing and grinning a comic thing, and the hitherto smothered mirth broke into open laughter, which for once the judge let pass without rebuke. He even smiled himself, seeing Mr. Duffy come down toward the railed-in enclosure to join the principals in the cast.

Syke groaned. The old cuss, he thought bitterly, the damned old fool. Don't he know any better than to act the clown at such a time! No wonder people called him crazy. Syke himself had come near to burning, half unread, Duffy's momentous communication of last January. It reached him a few days after his return from New Orleans. He opened it, standing by the red-hot stove in the back of the Emporium, which was also the post office. The letter appeared at first to be only a long catalogue of Mr. Duffy's supposed woes in the realm of conjure—three mortal pages of the murky stuff, ill-spelled of course and in a handwriting that would give you a headache all by itself. Long before Syke got to the end of it he was itching to open the stove door and let the roaring flames have the foolishness. But then at the top of the fourth page he read: ". . . what the black witch done to me ain't nothin' to what she done to others. I reckon you know who I mean. I don't know if she done it with somethin she slip in his food or what. Hit is all lock up in perfect darkness, what she done to him. But the eye of god can see throw the clouds of conjur. God know she got him so be-conjured he buy that yellow girl Lethe Im speekin of now whatever she want. He never brake that conjur long as he live ef he hadnt went to Georgy. . . ."

Followed the statement of Mr. Duffy's belief that Aimée was innocent of the crime she was charged with and his straightforward offer to testify in her behalf at her second trial. Syke in his sudden surge of excitement could summon a grin for the postscript: "If you was to git her a bag lik mine befor they try her agen, she'd mebbe have a better chance. The root-doctor I got mine off of is a old wobble-jawed black man by the name of Saul, belonging to a Mr. E. B. Davis near as I remember and lives 2 miles beyon Bates Ben on the River Road."

As Mr. Duffy stepped up to the witness stand, Tom Peters rose and spoke to the judge.

"Your Honor, we ask you to declare this witness incompetent. He is mentally deficient."

"Can you prove mental deficiency?"

"Yes, your Honor."

"Have you a doctor present to testify to such condition?"

"Well, no, your Honor. Duffy has never, to my knowledge, submitted himself to sanity tests. But we can prove by witnesses, as many as you consider necessary, that he is mentally unreliable."

The judge turned to Syke, who was standing, eager to be recognized.

"Mr. Berry?"

"Your Honor, discussion of this subject might prejudice the witness in the eyes of the jury—can it be conducted out of their presence?"

The judge nodded.

"The witness' competence will be argued in my chambers," he decided.

The lawyers followed him through the door to his quarters. At a hurried order a bailiff brought in chairs from the courtroom for them and they all sat down around the table, the judge at the end near the window, the two law teams facing each other, with a vacant chair at the farther end for witnesses.

"Now, gentlemen," said Judge Rusk, "it is obvious that you all feel the point in controversy is a serious one, since both sides have come prepared with witnesses. But I shall ask you to be as expeditious as possible and to remember that the final decision rests in my discretion. You may hand me your lists of witnesses and I shall call and question as many or as few of them as I need to convince me." The two lists were passed to him. As he ran his eye along them, he said: "Perhaps it will save time if before we begin you give me a brief outline of your contrary positions. Mr. Peters?"

"Why, sir, the man is stark crazy. He suffers a perpetual delusion relating to witches, conjuring and the like. He has lived hereabouts for a matter of ten years and anybody who knows him knows his obsession. He is totally insensible to the obligations of the oath. To attempt to bind him to truth by such means would be a travesty."

"Mr. Berry?"

"If superstition was to rule Duffy out, Judge Rusk, the State wouldn't a-been allowed air one of hits eleven Negro witnesses. If taking conjure-stuff for fact make Duffy crazy, then they're crazy, too, the last one of them. Didn't the State's own witness tell you how they all run like a turkey from believing that foolishness about the coroner's inquest?"

"Negroes," Tom Peters put in quickly, "are excused from the oath for that very reason."

Judge Rusk laughed, fumbled for his pipe and lit it.

"Gentlemen, let's take our coats off. What do you say?"

Their coats off and hung on a row of nails along the wall, their thirst slaked from the gourd dipper resting in the brass-bound, cedar water-bucket in the corner, their seats resumed, they received the witnesses whom the judge called, now one from the prosecution's list, now one from that of the defense and not in the order written down, but skipping about up and down the lists more or less at random. None of the witnesses denied that Duffy had a

[250]

tendency to drink to excess on occasion and held certain hoodoo superstitions prevalent among Negroes and illiterate whites. Some used the word "crazy" in relating his talk on such subjects. But the ginner and the tanner found his word in a business deal as good as any man's bond. Orrin Foote, employed at the Athens Emporium, said that Mr. Duffy as purchasing agent for Waverley at the store never so far as he knew was out in his calculations on any account by so much as two bits, and he quoted his employer Ed Ketcham as saying old Duffy was sharp in a trade but honest as daylight. One man, a shoemaker, the only person apparently who exchanged visits with Duffy on terms of personal friendship, said that Duffy possessed a copy of Hume's *History of England,* read it and could talk interestingly about the kings of olden times; that he had also a just estimate of American history and his conversation on that subject was pointed up with frequent references to George Washington, Thomas Jefferson, Andy Jackson and other big men; that, though Mr. Duffy did not vote, owing to his belief that one candidate was as liable to conjure as another, yet he attended political rallies, listened to the debates and could talk as sane as any man about the issues involved. Even Miss Harriet Hunt, who more insistently than any other introduced the word "crazy" in her testimony, had to admit that Waverley farm management and local business dealings entrusted to Mr. Duffy for ten years had been scrupulously attended to and that her falling out with him at last, as previously testified by her in open court, had not been due to his occasional sprees or even his irrational maunderings on conjure subjects but to a single defiance of her authority.

After the door closed behind each witness, argument between the law teams now and again flared up, a controversy in which the older, more experienced men kept their tempers and controlled their voices. Only Syke, excited by the terror that he might not be able to put Duffy on the stand after all, unrestrained now by the discipline of the courtroom, shouted and indulged in something dangerously near to vituperation. His insinuations that the State did not want Mr. Duffy to testify because he knew too much were barely veiled. John Oliver under the table laid a hand on Syke's knee and pressed it firmly. Then, smiling first at the judge and then at their rivals, he actually told—to Syke's horror—what

Mr. Duffy had advised to bring the defense luck. The laughter of the State's attorney made Syke writhe.

The clock in the tower overhead struck two and then two-thirty. The men in the small room sweated profusely even in their shirtsleeves and the air grew heavy with pipe smoke. Syke, going out to summon Mr. Duffy at last, noted that the courtroom was nearly empty. Such children as remained, so far from romping in the aisles as the judge, on retiring, had sternly forbidden, were napping on their mothers' laps or listlessly munching biscuits. It was a scene of complete apathy and it filled Syke with discouragement. Even if the judge should let Mr. Duffy testify, he somberly supposed it must be to half empty benches and the mere dregs of an audience, sodden with heat and fatigue.

In the judge's quarters, Mr. Duffy sat down in the chair reserved for witnesses and ran an anxious finger around the inside of his neckband.

"Mr. Duffy," the judge addressed him kindly, "by the law of our land every white person accepted to testify in court is required to take a solemn oath, as you know, ending with the words: 'So help me God.' And it is my duty to see that none take this sacred oath who are for any reason insensible to their obligation to that Supreme Being whom they thus invoke. . . ."

Mr. Duffy nodded solemnly. And the judge went on.

"It has been stated here by many who know you intimately, have known you for many years, that you hold ideas which—er, which are not usually held to be consistent with religious faith. That is to say, Mr. Duffy, witnesses whom I have examined state you put considerable reliance in—well, black magic, or hoodoo and conjure as commonly called. How about that?"

Duffy sighed.

"You gentlemen are all smoking. Mind if I chew?"

"Certainly not, Mr. Duffy. Make yourself comfortable."

Syke rose and sulkily dragged the cuspidor over with his foot. Mr. Duffy chewed, sighed again and strove with the question, his work-hardened, grimy hands clasped before him on the table.

"In the Bible there's what you call miracles—that right, Judge? Back in them days a thing happen folks don't understand they call it a miracle—Christians, they was, too. Well, there's a heap happen round me ever' day I live that's a mystery to me." He paused and spat carefully into the spittoon through the crook of his elbow. "Take like that wire they got strung all the way from New Or-*leens* to Washington. I can see how they make lightning run on it, but how they can git it to talk I ain't anyways able to figure out. 'A miracle of science' the paper call it. I don't know. Same with conjure. I don't know why some needles and pins and a pinch of graveyard dirt and a mite of dried snake's head pounded up and wrop all together in a scrap of red flannel got such almighty power in 'em. I just know they have. I seen it work too many times. That answer your question, judge?"

"Why, yes, Mr. Duffy. Thank you very much."

As the door closed behind Duffy, the judge stood up, announcing casually that he had made up his mind. When Tom Peters started to protest, Judge Rusk checked him with a gesture.

"On this record I hold that there is a failure by the prosecution to make any showing of the witness' incompetence. You will have, gentlemen, the usual opportunity in cross-examination to impeach the witness' credit—indeed it seems to me you have already laid the predicate pretty thoroughly through your own witnesses. It will then be for the jury to decide whether to believe part of his testimony and disbelieve the rest or whether to consider it wholly true or wholly false. I shall, further, make this clear in my instructions. Meantime I consider this witness no less competent than many of those introduced by the State."

The Yam stood, smiling and clasping his hands to his breasts, and declaimed in a lisping, sweet voice:

"O Romeo, Romeo? Wherefore art thou, Romeo?
Deny thy father and refuse thy name;
Or, if thou wilt not, be but sworn my love,
And I'll no longer be a Capulet."

Tom Peters grinned and spoke across the table:

"You're coming tonight, aren't you, Syke, you and Mr. Oliver? The Yam does it much better in his nightshirt."

John Oliver answered.

"We're coming, maybe not together, but in turn. We wouldn't miss it for the world."

Syke only scowled, trailing behind as the judge led the way back to the courtroom and mounted to his high seat. The benches were refilling with a rapidity and intent silence that Syke wouldn't have believed possible if he hadn't seen it with his own eyes. His spirits shot up with corresponding speed when the judge lifted his gavel and announced his decision.

CHAPTER 5

MR. DUFFY, having been sworn as a witness, was not disposed to hurry. He considered his personal history every bit as interesting and important as Dr. Gregory's, Miss Hat's and old Jerry's and, whereas they in this trial, like most of the other witnesses for the State, were testifying for the second time—or the third if you counted the Grand Jury —he was making his first public appearance. He wished to make the most of it, and not all the State's frequent objections or Syke's eager prodding could quicken his rambling pace through the preliminaries. He wanted to tell all about his circumstances back in Alabama, how he happened to come with his man Dave and a real good Kentucky mule out to the Yalohatchie country in the first place, the terms on which he had hired to Miss Hat, how good they had got on for ten mortal years and, of course, Mr. Duffy's long-standing trials from conjuration. But somehow Syke pulled and tugged him on to the first week of November last.

Asked to tell what he had himself observed of the prisoner's conduct during her stay at Waverley, Mr. Duffy reported, the first of any to have so testified, two fights between her and Lethe.

Q. Fights? With Lethe? You mean, of course, after Lethe's arrival on the afternoon of Saturday, November 8? They quarrelled, had words?

A. Words *and* blows. Yes, I reckon it was November 8, Saturday evening, anyways, close on to suppertime, their first ruckus was. I was crossing the yard. I hear 'em in the kitchen. So I pushed the door open and there they was a-tussling and a-screeching and Lethe had a-holt of May's hair with one hand and in the other she had a butcher knife she'd grab up and both of 'em was name calling. May say Lethe taken her earrings and Lethe call her a filthy liar. Well, the first thing I done was to git the knife away from Lethe and lay it up on a jice where she couldn't reach it and then I shove her up against the chimbley and hold her there while I send for Miss Hat. So then she come out and give 'em both a good talking to and then she make ever'body look for the earrings and there they was in a teacup up on a shelf. May say Lethe steal 'em and hide 'em there and Lethe say May hide 'em her own self. God knows who done it. But them earrings was the least thing they was fighting over. The real trouble was Mr. Kirk.

Q. This was, you say, Saturday, November 8. When was the second difficulty?

A. Round midnight the next night, Sunday, after Mr. Kirk got back. I set up real late, reading some New Or-*leens* papers he'd brought me. And then I stepped out in the yard to draw me a drink of real fresh water and I heard another row over in the kitchen cabin and I went and found them at it, hammer and tongs, in the firelight.

Q. Who? And what do you mean by hammer and tongs?

A. Them two, May and Lethe, May in her shimmy half tore off her and Lethe with all her clothes on, rassling and tussling. I separate 'em again and May claim she was laying in her bed in the shedroom when she hear Lethe come in the kitchen and start to feeling round on the shelves where the dishes stay. . . .

The State objected to the statement: It involved a conclusion and not even of the witness but of a third party. The statement was stricken. Syke prompted the witness:

Q. Leave out what May thought about Lethe's actions. After you come in and found Lethe and her in there fighting again and separated them, what did you do?

A. Told May to get back to bed and took Lethe to her mother's cabin and stayed, watching, till she was good inside. Then I went to bed. Next morning was when Miss Hat try to make me whip May. I refuse and she got Mr. Kirk to do it. And then we eat dinner like the others done told you and was all taken sick.

Q. Now, Mr. Duffy, when Dr. Gregory visited you in your house on the afternoon after the crime, and told you that he believed the illness of the family was due to poisoning you said that you suspected it had been done with Jimson weed. Is that true?

A. Yes, sir.

Q. Did you speak of this suspicion of yours to anyone else?

A. Yes, sir. I reckon I did. I written it, anyways, to Mr. Peter, when I offer to testify before. . . .

Tom Peters sprang up and strove for the judge's recognition. The judge addressed the witness instead.

Q. You did offer the District Attorney your testimony, Mr. Duffy? When was this?

A. I don't know as I can tell the date, your Honor—back in November when they was fixing to try the prisoner before.

Q. What did you say in making this offer?

A. I say I know some things about this case that he'd mebbe ought to know. I told him I didn't think May there done the business. I told him this wasn't the first time poisoning been tried at Waverley to my certain knowledge. Seem like, too, I say sump'n other about Jimson weed being used before.

Q. And what was Mr. Peters' reply?

A. He didn't make none, your Honor. Leastways I receive none.

The judge addressed the District Attorney, who was still standing.

"Mr. Peters?"

"Your Honor, the State at that time held, as it still does, a doubt of this witness' competence. . . ."

"The question of competence has been settled by the court, sir."

Mr. Peters subsided. At a sign from the judge, Syke turned back to the witness, who had his plug out, looking at it hungrily, handed him Exhibit D and asked him to tell what he knew about it. Mr. Duffy pocketed his plug and fingered the bottle fragment instead.

A. I think—I wouldn't want to swear to it. Hit's like any other little old burned piece of glass, ain't it? But, anyways, Lethe had a little bottle some whiles back, she carry around with her. I seen it several times. I know she had it way back last August in the wagon on the road the day I taken her in to hand her over to the reverend's folks, and it had some kind of little yellow lumps in it. She been a-crying and a-taking on ever sence we pull outer Waverley. Hit was kinder gittin on my nerves, I reckon. Anyways I try to cheer her up a little, talking. I says, "Lethe," I says, "town ain't so bad as all that, you know. More going on than way off out at Waverley. Town's real cheerful, side of the country. You ain't going be homesick long, Lethe," I says. Well, sir, she turn around and haul this yellow stuff up outer her stocking and she says: "I got a medicine here will cure homesickness," she say. But I didn't pay her no mind. I never see a Negro yet would kill theirself, nor never heard tell of one neither. In ginnerl they don't—

Q. You didn't believe it was really a dangerous drug then?

A. No, sir. I thought she was just funning.

Q. And did you ever see the bottle again?

A. Yes, sir. I reckon so. Somewhere round daylight the morning after the poisoning Dr. Gregory brought this here burned-up piece of bottle out to my house and asked me did I know who it belonged to. First I said No. And then he said Miss Hat been missing a bottle of her yellow arsenic dye and that put me in mind of the little bottle I seen Lethe with and I told him she the one had it a while back anyways. Well, then I left there soon as I could straddle a horse that morning and that's how come me to be so surprised when I hear it was May they was fixing to try. . . .

A motion to strike that last sentence was heard by the court and the sentence was stricken. Syke shrugged his shoulders and smiled encouragement at his witness.

Mr. Duffy's examination had already lasted overlong, and Syke, in his heavy clothing, was sweating hard. But he was pleased with his witness so far. Several important points were now established: Mr. Duffy's offer to testify at May's first trial, Lethe's malice toward May, her, Lethe's, long-continued possession of the poison and her presence in the kitchen the midnight before the crime. The witness, though he had made such a slow, rambling start, had been guided safely past the shoals of conjure without foundering there. His testimony had been given in a sober, earnest manner that surely commanded attention and maybe even respect. It would be a simple matter for Syke to recall this to the jury when, by contrast, he held up to their scorn the frivolous fabrication of the State's over-coached darkies, in particular of that little black flibbertigibbet, Fender. Yes, he was pretty sure his chief witness had so far made a good impression. Even the judge had sharply defended his ruling of competence. Maybe the time had come to try to play the trump card. He glanced questioningly at Mr. John and received a nod of confirmation. Syke mopped his brow and moved closer to the witness.

Q. Mr. Duffy, a little while ago you referred to a previous occasion at Waverley when poisoning was attempted by the use of Jimson weed. . . .

Tom Peters was on his feet.

"We object. Your Honor, it has been proved by Dr. Gregory and Professor Starness that the poison intermingled in the tea sent from the Waverley kitchen to the dwelling house on November 10 last was arsenic. Counsel for the defense has already conceded in his opening that it was probably the arsenic dye king's yellow missing from Miss Hat's shelf. We have seen how the prisoner got this stuff into her hands the night before the crime. We have proved she was alone in the kitchen with the child Fender when the fatal tea was brewed. Surely there is no point in bringing up repeatedly a poisonous weed in no way connected with the facts in issue, no earthly excuse for random insinuations about a person known to be far away from the scene of the crime at dinnertime November 10. Surely there have been more than enough of these irrelevant hints."

"Your Honor," said Syke, "we don't aim to do no more hinting. What we want now is to let this witness tell the jury exactly what happened before his face in that kitchen at Waverley on a morning back in July, three months before the prisoner ever set foot on the place."

Tom Peters objected that no event three months prior to the prisoner's coming could possibly be relevant. The defense contended that where the prosecution depended on circumstantial evidence alone the accused must be allowed a counterhypothesis whereby the crime could be attributed with probability at least to another person. Here was a story never told before to coroner, District Attorney, Grand Jury, or at the previous trial. Why not hear it? The judge interposed a question: Can the defense, if allowed to set up this contrary hypothesis, show motive in some alleged other person? Yes, your Honor. Motive is not enough, cried the District Attorney. The poison was administered in a pot of tea prepared that day in the Waverley kitchen. Even the defense concedes that. How could anybody but the cook have had opportunity. . . . ? Can counsel for the defense prove opportunity? the judge asked.

While the tug of war swayed this way and that below the rim of the judge's high desk, while he dropped over into the struggle the questions strictly incumbent on him as umpire to ask, he reconsidered not only the legal aspects, which certainly grew no simpler as the trial progressed, but also the human factors, which, with the hints about Lethe, grew more and more deeply entangled. The State had massed its dozen-odd witnesses with their multiple stories pointing unanimously to the guilt of the prisoner. She, on the other hand, had no one to testify for her but Duffy—for the character witness Arnaud, so distant at the time of the crime, hardly counted. Duffy's reasons for suspecting Lethe might be worthless, yet the attempt of the State to prevent his taking the stand looked bad. And Duffy's claim to know something of an earlier poisoning at Waverley (a story never yet told, as the young rooster so shrewdly pointed out) was probably the prisoner's one hope of an affirmative defense. . . .

"You may tell your story, Mr. Duffy," the judge ruled, "but counsel must understand that the court reserves decision on relevancy. If the testimony now about to be heard does not prove to be competent, I shall entertain a motion from the prosecution to strike it from the record."

Mr. Duffy straightened his shoulders, faced the jury and carefully began.

On the morning after Mr. Kirk got back from Georgia with his bride, Mr. Duffy, having seen the field hands well started at the day's business, rode into the back yard, tied his horse down by the stable and went up to the kitchen to get him a cup of coffee. There was nobody in sight when he went in, although he saw on the table a tray all set and ready to carry breakfast for one up to the big-house—for the bride, of course, since Miss Hat and Mr. Kirk, he knew, had gone off riding an hour or so earlier. He got himself a cup off the shelves and went back to the hearth. He hadn't no more than straightened up with the cup in one hand and the coffee-pot in the other when Aunt Dosia come at him from the shedroom, yelling and screeching.

Lethe come in, too, from the door to the yard, and there he

had the two of them, complaining at him and trying to get the pot away from him. In the tussle he dropped it, its lid come open and all it held went sloshing out on the floor. And then he see why they was so excited. Tumbling out with the coffee and a good teacupful of wet grounds, came a little bag, or a rag tied up like a bag. Quick as a cat, he set the edge of his shoe against it to burst it open and damned if it wasn't Jimson weed they'd boiled up for that Georgy girl. He even remembered then how he'd seen Lethe out gathering the stuff in her apron at sun-up.

The effect of Mr. Duffy's revelation on Martha was profound. While he was telling his story, her first morning at Waverley had risen before her to the smallest, hitherto mysterious detail: the delay in her breakfast, the angry voices and scuffling in the kitchen, Aunt Dosia's barely veiled hostility, Mr. Duffy's warning in the garden. Again and again her eyes had widened and her hands crept to her throat. So they meant to kill her—just her that time, Martha herself, Martha alone. And they'd have done it, too, but for Mr. Duffy. Only he, this humble, ignorant overseer, had stood between her and death.

Even Syke, who had lived through this moment so many times in anticipation, was unprepared for the stunning impact of his surprise blow. He had been far from imagining in advance the awe-struck, breathless hush of the audience, the fixed and frozen horror on the white, upturned faces floating on air out there beyond the rail. Those of the two women of McLean's household in particular startled him—Miss Hat's, so drawn and painstricken, so dead white, with the lips parted and the long bent fingers raised, shaking, to hide them, and that girl's, frozen in horror. . . . It surprised him, rather, that he felt a stab of pity for them, almost of remorse.

The effect inside the railing, too, was obvious and profound. Tom Peters and the Yam stared before them with careful impassivity. The judge bent forward, motionless as a statue, his hands gripping the sides of his high desk. On the hand just under Syke's eyes the knuckles showed blanched and bloodless. The jurors, of whom Syke had a hundred times wondered: Will they believe or will they not? showed faces as fixed as those of men who have been slugged. Maybe later, when they'd come to, they could weigh and consider, know the meaning of such words as "reasonable doubt," but not now. Even Ed Ketcham, Kirk McLean's staunch friend, whose smiles and frowns as the lawyers' contest had swayed now this way and now that had been to Syke throughout the trial a kind of hated barometer, looked groggy, stupid, incapable of even taking in the thing that he heard, much less understanding it and relating it to the other evidence. Automatically Syke prompted his witness: How could he be sure it was Jimson weed?

Oh, you couldn't fool Mr. Duffy on Jimson weed, them big flat seeds he'd recognize anywhere, and the stink when he scrunched the mess under his foot on the hearth was a smell like nothing else on God's green earth. He ought to know, seeing as he got it all over his legs ever' time he brushed too close to the stuff growing all over the hog lot. . . .

And what happened then? Well, he ordered Dosia to scald out that pot and scrub it, too, and he made the next brew with his own hands and stayed there till he see the old witch carry it with the breakfast in to the girl. And later on in the morning he see the girl out picking flowers, innocent as a lamb, and he try his best to tell her to be careful without scaring her half to death. Of course she didn't believe him, thought he was crazy, like she told on the witness stand the other day. Naturally she couldn't make out, the poor creature, why anybody on earth would want to harm her. And Mr. Duffy didn't have the heart to spoil her peace of mind.

Syke interrupted.

Q. So you did not tell her what had happened. Did you tell anyone else?

A. Well, I try to tell Mr. Kirk when him and Miss Hat got home from their ride. But he just laughed at me. "Oh, come now. You've been suspecting Aunt Dosia of putting stuff in our food for ten years," was what he said.

Syke shot a glance of triumph at the jury. Surely the stubbornest man of the twelve, whatever his reservations till now about Kirk McLean, must yield ground on this point: McLean had had and long suppressed a knowledge of a prior attempted poisoning. Even after the crime he had continued to keep the Jimson weed business to himself. Whatever his motive, whether he had acted to shield Lethe from suspicion of the murder, as Syke suspected and hoped even yet to make him admit on the stand, the secrecy itself stood proved.

The District Attorney was on his feet to remind the court of the promise to hear a motion to strike all testimony relating to an alleged previous attempt at poisoning by Jimson weed. Syke spoke in support of relevance for a passionate ten minutes. Twice at least he referred to Kirk McLean's unnatural secrecy and once he hinted broadly at Lethe's long-privileged status.

Martha gripped her hands together hard: So it was Lethe her husband had chosen to shield, not her, his wife. Nothing she had suffered privately from the first, not even the public shame under which she had writhed this morning during his testimony, could compare to this greatest wrong of all now laid open to her eyes. He was indifferent to her very safety. Then he was not, and never had really been, her protector. The last shred of illusion was torn away.

It seemed a thousand years since that first morning when Mr. Banning had talked to her so kindly about young Syke Berry, offering healing for her bitter and personal judgments in his wise, dispassionate thinking. Far off, too, seemed that afternoon when she had been drawn to confess her doubts to him. How childish she must have seemed with her single obsession to know why, on a given date, a certain slave woman had been bought. As if it mattered. May, and all that concerned her, seemed unimportant now. Lethe, too. What difference could it possibly make to her, Martha, which of them had put a certain poison in a pot of tea last November? No wonder Mr. Banning had thought she was foolish to attach private significance to a public investigation. It had nothing to do with her, never had had anything to do with her. All that mattered was the feeling between her and her husband. And that had vanished long ago—or had never really existed. It had never been anything but a girl's dream, something she made up to believe in because she wanted to believe in it. She had loved an image, not a man.

Before Syke could sit down, the Yam was on his feet, demanding to be heard.

The Yam declared he felt the honor of the Mississippi bar was at stake. He told an anecdote from his own experience as a fledgling attorney. An older lawyer reading over the younger's brief in a certain desperate case shook his head sadly and said: The law and the evidence are against you, Dancy, my boy. I reckon there's not much you can do but muddy the waters—a suggestion which the Yam implied he on that long-past occasion had scorned to take. But in the case of the *State* vs. *Aimée,* the Yam feared, his brothers at the bar, young Berry there and his able and distinguished assistant, Mr. Oliver, must have reached a conclusion mighty near similar to that. At any rate, the waters here had indeed been muddied. Actually, as this case had unfolded from day to day, the speaker, and no doubt everybody else in the courtroom, too, had many times wondered just who was really on trial: the prisoner at the bar or Mr. Kirk McLean. The judge looked at his watch but the Yam didn't notice. Are we, the Yam asked, gathered in this court of justice to fix guilt as charged in the indictment or is the purpose of the defense to attack and force the prosecution to defend a man's honor? The speaker, now in his thirtieth year at the bar, had never before seen anything like the base, scurrilous, deliberate pollution of the clear stream of justice attempted here— and that, too, in the presence of ladies as pure and chaste in thought and action as any in our broad Southland. What shocked him most was the persistent ruthless disregard of the feelings of that little Georgia rose, fresh-plucked from God's garden of youth—

The judge rapped on his desk and ordered counsel to speak to the motion or yield the floor. The Yam in a bitterly aggrieved tone remarked that his Honor's patience seemed wellnigh inexhaustible when there was question of hearing the most wandering and irrelevant testimony by a witness for the defense, but that it was short indeed when an opposition attorney was speaking to a motion his Honor had promised to entertain.

Maybe every judge resents the imputation of bias more than any other insult. Certainly Judge Rusk did. By the great jumping Jehoshaphat, there was not a lawyer back in North Carolina would have dared such impertinence. But here in the Mississippi backwoods a little potbellied mountebank had dared. And if the judge should give him the rebuke that he deserved, this jury of strangers was quite capable of taking the judicial anger as proof of the partisanship implied. Better of course to ignore the bumptious fellow, the judge decided. But the measure of his resentment was apparent in the sudden leap and clawing of that pain, like a trapped rat, in his breast. As the Yam took his seat, smirking, the judge straightened the papers on his desk, took off his glasses, polished and returned them to his nose, took a small sip of water, cleared his throat and announced in even tones that the testimony in debate was to remain in evidence.

MR. DUFFY was cross-examined by the Yam, who almost gleefully turned his entire attention to those peculiar superstitions of the witness which Syke, when examining in chief, had so successfully kept in the background. Syke fought hard for his witness but the judge allowed the conjure quiz as in chambers earlier he had promised to do: "The credit of the witness is a fair point of attack, Mr. Berry." So poor old Duffy, amid general smiles and even occasional laughter bordering on hilarity, was speedily brought to disclose, with sheepish grins of his own, all his foolishness about his gun that wouldn't shoot straight after it was conjured, his charm bag, and a dozen other such follies. And all Syke could do was grind his teeth and pop his knuckles and stare at the chortling jurors. But as bad as it was, it came to an end at last.

The clerk called Lethe's name and Lethe rose and went forward. The other Waverley Negroes after testifying this morning had been dismissed from further attendance and sent home. So, except for the few town servants on hand as spectators and the prisoner, seated as usual at the defense table, Lethe, when she sat down again on the witness stand, looked out on white faces only. She did not at first seem to be afraid. She appeared scarcely less self-possessed than when testifying the day before and her answers to Mr. Oliver were no less clear and distinct. But she was not a docile witness, far from it. She was, indeed, so reluctant, that her questioner began almost at once to handle her roughly. Of course the prosecution protested: Was this, Tom Peters asked, an examination in chief or a cross-examination? But the only result of that was a ruling by the court that this was a hostile witness and so entitled to neither protection of the prosecution nor mercy from the defense.

Even so, John Oliver could not shake her statement that Mr. Duffy's story about finding Jimson weed in the coffee-pot that morning in July, was not true. There was no Jimson weed in the coffee. Mr. Duffy was mistaken. He had a very suspicious nature where her granny was concerned and that morning he was excited. There was nothing in the pot but coffee and coffee grounds.

Q. No bag?

A. Oh, yes, sir. There was a bag—my granny always tied up the coffee grounds in a little clean cloth. It made her coffee good and clear, she said.

Q. But when Mr. Duffy broke the bag open with the edge of his shoe, it was Jimson-weed seeds, as well as coffee grounds, that spilled out, wasn't it, Lethe?

She shook her head and smiled.

A. He thought so, I reckon. But it was just coffee grounds.

Q. What became of the Jimson weed Mr. Duffy had seen you gathering earlier that morning?

A. Pokeweed was what I was picking when he rode past me down by the hog lot, just pokeweed for my granny to make cow medicine with. Mr. Duffy had told her the day before he had a cow with hits bag caked real bad and ast her to make up some of her pokeweed cure. If you was to ast him and he was to study about it a little, I reckon he'd remember.

Syke went over and whispered in John Oliver's ear. John Oliver frowned, went closer to the witness, bent down and spoke in an altered voice, very stern to hear.

Q. There is no pokeweed growing anywhere near the Waverley hog lot, Lethe. You know that, don't you?

She drew back from him as if he had struck her and abruptly her confidence deserted her. But still she managed to answer.

A. Yes, sir.

Q. So it *was* Jimson weed you were gathering. What became of it? Come now. No more lies. What did you do with the apronful of stuff Mr. Duffy had seen you picking?

A. Give it to my granny like she told me.

Q. For her to put in that coffee?

[267]

A. I don't know, sir. She never told me what she want it for. And I didn't see what she done with it.

Q. Now, Lethe, about this bottle of poisonous dye—I see by the records of the first trial that your statement was (he took a paper from his pocket and read carefully): "I did have a bottle of yellow dye. I had it a long time. I had it when I went to Waverley Saturday, November 8. And I missed it when I got back to town Monday morning. I reckon I must have dropped it somewhere around the yard at Waverley and May, maybe she found it and picked it up." Is that what you told the court before, Lethe?

A. Yes, sir.

Q. Was it true?

A. No, sir.

Q. When you testified here as a State's witness yesterday you told an entirely different story, all about giving May the bottle in Uncle Jerry's cabin Sunday night, a very detailed story in which Uncle Jerry and Fender have backed you up. I suppose this one is the truth?

A. Yes, sir.

Q. Then why didn't you tell it like that in the first place?

A. I—I didn't remember when they first ast me.

John Oliver darted a smiling glance at the jury, walked a few paces away from the witness, turned and said gently:

Q. But later on you *remembered* this story which you now call true and Uncle Jerry and Fender also *remembered* it and you all three have now declared in court that May took the bottle with her when she left Uncle Jerry's cabin. We'll leave that for the moment, because I want to ask you about something else. At the beginning of August you were hired to the Reverend Mr. Simmons' family with the distinct understanding that you could visit home once every six weeks and no more. And you had already paid that agreed visit two weeks before the November dates we're discussing. Yet on that particular Saturday you went home again. Doesn't that seem strange to you?

The witness stared at him and answered faintly at last.

A. Yes, sir. I reckon so.

Q. Sometime during that first week in November you went to your employers with a trumped-up story that your granny was dying and demanded to be taken home again. Is that true?

A. Yes, sir.

Q. But your granny was not dying. You had received no message from Miss Hat as you claimed. Why did you lie to Mrs. Simmons, Lethe?

The witness' eyes were fixed upon her questioner but she seemed unable to answer.

Q. You saw the prisoner the day she got here, didn't you, Lethe? You were down at the boat-landing with Mrs. Simmons and her children that afternoon, saw this likely wench Mas Kirk had bought and sent up from New Orleans? Answer me, Lethe. You have to answer, you know. We can easily call Mrs. Simmons to testify about what you leave out. But it will be better for you if you tell us yourself. You did see May get off the boat that afternoon?

A. Yes, sir.

Q. You heard the jokes the bystanders made about her, didn't you—heard them saying they didn't believe she'd been bought for a cook?

A. Yes, sir.

Q. And it was that very night that you told Mrs. Simmons the lie about Mr. Duffy's having given you a message that Aunt Dosia was dying and that Miss Hat said you must hurry if you wanted to see her alive?

A. I don't know. I don't remember. I was homesick. I dreamed my granny wanted me. I dreamed it lots of times.

Q. But it was the very night of May's coming that this homesickness, these dreams made you lie to get out to Waverley somehow. And it was one week to the day after May's coming that Mr. Simmons yielded to your pleading and took you home, wasn't it?

A. Yes, sir.

Q. And the evening of your arrival at Waverley, Saturday, November 8, instead of visiting your grandmother, whom you had so longed to see, you were in the kitchen fighting with May? Answer, Lethe. Is that what happened?

A. Yes, sir.

Q. You were so crazy mad with this woman you had seen only once and had never spoken to before that you'd have killed her if Mr. Duffy hadn't got the knife away from you. Why did you hate this stranger so much, Lethe?

[269]

A. She accused me of stealing. I never stoled so much as a quilt scrap in my life. Ast Miss Hat. May there said I stoled her earrings. . . .

Q. The next evening, Sunday, was when you met May by chance over in Uncle Jerry's cabin, as has several times been related here, and the dye bottle was passed from hand to hand and sundry small jokes were made about it. Now I'm going to give you another chance to say whether May took it away with her or left it in your hands. But there's something else I want to clear up first. You and others have testified that you slept that night in your mother's cabin. But until Mr. Duffy came into court we had heard nothing of what happened between the time you left Uncle Jerry's and the time when you went to bed in your mother's house. I wonder why you all left that out? Whatever your reason, this secrecy will not be allowed to you now. Do you understand?

A. Yes, sir.

Q. This time you must not leave out anything, anything at all. The whole truth means the whole truth, Lethe. You are sure you understand that now—understand that if you keep back anything the court will regard that as a lie and can punish you just the same as if you spoke a falsehood?

A. Yes, sir.

Q. Go on, then: You left Uncle Jerry's a few minutes before nine. We know what time it was because Miss Hat said she noticed the clock when she sent Dub home and Uncle Jerry told us Dub came in right after you left. Mr. Duffy has told us you did not go to Mealy's cabin until he took you there somewhere around midnight. That's mighty near three hours. Where were you in the meantime?

A. Down to my brother Jim Crack's with him and Josie.

Q. What were you doing there?

A. Playing with my children till they went off to sleep. Then just talking and eating hickory nuts.

Q. How long did you stay?

A. I don't know, sir. A good while.

Q. Did you leave there by yourself?

A. Yes, sir.

Q. And then you crossed the yard yet one more time and went into the kitchen in the dark, where Mr. Duffy again found you fighting with May a few minutes later. Now, Lethe, before you tell us about that, I want you to go back and tell us something about that bottle of yellow stuff. I mean to give you one last chance to correct your earlier story about letting May have that bottle over at Uncle Jerry's. Think before you answer, Lethe. Isn't it true that the bottle, still in your own possession, in your apron pocket or in your stocking where you had carried it for months, you took out now and emptied into the teapot right then alone in the dark. . . .

A. No, sir! No. No. That's not true. I swear to God May done it. May the one. . . .

She was almost screaming. And she half rose from her seat.

Q. Wait, Lethe. Think what you're saying. That's why you were back at Waverley, wasn't it—to make trouble for May?

A. No, no.

Q. Then what did you mean when you told Mrs. Ketcham's cook Ida before leaving town that you would make that yellow woman wish she had stayed in New Orleans?

A. I never said it. God knows I never. Ida made it up on me. And now you're trying to put everything what May done on me. Lord, save me! Lord! Lord!

She was too incoherent to be manageable. But, after all, hadn't she yielded just about all the defense could want of her, short of confession itself? Syke got up and went over to confer in whispers with John Oliver. John Oliver said the witness was excused. Syke turned his face toward the bench.

"The defense rests, your Honor."

The judge declared the afternoon session at an end. As everybody in the courtroom got up and made ready to go, Miss Hat hurried forward to meet Lethe and led her out as quickly as possible, speaking to her in a reassuring undertone.

CHAPTER 7

HARRIET, after consoling Lethe as best she could, turned her over to Mrs. Simmons and got Mrs. Simmons' promise to have Dr. Gregory call to see Lethe tonight and give her something to quiet her nerves. Then she saw Martha off for home in Mr. Banning's care and went back to wait for Mr. Peters. She felt the need of something to quiet her, too, mighty near as bad as Lethe, and it was a real comfort to see Mr. Peters come bustling in at last with his ready, cheerful smile.

"Well, now, Miss Hat, what can I do for you, ma'am?"

"I'm worried," Harriet said bluntly, fetching a deep, shaken sigh. "I don't like the way things are going. It scares me. I want to know what you aim to do." Tom Peters smiled and said, Well, now, we mustn't give up the ship, Miss Hat. We've still got rebuttal you know. She echoed the strange word dully. "What does that mean, Mr. Peters?"

He sat down at his desk, pulled toward him a blank pad and drew his usual arcs and whorls as he explained patiently. The State can hereafter introduce no new matter in evidence. But new testimony by the defense gives the right to call witnesses for examination on any points the defense may have raised.

"Then you don't think we've lost the case as a lot of them were saying on their way out?"

"Lost the case? My goodness, no. We've got a lot of fight in us yet. I own Kirk's secrecy about that Jimson weed business was a bad mistake. Ostrich tactics. He's just laid us open to this surprise attack from the rear. And if we do fail to get a conviction and the Grand Jury gets an idea the Jimson-weed thing has to be gone into seriously, I'm sure I don't see how we can keep Kirk from appearing an accessory after the fact." But then when he saw how that frightened her, he quickly amended: "There now, Miss Hat. I shouldn't have said that. That's a bridge we'll cross when we come to it, if we ever do."

"May done the crime, Mr. Peters. I don't care how Lethe behaved just now, it was May done it."

"Of course it was."

"Duffy's crazy."

"So we hope to establish. Anyway we'll play our hand as it's been dealt to us and that's the best we can do."

And he got up to escort her to the door. Still she lingered at the threshold, wanting some reassurance he had not given.

"Poor Br' Kirk. I'm mighty near sure he done what he done partly out of consideration for you, not wanting to embarrass you with something that happened away back before May come on the place—if it really did happen. Anyways, I hope you won't say anything to him to make him any more worried than what he is already."

"Now, Miss Hat, you know I'm much too fond of Kirk to distress him needlessly."

On the outside steps she hesitated. She was to spend the night at the Ketchams' again and, even more than on yesterday afternoon, the thought of putting up with Creole ditties and Evvie's faded coquetry from now till suppertime turned her stomach, seemed like. She walked slowly off in the opposite direction. Ever since Dr. Gregory had cautioned her about her heart, she had got the habit of noticing, times like this when she was alone, that she wasn't, as he said, as young as she used to be. She wasn't old of course—actually only three years older than Br' Kirk, who, to her eyes at least, seemed as young as ever. But she was tired—or her heart was. And at the end of the day, like this, she was apt to notice it.

She turned west along the street toward the river. It was quiet and peaceful over there. Below the bluff the ferry was just pushing off with some over-river people who had been attending court. She could hear their laughter and gay voices. But except for the loaded ferry, the river was empty and the bluff itself was quite deserted. She went a little way up the shore and sat down on a rough bench against the cotton-gin wall, facing toward the sunset.

[273]

Even before going into court this afternoon she had been feeling ill. Br' Kirk's fight in the street had mighty near unnerved her, so completely had it taken her by surprise. You never can tell what's going on inside a man like him, now can you? Look like he hide his real feelings so deep down you never get an inkling what he'll *do*. There he was, so dignified and calm on the witness stand, answering *No* with a firmness that made her proud of him. You'd have thought his self control was perfect. And then no sooner was he down in the street than he was ready to close in on Syke Berry and try to thrash him. Not that she blamed him. His nerves was ragged, poor fellow. She was just thankful it had been no worse. What if he'd had his Colt revolver? She was glad he had escaped the grinding ordeal of the afternoon session, glad Dr. Gregory had persuaded him to go on out home and take a good rest. And she was glad Mr. Banning and Martha would soon be there to soothe and comfort him. Why, he was trembling all over after that fight at noon.

"Miss Hat. Excuse me, please, ma'am. . . ."

She was downright ashamed of the way she jumped and screamed. The boy—the Ketcham's houseboy, it was, sent out to find and summon her to supper, a half-grown boy no bigger than Dub—was a heap worse scared than Miss Hat, staring at her through the twilight and looking skittish enough to take to his heels. She laughed outright when she see who it was.

"My goodness me, boy, don't you know no better than to come up on a body, barefooted like that, and startle 'em out of their senses?"

She had sat there longer than she had realized—till nearly dark, in fact. The streets were almost deserted as she got up and hurried through them, the boy trotting along behind her. Lamps were already lit in the houses she passed and supper smells drifted out to her, scent of frying ham and fresh coffee mingling with the fragrance of moon flower and star jessamine on the vine-shrouded porches. In one lighted doorway Sue Ella Foote stood and called: "Orrin, supper's on the table." Mrs. Simmons came out on her front steps, swung a clappered brass bell briefly and turned back indoors without even seeing Miss Hat or without recognizing her anyway; and the Simmons children came running home from wherever it was they had been playing. Nearing Dr. Gregory's,

Harriet became aware of a man's figure lurching and weaving aim-
lessly along in front of her and she thought vaguely of crossing
the street to avoid passing close to him. But then, glancing back,
she saw the Ketcham's houseboy coming along behind, grinning,
tacitly promising support in case of need. So she pushed boldly
on. The man put out his hand in a fumbling way as she went by
and spoke to her in a thick, blurred tongue.

"Horse," he said. "Can't find m' horse. You know where m'
horse is, lady?"

Recognition flooded her in a dark torrent. Br' Kirk, oh, Br'
Kirk, she mourned. No use asking him what had happened or how
or why. No use asking anything, for he was beyond telling. He was
not safe at home as she'd been thinking. He was here in this—this
condition (for she could not bring herself to think the word
drunk), helpless in the street, an object for public shame and ridi-
cule unless she could quickly get him sheltered, hidden. She beck-
oned the boy to her side.

"Take Mas Kirk's other arm," she directed. "Come, Br' Kirk.
Come along with us."

He seized the palings of the fence alongside and clung. At
last they pried his hands loose and dragged him along with them,
he protesting, every foot of the way and Harriet bothering: Clara
won't talk, but Evvie? Can I make Evvie keep a close mouth for
once? Seem like, after all that come out in the trial today, it would
mighty near be the last straw was people to start gossiping about
this. Oh, dear, if only Mr. Ed was not locked up with that jury,
if only Mr. Ed was at home.

All mixed up with her sense of inadequacy, her flurried longing
for some man to stand by her now, was helpless anger at Br' Kirk
himself, which, if he hadn't been too far gone to listen, she could
have worked off maybe in a hearty scolding. Oh, of course he always did take a drink now and then like any other gentleman. He
was downright fond of her scuppernong wine, kept a bottle of
whiskey on hand, too, to share with visitors who wanted something
stronger. With the two elderly Lee brothers, who owned the land
adjoining theirs and who had been born in Virginia like him, he
drank an egg-nog at Christmas and a sherry at those odd times
when the Lee cows had broken through a Waverley fence or some
Waverley boy and some wench of the Lees' made necessary the

buy-or-sell offer customary between neighbors. But never before in all the years had she seen him like this.

At the Ketcham gate, he refused to enter. Again there were palings to be clung to. They'd never have got him in perhaps if it hadn't been for Mr. Arnaud. He was sitting on the front porch, smoking, heard the argument at the front gate and came down. He was the soul of tact and courtesy, almost like Mr. Ed himself. And Harriet was only too thankful to let him and the boy get Br' Kirk into the house and upstairs to bed.

She found Evvie and Clara entertaining company in the parlor. It was Miss Minnie. Harriet listened grimly while Miss Minnie told how she'd seen Miss Hat and that boy helping Mr. Kirk home and, fearing he'd been worse hurt in the fight than had first appeared, she'd just run right over by the back way to see if there was anything she could do. Harriet tilted her head toward the ear trumpet held out like an enormous greedy spoon, and wearily put into it the information that the doctor thought all Br' Kirk needed was a little rest. Miss Minnie lowered the trumpet, tucked a stray yellow-white curl under her cap band, smoothed her skirts and got up as if to go. But she did not go. She stood, simpering and babbling of Martha and Mr. Banning way off out there at Waverley by themselves.

"Of course when Miss Martha realizes her husband isn't coming home tonight, she'll probably send over for Mrs. Berry to come and stay—just for propriety."

Harriet reached for the trumpet one more time and bringing her lips close, reckoned into it that the proprieties at Waverley were well provided for by the presence of Mrs. Scales, the new overseer's wife, a real plain, good woman.

"Anyways," she added, "I'm aiming to go out home myself, because I wouldn't want Martha imagining accidents and worried all night for nothing."

The resolution, once spoken, was rock firm and she held to it as poor Br' Kirk to his fence railings. They all tried to dissuade her: She must be tired. She should think of her heart. Evvie and Clara could go and Mr. Arnaud would be happy to accompany them. But, no. She wasn't one to be turned aside from her duty once she saw it. She was going herself—as soon as that boy could go over to the livery stable and get her a hack.

CHAPTER 8

MARTHA, not finding her husband at home ahead of them as she had expected, seized upon another chance to talk privately with Mr. Banning. She asked him to go with her over to the creek where they were less likely to be interrupted and he went as simply and naturally as always. She tried first of all to apologize for behaving so badly toward him at noon. Then she said humbly that she'd like to tell him what she had asked the judge and what the judge had said in reply. He listened and, though he made little comment, his sympathy was clearly hers. For one thing, he said, she should not take the judge too literally. No man would want his daughter dead rather than undergoing hardship. And while a woman who breaks her marriage does invite bitter experience, she might understandably prefer that to living a lie.

She wept a little out of sheer gratitude for his perception.

"I reckon," she said rather shakily, "I'll just have to run away."

"Oh, no, Miss Martha. You can't do that. You can't—well, just step off into space with no plan, no objective."

She flushed and looked away from him. She had an objective but naming it proved hard.

"I thought," she said in a small voice, "I might go to New Orleans. . . ."

He got up and walked off, down the creek a little way and stood, minute after minute, staring down at the water. She could see only the top of his head but she watched him patiently. What was he thinking? He came back at last and sat down, not beside her as before, but at a little distance, looking down at the creek.

"You don't want me there," she said painfully. "If you did, I reckon it wouldn't be so hard to tell me."

"You don't understand," he said. "The world is merciless, especially toward a woman who has left her husband, as the judge tried to tell you. Disinterested friendship with a man would—well, surely you can see what people would think, Miss Martha."

A strange idea occurred to her. She stammered a little, trying to put it into words. Her face burned and she was glad he wasn't looking at her.

"Are you—I mean is there somebody—a woman—down there you wouldn't want to think *that* about us?"

"I? Good Lord, no. I don't care what people say about me. And there's nobody else who cares, not a living soul. It's you I don't want put in a false position."

"Suppose I don't care."

"You don't know what you are talking about," he said almost roughly.

Still he did not look at her, but away from her down into the green-shadowed creek with the yellow-laced, late sunlight along its ripples. Sitting well apart from her, his hands loose-clasped about his jack-knifed knees, he stared down into the stream quivering along below him as though he searched its depths for whatever answer there could be.

"Suppose," she whispered, "it wasn't a false position. Suppose we made it true."

He bowed his head. She wondered if he were crying. And that made her want to go to him and take his head against her breast and lay her cheek on his rough hair. But something held her where she was, waiting for him to speak.

"My dear," he said gently at last, "it is impossible."

"Because you do not love me?"

He got up and came to her, sat down on the fallen tree beside her, even took her hard, tight-locked hands in both his own.

"Because you do not love me," he said.

"Yes. I do. Or anyway, I could. I know I could. Nobody else has ever been so good to me, nobody."

"No, Martha. You have found me a comfort in a trying hour. You trust me. You have been able to confide in me. That is all. It is not love."

"How do you know?"

"Because—forgive me, my dear—you are not the first to make this mistake. It is a thing that happens to the family friend. When I was younger I could be, in fact I was, a time or two, misled. Not now. At my age, I know my place. . . ."

He gave the words a sly twist and his serious eyes held the hint of a smile. He released his grasp of her hands and patted them lightly as in leave-taking. She tried to smile back.

"What is your place?" she asked forlornly.

"On the periphery, my dear, always on the outer rim, often welcome, I hope, as here at Waverley, sometimes useful in a mild way, but never at the warm and glowing center. . . ."

That made her feel sorry for him but a little impatient, too, as though there were, or might be, something of a pose in his sweeping renunciation. After all, why shouldn't he be at the center as he called it, if he really wanted to be? Bachelors, her grandmother used to say, are very selfish. They'd rather be free than muss up their lives with a wife and children. But her grandmother never knew Mr. Banning. And selfish was the one thing he seemed not to be.

"Is it enough?" Martha asked him earnestly. "Don't you want more? Don't you ever get lonely?"

The question seemed to make him uncomfortable. He got up and left her again and again came and stood before her. Yes, he said at last, yes, of course, he was sometimes lonely, often, in fact, and her divining it did touch him. But he was used to his life, had come to accept his lot just as it was, even to be content in it. He asked her to believe him. It was partly, he supposed, a question of capacities. He had, he considered, a talent for friendship, loyalty, affection, sympathy, but not for love.

It was getting dark there by the creek and all about them the click and whir of a hot summer evening was beginning. The sound was monotonous and doleful. Martha's throat ached with helpless sadness. He was a shadow, a ghost almost, withdrawn into some world of his own where she could not follow, a chill place wrapped in twilight and fog.

"Perhaps we'd better go back to the house," she said.

It was supper time and they both supposed Kirk McLean must have got home by now. But when they reached the house, he had not come. And, although Martha had supper held back an hour, they finally sat down without him. Dub was serving them though and not until he had cleared the table and taken a message to Mrs. Scales that she was not to wait up, were they really alone again.

Martha went to the front steps and sat down there. A gust of wind tugged at the candle on the table and she asked Mr. Banning to blow out the flame. Half-turned about, she watched him shield the top of the hurricane chimney with his hand and bend forward over it. For an instant his face, strongly illumined, hung before her in the shadowy passage, a high-minded face, marked by self discipline. The family friend, he had described himself. Just that. He had taken the role and was content in it—or professed to be. But was he really? He seemed now, not like someone she knew well, but mysterious, remote, almost a stranger.

He came over and dropped down on the step beside her. For some time they sat silent, facing the bottomless ocean of darkness, with only the sounding monotony of locusts and far-off frogs to bear them company. The air grew close and threatening. Once a jagged crack of brilliance split the blackness and thunder rumbled. If it should rain, they'd have to go inside and light the lamps.

"Mr. McLean's horse behaves very badly in a thunder storm," said Martha.

He offered to ride along the road and look for Kirk if that would ease her mind. But she said it was far too late now. And besides, if it was going to storm, she didn't want him out on the road, too.

Sitting there beside him on the steps, gazing out into the dark, she felt the chill of utter loneliness. She would have liked to find her way back to that moment of intimacy down by the creek before he had shut her out but she did not know how to do it. It was all very well for him, with his coolly reasonable talk of his capacities and limitations, to say what he did and did not want. But what about her? Was his kindness to her all this week just an illusion, too? Was there nobody, nobody at all, to care for Martha?

"Why are you so quiet?" he asked at last. "What are you thinking?"

"It's hard," she said, fumbling for words, "not to be wanted—anywhere."

He said something tentative about her uncle and that only angered her. Her uncle's home, Savannah itself, she never wanted to see again as long as she lived. Imagine her kinfolks' chagrin after all the romantic pictures she had painted of her brilliant match. Imagine their mortification at having her back on their hands in disgrace. Imagine how she'd feel, huddled in some corner at Dessie's wedding. She was so indignant she could not answer one word. And he, not noticing her resentful silence, went on in that elder-brotherly tone that no longer satisfied her. He said she should try to be patient. Maybe she would feel quite differently when this week had passed.

"I'm sure you will be able to see your path ahead more clearly, Miss Martha, when the dust has settled."

"Oh," she cried, too annoyed by his determined detachment to contain herself any longer, "it must be wonderful to be sure about one's path. I suppose *you* never have the slightest doubt about yours."

His arm came around her and tightened in the strangest way— an embrace and not an embrace. He seemed half like a lover, half like a parent shaking a naughty child.

"Don't be cruel to me, Martha," he whispered. "It's too much. I can't bear it."

She felt his heart thud against her and the swift thought leaped in her: He is not a ghost after all, but a man, a very human man. He cares more than he will admit. . . .

Through the darkness came the faint, unmistakable creak of an axle and then, with increasing distinctness, slow hoofbeats, the crunch of wheels and even the silken swish of underbrush. Twin pencils of radiance pierced the distant woods, lighting stumps and low-growing bushes, switched out of sight and in again as the curving drive pointed the lamps now this way and now that. And at last a voice, Sis Hat's, surprisingly clear and close at hand, said there was a right bad tree root beyond the next curve and some-body'd better mind out if he didn't want to break a spring.

After Martha got into bed, Sis Hat knocked and came in. She stood close and spoke in a careful whisper to keep Mr. Banning overhead from hearing. She seemed to have it all ready in her mind, as though she had been rehearsing it on the drive out. Anyway she went straight through her curtain lecture without allowing

Martha to get in a word edgewise. At the end Sis Hat said it was only the appearances she was warning Martha to watch out for, because she knew as well as she knew her own name that there wasn't and never could be the shadow of anything wrong between her and Mr. Banning.

Martha laughed. The room filled with a watery green light, in which Sis Hat, erect in her long white nightgown, appeared like an outraged, holy priestess, invoking that awful crash of thunder that came rolling forth over Martha's sacrilegious mirth.

"How can you laugh?" cried Sis Hat.

PART V

The Verdict

CHAPTER 1

A HARD storm came on in the night—thunder and lightning and a driving rain. The young crops needed rain and many a farmer out through the country, rousing himself to close his windows against the downpour, remembered that and felt thankful about his cotton and corn even while he worried about the state of the roads and bridges tomorrow morning and whether he'd be delayed or even cut off altogether from getting in to hear the rest of the trial. It rained hard in town, too. The cabin in the Reverend Mr. Simmons' back yard had several leaks, a very bad one in the corner right over the built-in bed and two smaller ones by the chimney. Lethe during a rain always took up her bedclothes and moved out to the middle of the floor to keep herself dry. But tonight, under the influence of the sedative which the doctor had given her at bedtime, she did not wake until she was thoroughly drenched.

Then she sat up, shivering, her tongue and the lining of her mouth as dry as cotton. She hardly remembered where she was and she could not reason out why she was shaking so. The rain had stopped by that time. All she could hear of it was a tiny drip-drip from the trees in the yard and a harder, intermittent smack over by the chimney. Must a-been a-raining, she slowly made out. She dragged herself up out of the dank bedding, moved to the hearth and fumbled about for some light'ood knots to kindle her a fire. When she got it to burning good, she heated her up some coffee that was standing there in the tin pot on the hearth bricks. Drinking it, her palms curved greedily around the hot cup, her whole figure in the wet shimmy leaning close to soak up warmth from the flames that now leaped up from the sizzling, frying pine knots, she got to studying about her troubles.

She was raised as near white as any colored girl could be. It was Miss Hat herself learn her Bible stories and how she mustn't never lie or steal. Miss Honey learn her to read and write down in the well-house at Waverley. The bees were buzzing all through the wistaria vine and Miss Honey was laughing and saying, no, Lethe, that's not the way to make the letter E. You've got it backwards, child. And then Lethe squeezed the pencil hard in her sweating hand and sent it squeaking over the slate to make an E that faced the right way. . . .

But, in spite of her raising, she'd turned out bad. Bad was what she was most times, she reckoned. Like her granny say, hit's bad and nothing but bad to fool around with first one white fellow and then another. But hit never seem bad when it was Mas Kirk. She never meant him no harm no more than he meant her any. Time she come on him crying, face down in the cotton bin at the Waverley gin the day after Miss Honey taken down so sick. Or time he didn't hear them blowing the dinner horn and Miss Hat sent Lethe over to the creek to look for him. Laying on the ground he was that day, right on the cold, bare dirt with his face buried in his arms. And she kneel down by him and whisper: Don't, Mas Kirk. Please, sir, don't. It ain't going do Miss Honey the least bit o' good on this earth do you take on so and it just do you harm. He said nothing at all at first but then he said: Good little Lethe, in a voice that turned her heart to water inside her. Good, he said, not bad. . . .

A long time after that, a long, long time—Lucas was getting to be a great big young 'un and Lethe was looking for her next most any time, the one she named Henry—Mas Kirk say he reckon this one was his and nobody else's. Lethe laughed and said, Yes, sir. Are you sure, Lethe? Couldn't be nobody else's, Mas Kirk, this 'un couldn't. And he believed her. And when her next was coming, little Johnnie, that was her baby child now, he never even ast her was it his. He trusted her. . . . Well, it was over now, forever and forever. He always told her it would be, was he to marry. But it was Miss Hat made him hire her out in town. He'd a-let her stay on at Waverley, he'd a-had his way. She knew that. She'd be out there at home this minute, wasn't for Miss Hat.

All the time Mr. Duffy was testifying yesterday she had sat there on the bench behind Miss Hat, her hands twisted hard together in her lap, trying not to get scared. Mr. Duffy was just white trash and crazy white trash, to boot. Those jury gentlemen knew that. They must know it. As for her, her white folks would take care of her. Of course they would. They was the finest folks in this county. But even before the trial, for weeks and weeks before it, she'd worried about how Miss Hat and Mas Kirk goin' to take it when they come to find out about the fix she had got herself into, especially Miss Hat. Miss Hat was sure to be outdone when Dr. Gregory told her.

It seemed strange not to know whose baby it was inside her now. It could be Mr. Orrin's or it could be Mr. Paul's, Mrs. Simmons' brother from Alabama, that was here to see his sister back in February. Dr. Gregory couldn't tell for sure which one, from what all Lethe told him. But he was mighty near positive it was one of them two and not that stranger white gentleman was through here, selling chill cure, back around New Year's or that other gentleman steam-doctor that visit her the last time just 'fore Christmas, seem like it was. She reckoned she'd know for sure after it came. She'd more than likely be able to tell from the favor of it, the same as she had about her first. But it worried her a little, not knowing. It worried her some, too, thinking how it might turn out to be a girl. She didn't want a girl, bright color, like it was bound to be. Bright-color girls is hard to raise good, like her granny used to say. . . .

Up there before all those white folks it was like it was *her* they was trying stead o' May. She couldn't a-got no more scared if they'd brought in a rope and showed it to her. Lord, Lord. They scared her into lying again. She know better than that. She know hit never do no good to lie—hit just make white folks think you been up to something sho nuff. That white gentleman lawyer know she was lying from the first word she spoke. And when Mas Syke Berry come over and told him there wa'n't a sprig of pokeweed growing anywheres near the Waverley hog lot he frown at Lethe like the Lord God Himself. No more lies now, he said. She wanted to go right through the floor for shame when he said it. And poor Miss Hat, setting on the front bench, twiddling with her breast-pin and shaking her head so sad and sorry! It was like Miss Hat was saying:

Now, you know, Lethe, you was raised not to lie. I learned you the words myself—thou shalt not bear false witness.

The good Lord know it was her granny done that Jimson-weed business, not Lethe. Bad as Lethe felt when Mas Kirk come bringing a wife home, she wouldn't a-harmed her. The Lord know. He know she didn't have no more hand in that than in this here that May done. But maybe the white folks wouldn't believe that. What if them lawyers was to take and try her, sho nuff try her, like they was trying May? What if Miss Hat and Mas Kirk wouldn't stand by her and get her off?

"Poppycock, Lethe," the doctor said, when he come at bedtime to see her and give her that medicine to make her sleep. "Poppycock. Nobody's going to try *you*. This is May's trial and nobody else's. Court is nearly over. They'll wind this thing up tomorrow or next day sure. I doubt if there's time for any but the most trivial business after they bring in a verdict on May. Court always breaks up on Saturday. Don't you remember? The judge will go home to his plantation down in Copiah County and the Yam and all the other lawyers will go to their homes. Why, they couldn't put you on trial if they wanted to. There's no indictment against you and no time to get one. They can't even hold court again before next November. By then you'll be living up in Ohio. Mas Kirk will see to that. He knows you had nothing whatever to do with the murder. Miss Hat, too. They'll take care of you. Now take your medicine like a good girl and go to sleep."

"That lawyer gentleman thinks I done it, Doctor. But how could he—how could anybody—believe such a thing?"

Why, Lethe loved Hunt like her own. Hunt would have died the time he had pneumonia hadn't a-been for Lethe: Three nights running she never had her clothes off. . . .

"That's right," the doctor agreed. "I always did say the boy owed his life to you. Now listen, you're getting yourself upset for nothing, girl. They've got the criminal over yonder in the jail. I reckon everybody in his right mind knows that—except Mr. Arnaud and her precious lawyers. I don't want to be uncharitable. So I have to allow the woman has somehow managed to pull the wool over their eyes. . . ."

"You taken notice of that judge, Dr. Gregory? He's got a *hanging* face."

"A hanging face, Lethe? Well, now, that's nothing to worry you. That's May's trouble. She's being tried and nobody else."

"Doctor, would it be better if I was to tell the truth?"

"The truth! The truth! Hell's fire, girl. What *are* you talking about?"

She raised up from the pillow. Her fingers clutched his lapel, and her voice sank to a ghostly whisper. All that about what happened in Uncle Jerry's cabin was mostly lies. The truth happened in the kitchen at midnight in the dark. The truth was Lethe still had the bottle, as the lawyer gentleman had somehow guessed, and she laid it down on the shelf in amongst the dishes. God himself wouldn't name it sin to set a trap for a low-down nigger to tempt her to kill herself. It wasn't a thing they could hang you for, was it, Doctor?

"You simply laid the bottle on the shelf, left it there for May to find next morning and she did the rest? She, not you, put the stuff in the teapot? That is the truth, Lethe?"

"Yes, sir. And tomorrow maybe if I was to tell—"

"No, no. If you're sure you only laid the bottle on the shelf, securely corked, you are innocent of crime. You'll have to let the thing alone now, girl. They're through with you now. You'd just mix the lawyers up if you tried to change your story again now. Let it alone." Then he said sump'n other she couldn't quite call back to mind now, sump'n 'bout where there's so much evil stirred up and scattered abroad, couldn't nobody hope to come out with real clean hands. Ever'body just got to accept a little as his share. Maybe she's kinder lucky she got nothing worse on her conscience than a few small lies. "Now for God's sake drink this dose. In the morning you'll feel better. . . ."

It was morning now and she did not feel better. She felt worse. Her body was warmer at last, no longer shaking with chill, but she was still cold deep down inside. She been cold inside like that a heap lately. Hit started the night he come home from Georgy bringing a wife and it got a heap worse from the day she first set eyes on May. Take more than a few splinters of light'ood and a cup of coffee to warm that cold out o' her. She'd carry it with her to her grave, she reckon.

She heaped more wood on the fire, poured out another cup of coffee and drank it slowly. Ohio, it have a heap of snow and ice, folks say. Maybe the boys have to have shoes and stockings to wear when they went to that white school to study in their books. Wonder where she get the money to buy so many pairs of shoes and stockings, let alone books to study out of.

She opened her door and watched the sun coming up from over behind Judge Calloway's barn, started shaking again, remembered she was still barefooted and in her shimmy, turned and started to put on her clothes. While she dressed, she thought about what all she had to do over at the big-house. She'd have to make the kitchen fire and get in fresh water from the well and put the kettle on and the oatmeal and coffee and make up her biscuits and then run up and see was the three biggest children getting on their clothes all right. Mrs. Simmons looked after the baby herself but she'd want hot water brought and Mr. Simmons would, too, it being another court day and him feeling like he had to shave even on week-a-days with so many visitors in town.

She put on her best blue-and-white-checked dress, did her hair neat, wound her head handkerchief around it, tied on a clean white apron, shooed the cats off her doorstep, closed her door carefully behind her and started across the back yard like any other morning. The air was clean and sweet like fresh-washed clothes. And the sun on the star jessamine on the well-house made it smell good. It wasn't like town somehow, more like out in the country spring mornings. She thought of thick woods and of deep water running along in between a-whispering and a-gurgling like the creek at Waverley. . . .

All at once it seemed like she just couldn't go in there and fix the white folks' breakfast. It was mighty early, anyways, barely sun-up. The Simmons family was all fast asleep, their shutters pulled tight, not a sound of anybody stirring yet. She passed the house, opened the front gate gently—and not wide, because of that creaky hinge—and walked away down the street, past Judge Calloway's big brick house and the little office beside it where them lawyer gentlemen was staying, past the courthouse, locked up so tight and quiet, past the Emporium store and even the gin on the bank of the river.

WHEN the carriage drew in before the crowded square and once again the gaze of the thousand-eyed monster licked over it, Martha shrank back against the cushions and her fingers bit into her palms. From one day's end to another's beginning she almost forgot those searching, greedy eyes. And now, in spite of all her boasts about not caring what people thought of her, she was almost overcome by fear. She did not dare to look back even once at Mr. Banning riding up behind. She could hardly summon the will to step out to the ground. And the moment she did climb down she caught Sis Hat's bony, resistant arm and clung to it hard.

She heard a boy yelp in mocking falsetto: "Oh, Mama, have *I* got a head!" Following his glance and the slyly smiling ones of the people who stood near, she saw her husband coming toward her through the crowd. He had not shaved. His shirt was torn and soiled. His nose was swollen and discolored. His eyes were bloodshot. Martha's heart gave a lurch of dismay at the change in him. But Sis Hat roused herself to determined, helpful cheer.

"Good morning, Br' Kirk. I hope you slept well and feel real rested." Then she added with low-spoken, brisk competence: "We've brought you your razor and a change of clothes."

He seemed not to hear.

"Lethe's gone," he said.

"Yes, yes, Br' Kirk. We know. We've been stopped over and over to hear about it. Look like people just can't hardly wait when it's bad news they got for you. But try not to worry and get yourself all upset. Take your bag and go fix yourself up a little. Hit's bound to make you feel better."

When he had taken the bag and gone off, Martha somehow got separated from Sis Hat after all and had to follow with Mr. Banning. A bunch of rowdies in the porch, scuffling and goosing one another, left off to stare at them as they passed and one— she thought it was the Burgess boy—called out: "Yankee!" Of course Mr. Banning called himself that often enough and perhaps the slapstick jibe didn't annoy him. But Martha stopped in her tracks as if she'd been tripped and, turning about, cried furiously:

"That was very rude. Whoever said it should apologize to Mr. Banning."

The boys only giggled and backed off. Nobody apologized and Mr. Banning drew her firmly forward.

Court opened in an atmosphere of augmented excitement. The audience milling about the room traded high-keyed bulletins about Lethe's disappearance and pursuit. It had been considered neces-sary, it seemed, to put dogs on her trail. And the detail was passed from hand to hand with relish. Some said her running like that looked bad for her. As the judge called for order and the proceed-ings once more got under way, Martha sank back into her own inner debate. What became of Lethe or May could not matter when she still did not even know what was to become of *her*.

As from a great distance she heard the judge asking if the State wished to present evidence in rebuttal. She saw Sis Hat take the stand but she paid no attention to what she said there. Nor did she find anything worth her attention in the testimony of the doc-tor, who followed, and read a long, tiresome passage from a medical book, which, he said at last, shutting up the book, bore out his opinion, namely: If there really had been any Jimson weed in coffee prepared for Mrs. McLean on her first morning at Waverley and said to have been destroyed by Mr. Duffy, she could probably have drunk it without fatal consequences, with, indeed, no more serious result than headache, vertigo, temporary impairment of vision. . . .

As the doctor left the stand and the eyes of the audience were drawn backward, Martha, turning her head like the rest, saw her husband coming down the aisle in response to the clerk's call. He was shaved now and wearing fresh linen. He had even, she guessed as he passed close beside her, fortified himself with a drink or two. He gave her in passing a sidelong, debonair smile that only chilled her and erased from memory his first deceptive appearance of suffering and need. Then he sat down in the witness' chair and began to speak with that aplomb which to her seemed devoid of feeling. He almost laughed when he spoke of Mr. Duffy's Jimson-weed story, so like the poor old fellow's suspicions on "a hundred and one" previous occasions. But his manner, when Syke Berry rose to cross-examine, changed as before it had done.

Q. Now, Mr. McLean, it seems to me that the occasion when Mr. Duffy actually seen and destroyed a foreign substance in coffee prepared for your wife was kinder different from the "hundred and one" other times before that when he, without nothing to go on, taken up a notion old Aunt Dosia was mebbe slipping something into the white folks' food. You see that, don't you?

A. Really, Mr. Berry! These legal subtleties are quite beyond a layman's grasp.

Q. Well, then, say you feel you was justified in not reporting Duffy's statement to the sheriff last summer. But what about in November when the Grand Jury was investigating the cause of your son's death? Seem like some similarity in the two attempts at poisoning would have struck you forcibly enough to make you speak up then. But it didn't, did it?

The witness, by that time, was almost too angry to speak, but he managed to at last.

A. No.

His questioner walked nearer and bent over him, pitching his voice lower and indulging in a smile.

Q. Now, sir, I reckon you won't deny that May's relation to you, real or fancied, was mighty obnoxious to Lethe. Why was that?

The Yam rose and interposed delicately.

"We object. The witness cannot be interrogated on the feelings of Lethe."

The objection was sustained and the question was reframed.

Q. Were you for some years prior to last summer in the habit of having sexual relations with Lethe and are her two youngest children yours?

"Your Honor!" cried the Yam. "My young friend forgets himself. The prisoner at the bar is on trial, not this witness, a gentleman of high standing in this community, a husband and father.

Surely this interrogation involving the feelings of his innocent family cannot be permitted in decency."

The judge bowed his head and his long fingers plucked at his beard.

"The witness must answer the question," he ruled.

The witness' voice rang defiantly.

A. Yes!

As he stepped down from the stand he looked again toward his wife, but again she would not meet his eyes. She dropped her own to the fan she was opening and closing on her lap. For her, at least, the trial was over. She had drained the last bitter dregs of revelation and public exposure. She was incapable of taking in anything further. Remotely she heard the lawyers make one meaningless motion after another, watched the judge take out his watch and, cradling it in his palm, discuss with the lawyers how much time each would require for his summing up. She heard him say: Gentlemen, the jury is yours. And then she heard no more. Not one word of the avalanche of Syke Berry's oratory disturbed her anesthetic calm.

After the adjournment for the mid-day recess, the Waverley party paused at the foot of the stairs and looked at one another uncertainly. Nobody seemed able just at first to speak. Then Sis Hat, with visible effort, said, well, now, there wasn't any use in letting Mrs. Ketcham's nice dinner get cold, was there? But Kirk McLean said he believed he'd ask them to go ahead, presenting his apologies to Mrs. Ketcham. He wanted to go by the jail to see if there was any word yet from the sheriff about Lethe, and, since that would make him very late, he'd just get a bite in town somewhere. Then Martha discovered she'd left her fan in the courtroom again and asked Mr. Banning to go back with her to look for it.

CHAPTER 3

SYKE parted from Mr. John at the tavern steps and hurried off down the street. Mr. Duffy would be riding out of town in half an hour and Syke had undertaken by way of farewell to treat him and his shoemaker friend and Orrin, to set 'em up, as they say, at the doggery known as Judson's over on the river front beyond the gin.

It was hard to believe that his summation was over. In the first minutes he had been, he knew, distressed and awkward, his fingers playing at that plaster strip on his face, his voice thick in his throat, his feet shuffling. He could see himself now, squirming inside his too-new coat, the backwoods boy, apologetic before his betters, helplessly clowning: Up at Oxford us boys use to say, if it's in air lawbook Mr. John knows the name of the book and the very number of the page where it's at. He waited slyly for the brief flutter of laughter to begin and die away. Now, me, of course, what little law I know, Mr. John there learn me and it taken him the best part of three months to get it through my thick skull I got to say *irrelevant* and not *irreverent*. Again a wisp of a laugh trailed through the courtroom, but the judge frowned and twisted his gavel threateningly.

Syke saw he'd better stop fooling around and get down to business, and the moment that he did begin to speak seriously, confidence was magically his. He knew that he walked up and down, pounded the jurors' rail, grew red in the face, choked, returned to the table for a drink of water and rushed back, his arms flailing, but he hardly knew what he had said. Oh, he knew what he had *meant* to say. Hadn't he been making notes all week and longer for this supreme moment? But the notes had lain forgotten on the table by Mr. John's hand all the time he was talking.

And now all that came back to him were fragments echoing out of context: them two steamboat men, chipping in their two-bits' worth of hindsight at this late day . . . that chemist and his six-months-old crust in a teapot. . . . Do you believe for one minute that Fender *seen* May shake a bottle over that pot? The State's whole case rests at last on that. All their other evidence is bare suspicion. Now look at this prisoner. Believe her evil if you must, capable of doing what they say she done, but is she intelligent? Would a woman that looks as bright and smart as that commit a hanging crime under the eyes of a witness? You saw the woman Lethe on the stand yesterday, gentlemen of the jury. With your own eyes you saw her break down under Mr. John's questioning. Was that the bearing of an innocent woman? Does a woman with nothing on her conscience lie ever' breath she draw?

Three times Mr. Peters interrupted, once to have the clerk read from the record of testimony to prove Syke had misquoted a witness and twice, to protest that he was exceeding his time. At last the judge caught Syke's eye and, though he smiled a little, he nodded upward toward the clock behind him. Syke, twisting about and staring up at it, stopped abruptly. Twelve-thirty. He had been talking more than two hours after saying he could finish in one. He was hoarse. He was drenched with sweat. His knees threatened to give way under him. He glanced desperately toward his forgotten notes, having no idea at all whether he had covered the arguments mapped out in them. Then his eye fell on the court Bible where he had laid it, open and ready. At least he should not be robbed of his climax. "One minute, your Honor," he babbled. "One minute and I'm through." He leaped to the Bible, brandished it, shouted: "And now, gentlemen of the jury, I want to leave in your minds one sentence from the Good Book itself: 'The wicked flee when no man pursueth.' "

Had he made a good speech, a tolerably good or a downright poor one? Mr. John, as Syke flopped into his chair, mopping his face, said: "Good." But still Syke wouldn't have believed it if he hadn't seen the way the audience acted. The instant the judge's gavel fell, the company split apart like an apple in the hand. What Syke thought of as the McLean faction, the more well-to-do and better-dressed, the larger slaveholders and their town friends—all those who in the natural order controlled, and had expected always to control—faced away and drifted out on a backward flow, an ebbing tide, silent with chagrin. The rest, in numbers heartening to a backwoods boy born to bare foot plodding down a cotton row, came surging forward to leap the rail and pound his shoulders and yell in his ears. Mr. Arnaud beamed and wrung his hand. Conviction after that speech, he said, was simply unthinkable. Syke's family, hungry to greet and congratulate him, hung back a little on the outskirts of his more vociferous well-wishers, his mother with her gray sunbonnet alternately crushed to her breast and used in place of a handkerchief to wipe her eyes.

The draught of triumph was sweet but heady. He heard himself protesting to one after another: Well, the trial ain't over yet. The State's got the last word. Don't forget that. And once he glanced inquiringly toward the judge. The prisoner, led out toward the back stair, was at that moment just passing beneath the bench. As she went by, she looked up and smiled. His Honor snatched up his papers, turned his back and disappeared into his chambers. To such a dizzying pinnacle had Syke been pushed by the swell of acclaim, so insecure was his footing there, it wanted only that small shove to send him hurtling downward into a chasm of doubt.

Now, as he walked along under the noon sun, it was, somehow, the doubt that remained. Why was that? He bent and caught up a blade of grass to nibble at as he considered the question: If it *was* a good speech like they're all telling me, why do I feel so down in the mouth? All along, over and over from the first, Mr. John had tried to moderate Syke's passion: Only the State needs all twelve jurors, Syke. We can do with one. One, Mr. John, one? You expect me to settle for a mistrial? No, sirree. I'm going the whole hog. Your mama may not need that hundred-dollar acquittal bonus but Mrs. Berry does. Do you know, Mr. John, my mam never had a straw bonnet with ribbons since the one she trimmed herself to get married in and she's never owned a black silk dress in her whole life? I reckon you don't know, sir, what it feels like to see your mother going to church in a cotton dress and sunbonnet. . . .

At Judson's he found his party waiting impatiently. The place was packed and everybody there, it seemed, had something to say to Syke about his speech. That ought to have made him feel good but somehow it didn't. After he had gulped down the one drink the circumstances demanded, he shook hands with Duffy, put down money to cover several more rounds for his guests and made his way toward the door. As he was about to step out he heard his name called behind him. When he turned he saw Kirk McLean seated at a table alone in the farther corner of the room, holding up a glass and beckoning with it. Syke felt embarrassed and reluctant but he was curious, too, and it was his curiosity that pulled him across the crowded, smoke-filled room to stand by McLean's chair. McLean asked him if he would have a drink. Syke said No, thanks, he was in a kind of hurry to get back over to the tavern to join Mr. John at dinner.

"That was a remarkable summation, Syke," McLean said. "It obviously swept your audience off their feet. I suppose you know it may cost Lethe her life?"

Syke tried to smile.

"Aw, now, sir. If I mebbe got over to the jury a reasonable doubt of May's guilt, that's a long sight different from getting anybody else indicted and convicted. Why look—its six whole months till November."

"November? If you've really convinced the people here that Lethe should hang, what's to stop them from stringing her up as soon as she's caught and brought in?"

"Mr. McLean, honest, now. Don't you think you're seeing things ain't anyways likely to happen?"

"Perhaps. Perhaps it's more likely they'll just shoot her down resisting capture. And maybe the poor thing would be better off if they did."

An icy chill stole over Syke. Surely that was unreasonable. Lethe's flight *proved* her guilt. Of course it did. Then why did these fanciful hints distress him so? Why did warmth drain out of him like his lifeblood leaking away? If he did not stagger, it seemed to him that he did. Certainly he stammered: The poor wench ought not to a-been so foolish as to run. We was through with her. It was her running and the way she acted yesterday on the stand, a heap more than anything Syke had said in his summation, that had give people the notion she was guilty. But he hoped what Mr. Mclean feared wouldn't happen. He sure did.

"Sit down," McLean urged. "A drink will do you good. Do have one with me. I'm not—well, you see, it's a new experience for me to have to drink alone."

Syke felt a heap more like running, but he dropped into the opposite chair. McLean's eyes were cloudy but he sounded sober as he questioned his guest about his drinking preference and communicated it to a Negro boy in a dirty white apron. After the boy was gone, Syke held a watchful, uneasy silence, while his host suavely and at random commented on what a filthy hole Judson's was and how uncomfortably crowded. But then, he supposed, if the town had twice as many drinking places they'd all be full in court week. Strange what a fascination court holds for people. Had Syke ever asked himself why that was? Syke's drink being now before him and the conversation pointed into what seemed a safe, impersonal channel, he sipped and relaxed.

"Because ever'body likes a scrap?" he guessed. "Or because a heap of 'em's just Peeping Toms when you come right down to it?"

The phrase was unfortunate. It touched off McLean's latent hostility. He stiffened, his eyes dropped to that glass before him and his two hands tightened on it. He turned the glass round and round in his palms like somebody counting ten or twenty before speaking and then he forced a laugh and looked up at Syke again.

"At any rate you've had a rare opportunity to pay off an old grudge, haven't you?"

The word startled Syke. It was the very one Mr. John had used that night at Oxford: Look here, Syke, have you got a grudge against this man? Now Syke tried to laugh.

"Aw, sir, if it's that hiding you give me that time in the old judge's barn you mean, why, I never held that against you. Honest to goodness, I never. Us boys deserve that licking you give us about Lethe if anybody ever did. And, besides, I was so thankful to you for not telling my mam on me, seem like I couldn't be real mad at you."

Kirk McLean merely smiled.

"When you were appointed in November to defend this case, Syke, you accepted promptly. I assume the question of the prisoner's guilt hardly entered your mind."

Syke reddened and cut in.

"The law—"

"Oh, I know. The law allows the guiltiest criminal the right to counsel. And it might as well be you as another. Why not? She had no lawyer and you certainly needed the $25 we were required to pay. And in that first trial at least you implicated no one else. What I can't get is your almighty assurance this time—as though you were riding some goddamned holy crusade. You say it's not from personal ill will toward me. Certainly you can have none against Lethe. Then what is back of it? Money? That bonus you're to have for full acquittal?"

Syke stared. He knew the words he had to speak and somehow he spoke them:

"Mistaken I may be, sir. And right bull-headed, too, once I get started. But I ain't dishonest. Or anyways I don't aim to be. I'm poor all right. I need money, but—"

"All right, all right. I believe you. I apologize. All the same I can't make you out. Not that it matters. Luck's running your way. It certainly isn't running mine."

Syke got away at last. Kirk McLean signalled the boy to bring him another drink. Syke, looking back from the door, saw him turning the glass again between his palms, staring down into it. Was it true, as he hinted, that nobody would drink with him? Had his friends turned against him sure enough? Popular as he was, it didn't seem possible somehow. And yet . . .

As the judge was crossing the street to the tavern to get his dinner, he heard bare feet running up behind him and the voice of his boy Joe.

"Mas Sandy, I got the axles greased like you told me and I had the horses' shoes looked at. Us goin' to pack up now?"

"Yes, Joe. As soon as we've had our dinner."

"Us ain't goin' stay over for the hanging, Mas Sandy—even if they was to have it tomorrow?"

"No, Joe. But what makes you so sure there'll be a hanging? The woman may be acquitted, you know."

"They bound to hang *somebody*, Mas Sandy—they just bound to."

The judge shook his head, tried to smile and passed on to the public dining room. He found it crowded and noisier than usual and he had no appetite for the dishes afloat on the long grease-spotted table cloth. Syke Berry's speech was, of course, the topic of the hour and he found it distasteful. Frankly, the young rooster's fiery appeal to the crowd's primitive emotions had been hard to stomach. He took no part in the table talk, finished his dinner and climbed the stair.

The small travelling trunk which, strapped behind his buckboard, always accompanied him out on circuit stood open in his room and, beside it on the floor and two chairs Joe had gathered his few effects: his shaving kit, his writing case, his Bible, his shirts and underwear, socks and handkerchiefs, his extra pair of boots, even the little box of powders Dr. Gregory had supplied for relief of colic. Packing was done in a matter of minutes. He sent Joe for a glass of fresh water, took a powder and stretched out on his bed. His pain diminished or his awareness of it became veiled. Yet he never lost consciousness of the dreary tavern room with its two double beds and the rest of its jumble of poor furniture, never ceased to see the window open on a big hackberry tree outside, its branches rustling slightly and sparkling with sunlight, never left off hearing the voices of Joe and the stable-boy in the yard below, rehearsing the trial and betting on the verdict. He clearly heard the two lawyers for the prosecution, who shared his room, when they came up the stairs laughing and talking together. They entered of course without knocking. Sh. Judge is asleep. No, gentlemen, I have been dozing only. Now I am quite wide awake.

The Yam held a coin on his palm and jovially shouted: Heads, she's acquitted, tails, she's convicted. Slap of metal on bare table top. Heads, it is. Judge, you win. The judge shut his eyes, pretending not to hear. The attorneys left the room almost at once and he was free to doze again. But even the brief comfort of half-sleep was now denied him.

He did not claim to be without prejudice, God knows. Every man has his personal weaknesses. One of his was a marked tendency to side secretly with the underdog. He had discovered that in himself long, long ago as a young practising lawyer. In this trial, because the accused woman had already been once convicted and even more, perhaps, because she was being defended by a half-baked young backwoodsman with the forces of property and substance arrayed against him, the judge's private feelings had been engaged at first by the defense. Mixed with this, too, no doubt, was some championship of the wounded young wife who reminded him of his daughter. But, by the same token, as the defense had developed strength and public feeling had more and more swung that way, he had instinctively veered contrariwise. Sympathy for Lethe, cornered and panic-stricken, had automatically tugged him toward belief in her innocence even before the young prophet in the wilderness had unleashed his wrath against her. Actually, the accused woman had only to give the judge that one glance of premature confidence as she was being led out of court just now to make him turn his back on her. Yet even that involuntary gesture of repudiation had not altogether surprised him. He could not pretend that it had. Presumption of her guilt had begun to form in him as early as some time yesterday.

Such shadowy, irrational promptings would, all the same, be very unsafe leads for a judge to follow. His private intuitions are completely irrelevant. He cannot deny them, must indeed acknowledge them to himself in order to allow for his inner deviations as mariners take account of the vagaries of the compass. But it is the law and the evidence which are and must be a judge's sole concern.

Well, it would soon be over now. Tomorrow at this hour with normal luck he might hope to be starting home. On the road, facing south, this final term of the spring circuit, like the ones that had preceded it, would fade and dissolve behind him. He would be free to daydream, to summon about him the images of the dear and familiar on ahead: his darkies at work in his own fields down in far Copiah, looking up to shout glad welcome. Look a-yonder. Yonder come Mas Sandy hisself. Bless God. His wife smiling up from her pillow with little Mas Sandy in the curve of her arm. His big boys crowding, each with something to show or some startling piece of neighborhood news. The little fellows hugging his knees. Tall above them, Katherine, merry, relieved of all care. She was a young woman now, old enough to marry. God grant she didn't fall in love with some man with a handsome face and no heart. . . .

O, upright Judge. O, learned Judge. That ruling to leave the Jimson-weed testimony in evidence, now, are you quite sure it was given with calm and abstract justice, unobscured by the promptings of the natural man? And if, as a result of that decision, a guilty woman is cleared and an innocent put in jeopardy of her life, will the judicial hands be entirely clean?

He started up from his bed, went over to the table, spread his papers before him and, sternly fixing his attention, got to work on his charge.

A judge's first responsibility to a jury is to clear away the dust of conflict churned up by the lawyers, show them the case stripped back to its original simplicity. This, gentlemen, is what the State wishes to prove. This, on the other hand, is the contention of the defense. These witnesses have appeared before you in turn testifying to these facts. Of the evidence, I have to remind you, you are the sole judges. No matter what any lawyer tells you or—a faint smile relaxed his tense lips—as to that, any judge, you are each to regard only your own feeling as to the truth or falsity of any given fact in evidence. You are to review this evidence exactly as you heard it with your own ears, weigh and test it by light of your own understanding, decide its truth or falsity by your own conscience.

Thus, if one side would discredit a witness, as the child Fender by the implication that one so young should not be brought into court, you will discard the implication and decide solely on the basis of whether you yourself believe she spoke the whole truth, a partial truth or an outright lie. If the mental stability of a witness has been questioned, as Mr. Duffy's has, you will leave out of consideration as far as possible the hints of opposing counsel concerning his sanity in matters unrelated to the case and focus on his trustworthiness, or the reverse, in the particular events to which he has testified. You must question whether a prejudice in the witness Harriet Hunt, which might be strong enough to color her interpretation of motives, could so far mislead a woman of her obvious rectitude as to make her misrepresent a matter of fact. As to the unanimity of the Negro witnesses introduced by the State, it will be necessary for you to decide whether this is parrotlike agreement, as the defense represents, or indication of fidelity to truth. Just what, you will ask yourself, is the testimony of each witness worth? In regard to what has been called "muddying of waters," you will recall that this court in ruling relevant that evidence concerning Mr. McLean which was excluded at the former trial of this case, has been guided by the opinion of the supreme court of this state.

And now—he lifted his eyes from the notes before him and again his lips twisted in a bitter smile—it becomes my task to inform you of the law as it applies to this case.

Murder, with its essential ingredient malice aforethought. There can be no question here of a verdict naming a crime of lesser degree, as in cases when from the evidence it appears that death may have resulted from accident or an act done in self defense, and indeed the attorneys for the accused make no such plea. They grant the fact of the crime, murder by poisoning, even by a specific substance, an arsenical dye known as king's yellow. They have shaped their case and rest their appeal on one sole point; namely, the identity of the person who placed this poison in the teapot sent to the family dinner table at Waverley on November

10 last. Weight of evidence. Preponderance of evidence. Burden of proof.

Reasonable doubt is not a merely possible or imaginary doubt but such proof as precludes every reasonable hypothesis except that which it tends to support. It is proof to a moral certainty as distinguished from an absolute certainty. Absolute, demonstrable certainty is not essential to proof by circumstances. The legal test of the sufficiency of evidence, either circumstantial or direct and positive, to authorize a conviction, is its sufficiency to satisfy the understanding and consciences of the jury to the exclusion of all reasonable doubt of the prisoner's guilt. In the application of circumstantial evidence, the jury must discard from mind every impression arising out of any thing or act or knowledge except that derived solely from evidence admitted by the court and not derived from matters excluded by the court.

If the evidence in this case satisfies you, gentlemen of the jury, beyond a reasonable doubt arising therefrom that the defendant Aimée administered arsenic, knowing the same to be poison, to Hunt Ralston McLean and that the said Hunt Ralston McLean died from the administration of the same, as the indictment charges, the law presumes . . . that the defendant was actuated thereto by wilful malice and you must find the defendant guilty as charged. But if from the evidence it appear to you that any other person could have had both opportunity and motive to commit this crime, then this would constitute reasonable doubt of the defendant's guilt and it will be your duty to acquit her. . . .

He rested his elbows on the table at last and his face sank into his hands. No, it was too late. The woman had won. She had won in the moment the Jimson-weed story was ruled in evidence. Lethe's subsequent actions, the young rooster's violent argument, had contributed their part, but it was the judge's own decision that had yielded the reasonable doubt. There could be but one verdict. Whatever his charge contained or omitted, the jury would clear Aimée. He was sure—as sure as if he already held in his hand the foreman's note, opening it, reading: "Not guilty."

CHAPTER 5

CLAYTE BURGESS' boy, Clayte Jr., had lost his ball through an upper window of the court-house just before court opened that morning, and he took prompt advantage of the noon recess to look for it. He had to wait till the room emptied and even then he didn't find the ball right off—it had rolled, of course, and probably been kicked about a bit, be-sides. While he was searching, Mr. Kirk McLean's wife and that Yankee friend came back into the courtroom for something she'd left behind—a fan, she said. But they was right nice and helped him to find his ball first. It was her that found it, clear over to the far side of the room from where he'd been looking. After she gave it to him, she sat down on a bench like she wasn't in any hurry. So he hung around a little, talking to the Yankee. The fel-low had a funny way of calling his words that made young Clayte enjoy asking him this and that: Did he think Lethe was the one that ought to hang? And what did he think of Syke Berry's speech? Then Mrs. McLean seemed to get kinder restless and after while she said: Aren't you getting hungry for your dinner? Oh, thought young Clayte, so that's it, is it? Trying to get rid of me, humph? It put him in mind of Sue Ella Foote when her sweetheart from Bates' Bend come up to see her and they was so red-hot to get to kissing and hugging and all that lovey-dovey stuff they just couldn't be polite. Well, he knew better than to stay where he wasn't wanted, of course. So he went out along the aisle, but slowly and a little resentfully, too. At the big door he stopped and looked back. She had got up off the bench and was walking off toward one of the little rooms at the back with the Yankee following close behind her.

Downstairs in the porch old Miss Minnie Calloway and a bunch of other women were hanging around. They caught hold of him and started in to asking him questions: Had he seen them two up there and all about it. He could tell what they wanted him to answer. With Miss Minnie's ear trumpet held out to him, the temptation came clear as anything, to make out like, when he'd heard them two coming up the stairs, he had run and hid behind a door and seen and heard a lot. But he wouldn't do it. He just pulled loose and laughed and said: I don't know nothing, ain't seen nothing, ain't heard nothing, and now I want my dinner! And then he ran off toward home, laughing back at them over his shoulder.

His mother was cross about his being so late, and all the time he was eating, she went on about how nobody considered her in this house and how they all just come in when it suited them and expected a special meal served just like this was the tavern and she was Mrs. Howells. He tried to jolly her up a little with teasing: I know something I ain't goin' tell. And after he got her curiosity up, he told her who he was talking about.

"They act to me like they was sweethearts," he said, scraping his spoon around the bottom of his saucer to get the last bit of his blackberry dumpling and then licking the spoon carefully.

You'd a-thought he'd fired off a gun, the way she yelled out and took on.

"You ought to be whipped. I'll tell your father. Yes, I will, the minute he wakes up from his nap. The very idea. That sweet, pure little creature. And after all she's been through, too."

"Maybe you wouldn't think so much of her if you know what I heard and saw while I was hiding behind that door."

Of course he was only funning. But she took him seriously and the next thing she was waking his father and making him listen, and Clayte Jr. was too stubborn or scared to take it back. He even added some fancy touches borrowed from the time he came on Sue Ella and the Bates' Bend fellow on the bench by the gin that evening. . . .

It was still early—a good quarter of an hour till court would take in—when Sam Hardy left home. He lit his pipe and sauntered slowly back in the direction of the square. As he was passing the office of the *Free Press,* Clayte Burgess came to the door and asked him if he would step inside for a moment. Clayte seemed considerably excited and no sooner had he pulled Sam in than he closed the door and began to whisper.

"There," said Clayte at last in a normal voice, "what do you make of that, Sam?"

"What should I make of it? It's none of my business or yours either. And the less said about it the better for all concerned."

"What we ought to do," said Clayte smugly, "is to take that Banning fellow up on a fence rail and ride him right out to the county line, that's what I say."

Sam pushed his hat to the back of his head, scratched an ear reflectively, and hesitated.

"Well, now, Clayte, ain't you just a little impetuous? The conduct of a man's wife is a thing he's apt to be pretty sensitive about. And Kirk's a fellow that always kinder liked running his own business."

"There he is now," said Clayte suddenly and before Sam could stop him he had flung open the street door and hauled Kirk in.

Kirk, seeing Sam there, nodded and smiled—though how he could smile after all he'd been through and the way people had turned against him was a marvel to Sam. Then Clayte began:

"Now, Kirk, we're your friends, remember that. If we're making a mistake about this, please understand it's done from motives of friendship."

Kirk's smile faded and he drew a deep breath. When Clayte Burgess made an opening like that, it was plain he was getting ready to hit below the belt. But Kirk never thought of dodging— any more than he'd thought of clearing out, as Sam and many another had advised, before he'd been subpoenaed to appear as witness in this trial.

"All right, Clayte," he said crisply. "Let's have it."

He heard Clayte through without a word. And when Clayte had finished, still he said nothing. His silence seemed to make Clayte nervous.

"Now, Kirk, I hope you won't think hard of me. I thought it was my duty. Do unto others, I always say . . ."

And Sam said:

"Clayte wanted . . . and I told Clayte . . . that was right, wasn't it, Kirk? You don't want your friends interfering? You do prefer to handle this yourself?"

"Yes," he said.

Then he put on his hat and turned back to the street. Sam pressed close to his elbow.

"If there's any way I could be useful . . ."

"There isn't, Sam."

In front of the courthouse they found a crowd gathered about Dr. Gregory, who was helping Miss Hat into the Waverley carriage. Mr. Banning put Mrs. McLean in after her and turned around, smiling.

"It's all right, Kirk. Miss Hat's not feeling well and the doctor's told us to take her home and get her to bed."

Several bystanders added details: It happened right after she got back from dinner. She was in Mr. Peters' office, talking to him. He noticed nothing wrong and then all at once, she collapsed.

Dr. Gregory was most reassuring.

"Nothing serious, Kirk. She's excited, over-tired—probably ate her dinner too fast. That's all."

"You'll ride out with them, Kirk," Sam hinted.

"No," he said.

He watched the carriage turn out into the street with Mr. Banning wheeling to follow and then he faced toward the courthouse door with Sam still at his side. By now the corridor was aflow with movement toward the stair. They eased into the tide and let it bear them on and up.

CHAPTER 6

$\mathbb{S}$ITTING alone on the front bench with folded arms, Kirk McLean gazed intently at each speaker in turn, but the rounded periods rolled over him as devoid of meaning as waves pounding on a beach. Neither John Oliver for the defense nor Tom Peters for the State had any understandable message for him now.

He was recalling a morning long ago at the University of Virginia, a morning in May, cool enough for a bit of fire in Mr. Jefferson's minuscule grate but warm enough, too, for study windows to stand ajar and young men, in an hour of excitement, to hurry along the colonnade and over the Lawn, hatless and many in their shirtsleeves. His friends, surging about his study table, put the pistol in his hand in the very moment that they told him what young Carter had said about him, the "insult" they called it, some blackguardly bit of nonsense about Kirk's having an ace inside his cuff at cards the night before. He was half minded to laugh it off when they began. Me, he said, me cheat at cards! It's a joke, really. But then they gave him the pistol and he saw by their eyes it was no joke. Carter was on the Lawn now, expecting him, and he was armed, too. *His* friends had seen to that.

And then he was going out of the study door with the whole mob at his heels, turning and saying coolly, like a line out of some damned play: Gentlemen, keep back. You must understand I prefer to handle this alone. So then they did keep back and he went on by himself and came to the Lawn, enamelled green between the long white-columned perspective rising to the Rotunda, and stamped against the bright scene, cameo-sharp, the Carter boy's strained white face, the small chin wobbling a little, the pale blue eyes filmed with dread.

The two reports to Kirk's ear were simultaneous, but the witnesses, even Carter's half dozen henchmen all said No. Carter fired first and missed. So it was self-defense and nothing worse happened to Kirk McLean than being expelled and having to go to New England to finish his education. Not that he wouldn't see young Carter's face in his dreams for years. He saw it even now more distinctly than he saw the orator of the moment pausing to refresh himself with a sip of water.

In New England he had come close to it again, close to killing or being killed himself at nineteen. A duel it was that time, or was to have been, complete with challenge and rendezvous at dawn, seconds, and pistols again. But Parson intervened, driving up under the dew-wet, shadowy trees by the river in a rattling old livery stable hack with the town constable and a half dozen other irate citizens. Parson was the maddest of the lot. You fool, you damned fool, Parson raged, grabbing Kirk's pistol, emptying the charge in his own hand, and flinging it out toward the misty river. You and your infernal Southern honor. When will you learn that life is the precious thing?

His wife's fan, which he had found lying there on the bench as he was about to sit down, was in his inside breast pocket with his coat buttoned securely over it. He could feel the folded fansticks rigid against his ribs with every breath he drew. The small sensation was slightly uncomfortable. He could have put a stop to it by loosening a button or maybe even by lowering his clasped arms. But he did neither one. He wanted to go on pressing her fan hard against him each time he drew in a breath.

It was the fan she had come back for. He could hear her guileless voice mentioning her loss and asking Parson to go back to the courtroom with her. Yet she hadn't picked it up. She had forgotten it after all, left it lying for her husband to find and retrieve. If he should confront her with it later on, how would she behave? Would she give some natural, simple answer that explained everything? Or would she close her eyes in the way she had and take refuge in the silence of injured innocence?

In the wall behind the judge were three doors. The middle one directly at the judge's back under the high clock led into his quarters. Those to right and left led to the little rooms used, one by the jury when sent out of court during transactions considered improper for their ears, and the other, by witnesses during trials in which the judge ruled against their presence in open court. Of the three doors only the one at the right stood open now, revealing a barren dusty cubicle to its last dismal detail: its unshaded window in the farther wall; its two unpainted benches and three split-bottom chairs, a miscellany of mops, brooms and scrubbing pail in one rear corner and in the other the piano left over from the graduation exercises of the week before with a homemade school banner on a standard leaning against it. The door was folded outward against the courtroom wall and not flatly, but at an angle large enough to hide a spy and eavesdropper. At the hinged side of the door there was a vertical slit to which an eye or an ear could be applied.

Kirk McLean, ostensibly gazing at the speaker, gazed beyond him into the depths of the witness room, deserted now, but peopled for him by two phantoms, represented in boy language as hugging and kissing and calling each other love names like sweetheart and darling. Now and again he shifted his eyes slightly and gave over peering into the haunted room to re-examine that crack between the door hinges.

Sometimes the speaker would turn and walk a few paces, bringing his body directly in front of the hinged edge of the open door and making it necessary for Kirk McLean to bend forward slightly in order to continue his absorbing calculations. But he made the adjustment without noticing that he did so. Was that vertical slit really wide enough and at the right angle for spying *into* that room? Admitting that a boy posted behind the door could see anybody passing into the room, could even keep such person or persons in view a foot or so beyond the threshold, he simply could not see them once they were well inside—not without leaving his hiding place, which of course the little sneak would not have dared to do. It was an obvious lie, cast in spurious words. It rang as dull and hollow as a lead coin. A sane man would do well not to be taken in by it.

"If the defense in its greed for salacious and slanderous detail has dragged into this case mighty near every canard the mind of baseness is capable of concocting to divert attention from the accused, you, gentlemen of the jury, do not have to swallow the nauseous mess dished up for you. . . ."

It was the Yam who was speaking now. The muddying of waters, he had called it yesterday; and that was strange in a way, because that was how this thing had appeared to Kirk McLean all along. From that day in November when disaster had torn a breach in his fences and any and everybody had come pouring in like a herd of hogs to root and snuffle through his life, he had felt polluted. That was why he could not come near his wife—however impossible he had found it to explain to her. Even to talk of such things to her had seemed to risk defiling her. And the one thing he wanted, had wanted from the first, was to keep her high above all evil. . . .

He wasn't a religious man, but he had his faith all the same. A man must hold something sacred, inviolate, if he is to live—or even want to. Martha. Parson. Parson. Martha. Twin pillars of his last sanctuary. Topple them in the mud, trample over them, and what would be left? Nothing. Nothing at all. Nothing in the least worth living for. . . .

But the thing to do was not to believe it. He must not believe. It was a monstrous lie, made up out of whole cloth by his enemies, men who had been his friends while the sun shone on him and now turned on him at the first cloud of trouble. A lie. Of course it was a lie. Then why hadn't he said so? Why hadn't he landed on Clayte's filthy mouth one good blow of his fist? That was the right answer to a slanderer, the one he deserved and could understand. . . . But he hadn't given Clayte that single perfect answer. He had let Sam ask him if he preferred to handle this alone and he had said Yes.

The Yes was a promise, a bond, a sacred oath. It implied the deed, contracted to perform it. Vengeance is mine, saith . . . But, no, said Kirk McLean, not this time. This time it is mine. I will handle this myself. I prefer to. It is I who have been sullied. I must remove the stain. Life, the most precious thing? No, Parson, no. That is a Yankee shopkeeper's notion, I'm afraid. There are circumstances under which a man would hold life cheaper far than honor. . . .

"Listen." The Yam lifted one finger delicately and paused, as though listening himself for some message too high and thin for mortal ears. His tiny form with its protuberant belly and the enormous head of unruly hair was the figure of a gnome, a dwarf, rising on tiptoe, ear bent for occult vibrations. His voice, as always at his climaxes, dropped to a whisper. "Listen. Can't you hear the rush of eager feet along the dogtrot and a glad cry: 'Did you get it, Papa? Did you get me my gun like you said you would?' Ah, my friends, I see many of you wiping your eyes and I do not wonder. For, as you hear the echo of that sprightly call, so full of life and promise, you are remembering that only one day later it would be hushed forever."

Kirk McLean twisted restlessly on the bench and looked back over his shoulder, measuring the distance to the outer door and wondering if he could possibly reach it without drawing on his head the indignant frowns of the entranced listeners. No. They were down on him enough as it was. Better endure if possible. This was the fourth and final oration. It couldn't go on much longer. And, the moment it was over, he could seize the chance to slip out.

The crime. That was the Yam's grand theme. Let others dwell on law and evidence. His text was just the crime, called up by sheer artistry to happen again here before their fascinated eyes. No ballad singer of old ever had a surer sense of primitive poetry. He even had a blackboard brought in and set up with a drawing of the yard and buildings at Waverley upon it. Then he tapped it with his sorcerer's wand and peopled the scene as true as life, walking as Miss Hat walked across the yard, speaking as she spoke, answering now in the speech and manner of old Jerry, now with the carefree notes of the doomed child. He described the kitchen, the black cave of the fireplace and the pots on their cranes, showed the stranger cook, witchlike with firelight on her face, taking that bottle of arsenic dye out of her stocking, nursing it greedily, gloating, as he said, like a great dark spider.

Nearing his end, he dwelt in bitter contrast on that pure white rose of Georgia and—here he shook an indignant forefinger in the prisoner's face—"this thing."

"The accused," the judge mentioned automatically, "is a human being, sir. I shall not permit you to degrade her to the lower animal orders."

The Yam merely shrugged, substituted in a tone drenched with sarcasm, "this prisoner, whom his Honor compels me to call a woman," and rushed on.

Kirk McLean unfolded his arms, folded them again and shifted uneasily. Sitting through this was harder on him than he had bargained for. It was as though Clayte and Sam were there sitting beside him, nudging him, whispering: Get on with it, get on with it. What are you waiting for? What good is there in waiting? The deed hung there before him in time but already complete and finished, like a piece of music or a picture formed in the artist's mind. . . .

The deed that cancelled out shame, purged honor, cleansed the blood itself to let it pour red again. Wash me in the blood of the Lamb and I shall be whiter than the snow. The sacrifice. Men have always resorted to death in one form or another for redemption, haven't they? Purification by fire. And there is a kind of beauty in the utterly final act, the single deafening explosion and flash that clears the air of murk and the last creeping doubt. Whether . . . to take arms against a sea of troubles, and by opposing, end them. . . . Pshaw, he was no Hamlet. Thinking wasn't in his line, never had been. Everybody said so—including Parson. Parson was the man of words. He was one who acted and must act.

As the Yam at last took his seat, the judge laid his watch out, arranged his papers, put on his glasses and, looking over them at the audience, explained that, since he did not expect to finish his charge under an hour and a half, before six o'clock, that was to say, he must ask any who wished to leave the courtroom to oblige him by leaving now. Kirk McLean was already on his way out. A score or so more took the hint, women mostly, town ladies who had to get home to see about supper and country mothers whose children were getting restless. A number of those remaining took advantage of the opportunity to improve their positions. But, though the front center bench, where the Waverley household had sat all week, was now vacant and was of course the best seat in the house, nobody seemed to think of moving into it. The judge waited for the commotion to settle. Then he cleared his throat, addressed the jury and began.

Down in the street as Kirk McLean swung into the saddle, a boy ran up and put a note in his hand. It was a soiled half sheet from the sheriff. It read:

Lethe's trail come to an end on the bluff a couple miles this side Bates' Bend. I sent 2 fellows in a rowboat off from there and they come on her body drove hard against a old sawyer a little way off the nigh bank. I'm bringing it in soon as I git me a wagon and team.

HARRIET in her sleep felt all about her the frail, soft web of a bride's veil. The man standing beside her was a lanky youth in an ill-fitting suit like Syke Berry's. It wasn't Syke, of course, it—why, sakes alive, if it wasn't Caje Cumby! And him dead these twenty-five years and over. She couldn't a-been no more than thirteen when Caje got his mortal wound from a drunkard's knife that Saturday night at Judson's. The stuff between her fingers wasn't veiling, of course. It was just her old blue muslin wrapper she'd got into soon as she took off her town dress. She was almost awake now. But she kept her eyes closed and lingered on a while in the time the dream had brought to mind.

The mountain woman and her son come here as quiet as birds passing through and settled down in the old tumble-down Injun house on the edge of the big bottom, the winter after Ma died, it was. Honey was just a baby crawling over the floor and Harriet ten or so. They was strange folks who neither plowed nor planted themselves nor had air nigger to do it for them. Wonder how they make out to live, Pa used to say. But pretty soon the boy, as shy as a fox, having loped the long miles so deep with dust in summer and mud in winter would appear on soundless bare feet at the back door of Waverley with a bag of quail or doves or a brace of squirrels to sell. Or in a season when hunting was slack he'd turn up emptyhanded to hire himself to Pa for a day or so. Not that he was ever much good with a hoe or a plow or even at picking cotton. But Pa's force was small in those days and he often laid out more acreage than they could handle. He was glad enough to have the mountain boy's help, such as it was, and he never be-grudged him the big silver dollar he handed him at evening: Them's man's wages, son, but then I reckon you got a man's ap-petite, ain't you? Apt as not, Pa'd add a fat hen or a pat of yellow butter for him to take his ma. And then one Sunday at church the mountain woman—or the weavin' woman, as some was calling her by that time—out of gratitude to Pa was offering to teach Harriet how to weave on her loom that her son had made her. And Pa got so he'd leave Harriet at the Injun house whenever he went hunting in the bottom.

Sometimes Caje would be out hunting, too, and she wouldn't even see him. But sometimes he would be at home. One rainy day he made a toy banjo from a gourd cut in half with brown paper stretched over the opening and strung with catgut for Harriet to strum while he sang her mountain ballads and camp-meeting tunes. She didn't know how old he was, but in size he was a man grown, taller by half a head than Pa. He had big hands, hard and cal-loused. To this minute she could remember the way Caje's hands had felt, curved over hers to guide them on the little banjo.

Even after Caje's death her and Mrs. Cumby was fast friends. Once Mrs. Cumby, fingering the paper slips covered with numbers and labelled with pretty names like Morning Star, Tennessee Beauty, Rose in the Valley, come to one that made her stop and look up with tears in her eyes. This here one, Flowery Vine, she said, I had aimed to make for Caje's marriage bed if so be the good Lord had let him live to take a wife. After Mrs. Cumby died, they found a paper saying she wanted Harriet to have the loom and the box with all the coverlid pattruns in it. . . .

Many's the time Harriet, rummaging through Mrs. Cumby's old pattruns along with all those she herself had accumulated since, would come on the tattered one called Flowery Vine with its nota-tions faded almost to illegibility and consider whether she'd try that one next. She never had somehow quite wanted to. But now at last she did. And she'd do it right away. She was glad now she'd finished that nigger cloth before court opened. Her loom was empty. She'd draw in the web for little Harriet's coverlid first thing tomorrow. Maybe there's some as would think it was foolish to make a bride's present for a child only a few months old. But she'd do it. The Flowery Vine.

Underneath the memories brought by the sweet, small dream and the pleasant after-thoughts, stirred a sense of loss and abandonment. It was like she wanted to run out in the dogtrot and call: You, Martha, come here to me this minute, way she used to call Hunt when him and Dub been up to some mischief and was hiding from her in the bushes. Not that she thought Martha would do anything wrong. Of course not. As she had told the girl last night, it was just the looks of the thing. And a married woman off in the woods with a man no kin to her don't look right. Please don't go down to the creek, lamb. Think how it look—not to me. Sis Hat knows you wouldn't do nothing wrong and sinful. But evil-minded folks is ever on the watch to make something out of nothing. Can't you and him set quiet here at home till Br' Kirk comes? But Martha had gone anyway.

And now it was real late. The green boughs outside her front window were burnished copper and through the one at the back came a flood of homely evening sounds: Andy Scales calling their hogs, hoo-pig, hoo-oo-pig; Mrs. Scales chirping chick, chick, chick and then a whir of wings, the skitter of claws on hard-packed clay and at last the tap and ring of the emptied feed pan; from the stable the clink of plow-chains and the bump of each mule turned into his stall; rattle of milk buckets and the far moo of cows at the pasture gate.

Hit's most suppertime. I must a-slept mighty near three hours. Look like I'd feel a heap more rested than what I do. She turned over and tried to doze, but the sound of Josie singing to the baby beyond the dogtrot rose shrill and insistent. Black sheep, black sheep, where'd you leave yo' lambie? Down in the valley. The buzzards and the flies a-peckin' at his eyes, and the po' li'l lambie crying, "Ma-a-ammy." Harriet reckoned she would feel more cheerful once they all come trooping home to supper, Martha and Mr. Banning from over to the creek, Br' Kirk riding up from town. Maybe she'd sit up for supper and listen to Br' Kirk tell how the trial was coming on. Whichever way it end, she for one was determined to put the whole thing out of her mind for good, not holding any grudges, not even against the Berrys. They was neighbors and would be long after this trial was over and done. As for Br' Kirk, if she so much as mention his getting drunk yesterday, she hope the good Lord would strike her dead. Martha should never hear a word of reproach for the way she'd flouted Sis Hat's well-meant advice this afternoon. A step sounded in the dogtrot and she called joyfully:

"Martha! Is that you, lamb?"

But it was Mrs. Scales who stood in her open doorway.

"You want anything, Miss Hat? I look in twice before like *she* ast me but you was sleeping both times. You want a drink? The bucket's fresh-drawed. I made Dub get it in before he went to drive up the cows." As Harriet held the gourd dipper to her lips and sipped from it slowly, Mrs. Scales walked to the front window and looked out. "They sure must like it over yonder to the creek, her and him."

Harriet, returning the dipper, said coldly: "Mr. Banning was ever fond of the creek."

Mrs. Scales had only just gone when Br' Kirk's steps came along the dogtrot. Harriet called him and he came in. She asked him first if there was any news of Lethe and without comment he gave her the sheriff's note.

Harriet made a small soft clucking sound and as soon as she was able to shape words, they wasn't about Lethe, they was about the judge. She heard herself going on and on about him: If good old Judge Calloway had a-lived, this never would a-happen. Oh, she knew Syke Berry was a blundering upstart all right, but what's a judge for if it ain't to keep such as him in his place. A judge is supposed to know better than to give a wild colt like that his head. . . .

Br' Kirk walked along between loom and bed to the hearth-rug and, turning about, stood there facing her while he answered her, but it was like he had something else on his mind all the time. She hated to see him so worried and cast about for some comfort to offer, but nothing came easily to mind. So she said:

"I'm real sorry you had to set there in court all evening alone and then ride out home by yourself, besides."

"Oh, the doctor was with me, riding out, as far as the Lees' at least. He stopped there to see a patient."

"I wisht you'd a-thought to invited him to supper. We're having fried chicken and strawberries."

"I did invite him and he accepted. He'll be along by the back road soon—with an appetite, he told me to tell you."

There fell a silence and he looked intently at her.

"Where's Martha, Sis Hat?"

"Over to the creek. She come in and told me she was going if I didn't need her. I said of course I didn't, I thought it might do her good to have some fresh air."

"Parson go with her?"

"I think so, Br' Kirk. Seem like I heard them talking, going off."

"What time was that?"

"Why, I never taken any notice of the time."

He went back across the dogtrot and she heard him talking to Josie, heard the sound of bureau drawers opening and closing, wondered what he was looking for, supposed he'd found it, whatever it was, because he came into the dogtrot again, dragged a chair to the table and sat down. By hitching herself around on her pillows a little, she could see into the mirror over her chest of drawers. It showed her Br' Kirk sitting at the table with a bottle and glass before him, showed him taking something out of his pocket and looking at it. A fan? Yes, clearly a fan. Now how come him to have Martha's fan? He opened and closed it, laid it aside, poured himself a drink, drained it off and poured another. Oh, dear, she didn't want him to drink *now*. It might make him cross and quarrelsome. Seem like she couldn't bear it was he to be ugly to Martha—or to Mr. Banning, like he was to Syke Berry the other day.

"Br' Kirk!"

"Yes, Sis Hat." The chair pushed back and he stood at her threshold, glass in hand. "Want something?"

"It's getting late and Doctor's likely to ride up any minute now. I was thinking we'd better blow the supper horn. Will you do it?"

He shook his head.

"There's no hurry," he said and went back to his drinking.

She closed her eyes and prayed, or it was more like she was calling Martha, Martha. Time seemed to have stopped. At last she heard the chair scrape again and his feet going out along the passage and down the front steps. She reached over to her table, caught up a medicine bottle that was standing there, rapped it hard on the wood and called: "Josie, Josie."

Josie wavered at the threshold, hushing the baby at her breast,

[321]

her eyes wide and shocked, and before Harriet could frame a question Josie asked one herself.

"Reckon what he want with his gun, Miss Hat? Reckon what he aim to do?"

"Maybe he's gone after that moccasin Dub saw on the foot log the other day. Now run along out to the kitchen, Josie, and tell them Doctor's coming to supper."

Josie went off with the baby, singing. Harriet swung her feet around to the bedsteps and got up. Her slippers were handy in reach and she pushed her toes into them without stooping. She felt as strong as she ever felt in her life. She walked around the foot of the bed without touching it, passed the loom and crossed the threshold. Day lingered in the dogtrot. A level sunbeam fingered the whiskey in the bottom of the nearly empty bottle and picked up the gilded tracing on the sticks of Martha's half-open fan.

Harriet rested her hand lightly at the table edge a moment and then moved on to the rear end of the passage. Near the back steps she stopped beside the shelf where the water bucket stood and, reaching up to the log wall above it, lifted the horn from the peg where it always hung by its leather loop. As she took it down she felt for the first time a kind of faintness, or maybe it was more like the fear of faintness. Breath, she prayed, God give me good strong breath. Then she set the horn to her mouth and blew.

Dr. Gregory heard the horn as he was passing through the gate leading into Waverley from the Lees' place and the familiar note brought agreeably to his mind a good supper ahead, but then almost at once his thoughts took a sharp turn. The blast of the horn, after fading as from sheer exhaustion, began again more urgently than ever. He pushed his horse to a quick trot. Fire was an image that shaped in his mind. But when he rode out of the belt of woods he saw no raging flame or billowing smoke on the rise ahead but only the old double log house bulking staunch and secure under the red evening sky and down the nearer slope the cabins and outbuildings trailing off like so many brood chicks at the old hen's feet.

Somebody came running across the darkening field on his left and tumbled over the barred gate—Andy Scales panting hard.

"It scared me, Doctor," he gasped. "I was clear the other side of the pasture. I never hear anybody blow like that in my born days."

The doctor motioned him out of the way and rode on at a smart pace, waving off as he went, other shadowy figures running and calling: "What is it, Doctor? What's happened now?" By that time the horn was silent, but the echo of its urgency still throbbed at his eardrums. Somebody swung open the back-yard gate in front of him and crowding, wailing Negroes got in his way as once before they had done and again Uncle Jerry met him, bobbing his gray head and croaking fear. At the back steps the doctor swung out of the saddle, tossed his bridle into eager, dark hands, snatched his saddle bags and ran up into the dogtrot.

Miss Hat was lying on the floor, the horn rolled a little way from her across the rough boards and Mrs. Scales and several Negro women bending over her. The doctor put them aside, dropped to his knees and leaned down. That unholy blast would have done for a stouter heart than hers. While he opened his bag and tried his useless stimulant, he flung about him his equally useless reproaches: Why had she been left alone? Where was Mas Kirk? Where was Miss Martha? Where was everybody? Before he got to his feet, from the woods toward the creek sounded the crack of gunfire.

He ran through the dogtrot and down the front steps. It was almost dark under the trees, but his feet found the old path and followed it easily. He saw the woman running toward him, heard her panting, gasping breath long before he came near her and he called out:

"Miss Martha! Anybody hurt?"

She recognized his voice.

"Dr. Gregory. Oh—thank God it's you. Hurry, Doctor, hurry."

"Who's hurt?"

"Both of them," she sobbed.

He sent her on to the house for his saddlebags, holding onto her just long enough to prepare her for what she would find there.

"And a lantern, Miss Martha. I'll need a light, too."

There was some daylight yet in the little opening above the old swimming hole, plenty to see the two who lay there, one fallen along the sloping, white-shingled bank, the other half lying, half leaning against a prone tree trunk and able to recognize the doctor and speak. Go away, Doctor. Let me die. I want to die. The doctor passed him and went on to the silent one, with limbs bent stiffly like the blades of a pocket knife, opened and flung down. No use trying to do anything for him. The doctor turned back to the other moaning and protesting. Go away. Please go away.

THE jury had retired at six sharp. The hope of an early verdict held many country families in town through the evening. And the town people, as soon as they had eaten their suppers, hurried back to the square. The courthouse stood wide open, lamplight flooding out of its windows and doors as on evenings of Masonic entertainments or school exercises. Courting couples whispered and held hands upon the stairs and in the darker corners of the hallways. A party of young people gathered at the piano up in the witness room and their voices in plantation melodies and "Believe me, if all those endearing young charms" floated down with the lamplight. Outside under the trees children played tag and circle games and the Methodist ladies sold ice cream for the benefit of the new church carpet. The spring night was full of gaiety and laughter.

A good many saw the doctor ride up, tie his horse at the hitching rail and go into Mr. Peters' office, but nobody thought anything of it. He came out again almost immediately, moving in a hurry, but that was nothing unusual with him. Two or three said: Howdy, Doc. But they all knew better than to try to stop him, with that intent look on him. By morning at the latest they'd all know what bedside he was hurrying toward. One or two passers-by in the dark little side street where Will Stokes lived remarked the doctor's horse tied at Will's front gate a little while later, but all they thought was that Mrs. Stokes must have got another attack of her quinzy. Sam Hardy's man down at the livery stable pocketed the usual tip when he took the saddle off the doctor's tired nag to put it on a fresh horse. He said: Going far, Doctor? It's getting mighty late. The doctor nodded absently, spoke of the fellow he'd operated on yesterday out at the Lees', said he wasn't doing so well and rode off.

Syke Berry and John Oliver whiled away the hours of their suspense over in their office, counting on Orrin to call them back when the jury gave the signal. Relieved of Mr. Duffy's company, they talked more freely than they had ever done before. Syke confided every detail of his disturbing encounter with Kirk McLean over at Judson's at noon and even confessed at last the half-forgotten whipping in the hayloft. How come me to deny it to you, Mr. John, wasn't only that I was ashamed—though of course I *was* ashamed—but I didn't think it influenced me. I didn't go to do McLean any real harm. And you know, Mr. John, when I used to joke about wanting the bonus for my mam, I was just funning.

Then Mr. John, like the true friend that he was, made a confession, too: A long time ago, when he was a young lawyer starting out in practise like Syke now, he had been lucky, too. Judge Calloway and others had been generous, thrown cases his way and otherwise put him forward. At twenty-five, assistant to the District Attorney, he had got a conviction in a case rather celebrated because of the eminence of the family of the accused and the large sum of money involved—a forgery charge, it was. Neither the District Attorney nor his young assistant had had a shadow of a doubt. But later on, another person, caught giving bad checks over in Alabama, confessed to the Mississippi business, too. So then they knew they had convicted an innocent man. But it was too late. The poor fellow, overcome by the disgrace, had already cut his throat.

"Was that how come you to get out of active practise and go to teaching, Mr. John?"

"Yes, Syke."

"Me, I couldn't never know enough law to teach it. But, way I feel now, I wisht I'd stayed between plow-handles where I belong. Yes, sir, ever since I left Mr. McLean today looking like he'd lost his last friend, I been down in the mouth. Way I feel, I'd like to walk along behind old Jonas the balance of my days and never have nothing heavier on my mind than grass in my cotton or cholera 'mongst my hogs."

They had their coats off. Syke had kicked off his shoes, too, and lay sprawled on the couch, his head on his clasped hands, staring up at the ceiling. There came a knock at the street door. Syke whistled and sat up, breathing hard.

"There it is, Mr. John. The verdict."

John Oliver snatched up his coat, called, "Coming," and in two strides reached the door and flung it open.

Orrin stood on the steps, blinking at the lamp.

"The judge is going into court. You'd better hurry."

The courtroom scene was more than ever like theatre rather than real life: the lamplight, the hushed assembly and, under the clock with its hands nearing midnight, the judge unfolding the paper, reading from it the words "Not guilty." And then his even voice going on, speaking the rest of his part, like something memorized and often rehearsed—the thanks to the jury and a grave admonition to the prisoner to make something good of the life the law had granted her. And at last the sound of the gavel and the murmur and rustle of an audience rising, breaking up to go home. There was no evidence of any deep feeling one way or the other. Maybe it had turned out about as they expected. Maybe Lethe's death had appeased their need for vengeance. Or maybe they were merely drugged with fatigue. No doubt, with a good night's sleep, they would be restored and ready to fall on any new sensation the morrow might yield, with appetite as keen as ever.

The State's attorneys made prompt and manly overtures of reconciliation to the victors. Mr. Peters shook hands not only with the rival lawyers but with Mr. Arnaud, too, genially assuring him he might take the prisoner in charge and leave town whenever he wished, saying Mr. Arnaud had the owners' permission to give his check to their factors in New Orleans and receive a bill of sale at his own convenience. The Yam told Syke he had the makings of a great criminal lawyer in him and even tried to sound him out on serving as the Yam's assistant on a certain case coming up for trial in the county below at the fall term. Syke wiped his sweating face and hedged: "Gee, Mr. Boone, gee, sir. A case with you. Why, sir, that's mighty flattering." And John Oliver threw an arm about Syke's shoulder and said: "Better let him write you, Mr. Boone. The boy's too tired now to know his own mother's face." When Syke looked around, the judge was gone.

Outside in the night, walking slowly back toward the office, hardly speaking, John Oliver stopped to get his pipe out and light it. Syke watched his friend's lean, studious face grow ruddy and fade out again. Mr. John would leave by the morning stage. His bag was packed and ready. Syke felt lonely. It was dark under the trees that arched the sidewalks, though the ribbon of sky between was clear and bright with stars and the air breathed jessamine and moonflower and sweet olive.

CHAPTER 9

"SOMEBODY is in this room. Who is it? Why are you hiding from me?"

His voice quavered, like a sick child's.

"It's me—Martha. I put the lamp over here so it wouldn't shine in your eyes."

"I shot myself."

"Yes. In the shoulder."

"But I am not going to die?"

"No."

"Will Parson get over it, too?"

"No."

There was a silence and then, more terrible still, the sound of a man's sobbing and a harsh outcry, a name twice repeated: Parson! And then the sobbing again.

The darkness outside heaved with a tidal wave of mourning. The Negroes' wailing chants and prayers rushed over him like surf. The bed would not stand still. It rocked and swung like a little boat in a rough sea. Even the log walls swayed and tipped and the great smoke-darkened beams overhead came crashing toward him. He panted and sweated and clutched at the bed-rail. But the bed-rail dipped out of reach and he felt himself falling. She said coffee would make him feel better. So he drank the coffee. But his stomach rejected it. And again he lay back, sweating, groaning. And all about the bed in the dim light faces leaned, now smiling, now leering, now bursting and splintered apart. A pistol shot exploded in his brain and his eyes saw a rain of blood-red sparks.

The parents were lost in a fire. The child would have perished,

[329]

too, if his nurse had not gone back into the burning house and brought him out. His nurse saved him to grow up in his grandfather's family, one with the children of the old gentleman's third marriage, and yet not one of them really. His nurse saw to that. Aunt Sophie. She spoiled him. The old gentleman thrashed him as conscientiously as he thrashed his own sons. The tutors, one after another thrashed him. But through every bitterness, every injustice, one solace continued constant: Aunt Sophie's face, gingercolored, lit with uncritical love. . . .

It rained the day they buried her and he screamed with rage and grief to see the coffin lowered into a grave half filled with water. The current tutor, a Princetonian with a long chin and nearsighted eyes, read the service under an umbrella. Dust unto dust. Only it wasn't dust, but mud and yellow water churning under the pouring rain.

Lethe's face twisted with fear in the swirling, murky current. He had not seen Lethe drown but he knew that her mouth had jerked open at last, calling to him: Mas Kirk, Mas Kirk. . . .

The prisoner's face wore a mocking smile between two trembling hoops of gold. She killed my son and they will acquit her. The innocent perish and the guilty live on. . . .

Honey's face was white, fixed as a doll's above her bride's dress. Oh, why did Sis Hat insist on burying her in her poor little bridal finery?

The Carter boy's eyes were blue and wide in the last moments they looked on sunlight. He had flung up his left hand to brush a blond lock off his forehead as he raised his right to fire. . . .

Parson's face was angry under the trees by a New England river. He had emptied the revolver charge into his palm. You fool. When will you learn?

"I don't know what happened today," he screamed, flailing about him with his unbandaged arm. "In God's name tell me what happened down there at the creek. Can't you see I don't know?"

Somebody stood by the bed and a hand touched his. He opened his eyes and stared. The face of the woman who stood beside him was grave and still. His gaze clung to it in fascinated horror, expecting it, too, to shatter and break apart. . . .

"Who are you?"

She tried to smile.

"Martha."

A baby began to cry.

"Take it out of here. Why is it in here? Why hasn't Sis Hat got it in her room?"

The sound of the baby's crying went away. The door shut behind it. Now he was alone and drowning in a muddy torrent. His left arm was strapped down and useless, and there was no one to hear his cry for help.

Yet the door opened and she came to him.

"The doctor is not here. He had to go into town. I told you. Don't you remember?"

"He should not have left me. I am dying."

He felt his head lifted up and the pillow with it and then the steam of coffee rose again in his face. He turned his head away and fanned at the vapor.

"No. It's no use. I can't keep it down. Take it away."

"Try. Just once more. Please try."

At last he drank. It came up as he knew it would. She wiped his face with a damp cloth, murmuring words that made no sense. He pushed her hand away. His voice was harsh and bitter.

"Home-breaker, traitor, snake in the grass. That's what he was. I had to kill him."

She dropped to her knees and put a hand over his lips.

"Hush. It isn't true. Those men in town put that in your mind. But it's not true. You know it is not."

"That's what I called him before I fired."

"No, no. You didn't. You called him no names, none whatever. I have told you, over and over I have told you how it happened. It was yourself you meant to kill."

"How do you know?"

"Because you pointed the pistol at your own heart. . . ."

"Then how did Parson get hurt?"

"Trying to get it away from you."

Her face faded before his eyes. His hand slipped out of hers. Dark waters swept him away. . . .

He was asleep. He had swallowed some coffee at last, grown a little quieter, dozed fitfully and then gone off. The baby, too, was asleep in Josie's arms out in the dogtrot. Martha sent Josie off to bed, returned the child to its crib and came out into the dogtrot again, leaving the door ajar so that she could hear if either of them waked and wanted her. From sunset on she had moved mechanically, performing each small service that each succeeding moment required, automatically, unquestioningly, like a well-drilled soldier under orders. It was nearly midnight now. She went to the front steps and sat down.

Behind her the back yard was quiet: The lament of the Negroes had some while back first receded and then died out. In the well of darkness before her nothing moved. There was no sound but the drone of summer-night insects in the black trees beyond Sis Hat's flower-beds. Yet she went on hearing the echo of the Negroes' mourning and the cries of a man shattered by grief. I don't believe you. It wasn't an accident. He betrayed me. I had to kill him. But gradually that babbling, meaningless echo faded out, too, and merged into the low, innocuous hum of insects.

Only now was she able to listen to the small, far voices from her own depths, a whispering chorus that had been going on within her all these hours. She clasped her hands tight together on her knees and bent forward. In the empty dark she saw a courtroom packed with people gathered for the trial of a woman. The woman was not a quadroon of evil beauty in silk flounces and glittering earrings but Martha herself in the soiled, crumpled lawn dress she wore now, shrinking and cringing and hiding her face in her hands. The little Georgia rose, she heard someone cry mockingly, and a titter ran through the audience. The judge rapped his gavel and said: Let the indictment be read. And someone stood up with a long scroll in his hand and read: The death of Miss Hat, though apparently attributable to natural causes, was desired by this woman. It exactly suited her book. Miss Hat was in her way from the first. She always wanted to get rid of Miss Hat, always resented Miss Hat's making her feel unnecessary, was secretly jealous of the smallest act performed in service of her husband, her child. . . .

The second charge against the accused, the indictment went on, concerns her husband. A wife ought to realize what her husband is feeling. But *she* thought only of herself, how she had been hurt, how she could get even, wanting to make her husband feel somehow, feel anything, if only pain, loss, regret. That is the real motive behind this clandestine traffic with another man's heart:

She wanted to hurt her husband. She is, therefore, as guilty of her husband's death as if it had occurred, your Honor. It was only his friend who saved him, gave his own life to save him.

And now, your Honor, we come to the question of her guilt toward the dead man. He freely gave her friendship but it was not enough. She wanted more. She must be loved at all cost, if not by her husband, then by this blameless gentleman, this family friend. A woman who would tempt such a man to be her partner in infidelity. . . .

No, no, cried Martha. You shall not say that. It is a false charge. I did not commit this sin.

The judge opened the Bible and read: As a man thinketh in his heart, so is he. Can you deny that you were guilty of infidelity in your heart, Mrs. McLean?

You see she cannot answer, your Honor. She knows she is guilty.

Guilty, guilty, guilty, the whispering chorus echoed. The judge turned his face to the prisoner, hammered his gavel and told her to stand and hear his sentence. . . .

Darkness blotted out the brief, strange vision. There was no judge and no audience. Even the prisoner in the crumpled lawn dress, stumbling to her feet, wringing her hands and weeping, blinded by grief, drew off, grew shadowy and indistinct, like someone not really seen but remembered from an earlier time, a helpless girl, relying on others, never on herself. The woman sitting here alone on the steps stared at the fading image in cool appraisal. In all these months at Waverley she had never, the poor, silly fool, mastered even one of Sis Hat's manifold skills, never so much as bathed or dressed her own child. She had not the faintest idea how the dark, unshepherded flock back yonder were to be led out of wailing despair to the homely tasks which the livelihood of all demanded. The healing words she should offer a man unhinged by remorse were also hidden from her. Yet she, that inadequate, blameworthy girl who was also this woman, would somehow do each of these things—she must because there was nobody else to do it.

A shadowy horseman emerged from the woods, tied his horse at the hitching post beyond the largest rose-bed and came toward the house. Martha went out to meet him.

"Doctor!" she said. "But you're alone. I thought Mr. Stokes. . . ."

He made a vague gesture toward the woods.

"Coming along behind in a hack, Miss Martha. He's been a bit under the weather lately and can't sit in the saddle. But don't you worry. Everything's all right." Stokes, as coroner, would merely hear her story and return a report of death by accident. "He must, Miss Martha. You were the only witness and you are absolutely sure of what happened: Kirk had been drinking, got his gun and tried to kill himself. Banning interfered. That's the simple truth. We've got nothing to worry about on that score. Peters said so. Peters, after getting the coroner's report tomorrow, may feel he has to question you a bit himself, he said, just as a matter of formality, but that's all. We can rely on him absolutely. There'll be no trouble at all if only you. . . ."

His voice trailed off uncertainly. She made no answer and he bent toward her trying to read her face in the dark. It scared him to think how much depended on her. Did she realize her responsibility? Could she carry through? As a doctor he had seen, one way and another, quite a lot of womanly courage summoned in emergency. This girl's competence with basins and bandages in the first hour after the accident was a thing he was quite accustomed to. All the same he was worried, had worried all the way in to town and back. Hysteria in women was a part of his experience, too. It could overwhelm her yet, make her doubt her own story, garble it somehow. If anything like that should happen the fat would be in the fire sure enough.

The slightest wavering or uncertainty in her would contain, moreover, an even deeper danger to Kirk. For, clearing Kirk with himself was far more important and far less simple than convincing any outside authorities. The doctor knew that. He was mighty fond of Kirk. And he could see that Kirk was doomed to be haunted to the end of his days by doubt as to what really had happened down there at the creek, could see that over and over through the years she would have to wrestle with Kirk's dark angel. Over and over she would be called on to convince him that he had pointed his gun at himself, not at his friend. And, whereas the legal authorities, like the doctor himself, would believe her once and for all, the specter of Kirk's doubt would, perhaps, never be finally vanquished. It would rise to confront her anew at every step. Could she hold firm now and forever?

While he struggled with his confused, uneasy thoughts, unable to put them into plain speech, she touched his arm and pointed to the woods. Two wandering beams of light played through the trees and bushes, wheels creaked slowly nearer, and a soft voice spoke:

"Grab a tight holt now, Mr. Stokes, sir. There's a chunk of tree root 'long in here somewheres and I wouldn't want to jounce your misery ef'n I can anyways help it."

The doctor found speech hurriedly.

"Now, Miss Martha, he's a rough sort of customer, Stokes is. If he should badger you a bit or if Kirk, on being waked and questioned, should be irrational still, not able to stick up for you, you mustn't get rattled or uncertain or . . ."

She said gently:

"Don't be afraid, Doctor."

END